MURDER

in D Block

by

Dutch Van Alstin

For Mom and Pop
**No first names; because to me,
they're my Mom and Pop!**

CHAPTER 1

The noise here used to unsettle me. That was a time when my hair was tad bit shorter, my boots were a trace bit shinier, and my now confident rolling gait was a timorous skulking. My uniform was still stiff from the tailor's starch and the blue was vivid before the washing machine spun it round and round so many times.

I recall my first day here when I walked through the sterile cellblocks. I imparted a voyeuristic glare at the steel cages through the eyes of naivety and youthful exuberance mixed carefully with cautious surveillance. The rumblings of the cell doors slamming and bristling tête-à-tête meant something different to me when I was a *new jack*. The clatter would reverberate like a volcano in a thunderous roar off the sloped ceilings causing my neck to snap to and from between the confusion. I tried to hide my fear. I tried to show the prisoners, as well as the guards, I was strong and capable of managing any predicament levied at me at any time. The problem is that fear emits an order and I was chum to a sea of sharks hungry to act and react. The prisoners would snicker and jab each other as they passed by the new face.

Rows and rows of prison bars in narrow symmetry graphically portray life in a holding pattern, circling about, as the sands of time dribble out crystal by crystal. Dark hair imperceptibly turns silver and strong bones wither away as the once sleek skin grows dry and

Dutch Van Alstin – Murder in D Block

scarred. Without so much as the tick of the clock, the young and the vibrant grow old and cynical, scratching imaginary lines on cell walls in search of a tally that will never arrive. They hang on their cell door with their arms hanging out, peruse the traffic during the day, and observe the empty solitude at night.

Old Man Tucker in number fourteen cell keeps a tab of all his days here by adding a matchstick to an old coffee can. The last count was twenty-one coffee cans under his bed. He always looks at me in the morning and nods his head slowly at me as a perfunctory type greeting. He has a plastic bag full of his own hair when it was jet black. The midnights guard told me sometimes Tucker dumps that hair out on to his mattress late at night and runs his fingers through the locks.

The austere nature of D block is second to none in comparison with any of the other seven cellblocks. Prisons are merely cities within cities and in every city, there is a scurvy side of town where crime and violence breed. D block is that section of Briersburg. The dreary atmosphere reflects on the faces of both the guards and the prisoners. Perhaps the entire aura is a self-fulfilling prophecy, but the whole cellblock seems just a tad dirtier, a bit louder, and the foul stench is unparalleled by any other cellblock.

The galleries stretch some *fifty-seven* cells long, nearly twice as long as the next largest block, C block. The lengthy gallery makes every grim walk down it during the morning count a baleful death march.

If only the walls could talk.

Given the spectral history of D block, it is too easy for me to point out the irony of Donny's death. It is here, among the over *550* cells where I saw Donny's lifeless body lying on the bottom tier. The fall smashed his radio, automatically setting off a personal alarm that rings ominously over the airwaves.

I don't recall who charged into D block first but I was in the first wave of guards responding. The adrenaline pumps through the body when an alarm sounds making minute details of who was first and why irrelevant. Adrenaline may pump through the veins but not always for the right reason. All too many of my cohorts would rush to the scene, not prepared, but hoping for a fracas. But all that we expected and all that we predicted didn't prepare us for what we saw; Donny's motionless body lay completely sprawled outward with his arms stretched over his head. His uniform, still creased and ironed, was moist from the blood that dripped from his skull.

Still and all, I could not help see the Donny I knew alive and well. He and I weren't

Dutch Van Alstin – Murder in D Block

close. In fact, I didn't know him on a personal level. But as I knelt beside him in a pool of blood, I touched his face and his skin was warm and soft. The fact I was touching the face of a man who was alive, merely seconds ago, was a troubling and sobering experience, an experience I don't wish to encounter again. I couldn't help but flash back to only a few days prior when I stood in front of a soda machine with an empty wallet in my hand. Donny strolled up to me and slid a dollar bill in the machine for me and smiled. I said "thanks" in a tone of slight surprise. He just gave me a high five with the back of his hand and said, "Hey! No biggie, pal."

I never followed up on his gesture of friendship. Donny was somewhat of an inconspicuous person who talked to very few people. I believe he theorized I was a more cordial person than our contemporaries were. I can't help but feel somewhat guilty that I didn't extend the hand of friendship that I believe he so desperately wanted and needed. As Donny lay dead on the bottom tier, I knew I had lost a missed opportunity forever.

The cellblocks consist of tiers, or 'floors', to civilians, and D block has five. The fifth tier belongs to the special housing unit, affectionately dubbed 'the box' so it is sealed off from the remainder of the block. That leaves essentially four open tiers. But one less tier made little difference when Donny crashed down to the flats from the top. One need not be a physicist to understand the properties of inertia when *190* pounds of human flesh drops such a distance on to the cement floor.

Unfortunately nobody but Donny witnessed the fall, or leap. Since there were no living witnesses, speculation ran rampant.

The ability of prison guards to engage in rumor-mongering is unprecedented in the field of gossipy busy-bodies. The rumors ran rampant. I heard them all:

"He was drunk."

"He was showing off."

"His death was really a suicide."

"He was depressed recently."

"He was dealing underhandedly with the prisoners."

"He was having girl trouble."

Not a single guard actually knows whether any of the rumors even had a tinge of truth to them. But often even a lie has a tinge of truth in it somewhere. I would submit that none of the guards really cared one way or another to the validity of their words. Just the exercising of scandalous talk about a guard they didn't care for anyhow provided some excitement to an otherwise vapid lifestyle.

Dutch Van Alstin – Murder in D Block

I don't mean to lecture in some sanctimonious chatter; I never gave Donny the time of day either. I knew Donny as well as most guards, which is to say not very well at all. I am under the belief that speaking of the dead in an unfavorable light is very callous, but it is important to take note of Donny's peculiarity. I find it very difficult to pinpoint any one certain aspect of his character that I can label as *peculiar*. I can't even cite a particular exploit that Donny has engaged in. If I must arrive at a definition of peculiar, I would say Donny tried too hard to fit in with all the other guards. He would casually enter into conversations the other guards were having. At first he'd slink in amongst a cluster of laughs. Then Donny would murmur a few "yeah, I'm telling ya, ain't that always the way?" The guards would toss him a glimpse or two wondering when he arrived to the conversation and who invited him. Eventually the group would ramble off to the mess hall or the locker room and Donny never followed.

Donny talked to the tower guards at the morning line up sometimes. The guards in the towers tend to be old timers and love to prattle on about the days of the riot back in '88 and the time a C block guard was stabbed to death back in '85. I think Donny figured if the old timers liked him then he was 'in'. However, to the veterans, Donny was a trained seal who knew when to laugh, when to say "wow" and when to grab them some coffee.

Donny's fault didn't lie so much in the actual effort he put forth as much as the notion he believed he needed to impress his fellow guards in the first place. My criticism of my fellow guards is not meant to be a sweeping indictment of some inferior form of life, however, the notion Donny felt compelled to work his way up to fitting in with the likes of prison guards, as a whole, is a clear reflection of the lack of substance in his life.

The very thought of a young boy having grandiose dreams of becoming a prison guard is ridiculous. There are several reasons why a man is drawn into working at Briersburg and few of those reasons are substantive. The temperament needed to work behind the walls is quite specific. By definition, the word *specific* leads to a limitation of diverse personalities attracted to the profession. I won't stretch my beliefs to the point where I would claim a pack mentality exists, but I must point out there is a distinctively similar sub-culture to the life of prison guards. Their personal interests, political thought, their philosophy as a whole, their uncanny ability to use the word *motherfucking* as a recurring adjective, are all similar. The sub-culture has one unmistakable paradox, which is nobody seems to want to have anything to do with each other outside of work. Nevertheless, any sign of nonconformity is scorned and ridiculed. I liken them to a pack of robots waiting to be programmed on what to do and say next; an individual thought is not an option. And yet, I walk here among these people, as one of them, and I still refer to

Dutch Van Alstin – Murder in D Block

them as "them."

In a state known for its hugely German settlers, Pennsylvania is the home-state of the city of Briersburg, hence the name of the prison. The city's name cloaks the actuality of the strong Irish population that has dwelled here since the city's finding. It is nestled around a few obscure but sizeable lakes in the southwestern portion of the state. The city is relatively small, 35,000 or so, just enough to keep its status as a city. The city's history is deeply rooted in the prison. Many generations of police officers and prison guards live in town. A day doesn't go by where I don't hear a story about somebody's grand pappy that worked in Briersburg years ago and how different it was, *back then*.

Part of me sympathized, in a warped sort of way, with Donny. I, too, am glared at from the corner of many eyes, the son of a Norwegian immigrant, a farm boy from Minnesota, invading the turf of tough, Irish prison guards. The first day I walked in Briersburg with my snowy blond hair, judgmental snarls were hurled at me everywhere wondering where I came from. Nobody recognized me from high school or the local watering hole. I never attended a Steelers game on Sunday and I never knew anyone who knew someone who worked at Briersburg.

The simple truth is I was a guard who transferred to Briersburg because of the surrounding area. The county, Briersburg County, as I stated, is home to a few lakes with a famous reputation for fishing. The surrounding area reminded me of home in Minnesota. Minnesota is the land of a ten-thousand lakes and our 200 plus-acre farm we owned was within walking distance to one of the biggest lakes in the area.

Dad died when I was eleven and my sister and I helped take care of mom. The farmhouse still remains but with only thirty acres. When I "ran away" at eighteen, as my mom still refers to my leaving home, my aunt moved in with my mom and the two of them make a comfortable living dealing in antiques and operating a small catering service.

I met a girl from Franklin Park who was vacationing with her parents in Minnesota. I found myself pursuing her back to Pennsylvania only to learn that the summer romance ended in September. But I took a liking to my first taste of independence and just didn't want to leave the area. All my education was wrapped in a diploma from St. Alexandria High School. The opportunity to become a prison guard came at a very propitious time in my life and when I factored in my age and education, accepting the job seemed like the right thing to do at the time. The state was in the middle of a huge hiring boom due to prison expansion and I knew my chances of transferring to Briersburg were good.

Dutch Van Alstin – Murder in D Block

Briersburg's acidulous reputation is not unfounded or exaggerated. Although many transfer to Briersburg because of some indefinable status of machismo, my reasoning for coming here was explained earlier. I own a small, quaint cottage on Taupawney Lake located a few miles from the city, just inside Briersburg County.

My reception to Briersburg was filled with distrust, not to mention an aura of paranoia. There are two types of people the robots tend to greet with skepticism: The first and foremost are out of town types such as myself. They equate an unfamiliar face with a fully blown Internal Affairs investigation. The fact I was born three states away just fanned the flames to an already unfriendly fire. A bitter old Lieutenant, due for retirement soon, dubbed me with the nickname "Dane" referring to their version of history that all Scandinavian people are Danish. I was subjected to all the Viking wisecracks. I would frequently find pornographic versions of the comic strip, *Hagar the Horrible*, stapled to my time card.

The second are those who don't follow the internal pecking order. If my pride causes me to have no friends, then I'll keep my dignity and my dog. He may piss on the floor now and then, sniff his backside uncontrollably, but he likes me the way I am.

My God given name is Augustovson Caleb Erickson. My dad cursed me with the title of Augustovson after some distant grandfather of whom I never meet. My mother wanted Caleb because there was an aura of the Bible attached to it. Since everyone at Briersburg was conditioned to think Dane was my birth name, I just went along to try to smooth over the tension.

Donny went through some of the same juvenile scrutiny that I endured. The fact his last name was "Quinn" didn't seem to help his situation much since he wasn't a Quinn from Briersburg, but a Quinn from somewhere in the Florida panhandle. The ostracism Donny received appeared to concern him much more than mine did me. I watched him on a few occasions slam his locker door or peel his tires out of the parking lot after a sophomoric attack on him by the robots. When I find a trite, juvenile note on my time card or recipes for Swedish meatballs in my mailbox, I just consider the source and toss them in the trash. I watched Donny one time grit his teeth and tear the note up that was on his card, he then spit on the time clock. I said to him, "relax, man, raising your blood pressure is what they want". Donny snapped his head around and stared at me. It was obvious I startled him. He just mumbled a few words, trying to down play what he did, and walked out the front gate. In fact, it was the next day he bought me the soda in the lineup room.

I normally ignore the ranting of the prisoners. But there is one notion, I'm afraid, that

Dutch Van Alstin – Murder in D Block

they're somewhat correct in saying. Many of the prisoners contend, usually in a fit of rage, the guards compensate for being slapped around all during high school with a cheap, tin badge given to us at the academy upon graduation. This blathering is psychobabble, true, but with a tinge of truth underneath the lie.

Falsehoods need some sort of truth, however miniscule; to keep the lie supported. The robots taunted Donny frequently and they enjoyed every second of the torture. I guess being slapped around in high school can seem like years ago when you can watch your derisive words bring a man to his knees. Donny was a sickly, skinny guy and his facade was apparent to all that knew him.

The district attorney's office ruled Donny's death as a suicide and the internal investigation was inconclusive, but they did rule out murder as a possibility, leaving only accident or suicide as the options. Suicide is within the tenants of logic, but accidental seems to be a ridiculous idea. There is no rationale for climbing out over the rails on any of the tiers other than to jump. There were no witnesses to Donny falling off the tier, ruling out any antics or attempt to show off. And the union has successfully fought off installing cameras in the antiquated prison. I don't hide the fact I have veritable concerns surrounding Donny's death. Maybe I'm guilty of listening to the rumors, too. But my suspicions stem from the fact no one saw Donny fall.

No one saw anything. No one heard anything.

A prison is not a wide-open prairie. All the space is confined and there isn't a nook or cranny without an ear or eye in the immediate area. How is it possible there were no witnesses? Somebody, at the very least, heard something, if not actually witnessed the entire incident.

To stand toe-to-toe daily with tough gang leaders with a remorseless outlook on life requires a stronger personality than that of a man who spits on a time clock because of an infantile note taped to his card.

To Donny, life was a game; being a prison guard was a game. However, life inside the walls is furtive, stoic and hard-hitting; these are the rules by which no games are played.

Dutch Van Alstin – Murder in D Block

CHAPTER 2

I can never fasten the top button without cutting off my air supply. I despise wearing a tie; I always have despised it. I can't grasp the concept of how a piece of fake silk dangling around a man's neck gives him a more professional appearance. Unfortunately, when I have to work the visit room, a necktie is mandatory attire. I confess I do enjoy having a day out of the cellblocks and it gives me an opportunity to relax in the newly installed air-conditioning.

There are two sections of the room divided by a piece of decorative pressboard. The larger section is where the actual visiting takes place. Tables and chairs fill the room encompassed by vending machines of soda, candy, and prepared food. The color scheme of the wallpaper is between off-white and pale beige, with a dash of trim along the ceiling in the shape of blue diamonds.

I'm not alone in the visit room. Bob Andover works in here daily, only occasionally with me. We don't see each other enough to become friends. Our relationship is cordial at best. I don't sense any mutual interest to become anything more than co-workers. We usually sit and blather about the ineptness of Briersburg's administration, and recent knife attacks and brawls. Just typical guard jargon.

Fridays in the visit room are not too hectic. The visits normally consist of what I dub as "professional" visitors. They are the people who try to visit on days where the visit room is sparse and attempt to take advantage of that paucity by requesting a table near the back of the room, and away from the guard's peering eyes.

I recognize the first visitor, as her head pops through the entrance gate from the admissions desk as Rhoda Holloway. She has the dubious distinction to be labeled a *professional* professional visitor.

Such professionals often are hired by family members to marry their sons, brothers, or whatever the case may be, to qualify for conjugal visits. Rhoda Holloway is engaged to Buck Martin of B block. Martin will be her third husband in the past eighteen months; she has been handed back and forth between a few of prisoners over the course of time. The whole scam is clearly illegal, but trying to find a complainant is difficult, making an investigation moot. Moreover, the police don't consider the marriage scheme a high investigative priority. Rhoda always tries to wangle a table near the back away from the guard's eyes. Bob has caught her many times groping her men under the table, for this reason he makes Rhoda sit up front near the two of us. She calls us '*sicko* voyeurs' and slams her purse down on a table in the front row.

A couple of days before Donny died; he and I worked the visit room together. I remember the day well because Donny argued with a visitor then went home sick. A frequent visitor, Mrs. Hopewell, became in a wrangle with Donny. Donny actually slammed his fist on the table; Mrs. Hopewell grew scared. I hollered out to Donny, "Hey, ease up, pal, what's the problem?" He glared back at me and shoved his finger in Mrs. Hopewell's face and said, "This tart is giving me a hard time about everything".

"Mrs. Hopewell?" I said, searching for an explanation. She just got a confounded look upon her face and shrugged her shoulders. I looked over at Donny and smiled. "Donny," I said calmly, "go get some lunch or something and chill out. I know you're stressed out a bit." I thought to myself: "who uses the word 'tart' outside the U.K?"

Mrs. Hopewell is actually a very polite woman; I tried to calm Donny down with a placid tone of my voice but he stormed out of the visit room mumbling, "Bitch". He called the watch commander's office, and then went home claiming he was ill. I tried to smooth things over with Mrs. Hopewell. I figured Donny didn't need a complaint filed against him. "He just flipped out on me when I told him the soda machine wasn't working," Mrs. Hopewell said to me. "All I said was how tired I was of having the vending machines broken all the time. He ranted and raved about this not being a country club and the world was concerned with bigger problems." I slipped her a twenty spot for 'snacks' and she agreed not to report Donny. I said it earlier,

Dutch Van Alstin – Murder in D Block

Donny was peculiar.

Strolling through the visit room door with a visit slip in her hand is the young, curvaceous Mrs. Delgado. Mrs. Delgado is married to Raphael Delgado of C block. She doesn't fall under any category of a professional visitor. She is always polite and courteous. The two of them have never had a conjugal visit leading me to believe she is just a typical prison wife trying to get along until her husband is free. C block Delgado is an odd match for his wife since he is in his early forties and she can't be over twenty. Mrs. Delgado just seems to be more polished and refined not the usual *street trash* that is proudly married to a Briersburg convict.

My immature gawking at Mrs. Delgado stems from my amazement of how she got by the frisk area dressed the way she is. A red tank top style blouse, with frilled lace on the outer edge, drapes snugly over body. Her black skirt rides up her lean, tanned thighs. The golden tan stops at a pair of red high heel patent leather shoes that are capped off with an ankle bracelet of colorful beads. Her dark black hair lay in a bed of downy curls with a small, fiery red tint that glistens underneath the softness. Her skin is silky and delicate, worthy of fine China. The erotic pink lipstick, matching only her personality, delicately covers her full, pouted lips. A small, gold crucifix dangles from her neck draping down to her inviting bosoms. Her eyes are a cat like style, green and enigmatic. Mrs. Delgado gives me a wink and smile showing her straight white teeth, a crown worn in a court of femme fatale that needs more than a sweeping glance to capture.

"Is he here today, Mr. Erickson?" she says with a quip, dropping the visit slip on the desk.

"Yes, ma'am, he is", Bob interjects brusquely.

"Not unless he jumped the wall last night, Mrs. Delgado." I say with a smile.

"Where would you like me to sit, Mr.....Andover?" She says.

Bob points at a table in the second row, close enough to watch her, but far enough away not to hear our guard jargon.

"Thank you, Sir," she says, tossing her purse on the table and digging through her coins. She manages to drop quarters in every machine and dutifully displays a meal for her husband.

"A real looker, huh, Bob?" I say.

"She's married to a prisoner," he responds sanctimoniously, "I don't look at them that way."

"Then your eyes are missing a treat, Bobby boy."

"You know," Bob says, peeking over his logbook, "that *slutty* outfit of hers violates the

Dutch Van Alstin – Murder in D Block

dress code".

"You're right, Bob, I'll go tell her to take it all off."

"You're a sick bastard, Dane."

C block Delgado makes his way in from the frisk area where he receives a quick pat frisk. There have been situations where a prisoner has smuggled in a razor or a knife. Briersburg experienced a hostage situation last year when a prisoner took his girlfriend at knifepoint in a vain attempt to escape.

Mrs. Delgado cracks a smile and embraces her husband. She pats his belly politely to stop him from kissing her and he sits down.

C block Delgado sports a white dress shirt with the tails protruding out of his waistline. His jet-black hair is caked with gel along with his boyish mustache. He is a taller man with rugged good looks. His face has a small elongated scar under his ear from a past razor attack he must have endured during his prison career. The two top buttons of his shirt are undone, exposing a gold crucifix that rests on a mat of chest hair, a mat he seems to wear as a trophy. Delgado sips one of the sodas his wife bought for him. He quickly snaps his head around stopping at our desk.

"Hey, man, come on, Andover", he says, waving his hands wildly. "My wife and I need our privacy, ain't no one here anyhow."

Bob returns a disapproving shake of his head.

Mrs. Delgado taps her husband's hand to divert his attention away from Bob. She pulls him closer, whispers in his ear and laughs. She then walks over to another vending machine to buy him a cheeseburger and a chocolate cupcake.

The rest of the day is uneventful. Only the Delgados, Rhoda Holloway, and Martin filled the room today. Bob had to separate Rhoda from Martin because she refused to leave her hands above the table.

Both prisoners are strip frisked and sent back to the cellblocks. The guard with the littlest seniority ends up at the visit frisk post, crassly known as *nuts and butts*. Somehow, regardless of seniority, Donny always ended up with this unpleasant task. The other guards just bullied him into doing it and then make jokes about how Donny liked to see the men naked.

Bob collects his paperwork and leaves to turn it in to the watch commander. He gives me a friendly salute goodbye as he fumbles to situate his folders. Both visitors gather their items and walk toward the exit where I await them both with the ultra-violet light. In keeping with her irritating demeanor, Rhoda Holloway purposely puts the wrong hand under the light.

Dutch Van Alstin – Murder in D Block

"The other hand please, Miss Holloway." I say curtly.

"This is so damn stupid!" she rolls her eyes and sighs. "Do I really look like I could be Buck in disguise?"

"Other hand, please."

She shoves her hand under the light exposing today's yellow coded symbol. In a fit of histrionics, she throws her blond hair back and tosses her skirt tails, and then storms out the door.

"Mr. Erickson," Mrs. Delgado says softly. "Can you please help me with one the vending machines? That metal bandit took nearly three dollars from me."

"Sure thing, ma'am", I say, holding up my finger, "just one second, please". I signal to the guard at the admissions desk gate around the corner to hold up a moment.
Mrs. Delgado walks over to one of the machines in the back corner near the bathrooms.

"What's the problem, Mrs. Delgado?"

She smiles. "I thought, Mr. Erickson, I told you to call me April?"

"I'm sorry…April," I say, mounting a grin on my face. "But I also recall asking you to not to be so formal and to just call me Dane."

"I believe you did, Sir." She rubs her hands up my chest and pulls me toward her, pressing her lips to mine. She slowly pulls away and smirks. "Is that informal enough for you?" She says with her arms draped around my neck.

"For the visit room it is." I reply. "Tell me, April, why the *stage dancer* look today? Are you trying to tease me?"

"We're not all whores, Dane," April says while kissing my neck. "This stigma that all prison wives jump in bed with the first man we meet is a bunch of bullshit."

"That's not what I meant, it's just that you look so…ooooh……the way you look."

"Naughty, naughty, young man," April jokingly shakes her finger at me. She sighs. "It's just that Raph harped on me to dress a bit scantily and I didn't know how to tell him no."

"Are you going out tonight?" I say.

"Hmm, not sure, how about you?"

"Probably, I have the weekend off."

"Where are you going to go?"

"Not sure, maybe Cassidy's to get some chicken wings."

"Cassidy's, huh?" April raises her eyebrows up and smiles. "Is there a chance I might run into you there?"

Dutch Van Alstin – Murder in D Block

"As possible as it has been the last few times."

"Hold on there," April says, throwing her purse over her shoulder, "my running into you that particular night was purely coincidental."

"I know, I was just trying to make a--"

"If your next word is 'date' then I may be there around, oh let's say, seven or so."

"A date? Please, Mrs. Delgado, obviously I cannot be seen in public with--"

"If your next word is anything but foxy lady, I may raise my knee up and make you a soprano." April chortles slightly. "Besides, I don't like being seen with some thug like centurion either."

"I don't recall any complaints from you on those occasions." I say, massaging her shoulders.

April spins her neck slowly absorbing the caressing and inviting more. "Oh, Dane I think I can recall someone complaining."

"Who?"

"You, tonight", she kisses my fingers, "I have Aunt Flo visiting!" April pats my fingers and begins fumbling through her purse trying to find her keys.

"That bitch!"

"Hey, if we women had a choice, we'd skip that monthly meeting, too." April grows agitated as she finally finds her keys. "You know," she says, slinging her purse over her shoulder, "you can still come over, play some euchre or something."

"Define 'something'" I say with a grin.

April cocks her head at me. "Euchre!"

"Euchre? I thought you wanted to keep things...you know, 'light'?"

"That doesn't mean just because you can't toss me around the mattress that you still can't be company? Christ, Dane, I'm lonely in other ways, too."

"Don't you have girlfriends?"

April sighs in disgust. "I'm from Philadelphia. I'm alone here in this town. I'm asking you to come over have a beer, play some cards and shoot the shit; I'm not asking you feed my strawberries and have you recite Emily Dickinson. Can't your libido take a night off and just allow the rest of you to play euchre and have a beer?"

Embarrassed somewhat I replied quickly, "no, I...I was just following your rules." I run my finger along her blouse and grin. "If all I can play with is cards tonight then so be it."

"You're such a pig. " She laughs. "I better go that other guard is probably getting

Dutch Van Alstin – Murder in D Block

suspicious. I know how paranoid you guys are."

"It wasn't me who complained about the cards, it was my over active libido."

"I'll make sure it behaves tonight if you don't," April says sternly. "Like I said, farm boy, we're not all whores." April smirks and furtively blows a kiss at me before she turns around and walks out the gate.

I gather up all my keys, finish up some final duties like making a brief glimpse of the trash, a prime smuggling area for visitors to drop contraband.

I can't help mull over April's subtle decree as she walked out the gate. She knows the image most men, especially guards, have of a *prison wife* and having an affair with me complicates the matter all the more. April was noticeably uncomfortable after the very first night we bumped into one another at Cassidy's. Although we did know each other from the visit room, the relationship was strictly plutonic. I did not even know April outside of Briersburg. There were no fortuitous meetings at the supermarket or the gas station, just one fateful night at Cassidy's by coincidence.

I always thought she was extremely attractive but in my wildest dreams that I can conjure, I never believed or thought that anything remotely romantic would start between she and I. The first night we saw each other at Cassidy's a brief chat led to a laugh, which led into a drink, then another, and then, finally, a six-pack in my car out in the parking lot, which lead to "*prom night*", as we used to called it on the farm. April and I enjoy each other's company. The physical side of our relationship never strays too far in a serious direction past a kiss good night and then pinch on her ass and a near simultaneous slap to my face followed by a giggle. I do it to reinsert the levity into the relationship. She always says: "sex isn't always love." I don't know if that axiom is profound or not but, I agree with her anyway.

I don't know why I take the chances I do with her. She could blackmail me if she ever grew angry with me or she could play me for extortion. There is a real danger in getting caught seeing her for numerous reasons, the obvious being the loss of my job and public humiliation. However, if I carefully scrutinize my own question of why I am sneaking around with her, I can find the answer woven in my carefully chosen words of bravado. Life in Minnesota tended to be tame, and a venturous lifestyle appeals to me at this juncture in my life. I always get a gloating sense of self-satisfaction when April and I are together, as if I just pulled the wool over everyone's eyes.

Normally I spend the last forty minutes of my day sipping some java in the main entrance guard's booth. The temperature is hovering around ninety degrees today, but some hot brew still sounds appealing. Unfortunately, our somewhat neurotic watch commander, Lieutenant Garrison, now wants me to do security escorts for the remaining time. Briersburg has a host of non-employed personnel visiting on a given day. Volunteer workers, clergymen, and even an occasional candy vendor, have no security clearance and cannot walk around the prison unattended. With little enthusiasm, I walk to the main gate reception area where the guard on duty is haggling with a man over searching his suitcase.

"Sir, our protocol mandates you give me the suitcase so I can search it while you walk through the metal detector." The guard says calmly.

"It's not a suitcase, dummy", the young, brash man rebukes, "it's an attaché case."

"That's irrelevant, Sir. Briersburg Prison is not public domain and you will adhere to the same policies and procedures as everyone else."

"Problem, Sir?" I interject.

The course young man turns and looks at me. He is a sharply dressed in a silk suit that looks expensive enough to suckle my next three paychecks. His face has a fastidious glow about it and his demeanor seems replete with pomposity and arrogance.

"Yes, the problem is this…this…" the man waves his hands histrionically.

"Officer? Or maybe Gentleman??" I say with a stentorian boom.

The man grows slightly flustered and tugs at his lapels. My six feet tall frame towers over his dwarfish demeanor. He straightens his back up in a vain attempt to stand up to me. "I'm Bryce J. Pitt of the N.C.A. and I have duly sworn search warrant issued by the Federal magistrate himself. All I want is to conduct my affairs without the *Gestapo* getting in my way."

"Let me explain, Sir, the National Corrections Association is not a law enforcement--"

"Yes, but we do accreditation for Briersburg involving hundreds of thousands of dollars annually and--"

"I could care less about the accreditation procedure, Mr. Pitt." I say, jamming my palm up to his face. "Can I see the warrant?"

"Rudolph Hess here took it," he says, pointing accusingly at the guard.

The guard slips Pitt a mordant glare and hands me the warrant. I give the document a quick look over and pretend I understand the complexities of legalese. "The warrant appears to be legal and all, Mr. Pitt," I say, jamming the crumpled paper into his chest. "But that fact does not exempt you from normal frisk procedures. Now hand this gentleman your suitcase and walk through the metal detector and I will take you to wherever it is you need to go. Do we understand one another, Mr. Pitt?"

Dutch Van Alstin – Murder in D Block

"You cannot be present during the search--"

"I will be right next to you in the stall if you decide to use the bathroom. Where you go, Mr. Pitt, I go."

Pitt snatches the attaché case from the guard and pushes his glasses up on his nose. "I want your name and badge number, cowboy," he says, fumbling for his pen. "The proper authorities will be notified of your perfectly boorish behavior."

"You'll be given any pertinent information you request after your search is completed. But first, I need to know where it is you want to go and what you'll be searching?"

"The area stated on the warrant. Do I have to read that for you, too?" Pitt flattens the warrant out smoothly. "Right here, cowboy," he points at the bottom of the page. "The locker contents and personnel file of one *Donald A. Quinn.*"

CHAPTER 3

I normally have a stoic disposition, but Pitt's announcement visibly unnerves me.

"Donny Quinn? Why does the N.C.A want to delve into Donny's private business?"

"Being that the man is dead, I don't believe we are intruding in his private business any longer." Pitt says smugly.

"That doesn't answer my question."

"No, I guess it doesn't. How about this for an answer: I can't divulge any information, Mr.....," Pitt says while he squints his eyes obliquely and looks at my nametag, "Erickson."

"Can't or won't."

"Either way, Mr. Erickson, you don't get to know. Now can we please move it?"

"Right this way, Mr. Pitt," I say, waving him through the main gate.

Pitt begins to look sheepishly at the old steel barred doors with every step we take in the prison. He rubs his thumbnail against his tooth, looking around in a state of voyeurism mixed with quiet panic. His eyes dash back and forth at every creaking gate, neurotically expecting at cataclysmic event at every bend in the meandering corridor. I unlock a large iron door leading out to the enormous recreation yard, presently filled with nearly *600* prisoners, many of whom are staring at the unfamiliar face.

Dutch Van Alstin – Murder in D Block

"It's nearly lunch time around here, Mr. Pitt." I say, scanning my watch quickly.

"I hope there isn't an emergency or something that requires me to leave you here alone."

"Hold it….wha…what type of emerge--" Pitt stops his fretful plea and glares at me acrimoniously. "Wait a minute? Is this some sort of threat if I don't tell you the N.C.A.'s interest in Quinn?"

"Threat is such an ugly word, but it works just the same."

"So is 'fired', try that one on for size."

"If you want to tell my Captain what I did, you have that right. The trouble, Mr. Pitt, is finding your way back, alone."

"You're a real piece of work, Erickson."

"So I've been told."

Pitt peruses the yard again, as if by miracle all *600* prisoners vanished. He steals a quick peek at his watch and sighs. "Fine, what do I care if some gendarme wants to play Sam Spade."

"Shall we proceed back to where we came?" I gallantly gesture Pitt back through the door.

"Are you telling me Quinn's locker isn't even this way?"

"That's what I'm saying. The lockers are in the *Rooney* building, the building we started in to begin with."

Pitt shakes his head in disgust and begins walking. "When we get to the locker room I'll explain the details and I'll try to say it at a fourth grade level so you can follow along."

"I think you better explain now, I don't want to deliver the goods without seeing payment up front."

"You call doing your job 'delivering the goods'?"

"You're stalling."

"Okay, how about this compromise, I'll tell you long the way. I don't want to be out here in the sweltering heat any longer than I have to."

"Sounds fair," I say, walking Pitt back through the corridors. "Okay, Mr. Pitt, start talking. Why is the N.C.A. so interested in Donny's effects?"

"Who?"

"Quinn…he had a first name you know?"

"Yes, I'm sure he did." Pitt formulates a satirical grin on his face. "Anyway, I'm here because of the accreditation process. As you know safety is a big concern--"

Dutch Van Alstin – Murder in D Block

"Whoa, hold your horses there. I am growing tired of your doubletalk. If you were worried about some bogus safety concern, then you'd want to investigate where he fell. Now either you come clean or we walk back to the yard and I serve your carcass for lunch out there."

Pitt sighs dramatically. "Fine, I have a dinner date with the governor's aid tonight and I want to get the hell out of here."

"The N.C.A. doesn't sound too anxious to do its job."

"The truth is, cowboy, Quinn's death is of no interest to us."

"That's very sentimental of you, Pitt. Are you forgetting we're talking about a human being here?"

"I don't mean it that way, Erickson," Pitt remarks. "Do you want to hear this or not?"

"Go on", I begin walking again with Pitt tailing very close behind me.

"The whole scenario is I.A.'s baby. They have some concerns about Quinn's death and they felt if they dug too deep, or were too obvious, they would scare potential witnesses or snitches."

"Why is the I.A. interested? They investigated and ruled out murder?"

"True, but the final conclusion was there was no conclusion. Ruling out murder simply rules out one possible scenario. But let's face facts; the whole scenario just seems a little perplexing."

I wave to the guard in the booth to open the gate to the basement door. The guard has a long, wooden dowel and manages to push the button to open the gate without getting out of his chair.

"What is the I.A. looking for?"

"Meaning?"

"Meaning, what are they looking for? It's not a trick question."

"I don't know the direction of their investigation, cowboy. Our organizations don't share secret information."

I scoff. "What secret information does the N.C.A. have? How our garbage compactors work?

"My you're an angry, bitter man, cowboy."

"Spare me the amateur psychology, Pitt."

"The bottom line, Erickson is I don't know what the I.A.'s agenda is. I just know that they smell something funny and they want to get to the bottom of it before whatever it is takes on a life of its own."

Dutch Van Alstin – Murder in D Block

I follow Pitt downstairs and lead him to Donny's locker, number 714.

"If you don't know I.A.'s angle then how do you know what to look for?"

"Anything suspicious," Pitt says, shaking Donny's locker.

"There is a door, Pitt. That will allow you a little bit easier access."

"I know." Pitt pulls a key from his pocket. "I'm also privy to a master key."

"Do you have any idea what you're looking for?"

"The orders I received were ambiguous. I was told to keep an eye out for 'anything suspicious', those were the exact words." Pitt fumbles through some personal items of Donny's. "Hmmmm, hair gel, combs, extra uniform, broken down thermos, gym bag, couple of raffle tickets, crumpled up repair bill, nothing but shit."

"Perhaps the sign that read: 'ATTENTION! DRUGS HIDDEN IN LOCKER! LOOK UNDER FALSE FLOOR AT THE BOTTOM'! was stolen last week? Why don't you start there?"

Pitt stands up and brushes the dust off his pants. "My, but you are a comedian."

"What did you hope to find in a locker?"

"I'm not sure," Pitt says, clapping the dirt off his hands, "maybe a sign like you described."

"Look, Pitt, you don't know me, and I don't like you. But I admit I have problems surrounding Donny's death, too. Tell me what you have and I'll tell you what I have."

"What do you have, cowboy?" He gibes.

"Well, nothing concrete, just speculation."

"Ah!" Pitt says, nodding his head. "That's a very meritorious start in your intensive investigation. Sherlock Holmes would be proud."

"Come on, I was honest with you, tell me what you have."

"I was honest with you too, eventually," Pitt quips. "And as I already said, the N.C.A. isn't interested in Quinn's death. I'm here as a favor to a friend to see if anything unusual jumped out at me that shouldn't have."

"Look, Pitt, I can't threaten to leave you out in a yard full of killers anymore, but I have to believe the I.A. told you something more than just 'anything suspicious'?"

"You're right," Pitt replies, straightening his necktie, "you can't threaten me now".

"Is that your way of telling me to go to hell?"

"No, this is: *go to hell,* cowboy."

"It must be frustrating pretending to be important, Pitt. You really like this *Sherlockesque* living, don't you?"

Dutch Van Alstin – Murder in D Block

"Now who's being an amateur psychologist? Besides, look who's talking?" Pitt snickers sarcastically. "A guy in a cheap blue suit, with a badge devoid of enough tin to make a dime insults me? You're the one skulking around sounding like *Dirty Harry* and *Inspector Clouseau* combined. Face facts, cowboy, this Quinn guy probably awoke one morning and couldn't stand the thought of being a prison guard for another day and dove to the cement."

I pause trying to think of a witty comeback. "The insult notwithstanding, nobody just wakes up one morning and does a half-gainer off the top tier."

"As I said earlier, I don't care." Pitt dumps Donny's effects in the trash and claps his hands again, ridding himself of the grime. "If something furtive and clandestine was going on, it's not the N.C.A's concern. Now I'll still need a shadow to the filing room. Are you capable of that, cowboy or should I call a real cop?"

"I think I can handle that minor task, Mr. Pitt."

I walk Pitt to the file room and leave him with another guard. Before I go home, I trek back to the basement and retrieve Donny's belongings from the trash. I didn't want to take them in front of Pitt because I'm sure, even though he didn't want them, he would have confiscated them as evidence to flex his federal muscle.

A backward salute is all I offer the front gate guard as I saunter out of Briersburg and into a hot, sticky day. The humidity is so intense there is steam visible rising above the road.

I open the car doors wide and leave them open to let some of the heat flow out. The black vinyl interior absorbs every bouncing particle of heat.

I toss Donny's belongings in my trunk and rummage through the various items. There is nothing of value to be passed on to the next of kin whoever that may be. There seems to be nothing in Donny's bag, except typical guard items that we all have in one form or another such as boots, uniform, comb, gel, thermos…thermos? Perhaps the thermos does appear somewhat out of place. Briersburg has been experiencing a heat wave of sorts; besides, Donny worked primarily in D block. There was always a pot of coffee in the guard's bathroom in D block.

I shake the thermos a few times and listen for some coffee. The top is tight but I manage to unscrew it and take a deep whiff.

"Wow," I say, as my eyes grow watery. The booze in this thermos belongs in a cheap paper bag.

"Damn you, Donny, how could you?" I say, sniffing the aroma again, as if somehow it would vanish and I wouldn't have to believe Donny was smuggling liquor in Briersburg. I poke through a few more items and smooth out the car repair bill that turns out not to be a bill, but a receipt for services rendered. New floor mats, rust proofing, a bed liner, and a pinstripe package. Enveloped in the receipt is a credit card wrapped in a sales slip. The sales slip is for two tickets for *Cats* on Broadway in September and a hotel reservation for the same weekend.

Two tickets? I don't want to sound cruel, but Donny having a *friend* to take on a weekend rendezvous seems peculiar. Moreover, if he had a friend, I picture him being a little boastful about a trip, not to mention buying a new truck. Whom was he going on the trip with? Where are they now? I'm not a *psychobabblist* of any kind, but I am under the impression people who kill themselves give some sort inclination of their plan. I read somewhere people revert before a suicide attempt, but Donny wasn't reverting. Maybe his future plans and commitments were not extensive like marriage, or a new house, but why would a man who is going to kill himself spend *$2,800.00* the day before he leaps off the tier?

I smell the thermos once more and shake my head in antipathy. Donny certainly wasn't much of a drinker. I don't recall him bragging up his hangovers like the robots do all the time. Smuggling in hooch is not a lone bad act a corrupt guard would dabble into, there has to be more. If the prisoners could talk Donny into bringing in whiskey, they could talk him into more such as laundering cash, helping shanks be transferred from area of the jail to another; the inventory of sleaze is endless.

"Damn you, Donny, and your stupid little games", I say aloud to myself. "This wasn't some high school play you were involved in." I dump the contents of Donny's thermos on the ground and sigh in disgust.

"Because obviously somebody on the cast list wasn't just pandering to the cameras, somebody was playing for real."

CHAPTER 4

The sun slips faster and faster into the hillside as summer wanes down at the closing of August. I could easily lament the passing of summer, saying goodbye to swimming, barbecuing on my dock as I look over the lake; but the fall brings splendor across the valley that is unmatched by any swimming experience I may have.

The aging maples drop their colorful leaves into the lake creating a kaleidoscope image in the swirling waters. The symmetry of the water flow seems almost rehearsed by Mother Nature herself to maintain the perfection of her nature, chiding humanity and reminding us we live in an imperfect world. Combine this view with a hot cup of coffee in my hand, and floundering about in the water loses its luster.

I do my last second grooming on the porch while I watch the hull of my boat whack against the dock by the waves of a passing jet ski. The proper attire coincides with my grooming. There is an art to the *all you can eat* night at Cassidy's and, in my case, the clothes make the man. Part of the ensemble must include loose fitting, but stylish slacks, to allow me to chow freely without undoing the top button. A burgundy colored shirt, matching the color of Cassidy's secret sauce, is the key to hide anticipated spillage. My sometimes D block partner, Joey Gullo, suggested Cassidy's to me one night when I inquired about who served the best wings in town. I have made it a somewhat ritual to be there every Saturday, regardless of my work schedule the following morning.

    I met April on one of those very nights. She and I have never made a formal date to meet at Cassidy's, but we always let each other know when the other will be there. The lack of *formality* is the reason why I do not suggest we meet elsewhere. Cassidy's is a guard hangout, and in spite of that, I like to come here. But I know the robots at work would not look favorably upon me for fraternizing with the wife of a prisoner. I haven't convinced myself she and I are fraternizing or dating. Our time spent together in the bar seems to dwindle more and more each week because we tend to spend it with a six-pack in the front seat of my car and then capping off the evening in the back seat, or, on occasion, a room above the Shakertown Tavern uptown. I know if I suggest we meet in another location, then I have to admit to myself April and I are, in fact, dating.

    Cassidy's parking lot is filling up quickly and trying to find a space underneath a light is growing more difficult. I manage to slide into a spot near the front of the bar as I watch a man, whose drunken exterior is only matched by his drunken interior, stagger, and bounce through the parking lot. The man, trying to get from point A to point B without running into C, has a name, and that name is Randy McPherson.

    Randy became a guard during the state's hiring boom just as I did. During the boom, several people wriggled through the state's psychiatric test undetected. I often believe Randy was one of those *greased pigs*, as the robots refer to those who squeaked by. Randy repeats tales so outlandish and so frequently, he often can't distinguish truth from fiction. The first time I was privy to one of his allegorical fables, I sincerely believed I was part of some hazing ritual for new guards, testing my gullibility. I find it curious that Randy, or "Mack," as he is referred to by his friends and myself, creates such fantasies.

    Mack's physical appearance gives one an impression that he is no wimp. Unlike Donny, who was skinny and almost sickly, Randy stands over six feet tall. He carries a large midsection, but he still is abundantly muscular. His arms are not lean, but they are stout in size, quite stubby in fact, which allows him to walk with a natural swagger in his shoulders. He has bushy black hair that lays flat on his large, round head. His face is blemished with pot-mark patches that he tries to hide in a prematurely graying beard, and the noticeably cubic ears tuck way in along his rigid jaw line. Tonight he gowns himself in a blue denim jacket, torn at the elbows, exposing his red corduroy shirt that he wears with the tails exposed. He tucks his oversized khaki pants in a pair of old army boots that have been spray painted olive drab and wrapped at the top with duct tape. I attempt to drive by him, shielding my face away from the window.

"Dane! Dane! Over here, man!" He shouts.

I concede defeat and stop my car to roll down my window. "Hey, Mack, what's up?"

"Come'n in, man?"

"No, I just stopped to use the head. I'm supposed to meet my cousin later on downtown."

"No kidding? Your cousin?" Mack says, wide eyed, as if he knows my cousin.

"Yeah, were hitting the bowling alleys a little later."

"Hey, cool, sounds cool. Why don't you two stop by later and have a brew?"

"Is there any left?" I say, waving away the reek of alcohol.

Mack laughs. "Oh, Dane, I need a slut tonight."

"I'm sure one needs you, too, Mack."

Randy drops his body down, resting his chin on my windowsill. "Damn, man, bring your cousin back here and will all get some tang."

"As tempting as that sounds, Mack, I'll have to take a rain check, okay?"

"Whatever the wind blows," he says. "I'll be here all night."

I grudgingly shake his hand before I speed away around the parking lot. Randy frantically waves at my car as I pull around the corner. I motor back nearby where I was and watch Randy walk into Cassidy's. A group of four girls stands outside smoking cigarettes and giggling childishly as they slap each other's backside. Randy walks by and smiles at one of the girls. She responds quickly by giving him the old *one finger salute.*

"Is that an offer, baby?" He says, stumbling into the door.

I give Randy enough time to order a beer, annoy a few waitresses, and make his way back toward the dance floor.

After walking inside and passed the bouncer, I walk up to the bar and order my wings, giving a sweeping glance around the room for Randy. The bartender, Chuck, the owner's son, runs back toward the kitchen to speed up my order.

"Hi, ya, Dane, how's tricks?" Chuck says.

"Not too bad, Chuck," I say, looking away from him and out toward the dance floor.

Chuck wipes the bar sweat off the counter and slides the pretzel bowl down to me. He wrings out his rag and wipes his hands on his formally white apron. Chuck is pushing forty and has already lost most of his sandy brown hair. He attempts a comb over, but the battle has been lost.

Dutch Van Alstin – Murder in D Block

"Sorry to hear about your friend, Dane."

"My friend?"

"Yeah, that fellow that came in here now and then, Donny I think it was. I heard he had himself an accident?"

I motion toward the tap for Chuck to give me a beer. He spins a bottle in air before he slides it down to me.

"What did you hear, Chuck?"

"Not much," Chuck says as he continues wiping the bar, "just what the papers were saying: that he fell off a ladder or something."

"Not quite," I say, swallowing my beer. "He fell off the top tier in D block."

"Shame either way, Dane," Chuck says. "He seemed like a nice fellow." Chuck stops wiping and leans in closer to me. "Nothing personal, Dane, but you fellows, the guards I mean, well lots of times they cause trouble, see? My dad and I have been in here many a night watching tables fly around and all too often it's one of you guys. That Donny was never like that, never caused a lick of trouble." Chuck stands back up and wrings the rag out again in the basin. "He just sat here and took it easy; I don't know why more people can't just do that?"

"Donny came in here a lot?" I say, swallowing my beer once more. "I don't recall ever seeing him and I'm here a lot, too?"

"That don't surprise me none, Dane. Donny? He was just that type of guy. Nobody ever noticed him, but he came a lot, he like my wings too, just like you." Chuck says, wiggling his finger at me. "He'd come in and just shoot the breeze real calm and collective, he never mentioned the prison or nothing."

"I'm sorry Chuck, I can't hear you," I say, leaning forward to fight off the music. "What did you say?"

No, nuttin much, I was just saying how nobody ever noticed him. In fact, you patted him on the shoulder one night yourself?"

"Me?"

"Yeah, just last month sometime, that's how I knew he was a guard."

"I said hello to him?" I say in continued disbelief. "I swear I don't remember."

"As I was saying, Dane, that's the type of guy he was, nobody noticed when he was around."

I swallow my beer and let out a feint laugh to cover my slight embarrassment. "What did he talk about?"

Dutch Van Alstin – Murder in D Block

"Simple stuff, sometimes, well...sort of, you know...well..." Chuck stammers. "I guess you could say..." Chuck shrugs his shoulders and sighs.

"What?" I say intently.

Chuck shakes his head. "Nah, it ain't right to talk about someone when they're not around to defend themselves."

"What did he have to defend himself from?"

"Nothing really," Chuck says, "I guess you could say he was a bit eccentric."

"Eccentric?" I say sharply. "Come on, Chuck, Howard Hughes was eccentric. Civil service employees don't have the financial means to be eccentric. What you mean is *weird*, don't you?"

Chuck grabs my wings from the cook, spins them around once, and slides them to me. "Well.....I'm trying to be tactful because Donny was a real nice guy, really he was."

"Nobody's accusing you otherwise, Chuck," I say, attacking the first helpless wing with my molars. "I just meant I always had that opinion of him, too and I was just wondering what lead you to the same conclusion."

"Well..." Chuck pauses and clicks his tongue off the roof of his mouth. "I can't pinpoint any one particular thing he did, Dane. He was just, kinda, I don't know," Chuck says, growing agitated, "he just was, that's all."

"I know what you mean, I couldn't pinpoint anything either. I just know he was a bit of an oddball."

"You know..." Chuck says, untying his apron and tossing into the kitchen, "he did start sounding different the last few times I saw him in here."

"How?"

"He was a semi-regular, mostly on Tuesdays."

"Tuesdays?"

"Yeah," Chuck says, spinning around and pointing at a sign, "*ladies night.*"

"Oh, and I show up on *wing* night and call him nutty?"

Chuck forges a small snicker. "Yeah, anyway, he always came in and talked about the girls and stuff, but there was a time when he stopped coming in regularly. So one day, out of the blue, Donny pops in and sits himself down. Now mind you, he don't order nothing, he just says he's sorry for not coming in lately. The natural follow up question is; 'yeah, I know, how come?' I mean, I didn't want him thinking I didn't notice, right?"

"Right, right, go on."

Dutch Van Alstin – Murder in D Block

"That's when he got weird on me. He started getting real somber and serious and falling all over himself apologizing."

"Apologizing for what?"

"That's what I wondered? He said he'd been hanging out at *Beviars,*" Chuck says with phony French accent. It's a place up the parkway, snobbish really. It's a hangout for the social elite who are impressed with French names. The only thing French there is the prices, but that fit, too. Donny was flashing more money around before he quit hanging out here."

"Money?"

"Yeah, mostly small bills, but he always had a wad of them. He said he a second job of some sort and was saving up for a boat and a truck."

"Did he say where he was working?"

"No, never did tell me that, figured he was embarrassed about it."

"Embarrassed? Maybe nervous?" I say, flashing my mind back to the thermos.

"I don't know, Dane, I ain't no head shrinker. I just know he seemed embarrassed. I figured he was bagging groceries or mopping floors." Chuck rubs his forehead with the back of his hand and sighs. "You know, there was a time no man was ashamed to work, but I guess that's when work was for need and not greed."

"Maybe so," I say disinterestedly, "can you just tell me the *weird* part?"

"Oh, yeah, well he actually asked me about how I felt about him not coming in anymore."

"Huh?'

"I know, that sounds goofy to me too but that's what he said. He asked if my feelings were hurt. He said he hoped I understood that 'he needed to explore new avenues', crazy talk, you know?"

"Sounds it," I say, swallowing another gulp between bites.

"He started talking like one of those unemployed psychiatrist types, you know, the ones you see on those trashy daytime talk shows?"

"Did you ever see him after that encounter?"

"Only once."

"When did he do all this mumbo jumbo?"

"About....oh, I guess a few weeks ago."

"I never noticed much of a change at work either; then again I have nothing to compare personalities with, he was a clam at work, too." I swallow the last of my beer and tap the bottom of the bottle on the bar. Chuck instinctively reaches back and grabs me another twisting off the

Dutch Van Alstin – Murder in D Block

cap with his slimy bar rag. "He did flip out in the visit room the other day. He became enraged at one of the visitors who never give us trouble."

"No, Donny never gave nobody trouble."

"I meant the visitor, Chuck. She's real polite and quiet. Fortunately the visit room only had a few people in it that day to witness Donny's little fit."

"I got the feeling he was hanging around someone new, Dane"

"What makes you say that?"

Chuck leans back on his elbows and looks up at the ceiling fan. He dabs a spot of sweat of his head and lays the rag on his brow. "Because one of the last times I saw him, he said he had to head back to Bevier's to meet someone."

"Any idea who?"

"No, not really."

"Can you expand on *not really*? Did he ever meet anyone here that you know of?"

"He'd talk with some girls here now and then, but never for long. The girls would just let him buy them a few drinks and then they'd be on their merry way."

"Did you get a name of any of these girls? Are they regulars?"

"No, the closest I ever I ever heard to a name was when he thought he had a phone call here."

"Donny received a call? From whom?"

"Nobody called him; he thought he had a call once?"

"Chuck, trying to decipher you sometimes is like--"

"I just mean there was a call one night for Bonnie, and I yelled out 'phone for you, Donny'."

"Who's Bonnie?"

"She was a waitress I hired a while back, fired her for skimming the till, but anyway, her boyfriend called here one night but it was so damn loud in here, I thought he asked for 'Donny'."

"You gave the phone to Donny?"

"I did, and you should have seen how excited he was. Good, God, he grabbed that receiver, fumbled with it, and shouted 'hello' three times before he got it to his ear."

"Who or what can be that eye-popping?"

"I don't know, Dane, all I remember is him being so pissed off that he slammed down the phone. He started ranting about how 'it ain't for me, it ain't for me, damn it all'!"

"He got that mad over a misdirected call?"

"He did?"

"Was he expecting a call?"

"Not that he told me about."

"What did he do then?"

"Naturally I asked him what the matter was."

"And?"

"I thought he said 'it was *a list'*."

"List? What list?" I say inquisitively.

"That's when he lost it, Dane."

"Lost what?" I say, motioning for Chuck to speed it up a bit.

"He said: 'damn you, old timer, get your hearing checked! I said *Chris! Chris!* Not list! How do you get *list* from *Chris*?"

"He got that mad?"

"That's what I'm saying, Dane, he wasn't himself."

"That doesn't sound like the Donny I knew."

"Me either, Dane," Chuck says, shaking his head. "After that he slammed his hand on the bar and walked out. I ain't seen him since."

"Nothing personal, Chuck, but your sure he said the name Chris this time?"

"Believe me, Dane," Chuck says with a smile, "everybody in the place heard him."

"Chris?"

"That's what the man said."

"Who the hell is Chris?"

"I don't know, Dane, but whoever he was, he was sure important to Donny."

CHAPTER 5

I don't recall an *all you can eat* night where Chuck didn't make some disparaging, albeit humorous, remarks about his kids not being able to afford college due to my overindulgence. I swirl my beer around in my bottle, taking an occasional sip of brew growing flat and warm. The intrigue surrounding Donny is just growing more cryptic.

"Donny Quinn?" I think to myself. It seems like a simple name, yet labeled to a complex man. Jumping from D block? Weird! Weird?

A raucous from the opposite end of the bar startles me. I capture a glance of a man being hurled across a table, taking several pitchers and mugs of beer with him to the floor. The disc jockey's music halts abruptly and patrons stand motionless, witnessing the man floundering on the floor and being held down by two large men. I creep in closer and notice the floundering fool is Mack.

"Get off me, assholes, I'm an officer of the law," Mack shouts.

"So am I, fat boy, now shut the hell up and keep still," one of the men shouts. The man, to Mack's dismay, has a badge on his belt. He seems to be an off-duty rookie Briersburg City cop.

"Excuse me, officer," I say loud enough to be heard but soft enough to sound respectful. "Why don't you let me get him out of here; he and I work together at the prison and he found out

Dutch Van Alstin – Murder in D Block

tonight that his house burned to the ground."

The young policeman looks at me half sympathetically and half pungently and sighs. "I don't want to do three hours of paperwork tonight anyway," the cop says, looking up at Chuck for approval.

"Just get 'em out of here," Chuck says, "and I'll forget the whole thing happened."

"Thanks, Chuck," I say, lifting Mack off the floor. Nobody volunteers to help lift the ignoramus on to his feet.

"That's what I was talking about, Dane," Chuck says, pointing to Mack. "It's guys like this that are screw ups. Maybe Donny was a bit weird but he wasn't like this guy."

"I know, Chuck, I'll get him out of your hair."

Chuck throws a sarcastic look my way.

"Sorry," I say quickly, "I should have used a better metaphor."

"My house burned?" Mack says amidst a simpering whine.

"Shut up, Mack," I whisper.

"When did this happen?"

"Mack, your house is fine, now shut up. I'm trying to get you out of here."

"Actually, Dane, my ex-wife got my house in the divorce."

"Who cares, Mack," I say, pulling him toward the door, "you've got to go before they take you downtown." I motion for Chuck to call me a cab for Mack and wait outside in the parking lot. My hopes the night air may perk Mack up some diminish when he stumbles and vomits near a trash can. Mack then tells me he loves me and mentions what a great friend I am, and then, he falls down and passes out on the hood of a Volkswagen.

The cab pulls up and I dig some cash out of Mack's wallet pull out a twenty-dollar bill. I find Mack's keys hidden in his sock and hand both items over to the cabby, along with Mack's address.

"Andy Jackson for a three dollar drive? What gives?" The cabby asks as his cigarette bounces around in his mouth.

"The money left over is your tip if you drag the palooka in his house and dump him on the floor."

"For a seventeen dollar tip I'll even make sure he lands on the carpet."

"Don't go to all that trouble," I say, patting the hood of the cab.

The whole night is heading for, if it hasn't arrived, for a complete disaster. I look up by the lamppost only to spot April standing on the steps. She is dressed in a pink blouse with ruffled sleeves and a pair of tight white pants. Her hair is little different than it was this afternoon; she drapes her bangs down in a loose curl just above her eyes.

"Hi, stranger," she says.

"How long have you been here?"

"Oh," she stares at her watch intently, "long enough to witness your gallantry to your friend."

"Wait a minute," I say defensively, "let's use the word *acquaintance.*"

April walks off the steps with her arms are delicately folded to fend off the chilly night air. "Either appellation used, you put your neck out for him and that's sweet."

"I prefer *instinctive,* I equate sweet with sap and donuts, the latter being the only useful of the two."

"What's the matter, big boy," she says, draping her arms around my neck, "big, tough prison guard don't like to be seen as sweet?"

I tense up some and move her arms off my neck. "I'm sorry, April, I'm going to call it a night. I have a lot of things on my mind and I just want to relax."

"I understand." She folds her arms up again and shivers. "I would have whipped your hillbilly ass in euchre anyhow." She shivers somewhat exaggerative once more and rubs her hands together. "How about you and I go somewhere for a cup of cappuccino and just talk? I'll even buy you that donut; I believe you let out a Freudian slip with your analogy."

For reasons unknown to me, I laugh. "Sure, why the hell not?"

April, somewhat affronted, manages to concoct a giggle. "That's not the response a girl likes to hear."

"I don't mean it personally; it's just my way of overruling my better judgment."

"Oh," she laughs. "You're just wooing me over tonight, Dane."

"I didn't mean that either, I've had a rough night. I'd love to have a cup of coffee".

"You're driving, I don't own a car."

"How did you get here?"

"I only live a few blocks away from here, I walked."

"Step this way, me lady," I say, motioning her toward my car, "your chariot awaits."

"Your chivalry is impressive."

"And artificial, open your own door."

April hops in the front seat and fumbles with her hair. I find an out of the way coffee shop near the out skirts of town. The coffee is notoriously bad, but the view of Kingfish Lake is

Dutch Van Alstin – Murder in D Block

what draws people like me to stop anyway. The café sits atop a knoll looking down over the water. When the weather is warmer, people sit outside on the veranda.

A waitress devoid of any signs of merriment paces slowly to our table and stands silently.

"Two cups, please," I say.

"Want cream or sugar, it's five cents extra."

"None for me."

The waitress treks over and slides us two mugs, and yet, she puts them on saucers. I sip the vile brew carefully and cough slightly.

"Where are you from, Dane?" April blurts.

"Me?"

"Um, yep". She says with a smirk.

I didn't expect her to ask me where I was from but I guess it's a good a place as any to start. I proceed in telling her of my humdrum upbringing on the farm in Minnesota. April smiles a few times during the homily of homespun lifestyles on a farm. Her smile seems sincere and not just a veiled attempt to cover boredom.

"So what you're saying is your life was full of *bullshit?*" she says with a snicker.

"That's a layman's way of putting it, but you got the gist of it. What about you?"

April takes a gulp of coffee. "What about me?"

"My roots were in *bullshit*, how about yours?"

April smiles and moves her coffee from one hand to the other. "Let's just say my roots were in sand so I pulled them up."

I nod my head affirmatively to let the subject pass. April seemed unwilling to divulge too much information about her past. I don't imagine it has been a fairytale, however, she did mention she was married two years ago before C block Delgado went to prison.

"Two years ago is all?" I say incredulously. You must have been pretty young since you can't be over twenty-one or twenty-two?"

"Let's just say I'm a big girl now," she says, tapping my hand and winking to end the inquisition. April takes one last big gulp of coffee and throws her spoon in the empty mug. "Summer's almost over, Dane," she says buoyantly. "How about we take a stroll along the lake. The view is totally gorgeous this time of night especially on a clear night like tonight." She sighs. "I come here a lot and just look at the sunset."

I fool myself into believing I am mulling over the repercussions of saying yes, before I do,

Dutch Van Alstin – Murder in D Block

in fact, say yes. We walk out into the August night and the air has grown cooler, so much so that April wraps her arms completely around her waist and shivers.

"Brrrr, it's chillier than I thought," April says.

I drape my coat over her shoulders. April grabs my hand, helps me situate the collar over her shoulders, and continues to hold it tightly when I'm through. She nuzzles her body into my chest and buries her head on my shoulder. "I'm really cold tonight."

We stroll together up on the hill, sit, and gaze down at the lake. The lake is calm as the twilight from the moon glistens off the water. The ripples of the docile waves paralyze us and could easily lull anyone to sleep in seconds. An occasional leaping fish breaks the tranquility of the sultry waters as a slight breeze blows through April's hair.
Just by looking at her, I can see she is miles away in her mind with her eyes closed and a gentle smile perched upon her face.

A peaceful serenade surrounds us.

There are no gray walls, no wedding bands, no April Delgado, nor any Dane Erickson. There is only us, in the crisp summer night being absorbed by the hypnotism of fantasy. I rub my hand along her arm and pull her closer. She sits in silence. All her thoughts she speaks with her seductive green eyes. April rubs her hand along my face and draws me near. The wetness of her lips dampens mine. She slides back momentarily and kisses my neck numerous times. Her fingernails lightly graze my face as she slides her lips along my nape. She sighs, strokes my face. And, amidst the moment, she whispers: "Dane…it's late."

"Yeah…uh,….I know, I know, you're right."

"I'm sorry, Dane," she says, sliding her body back, "it's just that, uh-"

"No, no, you're absolutely right, it's late and I'll, ah…bring you home."

My last sense of chivalry causes me to stand up and reach for hand to help her up. She stands and hides her embarrassment in a veneer of cheerfulness.

"The ground, it's so dirty sometimes," she says, brushing the grime off her pants.

April puts her hand in mine and then quickly pulls it back to fix her hair. She then slides her hand into her pocket. She climbs in my car and remains veritably silent. With the exception of telling me her address, April stares intently out my widow with her head resting on the sill all the way to her apartment.

"Is this it?" I say, pulling into a small apartment complex.

April pops her head up and grabs her purse. She looks at me as if it is taking great effort to look me in the eyes. With a peck on the cheek and a blurb of *goodbye,* April hurries herself in the door without looking back at me.

When she's out of my sight I pull out on the road and try to put the night into perspective. I'm glad she said goodbye because goodbye is what is needed. The whole thrill of the perilous roots of our relationship began to take a very dangerous off ramp from casualness to seriousness.

I took a small bite from the apple, now I need to walk away from the temptation of the orchard.

CHAPTER 6

The sample of fall Friday night was merely Mother Nature's way of teasing my senses. The sweltering heat that has plagued this month of August has returned at Monday's daybreak with reprisals. The lake looks stagnant and still, afraid, it seems, to cause even a ripple in its glass coating in fear of causing an undaunted surge of waves. Rather choosing a more pragmatic and conventional existence, causing no one discomfort or difficulty in their daily lives. Boats whisk through the mirrored surface unchallenged and uninhibited by the lakes potential powers. Anglers relax in the solace provided by nature's fleeting repose, knowing that its passions and tumult will rise again at a whim.

The midnight tower guard walks out onto the platform, stretching and yawning, greeting the morning sun.

"Morning!" he shouts to me as he opens the gate.

"Is that a greeting or a question?" I say with a quip.

"Not on my watch, farm boy."

I change into my uniform and grab a cup of coffee from the *line up* room, carefully giving the aroma a whiff. My eyes nearly tear up at the odorous brew and I dispose it in the trashcan. Being early to line up is a rarity for me, I take the opportunity to slide my feet under a chair and close my eyes, and rest before the chart sergeant arrives.

"Hey, Erickson, move it," a voice says as I feel a slap on my leg. I peer up at a guard I recognize by sight only.

"Only *A* block guards sit here, now move it."

Most scenarios, such as the one before me, I would argue the point, or lack thereof, but the overwhelmingly absurdity of the guard's contention renders me speechless. I sigh in surrender and move to another area of the room.

"Get some time on the job, Dane, and maybe you can sit with us," he says, amidst several laughs and *high fives.*

"I can't possibly want to anything more than that....someday, " I say with a smirk."

My comment brings forth some sophomoric barbs that I merely ignore. The kitchen guards sit huddled in their corner of the room. The kitchen crew tends to be less haughty about their jobs, much like the war veteran who hides the fact he was an army cook. I strike up a conversation with Mike Beacher, the kitchen's primary guard, in hopes he will send me ten extra baked chickens to D block at lunchtime. A request of ten extra chickens is not out of the ordinary for a cellblock the colossal size of D block. The wheeling and dealing begins. Before I can counteroffer twenty feet of coaxial cable I found in D block's basement, and a pile of confiscated pornography, Mack saunters in and spies me immediately.

"Hey ya, Dane," Mack says with a *Pall Mall* dangling from his mouth. The ash is about to fall off the end and Mack flicks the cinders on the floor underneath the *No Smoking* sign. "*Didja* tell these guys about the brawl Saturday night?"

"Brawl?" I say inquisitively.

Mack glances over at the kitchen crew, and regardless of the fact I am sitting next to him, he proceeds to lie out a synopsis, a synopsis I do not recall.

"This blond with a black leather skirt grabbed my ass out on the dance floor-"

"You dance, Mack?" Beacher says, dangling his pinky finger.

"Fuck no," Mack says, squirming a bit in his chair, "I just like to look at the bitches out there. Anyway, she asked me to take her home and that's when her boyfriend and three other punks showed up."

"From where?"

"From somewhere, you know," Mack says, exhaling his smoke into the air. "All I know is they jumped me, and remembering my hand to hand combat from the Marine Core, I laid 'em all out until some off duty pig showed up and bashed me with his nightstick."

Dutch Van Alstin – Murder in D Block

"Hold it, Randy," another kitchen guard interjects, "if he was off duty, why did he have a nightstick?"

"It took all six of 'em to knock me down, but not before I broke the one guy's nose. I think that's who the cop was friends with."

"First off," Beacher says, "that only adds up to five and secondly, that doesn't explain why an off duty cop had a nightstick with him?"

"I don't know," Mack says, shrugging his shoulders. "Maybe he borrowed it?"

Sitting a few chairs away from us is Officer T.J. Armstrong. Armstrong is one of the few guards we can all admit we respect. Armstrong's physical appearance is not intimidating at first glimpse. He stands just less than six feet tall but his build is solid, well-hidden muscle. His hair is torn between a red and brown. The color is hard to discern because he cuts it so short in a military style with a *wet like* fullness on top. Armstrong's face is square with strong cheekbones riding up beneath his cagey eyes, capped off with bushy eyebrows stretching from one eye to the other. His uniform is always impeccable and neatly ironed with full military creases, magnifying his old army boots that glare with an illustrious polish. The image Armstrong presents is the image he maintains, tough as nails and steeped in jail savvy.

The first time I worked with him I studied him as he worked by the arch gate, the big iron gate that links the two recreation yards together. The prisoners were looking at Armstrong as they passed by and they would instinctively lower their voices. It seemed as though out of nowhere Armstrong taps a passing prisoner named Cardozo and motions him to come over toward the gate. Cardozo was visibly agitated.

"Come on, Armstrong, I only gets a certain time out of that cell and I can't be wasting it talking the breeze with you," he said caustically.

Armstrong glared at Cardozo and squinted his eyes a bit as he went eyeball to eyeball with him. "Quick pat down and you can go," Armstrong said.

Cardozo bellowed out an exaggerative sigh and slowly placed his hands on the wall. Armstrong it seemed at once went for Cardozo's belt. "Take off the belt, Cardozo," Armstrong said. "Whatcha got under there?"

Cardozo shrugged his shoulders. "Why you jackin' me 'round, Armstrong? I ain't never given you no beef 'bout nothing."

"The belt," he said again without missing a beat.

Cardozo pulled his belt off slowly, dropped it on the ground, and then put his hands back on the gate. "Fuck you, Armstrong. Fuck you! Fuck you!"

Dutch Van Alstin – Murder in D Block

Armstrong bent down, never taking his eyes off Cardozo. By this time, I had my club out and ready. Armstrong lifts up the belt and three razor blades were taped to the inside.

Later I asked Armstrong how he knew and he just replied in that reclusive, furtive but slightly braggadocios manner of his, "I just do."

But even Armstrong, with his introverted nature, feels compelled to chime in on Mack's tale. "Mack, do really believe all this stuff?"

"Yeah, Armstrong, I'm on the up and up here," Mack says firmly, "just ask Dane, he was there, too."

Armstrong stares at me derisively. "You went to the bar with McPherson?"

"No, I just ran into him there, really," I say in a quick response.

"Well?" Beacher says, "how about it, Dane?"

"By the time I got out to the dance floor, the whole thing was over."

"Ya see?" Mack says as if my response was some sort of vindication for him.

The chart sergeant calls line up and the first order of business is a diatribe by our megalomaniac watch commander about how dirty the prison has become and how the N.C.A. will not accredit a dirty prison.

I grab the D block keys from the arsenal and march downstairs to the cellblock areas. The corridor guard, Calvin York, and I usually exchange a few brief amenities but today York is off and his replacement unlocks the corridor gate. Gullo and I exchange morning pleasantries as I dump the key bag on his desk. Joey shuffles through the bag, jingling the brass as he gives the D block guards their keys. I shuffle through Monday's monotonous paperwork in preparation for the morning count.

The morning count goes quickly and routinely allowing me to get my *feed up* workers out of their cells and begin preparing the breakfast. All the prisoners slide a bucket up to the cell door awaiting my block porter to march down the gallery with the hot water tub. Briersburg's most recent renovation in the early 40's didn't hook up any hot water plumbing to the individual cells. Rivera, the porter, hands out hot water twice a day, once in the morning and the other time is after supper. The prisoners dip their washrags in the steaming wetness and wipe their eyes preparing for the day ahead of them.

The food arrives in the block from the kitchen and the *head* feed up man, if any such title is appropriate, begins packaging the food into trays for the prisoners under the status of *keep lock*. Keep lock prisoners are prisoners locked in their cells for twenty-three hours a day due to disciplinary reasons. A keep lock is allowed out only one hour a day, not unlike the box. The

Dutch Van Alstin – Murder in D Block

only real difference is they are not separated from general population. They serve their disciplinary time in the cellblocks. Since they cannot be let out for meals, we have the food sent to the cellblocks and feed them in their cells.

I paw through the food pans searching for the breakfast sausage and create myself a makeshift sandwich. The head feed up worker, who goes by the name *Rook,* gives me a shameful glare for daring to eat state food. Rook is a tall, lanky black man with light skin features and a large head. On the streets Rook was in the realm of kings; here in Briersburg he locks in D-1-#11 cell and is told when he can and when he can't go somewhere.

"Someone may have pissed in dat, Viking." Rook says.

"Mr. Rook, just go about your business." Gullo shouts from his desk.

I scoop out a heaping portion of eggs and delve into them as I give my belly an affectionate rub.

"Dat ain't right, Viking, dat there is state food for inmate consumption only."

I hold my hand up to Gullo to thwart his sure reply. "You're a regular walking rules committee today, Rook. Remember that strict adherence to rules when you walk around with the food today passing out and picking up cigarettes and cans of salmon.
Maybe I'll start invoking every petty, bullshit rule, too; especially the one forbidding the exchange of articles during the feed up process."

"You got dat," Rook says, "I don't want my enterprise muddled with. One hand washes the other, right?"

"No, you just mind your own damn business, and what would you know about washing your hands anyway?"

"You are a crackpot, Viking," Rook says with a laugh.

"Maybe so, Rook, but I'm a free crackpot," I say, fighting off a burp. "My toilet isn't three inches from my bed."

The feed up runs smoothly and Rook rakes in thirteen cans of salmon for no more than five packs of menthols. The salmon will be used to bargain with the Dominican and Puerto Rican prisoners in exchange for other contraband, legal or otherwise. A part of me is impressed at the Laisseze-Faire economic system flourishing among the prisoners. Supply and demand is the measuring device used to set prices for all the commodities inside the walls just as it is in Wall Street. The only exception being is on Wall Street; a bad deal won't result in a shank to the back in the toilet stall.

The morning meal ends and the mess halls empty as the morning let in from the

Dutch Van Alstin – Murder in D Block

recreation yard begins. In anticipation of the beginning of morning programs, a slew of felons retreat back to their respective cellblocks to lock back into their cells.

The bell rings signifying the official end to the let in. The let in runs smoothly, which is to say without any fights or disturbances. The cellblock grows quiet and if I were anywhere except Briersburg, the serenity would be peaceful. I await the morning recreation bell with my feet high upon Joey's desk. Joey, however, spends his time monitoring the porter's mopping job.

"Joey, sit down for God sakes, you're making me nervous with all that pacing."

"It's not pacing, Mr. Erickson, it's diligence."

"I see," I say with a skeptical raise of my eyebrows. "In that case why don't you sit down and I'll change your oil and recharge your battery cells."

"Oh, humor, the last refuge of a scoundrel."

"I believe the word you're searching for is *patriotism*, but thanks just the same."

"Whatever the case may be, the warden is rumored to be making rounds today."

I scoff. "I doubt that, Joey. The warden is scared to come out of the Rooney building, not to mention entering this hell hole."

"Be that as it may, Mr. Erickson, we need to get this place shipshape if he does, in fact, arrive."

"In that case we better batten down the mizenmast, matey, and I'll grab us some grog below on the poop deck." I say in my best pirate tone.

"More humor, Mr. Erickson, well humor never fed the Admiral's cat." Joey says, looking at me out of the corner of his eye with a smirk on his face.

"Good, Lord, boy, you're human after all."

"The truth is, Mr. Erickson," Joey says while turning his body around.

"Hold it, young fella," I say, "every time you say the word *Mister*, I turn around looking for a man in a bad haircut wearing a barbecue apron. How about calling me just plain Erickson, or even Dane?"

"That would be acceptable," he says.

Joseppe Anthony Gullo is the first and only child to an Old World Italian-Catholic couple. Joey's mom was unable to have any more children after he was born and in retrospect, they sheltered Joey. Joey earned a bachelor's degree in public administration before he became a prison guard; his parents have always had high hopes for him. The robots chide him about his degree. Joey, not unlike Donny, takes their insults to heart and usually fights back and a war of words ensues. Joey wants to work his way up to a commissioner some day and aspirations of a guard striving for something better is a threat to the robots. The fact he just turned twenty-three and is still wet behind the ears makes him easy prey.

Joey isn't very physically intimidating although he does stand over six-feet tall and has a football player's build, in particularly his neck. His neck is wide and it's hard to make out whether he even has a neck. He slicks his jet-black hair in oil with no specific style in mind, not unlike the infamous *Moe Howard* hair-do. His nose is small, but crooked, causing him to forever tug on it unknowingly. His biggest dilemma seems to be his baby face that he tries in vain to cover by growing in a thick, bushy mustache.

When Joey first arrived in D block he implemented the old New Haven theory of *broken windows*, take care of smaller problems and the big ones will diminish. He started by actually fixing broken windows. When the heat grows to vast temperatures, the prisoners will throw cans of tuna or any heavy object out of their cell door and into the windows up on the top tiers. Most of the guards grew tired of fixing them, until Joey arrived here. He then pressured the porters to actually clean, mop, wax and he managed to finagle some paint from our parsimonious administration.

On the surface the idea sounds like intellectual, blowhard conjecture, but when the theory is put in practice, Joey was right. D block will always be D block, but the atmosphere has changed somewhat since he's been here. The prisoners have a mantra they like to repeat often and that is that *we work where they live,* implying we are trespassers. One morning Joey took on that premise by ringing the grating, raucous, outdated morning bell for eleven minutes straight instead of the usual twenty seconds. The prisoners were screaming, hollering, starting small fires and throwing trash on the tiers. Joey then clicked on the P.A. system, blew into it like the character *Radar* on M*A*S*H, and bellowed out his decree: "Attention temporary residents of my permanent work station. From the hours of seven A.M. until three P.M., five days a week, this is my, repeat, my cellblock. If there any arguments please feel free to vent them while the cacophonous morning bell is ringing." With that little speech, Joey has managed to turn those words around to: *they live where we work.*

"You know how I'm perceived around here, Dane, like some big, dumb kid in way over his head?"

"True," I say trying to sound sincere without being insulting.

"I still get a lot of heat from everyone and I want the block to be in shape at all times for when the brass from the Rooney building does visit."

"Why are they harping on you? The transformation in here has been positive and things

Dutch Van Alstin – Murder in D Block

are running smoothly, considering this is D block."

"I know," Joey says, leaning back in his chair. "But the brass is giving me a lot of shit over Quinn."

"What?" I say, dropping my feet off the desk. "Why are they on you, what did you have to do with it?"

"Nothing, but try telling them that. I'm in charge of the block; therefore, I am responsible indirectly for the accident."

"What makes you say it was an accident?"

"I don't know," he says, shrugging his shoulders. "What else could it have been?"

"I don't know either; I just thought you heard something I didn't."

"No, but the brass was all over me just the same." Joey sighs. "It's like when McDonald's cell was torched the other day, I got chewed out."

"Why? We weren't even here."

"Yeah, but it was only a few minutes past shift change, and, well, you know the brass, they're all over the day shift about everything."

"Not to change the subject, but what did you think of Donny?"

Joey sighs. "At the risk of sounding insensitive, he was a flake."

"How so?"

"I know you criticize me for letting the other guards get under my skin, but Quinn really let it bother him to the extreme. You know that nitwit Sergeant Pound?" Joey asks rhetorically.

"Vividly," I say while rolling my eyes.

"You don't know the half it, Dane. I grew up down the street from him when I was a kindergartner and he was in his early twenties. Bert Pound used to kick our lunch pals out of our hands, throw snowballs at us, and laugh. He was an egotistical bastard who thrived on humiliating those weaker than he and Quinn was his favorite kick toy."

Joey reaches into his drawer, grabs a lunch bag, and pulls out a sandwich with the crusts neatly trimmed. "You know how Pound likes to come up behind the guards and pull their batons out of the holster and then browbeats 'em about how easily the prisoners can do the same?"

"Do I ever," I say, shaking my holster. "That's why I put one of these straps around it, now a gorilla couldn't yank it out of there."

"Yeah," Joey says, pointing at my holster, "Quinn got one of those, too, afterwards. But when Pound first yanked out Donny's baton, Donny was nearly in tears. Pound knew Donny

Dutch Van Alstin – Murder in D Block

was about to start bawling so he stepped up the assault. The vindictive asshole wanted him to cry in front of the other guards so bad. All the other guards were snickering and elbowing each other as the tears welled up in Donny's eyes."

"Makes you proud to be guard, huh Joey?"

"The next day, after Quinn got one those straps and he tried to get Pound to grab it again."

"Did he?"

"No, instead Pound kept sneaking up behind Quinn and saying, 'better hold on to it, sweetheart'. Donny was fuming and wanted to belt Pound in the chops."

"I wish he had."

"Pound knew he was pushing Donny and goaded him into punching him. Donny just stormed off and Pound, McPherson, Doyle, and a few others just laughed."

"There's an impressive clique."

"Yeah, but they were tight lipped when Quinn jumped."

"Now you say jumped? What happened to fell?"

Joey laughs agitatedly. "Because when I said accident last time you nearly freaked."

"I'm just blowing smoke, Joey. But really, what reasoning did the brass give for blaming the matter on you?"

"Because nobody saw anything."

"That's typical administration logic; nobody sees or hears anything--"

"Oh, I did hear something," Joey says.

"You did? You heard him fall?"

"No, but while I was at my desk matching inventory logs with my supply requisitions, I heard a baton hit the floor. You know what an eerie sound that is, it always spells rumble somewhere."

"But?"

"I walked out and peeked down both of the flats, no rumble, no baton, no ruckus."

"Then?"

"The alarm went off and you know the rest: Quinn dead in the back of the flats."

"What was that noise that sounded like a baton?"

"That was his baton, Quinn's baton was found a few yards from his body. Where his body lain, I couldn't see it from the front of the gallery."

"One thing makes no sense, Joey?"

Dutch Van Alstin – Murder in D Block

"What?"

"If Donny kept his baton strapped in, how did it fall out of the holder? I told you, it takes a gorilla to yank it out of there."

"Maybe he didn't have it strapped right then?"

"As paranoid as he was about Pound? Hell no, he had strapped in all right."

"What are you implying?" Joey says. "That Donny had his baton out for some reason?"

"He had to have, Joey, there's no other explanation just another question."

"Which is what, Sherlock?"

"Scoff if you must, but I have to wonder why Donny had his baton out while he was all alone on the top tier."

"What are you saying?" Joey says, growing more curious.

"Nothing, Joey." I say somewhat derisively. "I'm just running off at the mouth, you know, over thinking, I guess." I sigh and run my hand over my face. "I just hate this place sometimes."

CHAPTER 7

"Oh, come on now, Dane," Joey says. "You're grasping at straws here."

"Wait a minute, Joey, admit it, you're thinking the same thing that I am about Quinn's baton. He had to have had it out of the holster and ready to fight."

"No way, things like that just don't happen."

"Look around you," I say, waving my arms frantically, "do you see all these prison bars? Men who have proven their commitment to the ability to kill live all around us."

"I know, but maybe he was just playing around with the baton and it slipped out of his hand?"

"Playing around just moments before he's found dead? I'm not a big believer in coincidences."

"I know the I.A. has dropped it, Dane," Joey says, reshuffling himself in his chair. "Maybe you should just drop it, too."

"Let me tell you what the I.A. is, they are a bunch of miscreants who roll into town, pop their head inside, and then zip off to the nearest chop house to pad their expense account."

"Yo, Erickson," a voice from behind me chimes. "Since you ain't doing nothing important, how about you opening my cell?"

My porter and waterman, Carlos Rivera has a bad sense of timing sometimes.

Dutch Van Alstin – Murder in D Block

"Where the hell have you been, Rivera," I say. This isn't some sort of country club when you can just come strutting in whenever you damn well please."

"Whoa! Whoa! there, chief!" Rivera says, flailing his hands up as a shield. "What side the bed didja wake up on this morning?"

"It don't matter, Rivera because--"

"Yeah, yeah, I know," Rivera interjects, "your toilet ain't three inches from your bed; you told me that one already."

"All right, Carlos," I say, composing myself. "But I need to speak with you real quick like in my office."

"What do you two do up there all the time?" Joey asks inquisitively.

I just glance back at Joey unable to retort with something witty, and motion Rivera to follow me.

"S'up today, Viking? What surreptitious plot we doin' today?"

"Surreptitious?" I say, surprisingly. "Mommy send you a dictionary for your birthday?"

Rivera goosesteps through the supply room door, also dubbed my office, and plops down in my chair and props his feet up on my desk.

"Ahem", I clear my throat, "I--"

"Went off without a hitch, Viking," Rivera exclaims. "Old man McDonald went to the yard and 'poof', his cell went magically up in flames!" Rivera laughs. "Some of my best work, ya know?"

"As long as I wasn't here at the time, Carlos, that's my concern."

"You was zipping down the interstate by then, I covered ya."

"What did you use? I heard it was a regular inferno?"

"I got some--"

I hold my hand up to thwart his response. "Never mind, I don't want to know. I just wanted that shit bag molester gone off my gallery and he is."

"Now, how about given my man on five gallery another mattress and look the other way with his hot plate?"

"Done," I say, "but I can't guarantee other shifts and other guards."

"He knows that." Rivera says. "How 'bout that Italian sub from the deli."

"It's in my blue cooler downstairs, help yourself."

"It's a pleasure," Rivera says, walking back downstairs.

"Carlos--"

Dutch Van Alstin – Murder in D Block

Rivera looks back at me almost sensing what's coming next.

"I know you're no snitch--"

"Since we understand each other, don't ask, Viking."

"You must know something."

"If I did, Viking, I wouldn't tell you, but..."

"Yeah?" I say, with my interest peaked.

"Truth is, from my heart," he taps his chest, "it's weird, I really don't know nothing. People is clamming up about it."

"Find me someone who knows and who will talk."

Rivera emits a derisive chuckle. "Ain't no one gonna talk in D block, Dane. You get a shank stuck in ya real quick like, and you know that." Rivera starts walking out again and I block his exit with my arm.

"Hey, yo, man, we don't want to do this." Rivera says, tapping my arm.

"No, I know...I just want you to keep your ears open...find some dupe child molester to tell me, let him get the shank to the back."

Rivera sighs. "I'm going to get my sandwich now." He smirks. "Services rendered, ya know?"

"Yeah," I say, letting him out the door. "Just think about it, Carlos...please."

The two o'clock yard-run ends and the block is nearly empty. Joey is busy lining up his filing cabinets in some sort of order. At first, he arranges them by the color scheme, dark to light. Instead, he has Rook paint all of them same color and lines them up by height. Joey and I only exchange brief words. He doesn't mention our conversation about Quinn anymore. I can't tell whether he is reflecting on what we discussed or if he is just dismissing the entire interaction as mere gossip and innuendoes. Joey remains relatively quiet to me for the remainder of the day. He is a funny kid and hard to figure out sometimes.

Danny Ford, Briersburg's fire and safety guard, walks in the block and signs the logbook. He gives Joey and I a backward salute and walks down the gallery, whistling some inane melody.

"Hell of a mess," Ford shouts from McDonald's former cell. He steps in and out of the cell repeatedly. He looks up at the gate and then down toward the floor.

Having Ford conduct the investigation doesn't concern me as much as the State Fire Marshall. Ford will look into the cause of the fire, the Fire Marshall will scrutinize who, what, where, when, why, and how. Ford walks back up the gallery still whistling the same, unfamiliar tune.

"It was a pretty big blaze, but I'm going to recommend the Fire Marshall pass on the investigation."

"You can do that??" I say ecstatically. Perhaps too ecstatically.

Ford laughs and scratches his ear. "I can make recommendations," Ford says, trying to light a cigarette. "However, they're not binding, the Marshalls can do whatever they damn well please." Ford repeatedly flicks his lighter. "They usually take my recommendations; an investigation would just interfere with their midday poker games."

"So the fire wasn't arson?" Joey says.

"Hell yes, that's obvious to a duck, but tell me guys, how uncommon is that in this shithole?" Ford says, exhaling a cloud of smoke.

"Not very," I say.

"I heard this McDougal character was a *toucher*, is that true?"

"It's McDonald," Joey says.

"His name ain't important, son," Ford retorts.

"Yeah, Danny," I interject, "he was a toucher of his own daughter."

"Then it's too bad the lame fuck wasn't in there cooking like a stuffed pig!"

"True," I say.

"Who says arson is a bad thing, Dane, Joey?" Ford says, smiling. "Sounds to me, boys, like the guy had it coming, the arson I mean. What do you think?" Ford says with a laugh.

I scratch my head and adjust my notebook in my pocket. Ford stares at us and laughs some more. "Well boys, what do you think?"

"I try not to think too much, Danny," I say.

"That's what I like to hear," Ford says. After an uncomfortable pause with Ford staring at Joey and me, Ford laughs and signs the logbook. "I guess this block has bad karma, aye, boys?"

"It seems to be a magnet for trouble," I reply.

"If we ain't got blazes that make the Chicago fire look like a weenie roast, we got half-crazy guards doing swan dives from the top tier."

Joey throws me a quick glance.

"Dive?" I say inquisitively. "Is that how they're ruling it?"

"That's how the brass sees it," Ford says with a sigh. "I'm supposed to come up with some recommendations to seal off the gallery so nobody can jump, leap, get tossed, or whatever. That Quinn is causing me more grief now than when he was alive."

"How'd he cause you grief?" I say.

"The fucking nut kept leaving the fire hose boxes at the end of the galleries open. I must have found 'em open five or six times; after a while, I get shit from the brass because I supposedly ain't training these idiots correctly."

"Why was he opening them...I mean, they're locked up all the time?"

Ford develops a peculiar look on his face, "I dunno...good question". Ford exhales a cloud of blue. "Too bad he ain't here to ask."

Joey looks at me reproachfully yet with some curiosity.

"Gotta go, boys," Ford says amidst a backwards salute.

"Now that Danny is done, I'm going to open up some of the workers to start painting and cleaning McDonald's old cell." I say.

"It probably wouldn't hurt to make one last go around of the flats, Dane. You might want to check the fire hose boxes." Joey says with a twinge of sarcasm.

"I guess it wouldn't hurt," I say, walking down the gallery, ignoring Joey's slur.

Rook, Rivera and an inmate I know as 'Toes,' begin the excavating of McDonald's cell. Toes grins at me as I walk by, never losing eye contact with mine.

"May I speak with you a moment, sir?" Toes says mindfully.

"Concerning what?"

"I'll be brief, sir, please?"

Rivera stares at Toes and shakes his head disapprovingly.

I glare back at Rivera, trying to read his thoughts. "Okay," I say, still staring at Rivera. "Follow me around the back way; I have to walk up the other side of the flats anyway."

Toes leans his broom up against the bars and wipes his hands on his pants. He smirks and motions for me to walk ahead of him. We walk to the end gate and I open it allowing us both to the back of the cellblock. I begin locking the gate behind me when Toes says, "How about that?

"All right, get to the point, assuming you have one."

"No point, per se, just a few words from you is all I need."

"What's your problem?" I say, growing irritated at Toes' futile attempt to appear enigmatic.

"I ain't got no problem, Viking, no problem whatsoever."

Dutch Van Alstin – Murder in D Block

"Then what are you talking about?"

"Same thing you is, man, I'm talking about the fire."

I stand steadfastly and put my keys back on my belt. "Get to the point."

"I want some whiskey, Viking."

"*Want* can be an ugly word, especially when there's an aura of threat behind it."

"Don't go that route with me, Viking," Toes says, waving his hands in the air. "I helped with the torch and I want my pay."

"Assume I know what the hell you're talking about," I say, leaning up against the bars, "Rivera hired you, not me."

"He gave me a down payment, now I want the whole balance."

"I think you're just trying to shake me down." I reply.

"Ain't no shake down, man. I just want what's mine."

"Then go put your orange juice on the radiator like the rest of the convicts."

"You know what I mean; I want some street stuff, not this homemade shit in here."

"You're looking up the wrong tree for your possum, fella."

"Ain't nothing to it," Toes says. "You just put some in your thermos and--"

"Whoa, whoa, whoa...what do you know about smuggling hooch in with a thermos?"

"Don't get so self-righteous with me, Viking. We both know you guys do it all the time."

"Not me," I say adamantly, "I don't break the law in my endeavors."

"Oh, I see," Toes laughs, "has arson become legal recently?"

"I'm not going to let you box me in on a technicality."

"Is that what you call it? A technicality? Well, man, hooch ain't no more than a *technicality* either."

"Yes it is and you never answered my question about what you know about whiskey in a thermos." I slide the end gate shut all the way is if somehow that will prevent our conversation from being heard.

"That crooked cop who got tossed from the top tier use to bring it in all the time."

"Tossed?" I say curtly. "Start talking, Toes."

"Kiss my ass, Viking, I ain't telling you shit," Toes says, stepping toward me. "You bring me in some whiskey or I sing to the sergeant."

A quick snap of my baton holder is followed by a sharp thrust in Toes' midsection. Toes grabs his stomach and gasps as he drops to his knees and gasps again. I grip my baton tightly and hover over a hurting Toes.

Dutch Van Alstin – Murder in D Block

"You-fuc-king-ass-" Toes murmurs through his search for air. Toes lets go of his stomach and grabs a rail and attempts to pull himself back up from the floor. I ram my baton sideways across his neck and pin him against the wall. Toes squints his eyes and screams.

"You son of a-" I say, slamming my knee in Toes' groin. He falls to the ground in a stridency of whimpers. The end gate slowly creeks open as Rivera peeks his head in and looks down at Toes. He closes the gate behind him and kneels down by Toes.

"You included this idiot in your plans?" I shout.

"You stupid mother-fucker," Rivera says to Toes, slapping him in the head.

"You included this idiot in your plans?" I say again, still hovering over a wriggling, moaning Toes.

"He works in the machine shops, Viking, he gets me the gasoline."

Toes attempts to pull himself up again by grabbing the rail. His movement draws my attention again. I abruptly drive my boot into his stomach once more. Toes drops back to the floor with a drip of blood protruding from his mouth. He stares up at me, silently, trying to catch his breath once more.

"This lame fuck was pushing up on me, Rivera. Didn't you pay him his money?"

"I did," Rivera says, looking down at Toes, "and I told him not to push up on you for nothing."

"Your soldiers listen very well."

"He'll listen this time, "Rivera says, "I'll take care of his ass."

"Leave me out," I say, sliding my baton back in the holder.

"Come on you damn fool," Rivera says, grabbing Toes by the shirt collar.

"Carlos, what are you doing? Gullo is sitting at the desk?"

"So?"

"So, I think he'll get suspicious if he sees you dragging this slug along the floor."

"Doesn't he know?" Rivera asks quizzically.

"Of course not Carlos," I say incredulously, "what are you thinking?"

"How the hell do I know whether he's in on it or not?"

"Think, Carlos, think, he's already wondering why the three of us vanished back here."

Rivera looks down the gallery and says Joey has his back turned fiddling with some wires. He drags Toes back to his cell and tosses him on the bed. I lock the gate back up as Joey continues fidgeting and rearranging some wires.

"We'll continue this conversation tomorrow, Toes." I whisper in his cell. Toes rolls over on to his back and says nothing. He lifts his head up some and stares over at me briefly before he grabs a towel and dabs the blood off his chin.

The three o'clock hour rolls in and Joey and I leave the block together. We walk through the corridor and out into the main yard without Joey saying so much as a word.

"Why are you so quiet?" I say.

"Huh," Joey says, snapping out of his reverie, "oh, I was just thinking."

"If you really want to be a warden someday, don't let the state catch you thinking on your own."

"No, I was just thinking about how much you hated him."

"Who?"

"McDonald," Joey says reproachfully, "you hated his guts."

"Yeah, so, I never hid that fact from you."

"I mean you *really* hated him, you had a screaming match with him just one day before his cell went up in flames."

I continue walking and say nothing.

"Am I right?"

"So what, Joey," I snap, "I hate a lot of these guys, they hate me, we hate each other. That's what a prison is, Joey, it's a hate factory and there is plenty being produced daily. I just have more than my share. I guess that's just part of my greedy, capitalist nature."

"I saw Rivera and Toes by the cell before it went up. I remember because I shagged them both off the gallery before I left for the day. A half hour later, the alarm sounded."

"Joey--"

"You did it, didn't you?"

My boots halt on the pavement and I hurl my body toward Joey. "Look, Joey, don't concern yourself--"

"That is so cool."

"Excuse me?" I say.

"That is so cool. You had those two jokers burn his cell. That is so cool."

"Okay, Joey, it's real cool," I say calmly as I begin walking again. "Now let's just keep this secret between the two of us, all right?"

"Who else can we burn out?"

"Whoa there, partner," I say, halting my footsteps again, "you keep talking like that and

Dutch Van Alstin – Murder in D Block

the next people to get burned are us."

"Why didn't you include me in on it?'

"You?" I say skeptically, "a man who sewed wire into his pants to keep his creases straight?"

"I quit doing that!" Joey snaps.

"Ooh, living on the edge are we?"

"Well, I mean now that I see how easy it is. I mean, *poof*, and he's gone."

"Yeah, Joey, poof, and he's gone. Now settle down, I don't want to see you come in tomorrow with a can of gasoline in one hand and a box of matches in the other."

"I'm off for the next three days."

"Joey." I sigh. "You missed my point."

"No I didn't...what fire?"

"Now you're getting it," I say, walking out the main gate. "So what are you going to be doing on your three days?"

"Mowing my mom's lawn."

"All three days?"

"Nah, I got stuff to do," Joey says, "I'll see you in a few."

We part ways at the parking lot and I walk out to my car. I spot something jammed in the windowsill and even with a strong squint of my eyes, I can't make out what it is. As I close in on my car, I can see what it is. I see a heart shaped envelope with a pink lipstick kiss sealing it shut.

CHAPTER 8

The envelope is misty pink with white paper lace surrounding the edges. *Dane* is written in a bright red fancy script encircled by a sketch of a heart. An overwhelming curiosity causes me to tear into the envelope. I would be a liar if I said I knew April would contact me again. I truly believed our last meeting was in fact, our last meeting.

> *Dear Dane,*
>
> *Please come tonight and have supper with me. I'm making an old family recipe and I promise you'll love it. I swear you will not regret coming. Let me make Friday's debacle up to you! Be there at 6:00!!*
>
> *Love,*
>
> *April*

I consider all options as carefully as can be expected in a situation such as this. I know continuing any type of relationship with April won't remain the casual, carefree one it once was. I have my fingers gripped tightly on Pandora's box. The question before me is do I want to open it?

I need a haircut.

Dutch Van Alstin – Murder in D Block

I arrive a few minutes early and knock on the door briskly.

"Dane?" April shouts from inside

"Yeah, it's me, April."

"I'm in the oven right now, come on in and sit down, the door is unlocked."

I grip the handle tightly and open it. "April?" I say, walking in and looking around the apartment.

April walks out of the kitchen wiping her hands on an apron. "Hi, Dane," she says with blanketed nervousness.

A brief pause seems endless with the two of us nodding our heads at one another and formulating a frozen smile.

"Well, Dane…just have a seat and make yourself comfortable," she says, pointing into the living room. "I just have a few loose ends to tie up in here." April ducks back into the kitchen and clangs a few pots around. "Do you want a beer?"

"Please," I say, plopping myself down into a soft, suede chair.

Silence.

"Nice place, April."

"It's a shit hole," she bellows, walking out of the kitchen with an alligator shaped oven mitt on her hand.

"That's cute," I say, pointing at her.

"Thanks," she says, tugging at her blouse, "I just bought it yesterday on the clearance rack."

"Oh, yeah…you do look great too."

April smiles and bites her lip. "Oh, you were talking about the oven mitt, weren't you?"

"No, really, you look sexsational, I mean sensual, uh,… s,s,s,sensational," I say, gesticulating my hands with every stammered word.

"April pulls her lips together tightly trying to fight off a laugh. "Obviously I'm not the only one who's a bit uncomfortable here?"

"Sure you are," I say, wiggling in the chair. "This is the most comfortable chair I've sat in for months."

We fail to battle off an impending smile and begin laughing. April breathes out a long sigh of relief. "I feel so much better now," she says, squatting down next to the chair. "I knew something would have to break the ice; I was so nervous about leaving you that letter. I swore up and down to myself that you wouldn't come, I'm glad I was wrong."

Dutch Van Alstin – Murder in D Block

"So am I," I say, pinching her cheek. "Now tell me what that tangy aroma is?"

"Oh, my," she gasps, "I forgot all about it." April hurries back into the kitchen, again, wiping her hands on her apron.

My erred attempt at complimenting April's appearance is an injustice to how radiant she really is tonight. The halter top that I overlooked in place of an oven mitt, is made of a soft, velvety pink, that seemingly should have gone out of style with platform shoes and schoolgirl crushes on Bobby Sherman, but on her, the blouse is exquisite. Her skirt is ebon black silk with a fashionable zipper riding up along the side. Her hair, that I childishly swoon over, has loose curls that fall over her bangs causing her to periodically toss it back away from her eyes.

Me? I have on boots, jeans and an old Minnesota Viking training camp shirt.

Curiosity draws me into the kitchen where I watch April pull a dish from the oven. I never would have believed a woman could look so sexy while cutting into a pan of pasta.

"Manicotti," I say energetically.

"You bet, good old manicotti," she says, dipping her finger in the sauce. "The recipe is one of my mom's finest creations." April licks the sauce off her finger and mulls over a reaction. "Ah, not too bad," she says, tossing a sprig of garlic over the top of the pan. She dips her finger in the sauce once more, "slowly but surely," she says, sliding the pan back in the oven. "I know the thought of manicotti sounds simple or trite, but actually it's an art form requiring just the right touch."

"For me it's a matter of what portion of the plastic to fold back before I stick it in the microwave."

"Well then, at the risk of sounding aloof, you sir, are in for a treat," she says, tapping my nose affectionately.

The aroma didn't do the meal justice. I'm not sure if my admiration stems from missing home cooked meals or because April's cooking truly deserves the kudos I give her.

"You weren't being aloof at all," I say, thumping my belly.

"You're just being polite."

"April, nobody has three portions and rudely burps just to be polite."

April laughs and walks into the kitchen. "My father always said a good burp was the crowning glory to a hearty meal."

"Your dad, huh? Well I couldn't (*burp*) agree more."

"My daddy always had an axiom for every occasion, serious or otherwise." April walks

Dutch Van Alstin – Murder in D Block

out of the kitchen with a tray full of cookies and a coffeepot.

"Wow, you think of everything," I say, delving into a cookie.

"If you're not a gracious host, then what are you?"

"You're me."

April laughs and pours us both a cup of coffee.

"I'll bet your dad liked your mom's cooking too," I say.

A faint smile grows on April's face as she fidgets with the tray.

"I'm sorry," I say, sensing her uneasiness. "I guess I should just mind my own business."

"No," she says, swallowing a sip of coffee, "there's nothing to be sorry for, I'm okay."

I struggle to manipulate the conversation and steer it toward April's family. I doubt my own sincerity in wanting to know about her family. If I were to be honest with myself, my reasons stem from curiosity borne about by her reluctance to discuss the annals of her family history.

I clear away the tray and the dishes and relax with my coffee. April sits and stirs a spot of cream in her coffee. I anticipate the lull in the conversation will lead to call it a night.

"I'm sorry about being so reticent about growing up in Philadelphia but when I mention it, people get a queasy look in their eyes. I know they think I'm just sort of inner city street trash."

"The City of Brotherly Love?"

April scoffs. "*Brotherly* and *love* were palliative clichés in my neighborhood."

I nod, trying to look comforting to her.

"Can you blame me for not wanting to talk about it?"

"I don't follow what you mean, April."

"Be honest, Dane," April says, putting her coffee down on the table. "Imagine this scenario: you meet me, you learn I'm married to a prisoner and I hail from some shitty 'hood in Philly, and the highpoint of my success is graduation from cosmetology school, what conclusion would you come up with?"

"Well," I say, setting my coffee down on the table as well, "I would-"

"Be straight, Dane," April interjects. "I'm not blaming you for what you'd think but given all that information, do you see why I wait for people to get to know me? If you and I hadn't talked and, well..." April blushes. "If you hadn't known me for the few months you have, wouldn't you assume I was just some slutty *prison wife*?"

I sigh. "I see your point."

"My life hasn't had the most auspicious beginning and that's what people judge you on

Dutch Van Alstin – Murder in D Block

when they have no other information to judge against it." April leans back on her couch and sighs, trying to regain her composure.

"We don't have to talk about this, April."

"Dane," she says with a cracking voice, "my parents were good, hardworking, decent, honest, God-fearing people. But because they were Latino, people concluded they were trashy spicks. April stands up and walks aimlessly about the room, stopping and staring at a floral painting hanging near her hallway. She rubs her fingers along the brush strokes pondering her words and delving into thought.

"April," I say softly, "are you okay?"

"Mom died when I was about ten years old in a car accident while driving home from work one night. She cleaned rooms at a hotel nearby and she was driving down the Pennsylvania turnpike when a drunk ran a red light and smashed---" April clenches her fists and gasps for air. I quickly stand up but she shoos me away. "He just smashed into her like she wasn't important. He didn't know who she was or what she meant to a little girl less than a quarter of a mile away. To him, Lila Cruz was somebody who got in his way one night. He didn't care that she walked me to the park every Sunday. He didn't care that she bought me my first communion dress with tips she scrimped and saved for six months. He didn't care that she cried every day when I went to school because she knew I'd be coming home to an empty house. He just didn't care, Dane. To him, she was nothing. To me, she was Joan of Arc and Mother Mary rolled into one. I had to watch as my father received the phone call from some cop who callously said 'your wife's dead, come down and I.D. the body by noon'. I watched my father hit his knees and sob like a baby, like a baby, Dane!" April spins back and looks at me.

"A man who knew from that moment on that his only true love was gone from our earth for an eternity. From that day on it was just pop and I. He worked fourteen hours a day at the shipyards before they closed down. I'm ashamed, Dane, ashamed! Pop worked hard to help me get a good start in life. He always said to make my mom proud and look what I've done to her, to him, to me?

"April, "I say with some uneasiness. "I have a major flaw in my character; and that is I never know how to say or do anything to console people. I'm sorry, but I think you're selling yourself too short."

"Too short?" she says with a sarcastic laugh. "My dad died of a heart attack when I was sixteen and in six short years, I've forgotten all the values he taught me. I'm just at the point where my life is a daily struggle to make sense of what I've done. I've dishonored their

Dutch Van Alstin – Murder in D Block

memory." April walks slowly into the kitchen and grabs a dishrag. She dabs both her eyes and sighs. "My dad once said: *a small garden of righteousness will feed you for a lifetime whereas you will starve in a field of sin.*"

"That's very profound, especially from man who said a good burp was a sign of a good meal."

April struggles to laugh and wipes her eyes again.

"I'm sorry, April."

"It's not your fault, Dane."

"I mean, for what I thought about you."

April stares pleasantly at me smiles. "I believe you really mean that."

"I do."

"There's nothing to be sorry for, Dane," April says, walking toward the balcony.

"I'm the one who walked away from the garden and planted seeds in the field."

An overriding compulsion causes me to slide in behind her and rub her shoulders. April tips her head back slightly and puts my fingers in her mouth and slowly kisses them individually.

"Why did you marry him, April?"

"I guess," she says, dropping her eyes downward to the floor, "since I'm already airing my dirty laundry, I'll tell you. Money! He had lots of money and he spent it on me all the time."

April slides open the balcony door and invites the night air inside. She pulls her hair back from her eyes, tips her head back, and twists her neck back and forth. "I know that sounds shallow, and it is, but greed is part of the field. I overlooked where he was getting all the money. I believed he was an investment broker like he said he was. Raph worked 9-5, no weekends or nights. Drug dealers in my neighborhood skulked around till all hours. Raph was an *executive* in the drug business, he worked banker's hours." April walks back into the kitchen and picks up the percolator. She swishes the pot bottom brew around in the canister and then dumps it in the sink. Her face turns red and she digs her fingernails into her face and screams.

"God damn pot is empty!" She hurls the percolator in the sink and begins sobbing uncontrollably. "I just don't have control of my own life anymore, Dane! I just can't take it anymore!"

I step toward her and she buries her face in my chest. My eyes dart around the room as I systematically rub her back.

"He'll kill me, Dane; he'll kill me if I try to leave him. He has friends everywhere." Her body begins to shake as I search vainly for some comforting words.

Dutch Van Alstin – Murder in D Block

"I'm sorry for dumping on you, Dane."

"Don't be," I say, kissing her on the head.

"I...shouldn't be though."

"Maybe I'm out of place here, April, but you talk as though the fight were over. You're a young twenty-two and have a life ahead of you that you can steer into any direction you want."

"Oh, Dane," she says, wiping her eyes on her sleeves, "where were you when I was roaming the streets."

"Roaming through cow shit."

A smile is followed by a giggle from April. "How do you turn a moment of turmoil into a laugh?"

I shrug my shoulders.

April steps closer to me and kisses my cheek. "You're sweet."

"April, you're a flower. You're a flower growing in a garden of weeds; don't let those weeds choke you."

Our eyes lock as I grow uneasy. We stay silent, staring and searching for words. At the height of her vulnerability, April kisses me. She kisses me hard and throws her arms tightly around me. She moans softly and pulls me tighter. I gently slide my arms down between us and slowly push her away from me.

"What?" She says anxiously, "I know you find me attractive?"

"That's not it; I just can't do this while your emotions are all churned up inside of you."

"Sex was easier when it meant nothing?" She says incredulously.

"That's not what I mean; I just don't want to take advantage of you."

April sighs and fixates a sorrowful glare at me. She wipes her hands on her shirt and walks away toward the balcony again. The wind picks up and her blows back around her ears and she folds her arms to keep warm.

"Do you know how many men would have just taken me right there, right then, with no questions asked?"

"One less than you thought?"

"Regardless of how I felt, or how he felt, he would have fucked me on the floor right then." She repeats.

"I can't prey on someone's weakness; I just wasn't brought up that way."

April turns toward me and cocks her head sideways like a lost puppy. "Maybe, I just

Dutch Van Alstin – Murder in D Block

don't excite you anymore?" She says with a mock coquettish look on her face.

"Oh, my, no, that's not it, we both know better" I say, digging my nails into my leg. "You excite me very, very much."

"I know," she says with a beguiling smile. She walks toward me and kisses me on the cheek. "You just have some decency about you, that's all. A girl just likes to know she still has it."

I turn my head sideways a few times and murmur a few phonetic noises.

"I guess that's a yes?"

"It's something."

April smiles and looks at the clock. "How about we just put in a movie and curl up on the couch?"

"Sure." I say with a smile.

April fumbles through a stack of old DVD's and slides one in her player. She sits close to me and rubs my chest as she lays her head on my shoulder. She peaks up at me and smiles, and gives me a furtive little wink. She lays her head back on my chest, sighs, and relaxes.

The sound of gun shots from the movie causes my eyes to peak open, and for a split second, forget where I am. I look down at a sleeping April and nudge her slightly. "Hey, sleepy head...wake up."

"Huh," she says, nuzzling my neck, looking around the room. "The movie?"

"Over," I whisper softly. "We fell asleep."

I stand, stretch, and begin the hunt for my shoes. I feel April's hand touch my back and rub her fingers in my skin. "Dane," she whispers.

I grab my shoes from behind the couch and toss them on the floor in front of me.

"Dane," she says more intently, rubbing my back briskly.

"April," I say defensively, "I should just go home."

"Shhh," April says, pressing her finger to my lips. She unfastens her top button, all the while fixing a hypnotic stare into mine, exposing my passions.

"April..."

April shakes her head slowly and undoes the next button, moving her body closer to mine.

"April, this whole thing, us, it's wrong."

Dutch Van Alstin – Murder in D Block

"I know," she says, nodding her head. She slides her fingers inside her blouse and drapes it off her shoulders and on to the floor. She rubs her fingers across my lips and sighs. "I know it is, Dane."

Before I can utter a sound, April turns off the light.

CHAPTER 9

I am awakened by the sunlight that peeks through an unfamiliar window. I gaze around the room with sticky, watery eyes, searching for an alarm clock. I look down at a slumbering April with her arms draped over my chest.

I stare down at her and think about last night. Last night was the easy part. Giving into primal needs is natural and often necessary, but the repercussions that boomerang back where they once were is the difficult part to handle. I'm not equipped to handle the aftermath of a lustful romp that promises to be a harbinger to romance with a vivacious, intriguing, and most of all, forbidden woman. The fear of this day arriving was clouded last night in the heat of passion and the mist of want.

I'm here now; I'm no longer there. *There* seems like light years away, out of my reach, out of my control. The paradox of all this is never in my life has my fear and uncertainty felt so good and felt so right; doing what is wanted and not what is needed. Impetuousness was always a spectator sport to me, being in the game required risks and risks require a hunger and desire for the uncharted. Am I wrong? Am I crazy? Am I still just a little euphoric to even be rational? Maybe I'm just hungry for more? Maybe I am just hungry for breakfast.

The question is how will I ever know?

I reach across April in hopes of retrieving her watch on the nightstand, but it causes her

Dutch Van Alstin – Murder in D Block

to flutter her eyes, fighting off the morning glare. She wriggles some but remains sleeping. Mickey's hands signify it is only six A.M. leaving me ample time to engage in my morning routine. I carefully slide April's arm off my chest in an attempt to let her sleep. To my chagrin, April flutters her eyes once more and focuses them squarely on me. "Is it morning?" she says with a squeak

"It's almost six o'clock," I whisper, while searching for my clothes, "go back to sleep."

"You're not leaving?"

"I have to work."

"Call in sick, Dane and stay with me today."

I manage to locate my jeans and gingerly slide them over my legs. The search continues for my socks and underpants. "I can't today; I need to follow up on some things at work."

April rolls over on to her back and a sudden gust of modesty causes her to pull the sheet up over her body. "At least stay for breakfast, Dane."

"I need a shower and I have to brush my teeth."

"I have a shower," she says anxiously, "and you can use my toothbrush. I doubt you're concerned with germs now."

"Uh…" I look around the room in search of an excuse to decline.

"Dane," April says, sliding her arm up under her head. "How about it? Breakfast?"

"I'd like to."

"But?"

"Ah…I didn't say 'but'…in fact, I'd like some chow before I run off to work."

April smiles. "I'll make you a breakfast like you use to get on the farm."

"Only if you have a freshly slaughtered pig draping over a cutting board in your kitchen, and I'll bet you don't."

"That's gross."

"Where do think we get pork, ham, bacon, and sausage from?"

"The supermarket," April says as she stretches, "end of aisle six, near the deli."

"How about pointing me to the shower?"

"Wait," she says, flinging the sheet off her body. "I'll give you a personal tour."

"Only if you let me wash up," I say, waving a scolding finger.

"I'll just help you wash certain areas," she says with a sinister laugh.

April slides in the shower slowly, complaining of the cold water.

Dutch Van Alstin – Murder in D Block

"The Minnesota in me likes the water a bit nippy."

April glides her body in behind me, rubbing her hands up my chest. "How about if I cook you dinner tonight again?"

"No, not tonight," I say, scrubbing the suds from my hair.

"Why?" She says dispiritedly.

"Because," I spin my body around toward her, wishing I could hide from my ten extra pounds, "I'm going to cook for you at my place."

"Oh, can you really?"

"*Can* as in able, or *can* as in willingness?"

"Oh I meant willingness. I'm so excited. What time do you want me there?"

"Sixish," I say, rinsing the last of the shampoo, "I'll pick you up after work and take you out to my cottage."

"Cottage?"

"Yeah, I have a small cottage on Taupawney Lake and if the weather holds up, I'll take you out on the boat too."

"Boat?" She says surprisingly. "Are you guards rich or something?"

"Something."

"Oh, I can't wait."

"Look, April, I have to take a rain check on breakfast. I forgot about my dog needing to go outside. He'll never be able to wait until I get home from work; his little nibs will burst."

April snickers. "Okay, sure, I mean I don't appear needy or anything."

"No, ma'am, you don't."

I hop out of the shower, shivering from the cold as I search for a towel. "Until six then, my dear."

April bores her head out the shower and kisses me twice. "Okay, I'll be here." She grabs my ears, kisses me again, and pinches my cheeks spiritedly. "If I'm not here, just let yourself in and make yourself comfortable. I work until four o'clock today."
She envelops my neck with both arms and intently kisses me. "Bye," she says softly.
I try, abortively, to towel myself and kiss at the same time. "Bye, April," I say, pulling away from her. "I really have to go."

"Bye."

"This is a recording."

"I'm sorry, she says with a snicker, followed by another kiss." Go, get, be gone from my

Dutch Van Alstin – Murder in D Block

sights," April says with a mocking wave of her hand.

I scamper at a breakneck pace to the living room where I gown myself and begin the search for my keys. I spot my keys on the table near the entranceway next to a crooked plant stand and quickly grab them, nearly knocking it over. The irregularity of the stand causes me to wobble it from side to side. As I focus down to the floor and underneath the stand, I see a glass object protruding ever so slightly from the base.

When I pick it up I am greeted through the freshly cleaned frame by C block Delgado posing with two other prisoners. Judging by the background, I'd say the photo was taken in Briersburg's south recreation yard, the yard where we hold all the family festivals. The picture was obviously hidden intentionally and rather hastily; telling me it is normally on display.

Euphoria has a train wreck.

I tuck the picture back, upside down, under the plant stand and walk out the door.

After my dog Bambino's initial onslaught at my entrance, he runs and frolics across our yard, cutting corners so sharp that he nearly hits the neighbor's birdbath. Bambino is visibly disappointed when I leave him again. I try to console him with a few scratches on his belly and the promise of company later tonight.

"I got to work, old boy."

He circles the floor a few times and then bites his leg to attack the little wingless bloodsuckers. I slip him a biscuit and jaunt on my daily excursion I call Briersburg.

Sipping some vulgar coffee, I begin to bemoan my discovery of C block Delgado's photo. My struggle is with why I am lamenting the unearthing of the photo at all. How can I be jealous of someone who isn't supposed to be any form of competition? My revelation to what end April and I have evolved so quickly is frightening somewhat. The ease and naturalness of how April became the degree of importance to me; enough so I become jealous, has left me puzzled.

The lineup room is clamorous and disorganized with the robots arguing over how their particular workstations are more dangerous than that of their counterpart. Some sort of erotic thrill is derived by the one man who can champion his argument to the prevailing masses of the hazards of his own corner of the world. Somehow, tonight, their steak will taste heartier and their ale a bit stronger, if they can prove to the herd that their manhood is unparalleled to no one. When the sovereignty of being a man is based on the high probability of being shanked in the back, then stop the world please, I want to get off.

One such man who is unconcerned of his machismo is Joey Gullo's D block

Dutch Van Alstin – Murder in D Block

replacement, Toby Sweet.

"Hey, Dude, what's happening today?" Toby says.

"*Toby* is the man's God given name, not a nickname. He is a salmon trying swim with a downstream with school of trout. His insufferable use of the word *Dude* is enough to grate the steadiness of nerves, but the real clincher is his imbecilic, nonsensical two tiered grin, widely exposing both the upper and lower sets of teeth. Toby is well over six foot tall, but I would be greatly surprised if he weighed over 150 pounds. However, he does wear his clothes very baggy making his build difficult to detect. Toby's face seems gaunt, but in a healthy way, not disproportionately thin like his twiggy body, but thin nonetheless. My blond hair is nearly identical to the color of Toby's leading the robots to chide us about being long lost brothers. I'm pleased Toby keeps his hair shaved tightly around his head with globs of gel on top. At least the style of his hair can be distinguishable from my own. His eyes are blue and sleek and his chin is slightly pointed at the tip. Many of the paranoid fringes of the robots peg Toby as an Internal Affairs agent. I believe, however, he lacks the moxie, fortitude, and the smarts to pull off something so covert. I can envision him as a soda jerk, dressed in one of those stupid paper hats, serving people with fake names like *Biff* and *Muffy,* as they discuss the awesome waves rolling over the coastline, all the while, never losing that exasperating grin.

"Hi, Toby, what's new?" I say cordially.

"Are you working in the *dog pound* today, Dude?"

"I'm not supposed to, but I switched with Tyler today so I could catch up on some paperwork."

"I guess we'll be partners today!"

When lineup ends, I pace my stride to D block quickly to avoid having to walk with Toby. York, already in the corridor, is singing Christmas carols.

"Morning, York," I say.

"Dane! The mighty Viking warrior has arrived to stop the flux of crime plaguing our fair city." York sidesteps to the gate and lets me in the corridor. "Tell me Dane," he says, following me to D block's gate. "Do you think Wilma and Betty engaged in lesbian sex while Fred and Barney were working? I mean it isn't as though they had housework to do since everything was made of rock?"

I shake my head while veiling a smile. "So is your head and it's the dirtiest thing I've seen."

"How so?" York says, rubbing his chin in contemplation.

Dutch Van Alstin – Murder in D Block

"A prime example is your song about Roosevelt yesterday. The one you titled *Is It Just His Wheelchair That Is Stiff?*"

"Ah, yes," York hyperbolizes an exaggerative sigh. "A classical piece of melodious treasure."

"At the risk of being unoriginal, if that's a treasure, then bury it quickly."

"And deny the world my musical--"

"Hey, fruitcake," I shout impishly, "let me in my damn block."

"Oh, sorry about that," he says, twisting the key in the lock and spinning the gate open for me. "Praise be to *the peak* for saving me from the evil powder, Dane. PRAISE BE!"

The midnight guards wipe their eyes and stretch when they see me. They relay to me some pointless information of goings on from last night in an effort to sound like they actually do something other than sleep.

I open my lock box and look proudly at the tag dangling from number thirty-five cell reading *VACANT*. Toby walks in behind me and tosses the key bag on the desk. "Is York all right?" He says.

"No," I say, spreading the keys out on the desk.

Toby sneers. "He just asked me a sick question about *The Flintstones*."

"Yeah, me too," I laugh, "so what do you think? Are they doing each other while Fred and Barney are away?"

"You're as sick as he is, Dane."

"No, I don't think so; nobody is that sick."

"How do you guys work with a goofball like that?"

"Lighten up, Toby, he's just kidding around with you."

Toby shakes his head knowing further debate on York's rationality is futile. "We have a couple of moves today, Dude. Four cell-to-cell moves and two block-to-block moves."

"What do we have?"

"Well, for starters we have D-4-45 moving to D-3-"

"Just the block-to-block moves, Toby, the internal moves can wait awhile."

"Whatever you say, Dude." Toby fumbles through some papers, searching for the right paper. "The first move is D-1-55 moving to P.C."

"Toes is moving to protective custody? Why?"

Toby shrugs his shoulders aimlessly. "I dunno," he says, "is there a problem?"

"Shit!" I scream and kick the desk, jostling Toby's papers. Toby grabs the desk as if it's

Dutch Van Alstin – Murder in D Block

about to tip. "No, there's no God damn, son of a bitching, mother fucking problem."

"Okay, then…" Toby looks at me cautiously and clears his throat. "We also have D-3-27 cell moving to C-11-7 and the C block is moving in D-1-35."

"I guess McDonald's cell didn't stay empty too long after all. Who's the creep moving from C block?"

"Uhhhhh," Toby stammers, searching through more papers, "Delgrado, Raphael Delgrado."

"Huh? What? Are you just teasing me?" I blurt out hysterically.

"Teasing you," Toby says curiously. "Why would that be teasing you? Do you have a problem with this move, too?"

"Problem? No, no problem, per se, but his name is Delgado, not Delgrado."

"For adding an 'R' to a name, you'll go nuts on me? Good, Lord what will you do if I dangle a participle? Kill me?"

"No, I just…never mind, Toby. It's not important; I'm just curious why he's getting a demotion from C to D?"

"I guess he failed a drug test and lost his program."

"Oh, how long is he keep locked for?"

"He's not," Toby say, shaking his head. "The A.W. cut him loose from serving any time."

"He kicked him loose for drugs? What is matter with that stupid son of a bitch?"

"I don't know," Toby says calmly. "Are you in a pissy mood today?"

"Hell, no" I say, swinging open my lock box, "everything is just peachy fucking keen." I open Rivera and Rook's cell to start the morning feed up run. Both prisoners trudge up the gallery listlessly, stretching and yawning all the way.

"Yo, Carlos, I need some help in my office for a minute. Rook can handle filling up the food trays by himself."

"Dat ain't fair, Viking," Rook whines.

"Neither is the fact you share a shower with sixty other men, but you've adjusted to that minor inconvenience well," I say, reaching for a cup of coffee. "Do you want a cup, Toby?"

"No thanks, Dude," Toby says, sliding out a thermal bag in the shape of Captain America. "I got some *Tab* to drink."

"I didn't think they sold that anymore?"

"The tab," he says, holding up the can. "Not around here, but my mom sends it up from my old neighborhood in California."

Dutch Van Alstin – Murder in D Block

"Actually, I meant the thermal bag."

"Can I get a cup of that java, Viking?" Rivera says.

"Sure, it tastes like shit anyway."

"You is all heart, man."

Rivera walks up the stairs, neurotically looking at back me repeatedly. "What's up, man?" He says.

"I'll talk to you in my office," I reply pointedly.

"Okay, okay, I'm just wondering."

I unlock the door motioning to Rivera to hustle some. He responds by standing outside and gestures for me to go in beforehand.

"Fine," I say, "we'll do it your way."

Rivera slides himself up on to a crate of toilet paper and props his feet comfortably on my desk. "Shoot, big man," he says, pointing and winking at me.

"What happened to Toes?" I say.

"Damn," Rivera laughs, "I knew this is what we was going to talk about."

"What happened to Toes?"

"He fell down and broke his crown," he says impudently.

"Not funny," I say, slapping his feet of my desk. "Now, why is Toes in P.C.?"

"Scared as a bunny rabbit, Viking. Toes wasn't what you call *astute* enough to play with the big boys."

"I'm growing irksome with your, what you call, *bullshit* you're spewing. Now, one more mother fucking time: what happened to Toes?"

"Damn, Viking, the last I knew you was flogging him with that stick."

I snatch Rivera right off the crate and hurl him against the wall. His head snaps forward and his eyes cross as he tries to maintain his balance. He shakes his head and grabs me, throwing me into a locker, and crashing it to the floor. "I ain't no chump, man," he says while huffing and puffing. "You touch me again and I'll bury your fucking ass, Viking! I will fuck you up!"

Instinctively, I grab him by the neck and slam his head against my desk. He grabs my knee and manages to tip me backward, causing him to fall back, too landing a few feet in front of me. I try to stand, but Rivera grabs my shirt, tearing off two buttons. My struggle continues and Rivera shoves me to the floor again. I leap up, snapping my baton out of its holder.

We both freeze and glare at each other.

Dutch Van Alstin – Murder in D Block

"Hold it, Viking," Rivera says, holding his arms out, "let's not you and me go down this road because we ain't got the usual cat/dog relationship no more."

I continue a fervent grip on my baton and watch him, trying to read the moment correctly.

"Put that damn stick away before someone gets hurt; most likely you."

Cooler heads prevail and I slowly place the baton back in its holder. "Okay," I say placidly, "let's start over again. Why is Toes in P.C.?"

Rivera unclenches his fists and walks backwards, feeling behind him, looking for the crate again. He sits down and leans forward toward me. "Truth is, Viking, I told him to sign in yesterday."

"Why, Carlos?"

"Fact is, Toes was too stupid to be having around no more."

"I wanted to talk with him today."

"Go," Rivera shouts, pointing off into space, "he's still in Briersburg, just in P.C."

"You're making it sound easier than it actually is," I say. "They keep detailed log records of who, what, where, and why every time someone walks in to the area."

"So? You wear one of the white hats, remember?"

"True, but what I want to discuss isn't in the normal course of my duties. Besides, if that weasel sees me he may panic thinking he's about to be tuned up again."

"You wanted to talk about that Quinn dude, didn't you?"

"What about him?" I say, straightening my body. "Be straight with me here."

"Forget it, man; the whole thing just ain't in your world."

"Meaning what?"

"I don't mean nothing. Quinn was just some homo bringing in hooch; you must know that by now?"

"Is it necessary to speak ill of a dead man?"

"Ill?" Rivera says looking somewhat mystified. "I'm being straight up here; Quinn was as gay as a three dollar peso."

"How do you know?" I say skeptically.

Rivera grows agitated and shakes his head feverishly. "Are you out in left field or something? I thought you knew what was up in this joint? Quinn was a fag; his man was in Briersburg, too."

"Who was he?" I say, slamming my fist down on my desk.

"Don't be starting that shit again," Rivera says, staring at my fist, "because you ain't

Dutch Van Alstin – Murder in D Block

gonna like the answer."

"I said, who was he?"

"Truth is, I don't know."

"This whole scenario is crap. Are you telling me Quinn was messing around with some prisoner?"

"Hey, fuck you, man. Don't be such a snob."

"Save your hurt feelings, Carlos, just tell me who he was?"

"I don't know," he says adamantly, "I do know it's not a prisoner, it's an employee."

"A guard?"

"I'm telling you, I-do-not-know."

I run my hands aimlessly through my hair and sigh. "Will you please find out for me, Carlos? I swear, I'll owe you big for this one."

"I'm telling you, Viking," Rivera says, shaking his head reluctantly, "ain't nobody talking about it. I mean, it's weird, nobody is saying a word."

CHAPTER   10

I seem to have a natural talent of complicating my life with little effort. Perhaps the solution is to just pull back the reigns and when things slow down, let them go. Donny is dead. None the snooping around I do is going to change that fact one iota. My zeal and ardor to dredge out what was safely buried has bounced back and blindsided me. In retrospect, the entire synopsis has been a sobering experience. I am not *Columbo*. I am not Sherlock Holmes. I am a prison guard at Briersburg State Prison, nothing more, nor nothing less. The pain and tumult I cause myself seems almost masochistic. The truly sick part of all of what I just said is I can't seem to allow myself to stop it all just yet.

I retire Rivera back downstairs to help Rook finish the feed up run. I follow close behind him and try to hide the torn buttons until I can get down to the front desk and fix up my shirt. Toby sits at the desk quietly and calmly writing in the daily logbook as Rook rants and raves to him about Gullo's dictatorial tactics on Toby's days off from the block. Rook peers over at me and stops in mid-sentence as he walks off, finishing the morning feed up run.

"Did the count officially clear the watch commander's office yet?" I say.

"What happened to your shirt?"

"I caught it on a door knob. Now, did the count clear yet or not? It's not a trick question."

Dutch Van Alstin – Murder in D Block

"Yes it did," Toby says, looking back at his logbook.

I attempt to pin up my shirt some where the rips are more noticeable. The pocket is easier to simply tear completely away and switch my nametag to where the pocket was.

The creaking of the rickety old front gate alerts me to Officer Armstrong's surprising visit.

"Where's Gullo at?" Armstrong says, looking around the block.

"Off for two, Armstrong," Toby replies.

Armstrong rests his hand under his chin and stares intently down my gallery. "Nine fire extinguishers and a fire hose."

"Where?" I say.

"I didn't mean they're down the gallery now," he replies. "I'm referring to the fire the other day. I'm curious to know why it took so much to put the damn thing out."

"It was a big fire, Armstrong." I say.

"It would have had to be, Dane," Armstrong says curtly. "What the hell happened here anyway?"

"It was arson."

Armstrong turns his head slowly toward me and grills me with an agitated stare. "I already know that, Dane. I meant a blaze that size tells me someone backed a gasoline truck up to the cell and unloaded. Didn't you two see anything at all?"

"If you're talking about the fire a couple of days ago, Armstrong, I wouldn't know a thing about it," Toby says quickly. "I wasn't even in here that day."

Armstrong leans on the dusty gray bars and continues his studious overview of the gallery. "I heard Ford found some type of accelerant way on the back wall? Wasn't the cell locked?"

"I'm sure it was."

"I'm sure it wasn't," Armstrong snaps back. "How else can you explain gasoline on the back wall?"

"A spray bottle?"

Armstrong pauses and smirks. "Quick thinking, Dane, very quick thinking. But even if they used a spray bottle, it doesn't explain why you and Gullo didn't see anything? We have guards acting like Greg Louganis off the top tiers, blazes that make Smokey the Bear come out of hibernation and nobody sees anything? What were you two doing? Building model airplanes? Rummaging through that porno Gullo has hidden in the bottom of the filing cabinet?"

I heedlessly glimpse over at the filing cabinet. "Ah, no, the block just gets real busy sometimes. Besides, when the cell went up in flames, I was gone."

"How convenient...and I know that the block gets busy, Dane," Armstrong says, trying to keep his composure. "But I don't want a *blue shirt* to be down at the end of your gallery someday with a shank rammed in his chest while you and Gullo are up here dancing."

"I understand," I say sympathetically, "but we keep a good eye on the boys when they're here."

"I know you do, Dane," he says, nodding his head in agreement. "I know you're very careful in the things you do."

"I try," I say, striving not to sound sarcastic.

Armstrong continues the accusatory scowl at me. "Okay," he says nonchalantly, "I have bigger fish to fry." Armstrong turns around slowly, taking an extra peek down my gallery. He walks to the block gate and puts his hand on the bars. "Dane?" he says, without looking back at me.

"Yeah?"

"I thought you were in here only two days a week?"

"That's all I'm assigned."

"Why are you in here today? I know Tyler is here, I saw him walking upstairs to the main tower?"

"I switched with him today so I could catch up on some paperwork."

"You gave up a gravy job like the tower to work in this *shithole?*

"Well, yeah, I, uh, really was falling behind on supply inventories." I say timidly.

"Okay," he says, opening the gate. "Oh, Dane? One more thing:" Armstrong says, without looking over at me.

"What's up?"

"Fix your shirt, it's ripped to shreds." Armstrong walks out and shuts the gate.

"Was the fire that serious, Dude?" Toby says.

"Oh that's right," I say mockingly, "you *weren't* here!"

The jingling of York's keys grows closer to the front gate. I focus my sights out into the corridor and spy Delgado with York. York laughs with Delgado over some obscure joke. "There you go," York says, playfully booting Delgado in the backside, "off to the dog pound with you, bad boy."

"That there is guard abuse, York," Delgado says lightheartedly, "I'm calling my shyster of a lawyer after I unpack my stuff." Delgado walks in and looks around the cellblock indignantly.

Dutch Van Alstin – Murder in D Block

"Damn, this here is one filthy cellblock."

"It's the maid's day off," I say sharply.

Delgado looks at me contemptuously. "Okay, send her to my cell tomorrow. By the way, what cell will she be coming to?"

"Number thirty-five cell, freshly painted and cleaned for your arrival. Now, are you going to unpack first, or go to the yard with the rest of the denizens?"

"I'll just unpack," he says, "the yard will be here tomorrow."

"As you will be, too."

"I can see," Delgado says, setting his bags on the floor, "it's going to be interesting being with you, Erickson. I've heard lots about you from my friends."

"You have friends?" I say with a cocksure smirk.

"Yeah," he says with a sigh, "and they gave me the 4-1-1 on you."

"I hope it wasn't all bad."

"Nobody is all bad; we all have a good side to us, somewhere."

"I haven't seen nor heard from mine in a decade. He and the *bad side* had a falling out one night and they split up."

"Oh, that's so sad," he says, picking his bags back up, "that can be so hard on the children; I wish you all the best though."

"Number thirty-five cell is right down there," I say, pointing down my gallery.

"Thank you, you are too kind." Delgado lugs his belongings down the gallery and gingerly places them inside his new dwelling.

"You make friends fast," Toby says.

I fix my sights on Delgado as he unloads his personal effects into his cell. A contempt unknown to me before boils inside my soul. Every scurrilous plot I can formulate in my mind races around, searching for an exit. I want to hurt him and hurt him severely. I want to shout to him that I just left his wife in the shower only hours ago and that we made mad, wild, fiery love the night before. He should know she uttered words of ecstasy and ardent passion that he can only imagine in some unattainable dream.

"Is there some type of trouble between you two, Dude?"

"I'm going to my office," I say, ignoring Toby's question.

"Look, Dane, if there's a problem with Delgado and you, I need--"

"I said, I'm going to my office."

"But I need you to--"

Dutch Van Alstin – Murder in D Block

"Put it in my *in* box, Toby and I'll get to it later."

The bell shrills from B block next door signifying their lock in time. The blue smoke from the slew of cigarettes rises up to the top tier and spreads out along the ceiling, making the chalky gray paint difficult to see. I tip my locker over on to its side and unscrew the bottom shelf. I reach inside and pull out two, sharpened, chrome-plated shanks I keep hidden from my enemies, both in orange and blue. The jagged tip rubs along my fingertip, prodding the callous covered skin as I indulge in a bit of reverie.

The shank is pulled out of Delgado's floor drain or the binding of Bible right in front of his startled eyes. "How the hell did that get there?" He'll say. Nobody will believe his story. I could plant the shank tomorrow, tip off the night guards and *POOF*, Delgado's gone.

A spot of sanity urges me to place the shank back where it belongs. A trip to the box amidst the feet of the robots is not some panacea to this whole fiasco. Such a plan will not get Delgado out of my life, out of April's life.

My car swings into my driveway causing Bambino to pop his head up in my window. His tongue dangles out and his head swings frantically about. Bambino is a black/brown, mangy, midsize, mutt. I find describing Bambino difficult, he's just your average, run of the mill dog. He is, however, as faithful and true as a Boy Scout. He has been with me through thick and thin and I recall all of his loyalty as I enter my humble abode and scratch his ears. He charges around the living room, leaping on to every stick of furniture and knocking over my candy dish.

"Settle down, boy," I say. "You'll destroy the place before you meet April."

I shuffle through some recipe cards I received free in the mail years ago as an advertisement. If I correctly recall, there was a description of a tuna casserole in the mix. Reading off the ingredients, I am overcome with juvenile tendencies that cause me to juggle three eggs in the air. Alas, the fragile shells crash to the floor sparking an interest in Bambino. He trots over excitedly and smells the mess, lifts his nose, and walks away disappointedly.

I slide the casserole in the oven and seek out my wading boots. The hour baking time invites me to a sprig of fishing off my dock.

The lake air blows along my face, cooling down what was a humid day. I toss the line in the water and wipe the sweat from my brow while I reluctantly conjure up the day's events in my mind. The serenity I normally equate with fishing trickles away with every complexity I face. The struggle of Donny Quinn creeps into my psyche once more. Questions that have been answered only bring to light more, unanswered, questions. To prophesize that Quinn being gay is directly linked to his death may be a little short sighted of me. What could his gay lifestyle play? Where does the liquor fit in and does it? Directly or indirectly? His death is tied to something specific. If a prisoner is responsible, I don't believe it's linked to the usual cat/dog animosity plaguing prison life on a daily basis. There are three facts I am totally convinced of:

One: Someone other than Donny is directly, or indirectly, responsible for his death.

Second: His murder was planned and orchestrated by a person, or persons, involving something Byzantine.

Three: I haven't a clue of who or what.

The casserole's time draws near, but I feel a wiggle at the end of my fishing pole. I pull the line a few times and jerk the pole hard. The hook flies into the air with nothing but a clump of seaweed attached leaving me to ponder if there's anything in the lake to catch.

I wrap the casserole in foil and leap in the shower and dress quickly, simultaneously running a comb through my hair and searching for my keys. I dart my eyes around the room until I realize the entire ring of keys are dangling from my mouth.

When I arrive at April's, she is waiting by the window with all the eagerness as Bambino exhibited earlier. She smiles and hastens downstairs with her coat and purse draped over her arms. Upon getting in my car, April seizes my rearview mirror and begins fussing with her hair.

"You look fine," I say, retrieving my mirror, "stop pampering."

"I'm a girl, that's what we do."

We chitchat about various subject matters, not including our night together. I'll assume she is trying to point out she is not a needy person, but the possibility she is just a little embarrassed is plausible.

Bambino, again, waits patiently by my window. "I guess I should warn you, April that my dog goes crazy when I get home."

"Oh, that's so cute," April says, "What's his name?"

"Bambino."

"Bambino?"

"Yep, I named him after the greatest baseball that ever lived, Babe Ruth."

Bambino, true to his nature, charges me at the door. "*Yip Yip Yip,*" he barks as he lunges toward April.

"Damn it, dog, get down," I shout.

"Oh, stop it, you old grouch, he's fine," she says, squatting down to scratch his ears.

Dutch Van Alstin – Murder in D Block

"Yes, you're a good puppy dog, is your master mean to you?"

"Supper will be ready soon, I didn't promise you the Ritz, but how about some wine?"

"I'd love some."

I pick at the cork from the near empty bottle of wine sitting by my dirty casserole dish. April is either very good at lying or she super wasn't as bad as I feared. I'm inclined to believe the former since I know my cooking is not that tasty. She ate most of her food, leaving a few bites as every woman does. I pour the last drop of Chablis' into her glass and we clink them together in a toast.

"To love, to peace, to togetherness, to unity, to relationships, and, to us," April says as she gulps the last of her wine.

"I can drink to all that," I answer cheerfully, swallowing my last gulp. "And more for that matter."

"Let's swim," April blurts out.

"Huh?"

"I said swim, lets' go take dip in the lake while the moon is full."

"Did you happen to bring a swimsuit with you?"

April commandeers my glass of wine and drinks the remaining spirit. "Grab me a T-shirt and we'll run down to the lake."

I rashly strip off my own and give it to her. April slips off her blouse and slides my shirt over her body, tossing her head back and forth as her hair catches in the neckline. "Come on, Dane, it's your turn."

I quickly, and almost systematically, strip to my underpants and throw my clothes over the couch. April giggles and pulls me out the door with Bambino close behind. She runs full bore into the water, throwing her arms in the air. "*Weeeee*," she shouts ecstatically, "get in, Dane." She continues splashing wildly, sending tiny droplets into the air. Slowly I walk in and April charges at me, plowing into me, and knocking me in the water. She runs her hands through her slick, wet hair laughing uncontrollably. "I love this, Dane, I just love all this. I'm free, for the very first time in my life, I'm free. Look what you've done for me, Dane, I'm free!"

"I think the wine played a small part as well, April."

"No it didn't, I know I drank a lot of it, but it's more, much more than the wine. I know we've only known each other for a few months but they've been the best months of my life. I'm not trying to scare you away, Dane, but I just can't help myself, you're the best thing that ever happened to me, ever."

April continues her frenzied frolic through the water as I search, in vain, for a reply.

"Take my hand, Dane, don't be afraid, it feels so right to me."

"I'm not afraid."

"Don't be embarrassed, Dane, we all get afraid sometimes, but when I'm with you, all my fears seem so far away. Do you believe in love at first sight? Do you, Dane? Do you believe it can happen? My mom and dad fell in love at first sight; do you think it can happen again? I do, I believe it's true, do you?"

"Sure I do, April, you've stole my heart, too." I say sheepishly.

"Oh, Dane," she says, draping her arms around my neck, "we're going to be together, I can just feel it in my soul."

April strips away her T-shirt and dives backward into the water. She comes back up, spitting water in the air that flows over her face. She leaps up and grabs my arm, pulling me deeper in the water.

"Where we going?"

"It doesn't matter, as long as it's together," April says, caressing my shoulder. Her attention is captured momentarily by a boyhood tattoo on my arm. She rubs the near faded letters with her thumbnail. "Who's Ace?" She says curiously.

"No, that's A-C-E, my initials, my real name is *Augustovson* and my middle name is *Caleb*."

"Oh..." April catches her breath and pauses. "I never knew that."

We kiss.

CHAPTER 11

We are awakened by the sound of the seagulls squawking around the lake. They swoop harmoniously in a polite procession, each awaiting the first to collect the bread chunks tossed in the water by a young neighbor boy. The sun's emergent glow is unimpeded by any cloud cover allowing the burnt orange to radiate and whisper to all its children: *"morning is here."*

My cottage rests about twenty yards off shore with an old stone path leading from the waterfront to my front door. Two sapling oak trees, trembling toward the sun, sway mildly back and forth on each side of my gravel driveway. The dawn breeze energizes my neighbor's wind chimes bringing forth a precise but sedative melody that can be heard through my bedroom window to my awakening senses.

The cottage itself is a relatively small, *Cape Cod* style edifice covered in dried out, aged shingles that lost the sea blue luster they once had. An abundance of the little homes sprang up following World War II in a small development project built by the Veteran's Administration. My cottage was apparently built as an afterthought because it was constructed on a corner lot, giving me less than a quarter acre of a front lawn and no back lawn to speak of. The concrete steps on my front porch are chipping chunks of cinder on to the ground almost every day giving way to my handrail, being held in place by some wire and a few nails. A handful of shingles are sporadically arranged along my rooftop.

Dutch Van Alstin – Murder in D Block

There are occasions when I awake after a turbulent storm only to be greeted by a few of my shingles floating in the lake. I have been contemplating, as much as the antiquated charm of my cottage endears me, tearing down my humble domicile and replacing it with one of those new, prefabricated homes that can be livable in a matter of two or three days. The future is now.

I reach my arm across the bed, looking for April. I stroke her back gently as I try to wake her. "Time to get up, April," I whisper. April yawns and stretches like a cat rising from hibernation. Her eyes fight to focus against the peering sunlight through my window. She looks at me warmly and smiles.

"Good morning." She says.

We share a picturesque breakfast out on my dock where I have a small picnic table shared by nobody, until today. April and I occasionally glance up at each other and smile. We watch intently as the neighbor boy feeds the ducks that swim near his dock. One duck sinks his head far under water to retrieve a fragment of dough leaving his backside in mid-air to wiggle frantically. We laugh at this lighter side of nature's comedy.

The drive retreating to April's apartment grows ominously quiet as April stares pensively out my car window. As I pull in the parking lot, April remains fixated in her thoughts, staring out at nothingness.

"Dane," she says, never taking her eyes off her sights. She pauses and sighs.

"What?"

April presses her hand to her pursed lips and, again, sighs.

"Is everything okay?" I say.

"I'm...telling him I want a divorce today. Whatever the circumstances surrounding you and I are, or will be, are irrelevant. I'm divorcing Raph anyway. All I'm trying to point out to you is that I'm not pressuring you."

"I know."

"I don't love him," she snorts embarrassingly, "obviously."

"I know that, too."

"I love you, Dane," April says softly, still focusing her sights out my window. She remains sullen, not looking for a reply from me. "Please don't think I'm crazy, I know we've only been seeing each other a short time."

I rub her shoulder and she stretches her neck back and kisses my fingers. "Where's this going, Dane?"

Dutch Van Alstin – Murder in D Block

"That's a question I can't answer, I am not a clairvoyant." I sigh. "However, I do know that I love you, too."

April turns her head and smiles. "You're crazy."

"Yes, ma'am, I am," I say proudly, "about you."

April leans in to me and kisses my nose. "I'll visit him today and tell him."

"I'll call you about six or so then."

"I love you, Dane, thanks for being there for me."

"As you were for me."

The robots gape at the beaming smile on my face as I extend affable greetings to Lieutenant Garrison, A.W. Edwards, and others where animosities are rampant and amenities are few.

"What the fuck, Dane," one robot bellows, "did you get laid last night?"

"Couldn't be," another robot chimes, "his *boyfriend* is out of town."

A raucous of laughter follows that I delightedly share in as well. Not even the insufferable clanging of the robots will irk me now.

Today is my *float* day where I am at the mercy of the chart sergeant. I normally fill in for other guards to cover sick days or vacation days. If the staff isn't too short handed, I usually end up as an *extra* in the main recreation yard with Sergeant Flannigan. While there, I will be at Flannigan's mercy.

Sergeant Flannigan is an endangered species in the domain of prison guards. Flannigan, or *Red*, as he has always been referred to since I've been in Briersburg, is a guard's ideal prospect of a sergeant. Red is informal enough to be on a first name basis with everyone, however, the respect he commands from all of the guards is unparalleled. When we, guards and prisoners alike, are in the main yard, there is no doubt to all present who is in charge. As much as Red Flannigan reveres the guards, he will not hesitate to chew one out if he has it coming. And if Red Flannigan reads the riot act, it was warranted.

I walk alone through the near vacant yard to the sergeant's post. The fog is just lifting off the rooftop exposing the gun turrets mounted along the cellblocks. The pigeons swoop down like kamikaze dive-bombers into the yard to pick up scraps of debris spewed along the cement. Two prisoners near the commissary entrance toss bits of stale crackers on the steps by the showers and laugh in amusement at the pigeons fighting over the broken morsels.

Red strolls out of B block with a hot cup of coffee in his hand and a cigarette wedged

Dutch Van Alstin – Murder in D Block

between his yellowed fingers. "Morning, boys," Red says, nodding at each one of us individually.

"Morning, Red," we respond in near unison.

The breakfast bell sounds and the yard is flooded with the orange clothes of the prisoners as they proceed to the mess hall. Red scans his sights over the mass as he sips his coffee and takes a drag off his cigarette, all the while chewing on his hearty peppermint gum. Red claims the gum simultaneously *freshens* his stale breath from the coffee and cigarettes.

A large prisoner muscles his way through the crowd toward the observation deck of the sergeant's post. His sleeves are intentionally cut-off at the shoulders, exposing the taught muscles and several rogue tattoos. His brisk charge at the post is meeting with a stiff-arm tactic of Officer Armstrong. "What do you want?" Armstrong says sternly.

"I'm here to talk to the sergeant," the prisoner replies.

"Why?"

"Personal reason."

"We're all one big happy family here," Armstrong says, "we don't have secrets from one another. You will tell me what you want and if I feel it merits a conversation with the sergeant, I'll allow you to speak with him."

"Let 'em through, boys," Red says, climbing down from the deck. "This here gentleman and I have already meet last week."

Red is a short, but very stocky man who purposely hides his muscle in oversized shirts. He slicks his salt and pepper hair straight back and keeps the length as long as he can without violating the dress code. Red trims, daily, his sideburns just under his earlobe blending in with his permanent *five o'clock shadow*. The rough whiskers fail to hide his rigid, stern jaw line. His eyes are gray, cold, and emotionless. If the eyes are truly the mirrors to the soul, then the icy, inimical spirit residing within Red's soul is disturbed and angry.

Red shoos us all back away from the post. We comply readily but stay within hearing distance.

"Yo, Sarge, you stole my smokes last week and I want 'em back."

Red smirks. "Why didn't you ask me?"

"I did, man, I filed a grievance report three days ago and--"

"No, no, no, no, asshole," Red says sharply. "I said, why didn't you ask me personally, not file some faggot-ass, whiney, schoolboy complaint with the warden."

"Look here, Sarge, they are my smokes and you--"

Dutch Van Alstin – Murder in D Block

"You were in *my* yard with thirteen packs of cigarettes that day," Red interjects, poking the big man in the chest with every syllable. "Nobody comes to the yard with thirteen packs of smokes unless he's using them for a payoff somewhere. Here in Briersburg, all gambling, prostitution deals, drug running, bribes, extortion, weapons traveling, are **never** done in my yard! We like peace and quiet out here, don't we boys?" Red says, without dropping his menacing glare.

We all nod affirmatively.

"Do we understand the rules here? Are you and I in sync now?" Red says.

"I got it, man..." the prisoner stammers and swallows his words. "I mean Sergeant."

"Good, now as a celebration of our agreement, I happen to have your smokes in my post," Red says, reaching up on the deck. "Here you go." Red tosses the prisoner the paper bag full of cigarettes. The prisoner reaches in and begins fumbling through the contents.

"What the fuck do you think you're doing?" Red says irately.

"Uh, counting 'em?"

"I'm not a thief!" Red shouts. "Get the hell away from my post!"

The prisoner sheepishly walks away, occasionally looking back at Red trying to read his demeanor.

"Is he a new prisoner, Red?" I say.

"Him," Red says, pointing at the retreating man, "yeah, he's new."

The yard phone rings as the robots scramble feverishly to answer it first. Red calmly reaches over the crowd and takes the receiver. "Main yard, Flannigan."

Red nods his head a few times and mumbles. "Okay, I'll send a man in." He hangs up the phone and surveys his guards. "Gillian, go into D block and escort a prisoner to the visit room."

"I'll go," I say anxiously, hoping to see April.

"I know you would, Dane, but I said Gillian."

"Who is it, Red?" Gillian asks.

"Some creep named Vinetto," Red says, "locks up top somewhere." Red sighs. "Try not to fall off the top tier, okay, Gillian?"

"I can walk and chew gum at the same time, Red," Gillian says with a snicker.

"Vinetto?" Armstrong says suspiciously.

"Something up with him, T.J.?" Red says.

"No, not really," Armstrong says, "It's just that Vinetto has been here seven years and I

Dutch Van Alstin – Murder in D Block

don't recall him ever receiving a visitor until one time a few weeks ago and now today."

"I don't remember him having one a few weeks ago, either," Red says, "but I know he's being paroled next week. Maybe that has something to do with it?"

"You were off that day, Red," Armstrong says. "Bert Pound was here, in fact, he insisted Quinn walk him up. But, I'm just being overly paranoid," he says, shrugging his shoulders. "I guess I'm just naturally suspicious."

"That's why you get the big money, Armstrong."

Armstrong flips open his wallet and stares disappointedly at the vacant contents.

"Why would Pound let that fuck up escort anyone to the visit room?" Red says.

"Pound liked to bust Quinn's balls." Armstrong replies.

"What was so bad about Quinn," I ask curiously.

Red peeks up over the partition at me curiously. "I don't know, Dane, other than he was a fuck up. He sure as hell was no drinking buddy of mine." Red snickers caustically. "The lame fuck can't even walk down a gallery without killing himself."

I demur at questioning Red any farther. His stoicism and gruffness do not make him a good candidate for my brand of repartee type interrogation.

The clock ticks on and on and on…

"That's lunch, boys," Red shouts. "Go grease up!"

The menu of fried liver and onions leads to a quick run of the afternoon meal. Red looks down at his watch and gives us thirty minutes to eat lunch. The kitchen guards will only be too happy to part with liver and onions today without much bargaining on my end. Liver is not high on the preference list in delicacy for most people. I, however, have a voracious appetite for calf's liver, but cheap, prison cooked beef liver still appeals to my bucolic upbringing. According to the clock hanging in the mess hall's gun nest, I have only minutes to return to the yard.

I return to the sergeant's post with the others as Gillian walks out of D block snickering like a schoolboy. "No wonder you were so eager to go to the visit room, Dane," he says.

"Meaning?"

"You wanted to see that porno act live and in person."

"What are you jabbering about?" I say.

"I took Vinetto up to his visit and there was this whore-bag crawling over her husband so bad, Andover moved them in a *non-contact* room. They have a conjugal visit coming up, but the way they pawing at each other, like sex starved savages, that should count as the actual visit."

"That's gross," a guard says.

Dutch Van Alstin – Murder in D Block

"No way, this slut was a fox," Gillian says.

"A prisoner's wife?" Armstrong interjects. "You're a sicko, Gillian."

"You would have had to see this bitch and what she was doing to him, talk about hot."

"Damn, Gillian, you're getting a *woody* just talking about her. Who the hell is this slut anyway?"

"That guy who moved from C block over to D yesterday," Gillian says. "Delgado, Raphael Delgado and his wife."

CHAPTER 12

"Delgado? Raphael Delgado?" I say excitably, "the guy who moved from C to D yesterday, that Delgado? Are you sure it was him and his wife?"

"Yeah, yeah, that's him, settle down," Gillian says, holding his hands up in condescending fashion.

The robots begin verbally assaulting in a pejorative manner the woman I love and left in the shower only hours ago. My eyes dart from man to man, as they belittle and besmirch a woman they know nothing about.

"Red, can I go into D block and use the can?" I say.

Red glances down at his watch and nods. "Yeah, you may as well stay in there. The keep lock recreation is about to run in the yard so stay in there and help that Toby character." Red shakes his head in disgust. "He's another fuck head."

"Open up!!" I shout into the desolate corridor.

The jingling of brass on York's belt closes in on my quickly. "What's up?" York says excitedly.

"Nothing, I just want to come in, that's all, there's no problem in that, is there?"

"Jesus, Dane," York exclaims, "you sounded so riled."

"Thank you, Dr. fucking Phil, now open up the fucking gate."

Dutch Van Alstin – Murder in D Block

York laughs and opens the gate. "Dane, my brother! Love the world and love yourself. Anger is a demon seed planted by the wicked."

"Stick that fucking, marshmallow, pansy-ass, faggot talk you learned on *the peak* and shove it up your oversized, cocaine loaded nostrils you fucking freak of nature."

"Wow," York says, pretending to wipe sweat from his brow, "if I were a different kind of man, I'd think you didn't like me."

"Are you really this stupid?" I say, "Or are you just deaf?"

"I still love you, my son," York shouts.

"I mean it you sick, deformed, mutated abnormality, shut the fuck up," I scream, kicking over a metal trashcan, sending it clattering to the floor. The impact of the crash in the stark corridor creates an ominous echo, causing a handful of guards to charge out of B block with their batons drawn. They stop and stare at York and me alone.

"What the hell was that?" One guard yells?

"Nothing, Dane just blew his top," York says with a picayune grin. "But not to worry, I will not allow him to take the white powder train of hell." York shouts in an evangelical style.

"You're a sick pup," he says to York, "and you," he points his baton at me, "throw your fucking temper tantrums out in the playground with the other children."

I scowl at York with an apocalyptic glare. York smiles back at me and waves his pinky finger. Toby, in keeping with his paranoid form, has the outer gate to D block latched tightly.

"Toby, let me in the damn block, nobody's going to hurt you."

"Sure thing, Dude."

"Dude! Dude!" I rave, "what the hell is the matter with you anyway? Get in the game or at least get a program so you can follow along with the rest of the world."

"That means a lot from someone who beats up unarmed trash receptacles," Toby says with an obvious pang of sarcasm.

The ice-cold water from the bathroom sink shivers my sweaty skin. The face in the mirror is the target of my rage. "You dumb bastard," I say quietly, "what made you think you could trust a prisoner's wife?"

Collecting my composure seems futile, but action is needed, not histrionics.

Clearer heads prevail and I grab my keys, unlock my lock box, and place a *keep lock* tag on number thirty-five cell's handle. Next step: Delgado will want to know why he is keep locked when he returns from his work duties. I reach over Toby's shoulder, snatch the Keep Lock Logbook, and flip through the pages.

Dutch Van Alstin – Murder in D Block

"Locking someone up, du--ah, Dane?" Toby asks.

"Nope, just browsing."

I scratch out Delgado's name under the column of *new keep locks*. The next column requests the name of the person authorizing the keep lock status.

Hmmm, I look out the corner of my eyes in neurotic fashion and write in the name *S. Brannigan*. He, obviously, does not exist in Briersburg, but by time the snafu is discovered, the conjugal visit will have gone by already. I scribble a note for the night shift to tell Delgado he has been keep locked and sign Brannigan's name to that as well.

Now I have to apologize to a man, albeit, a lunatic, who was the target of my childish rage.

"Oh my, no, Dane," Toby squeals, "you can't go out in the corridor with the keys."

"Relax."

"No, I can't," he says as his body cringes and twists like a boy waiting to go to the bathroom, "you just can't leave the block with D block keys."

Toby is technically correct. The 1984 riot, where Red was beaten to a pulp, started because a guard walked in the corridor with the B block keys and was subsequently jumped by three prisoners. They commandeered B block and when it was over, four guards were beaten to death and one hung from the gallery bars.

"Okay, Toby," I say passively, "you win."

Before I can hand him my keys, the clanking and clinking from the upper tiers signifies the keep lock recreation has begun. The prisoners promenade out the block and into small yards designed for them exclusively. I stand poised by Toby's desk as the march continues outside.

A short, hebetudinous prisoner named Ludlow stops at the desk. "I need a Sergeant right now," he says.

"Uh, after you return from the yard, okay," Toby says softly.

"I ain't waiting for no mother fucking yard," Ludlow says, swinging his arms wildly. "I want him now."

"Please, Mr. Ludlow, just wait until the yard returns, okay?" Toby pleads.

"I need my cell painted."

"Not now, Ludlow, okay?" Toby continues in an almost desperate fashion.

"Look here, man--"

"Hey," I shout, "do you have rocks in your head? The man said you wait, you will fucking

Dutch Van Alstin – Murder in D Block

wait! Now get out to the fucking yard and do it fucking now, you stupid shitbag!"

"Who's talking to your *motherfuckingass* anyway?" Ludlow says, throwing his hands out at me. He turns around, mumbles, and begins walking out the gate.

"Hold it," I roar, "get your goat-smelling ass back here now!"

Ludlow continues walking away but does give me the *old one finger salute* as he exits. I follow close behind into the corridor where nearly forty prisoners are huddled. Toby charges to the gate and stops his feet as if he stepped in wet cement. "The keys," he says, "you can't have the keys."

I leap on Ludlow's back and slam him to the floor as I fall directly on top of him, jamming my knee in his back. After a few wild slugs to his body, I pick him up from the floor and drag him back into D block and, again, slam him to the floor and continuing pounding on him. I shout words that mean nothing to anybody.

The prisoners stand fast in the corridor.

Red points at the unsettling mob. "Outside, now, unless you want trouble."

The prisoners grumble some, but, reluctantly, they walk outside, looking back at Red.

I snatch Ludlow from the floor by his ponytail and hurl his flabby body against the wall. Ludlow drops to the floor and covers his body as the pummeling continues. "God damn son of a bitch," I shriek as I go completely out of control and far away from my wits. I drag Ludlow in the storeroom where he encounters more battering, this time from other guards as well. I forgot why I was mad and if I ever was.

"Enough!" Red bellows.

Instantly, the beating ceases. Red plucks Ludlow from the floor and pulls him in tightly to his chest. "What did you do to piss off one of my men so badly?"

"Damn, man, I didn't do nothing," Ludlow stammers, "I ...I...I just asked if I could have my cell painted and this crazy bastard goes *postal* on me."

Red throws Ludlow into the arms of an awaiting guard. "Get 'em the hell out of here," Red says.

"Holy shit, man, I ain't never been in a joint like this. What do you do if a man wants his toilet fixed? Stretch 'em on the rack? I ain't never seen nothing like it."

"Well then, son," Red says, slapping Ludlow's face gently, "welcome to the *Briar Patch*. Now get out of my sights. That goes for all of you, out, now."

I stare at the floor like scolded boy with a slingshot in his pocket as I casually begin walking out with the others. "Not you," Red says, shutting the door. "Do you know how lucky

Dutch Van Alstin – Murder in D Block

you are you flipped out on a white guy? Do you know how many creeps were in the corridor waiting to avenge Rodney King, even to this day?"

I nod my head.

"Do you want to explain what all that was about?" Red says.

"I…I just," I pause briefly. "I just am having a really bad day."

Red nods his head subconsciously and sighs. "Yeah," he says, slapping me on the shoulder, "you sure *were*."

Red opens the door and coolly strolls out of the storeroom.

CHAPTER 13

The robots amassed all their disparaging remarks and hurled them at me for the remainder of the day. Just like dominoes, they hounded me one after another until I went home. Even at the conclusion of my day, I could not escape the sophomoric barbs because when I went to punch my time card out, there was a note stapled on it that read: "Dane's new phone number - 1-800-*T-E-M-P-E-R-T-A-N-T-R-U-M*." At the bottom of the note was a rudimentary sketch of a baby crying.

The whole situation seems incongruous to me. I was always under the impression we were in an '*us* versus *them*' type atmosphere. Lately, trying to differentiate who qualifies as an '*us*' and who qualifies as a '*them*' is growing significantly more difficult. Mack, of all people, was the only guard to be somewhat civil to me. All he said was, "I like the cut of your jib, country boy," as he spun the wheels of his new truck in the gravel on his way out of the parking lot.

The robot's derisive comments are small potatoes to me when juxtaposed up against other more pressing matters. The fact there is a conjugal visit scheduled with my girlfriend nettles my nerves almost as much as the torrid tryst in the middle of the visit room. April never mentioned anything about the conjugal visit. The goings on in one of those trailers during conjugal visits is far removed from the warped mind of Larry Flynt. D block Delgado is not going to lay one hand, utter one groan, on my girl. My girl!

Dutch Van Alstin – Murder in D Block

The first line of attack has to be confronting April on what I know to be true. The phone is the method of choice. Confrontation made simple.

My drive home is somber and melancholy. I don't cry because, I don't cry.

I shoo Bambino off me when I get home. The slobbering love he has for me is not welcome at the moment. I grab my cell phone and crank up my boat's motor and putter aimlessly around the lakeside. My impatience grows. I know April is not due home from work for nearly an hour but that fact fails to repress my desire to call anyhow.

The phone is answered on the very first ring. "Hi, Hon," April says.

I pause. I try to think what needs to be said and fast.

"Helloo, Dane, hello, I know it's you; caller I.D., remember?" she says impatiently.

"It's me," I say phlegmatically.

"Hello, me," she says coyly.

"Don't be cute, it's Dane."

"I know, Silly. Hi, Sweetie," April says exuberantly, "how are you?"

"Lousy."

"Why, Hon, what's the matter?"

"I got in a fight today."

"Oh my Lord, you weren't hurt, were you?"

"No."

"You sound sad," she says, "come and get me."

I lapse in my words briefly; dumbfounded at her *se la vie* attitude. My pause causes her to say "hello" a few more times.

"I'm still here," I say.

"Dane, what's the--"

"You visited your husband today, didn't you?"

"Huh," she says confusedly, "you knew I was. Why does that make you mad?"

I erupt. "I heard you were pawing at him so damn bad, the guards had to move you two sex-crazed *nymphos* up front to a non-contact room? I've been at Briersburg a long time and I've never heard of a visit getting so lewd that the people needed to be isolated. What was the matter? Didn't Andover have a bucket of ice water to dump on you two cats in heat?"

"I would tell you to think before you speak so you won't regret something you say, but...too late for that." April says.

"I regret nothing!" I say with all the fervor of a man in the gallows.

Dutch Van Alstin – Murder in D Block

"You have the story all wrong, Dane," April says pointedly. "Come and pick me up here so we can discuss this like two, civilized adults, you jackass."

"Never mind," I exclaim, and then ended the call.

I return the boat to the dock and march into my house and pop open a beer. I turn my ringer off on my phone, sit, and watch TV. My ruminations are interrupted while I watch *Pepe LaPew* chase around that damn cat he believes is a skunk. Is he some kind of fool? Can't he see what she really is?

A loud wrapping at my front door jostles me. A visitor at my door is not an everyday occurrence. The last caller I had at my door tried to convince me I would be unable to survive without a new and improved *Wesso* brand vacuum cleaner. The loud wrapping is now being replaced with loud pounding.

"Open the God damn door, Dane now," April screeches.

"April?"

"Have you pissed off anyone else enough to come and pound your door today?"

I leap up, trying to remember I am angry, and open the door. "How the hell did you get here? You said you don't own a car?"

"I got a thumb, don't I? She says, shoving the appendage in my face.

"You hitchhiked? Are you insane or just plain stupid?"

"Neither A or B, just pissed off at your ignorance beyond belief."

"At me," I say with great incredulity, "how dare you!"

"You didn't have the decency to listen to what I had to say, how-dare-you!"

"I can't believe you have the audacity to be mad at me after what you did?"

"I didn't do anything wrong, Dane, listen to me for a second and shut your mouth."

"He was there, April."

"Then he's a lying scumbag, Dane."

"He dropped off a visit today and saw you, it's as simple as that," I say, pounding my fist in my hand.

"No, it isn't," she replies, mocking my fist gesture.

"Are you trying to--"

"Whoa, hold it, wait a minute here," April blurts out, "are you telling me the guy who laid this crap on you wasn't that Andover fellow?"

"No, but he was there."

"Did you bother to take a minute of your life and ask Mr. Andover? Or wasn't I worth all

Dutch Van Alstin – Murder in D Block

that extra trouble?"

"Meaning what?" I say curiously.

"Ask Mr. Andover and he'll give you a whole other version, a version I like to call *the truth.*"

My interest is peeked. "What version?"

"I visited him today, like I told you I was, and I hinted here and there about divorce."

"Why didn't you just come out and tell him?"

April scoffs at me. "Maybe that's the way they do it in East Tuna, Minnesota, Dane--"

"St. Alexandria."

"Whatever," she says, growing irate, "that's not the point. Here in the real world, we don't blurt out, 'hey, we're history' to a raving madman like Raph."

"Okay, sorry, continue."

"As I was saying, I dropped hints about how young I was, how long he's in prison for, etc. Raph is no fool. He knew what I was hinting at and he started pawing at me and kissing me, trying to keep me from talking. That's when I made an excuse to leave the table. I told him I needed to use the ladies room and when I came out of the ladies room, I stopped at the desk and told that Andover guy what Raph was doing and could he please move us to a non-contact room. I figured that room would be safer to tell him. When Raph asked why I stopped at the desk, I said I was reporting a leak in the sink. Now, if you need to verify my story, then ask Andover tomorrow."

"I don't need to ask, Bob," I say apologetically, "I believe you."

April sighs and takes my hand. "Let's not let this happen again, for all this to work, you need to trust me."

"I'm sorry," I say, kissing her forehead, "I do. But what about this conjugal visit coming up?"

April looks up at me discontentedly. "I don't know; I forgot that it was coming up soon. I thought when he failed the drug test; he'd lose his conjugal visits."

"That's normally the procedure."

"I know, but he said the assistant warden gave him a waiver for the visit."

"A waiver?" I say skeptically, "I never heard of such a thing; even from that dickhead A.W."

"Neither have I," she says. "When he told me that, I was so shocked, I never got around to telling him about the divorce."

Dutch Van Alstin – Murder in D Block

"Conjugal or no conjugal, most prisoners would be a little nervous."

"Why?"

"A favor like the one the A.W. did for him smacks of nepotism."

April shrugs her shoulders. "I don't follow."

"A snitch?"

"Not Raph," April says, shaking her head, "he's not snitch material."

"Whether he is or isn't doesn't make any difference, it's how the other prisoners perceive it is what counts. None of this makes sense, April. This guy seems to have clout with the brass and some of the guards. York was joking around with him yesterday like they were old college roommates, A.W. Edwards bends over backwards to free him from keep lock and Pound sniffs around looking for trouble because of him, it doesn't make sense at all."

"I just don't know, Dane," April says somberly. "I'm running out of ideas. Do you have any?"

"No, I don't."

"Well I do," she says, "I'm just going to serve him with divorce papers."

"That will take a few weeks, what about the conjugal in the mean time?"

"I don't know. I know I'm not going, but if I don't, he'll know something is up and I want to be the one to serve him first."

"How do you think he'll take being served?"

"I don't have a clue," she says with a forged smile. "How do most prisoners handle it when their wives take off on them?"

"Let's just say I'll make sure he has a nice strong bed sheet in his cell. Maybe he'll do us both a favor."

CHAPTER 14

The chart sergeant, again, sends me to D block. Only this time I'll only be there until noon to cover for a guard who is at a doctor appointment. York is off today and the corridor seems eerie without his buffoonery and bantering to make the day complete. I dump the keys on the desk and wave goodbye to the midnight guards as they put their shoes on, collect their coats, and go home.

Delgado's name is erroneously deleted from my keep lock list. It seems again that he squirmed off the keep lock status once more. I envision him and April in the trailer, in bed, with their clothes slung over the furniture. The guards are walking by, laughing and pointing at the trailer, making jokes about animals mating and slovenly prostitutes thrashing around under the sheets.

Joey walks in through the gate and we are shocked to see one another.

"I thought you were off today?" I say.

"I switched with Sweet, and you?"

"I'm only here until noon, but I do want to ask you about this keep lock list."

The block sergeant, Sergeant Pound, saunters in from the corridor. He gives the block a cursory glance, trying to appear saddled with overwhelming problems. Pound is only in the block two days a week to cover the regular sergeant's days off, but, when he is here, he makes

Dutch Van Alstin – Murder in D Block

the worst of every situation. Pound is a short, chubby man with balding black hair. His idle attempt to comb his hair over his gaping bald spot is humorous.

"Erickson," he bellows, "just the man I'm looking for."

"I never left," I say, writing out my count sheet.

"Is that a crack?" Pound says neurotically.

"No, just my vain attempt at humor. Is there something I can help you with, Sergeant Pound?"

"Yep," Pound says, spitting tobacco in the trashcan, "you can tell me where the hell your nametag is at?"

I rub my fingertip along the area where my nametag normally resides. "You got me on that one, Sarge, but surely there was something of importance you wished to discuss?"

"I don't like that chip on your shoulder, boy."

"Oh?" I say bitingly, "well I don't like being addressed as *boy* either."

"Okay, wise guy, I am officially writing you up for insubordination and failure to adhere to the adhered uniform."

"Fine, when you're done with all that, Sergeant Pound, do you think you can get to the original reason you were seeking me out?"

"Sure can," he says, spitting in the trash can again, "yesterday a man was keep locked on your gallery."

"So?"

"This man was illegally detained and the facts are clearly deleted to why he was illegally keep locked to begin with. To clear up these illegalities, I'll need the facts."

"Just the facts, sir?" I say. Joey turns his head away from us and bites his lip to keep from laughing. Pound, however, seems to have missed the entire insult completely.

"That's right, according to the logbook; one Raphael Delgado was keep locked per *S. Brannigan.*"

"Only one?" I quip.

Not funny, smart ass," he says, boldly. I'm trying to make a point here!"

"And that point is..." I wave my hands trying to elicit more information. "I wasn't in here yesterday and I don't know any S. Brannigan."

"There's a good reason for that too, there ain't one in Briersburg."

"There has to be," I say.

"Are you calling me a liar?"

Dutch Van Alstin – Murder in D Block

"I would never call you a liar, Sarge, but did you check with--"

"I called personnel, personally."

"How about non-security personnel?"

Pound shakes his head feverishly. "I just told you, ain't nobody by that name in the whole damn place."

"How about names that sound similar?" I say, realizing I am helping too much like the guilty party in an episode of Columbo. Joey glances over at me out of the corner of his eye.

"Nope," Pound says, "he checked *Finnegan, Flannigan, Barrington,* and *Brandeis.*"

"He?"

"A.W. Edwards is looking into the matter personally, so he asked me to find out what was going on and bring him the original logbook. As of now, Delgado is no longer subject to further keep lock status at this time."

"I got it," I say.

"See that you do," Pound says, spitting one last time before he exits.

Joey hands me my keys. "Brannigan, huh?"

"I guess."

"I sense a nuance of *Ericksonism* in the air."

"There's some air freshener in the back room if you need it."

I walk down my gallery to conduct my count. Slowly I pass number thirty-five cell and peek in on Delgado as he sleeps. When the count is complete, I open up Rook and Rivera's cells so they can begin on their chores and set up the keep lock's breakfast. I storm to my office and pull out of my shanks from the locker. I rub the rust off the tip with my fingernail before I allow Joey to see what I have discovered. The block bell, signifying breakfast, rings loudly. I hurry back to my gallery and let the prisoners out of their respective cells so they can go to the mess hall.

The block begins to quiet down after a few minutes of turbulent traffic pouring off my gallery. I turn to Joey as he rearranges his desk drawer, putting the pencils with the pencils and the pens with the pens.

"I need a cell frisk slip and a ticket, Joey."

"Why?"

"I found this," I say, holding up the shank.

"Where?"

"Number thirty-five cell."

Dutch Van Alstin – Murder in D Block

"When?"

"This morning."

"When, exactly, this morning were you in thirty-five cell to find it?"

"I was in thirty-five cell, at one point in time."

Joey snickers. "I know, but at *what* specific time was that?"

My ill-fated stare speaks for me.

"What the hell is the matter," Joey says. "Do you have a problem with that number?

I remain reticent and look unabashedly at Joey.

"The man just got here, what could he have done to piss you off already?"

"Can I help it if garbage keeps moving into that cell?"

Joey shakes his head and opens his desk drawer. "This is so cool."

"Just give me the paperwork," I say, amidst a big sigh.

"Is he keep locked as of now?" Joey says, giving me the papers.

"No, wait until he returns from afternoon yard, that way he'll find out after you and I go home. We'll just write the ticket so it looks as though we found it when Delgado went to the yard at two o'clock."

"We?" he says hesitantly.

"Okay, me then."

Noon comes and goes and the guard who was supposed to relieve me saunters in an hour before my shift ends. Before I stroll out to the yard with Red, Joey and I exchange a mutual nod to synchronize our thoughts.

"Where you been?" Red says.

"D block."

"All damn day?"

"I was supposed to be relieved at noon but the guy just showed up a few minutes ago."

"Okay, go sit over at the shower post. There's been rumors gambling debts are being paid off with prostitution and faggot favors, so keep an eye out."

"Got it," I say, walking briskly to the post.

Now an event that took place a few weeks back makes some sense to me. Pound sent Donny and I out to the shower post for the same reason Red did. The prisoners grow irate when we staff the shower guard station. Observing a man showering is the utmost indignity and it's not high on the guard's list of favorite things to do either. But as a very bizarre type protest the prisoners grab their penis and brandish it toward the guards. They behave this way regardless of who is staffing the station but Donny's paranoia must have been peaked because he was clearly uncomfortable. It makes me wonder why Pound sent Donny out here all the time unless he knew Donny was gay because Pound always has a sick reason for whatever he does.

The yard is packed with prisoners today and the color of the day appears to be purple. Gang members in prison often sport certain colored clothing enabling them to recognize each other. The Dominicans and the Puerto Ricans are trying to keep the other from circling around them. The Puerto Rican gang is dressed in purple but I am unable to distinguish exactly what the Dominicans are wearing to identify themselves. I see no similarities in color, but often they distinguish themselves by wearing their coat or their hat a certain way. Sideways, unzipped, backward, torn in a certain area, there are dozens of different ways they manage to communicate. I've never understood how they converse amongst each other between all the cellblocks and then spread the word of what to wear on a given day.

The yard was totally covered in blacktop after the 1960 riot. Prisoners hid weapons in the dirt and retrieved them once the uproar began. A week after the riot ended, the state came in with tons of blacktop, not leaving so much as a shrub. They did, however, install six basketball courts and painted a baseball diamond, complete with a backstop. Two tennis courts are on each end of the yard but for as long as I have been at Briersburg; I have never seen a net. A running track surrounds the entire yard but there is rarely room to run since most prisoners merely roam about and conduct business. Directly in the middle of the yard is the tallest gun tower in existence, also installed after the riot of '60. There isn't a square inch of the yard that cannot be seen by the human eye, or reached by gunfire.

I finally manage to spot Delgado near the telephones. He is being pushed around by a few black prisoners, although rather gently. Whether they are just horse playing or being serious, I cannot determine from where I sit. I have never been able to establish Delgado belonging to any certain group among the Hispanic population. He seems to keep to himself most of the time, which is peculiar for a guy who seems to have a lot of juice. I didn't know him too well when he was in C block but I noticed his cell is loaded with cigarettes, food and clothes. He has two or three legal visits a week from guys with expensive gray Armani suits and Edwards treats Delgado like he is his nephew and is trying to hide it from everyone. But not even Edwards can kick Delgado loose when he finds out about the shank in his cell.

"Bye, bye, Mr. Delgado," I say to myself. "Your presence is no longer required for this little melodrama to be carried out and you're being written out of any further episodes."

Dutch Van Alstin – Murder in D Block

CHAPTER   15

A sloppy, wet tongue licks my ears before the sun can even considers rising for the day. My failure to let Bambino outside when I arrived home last night has come back to haunt me in a manner I am not accustomed. Through the sand filled eyes, I can barely view my clock's red lights that read '4:02 am'. Conceding to Bambino's natural urges, I awake briefly to let him outside as I sit on the porch.

While I sat outside waiting for Bambino to do his dirty, sinful business, I was enraptured by the sound of the waves rolling into shore. I have lived in this old cottage a long time and I'm not sure if I ever had the occasion to sit, in the dark, and just listen to the hypnotic tone of the water crashing ever gently on the shoreline. The regularity and symmetry are of something man can't reproduce in some sterile, impersonal laboratory. The waves are guaranteed by Mother Nature to follow one after another after another. Each surge, each ripple is promised another will be close behind to help them make it to the lakeshore. What people have that type of promise that there will always be someone there at all times to help him or her make it ashore? Why does only nature have that promise when people need it more?

Bambino and I sat nearly an hour on my porch until the sun gave me sight. There was no point in staying any longer.

Dutch Van Alstin – Murder in D Block

"Erickson, D block!" The chart sergeant shouts at lineup. Some people say that familiarity breeds contempt, but for me, the familiarity of D block breeds comfort. I would rather be in the cellblocks than in a license plate shop or pushing papers. People tend to create their own misery. Often, when folks fail to discover nirvana, they believe the only alternative left is their own private hell.

York's insipid singing can be heard from the main yard as I walk, reminding me that an apology is due to the fatuous old guy. Just as Calvin breaks into the second chorus of *I Feel Pretty*, he spots me waiting at the gate.

Humility has never been my strong suit and I try to convey that to York with a modest smirk.

"Dane, old boy," York shouts, opening the gate. He bows to me and waves me on in to the corridor.

"You're really rubbing it in, aren't you old man?" I say.

"I rub nothing in except Ben-Gay," he replies.

"Look, Calvin, what can I say here?"

"Say about what?"

"The other day, you know, I was having a bad day and I took it on you."

"Me?" York says with a wry face. "You took it out on someone but sure the hell wasn't me." York mocks my tackling of Ludlow.

"Oh, him."

"Yeah, him," York says, "the one who got *bulldogged* by you. I have never seen any man get bulldogged like that before, that was great, Dane. You are truly a great Dane..." York freezes and stiffens his lip. "Ah, a *Great Dane!*" York begins to howl uncontrollably.

"*...and this is your brain on coke,*" I think to myself. "Hey, nutcase," I shout playfully, "no hard feelings then?"

"Huh, when, oh that, no, no hard feelings only if you promise to live free, Dane. Live life as if it were your oyster...unless," York pauses and rubs his chin, "you're allergic to oysters and then that would present a problem. I would never--"

I journey into D block as I continue hearing York babbling about the differences between lobsters and crabs and how unfair it is that a crab has an unfounded reputation for being crotchety. His voice grows faint as I walk to the desk where Joey Gullo greets me with a disappointed shaking of his head.

"Don't say it, Joey." I say, sensing his next words.

Dutch Van Alstin – Murder in D Block

"The A.W. kicked him loose again, and, to make matters worse, he moved him to G block last night." Joey says.

"How can that asshole A.W. justify kicking him loose when I find a shank in his cell?"

"From what I understand he whined about some conjugal visit he has coming up?"

"Oh, that warrants looking the other way when there's an ice pick being hidden in his cell?"

Joey slides his chair back and puts his glasses on as he peers down my gallery. "Delgado claimed the shank belonged to McDonald and was there when he moved in."

I sigh and close my eyes tightly.

"I know, Dane, I'm pissed, too. That Delgado is a real piece of shit."

"You have problems too?"

"No, but there's something up with that guy," Joey says, leaning back in his chair. "The other day he came in here with McPherson's wallet claiming he found it on the stairs."

"What?"

"Yeah, and when Rook and Rivera saw what he had, they said to 'leave them out' of it."

"Out of what?"

"I don't know, but soon after that, Armstrong and Flannigan dragged Delgado in here by the scuff of his collar into the storeroom. I could hear the three of them screaming, but I couldn't make out any of the words too clear."

"Delgado raised his voice to those two maniacs and he was still able to breathe on his own?"

"Yes, and when they were through, Delgado just went back in the yard before I could tell him about the shank."

"Why were you here so late?"

"The count didn't clear, there was a prisoner missing from the upholstery shop. They found him an hour later, sleeping in the closet."

"Was the guard assigned to the shop sleeping next to him?"

Joey turns and looks at me direly. "It was McPherson."

"You're kidding?"

"No, I don't like coincidences."

"But really, Joey, it could just be a coincidence. Nothing makes sense to connect the two incidences together. I mean, Mack isn't a brain surgeon; I can picture him dropping his wallet. And he could misplace an elephant in a sandwich bag."

Dutch Van Alstin – Murder in D Block

"None of this explains why Delgado is being treated like a prince around here."

"I can't argue with that, Joey."

"Just because it's mating season and some guy wants to lie on his primeval slut of a wife doesn't mean he should be forgiven for weapons in his cell."

I instinctively give Joey a nasty look, but take it back quickly. "Fuck this guy!" I scream, pounding my fist on the desk.

"Go get 'em, Bulldog," York shouts from the corridor.

The morning meal run passes smoothly and I plod upstairs to let a few kitchen workers in their cells. Officer Armstrong, pretending to be tired from the many stairs, walks over to me, jingling his keys casually.

"Hi, Armstrong," I say, "got a tip on some guy up here?"

"No," he says, rubbing his neck, "actually, Dane, I came to see you."

"Me?"

"Yeah, I heard what happened in the corridor the other day and I was wondering if maybe you're becoming a little stressed?"

"Nah, I'm fine."

"I'm sure you are, Dane, but I was talking with Edwards this morning and he's a little worried about some of the rumors flying around about D block."

"Edwards," I say disdainfully. "Has he told you he's been kicking every mother-fucker loose around here?"

"I know what the man is like," Armstrong says. "But he's concerned about prisoners beating up other prisoners, fires being intentionally set, cells being ransacked, planting shanks, and stuff like that."

"The old A.W. is worried, huh?" I say, opening the lock box.

"I know what it's like, Dane, working alongside child molesters, guys who would murder their grandma for her last nickel, and laugh when one of our own gets killed in some freak accident. Now all that's bad enough but when these same dregs throw shit and piss in our face and call our mothers and wives whores, we then have to hear from these upstart nitwits in administration claiming we are provoking these reprobates. I know how frustrating that can be, especially since we weren't on the streets to provoke them when they committed their original crime. All that frustration, unfortunately, can sometimes lead us to do things we shouldn't be doing."

Dutch Van Alstin – Murder in D Block

Armstrong sighs and looks around waywardly, aiming his words, but not his sights, at me. "I know how easy it can be to start our own little *hit squad*. We find a couple of prisoners who like extra cooking time or perhaps a shower whenever they want and then favors are exchanged. The problems begin when one, or even a gang of prisoners, finds out what is going on and want it stopped. Then, Dane, that's when you're going to find yourself all alone on the top gallery sometime and you'll be visited by a group of men wearing sweat suits and a bandanas around their faces."

Armstrong halts his words and lays a piercing cast upon his face. Like I said, Dane, I know what I am talking about. The question before you is: do you know what I am talking about?"

"I nod slightly. "Yeah, and thanks."

"I'm not sure you completely do," Armstrong says, slapping me on the shoulder. "I don't have anything against you personally, but the truth of the matter is you're inexperienced when dealing with certain issues. You have to have a firm grip on who you're messing with and why, because, all too often, you don't. Don't concern yourself   with things you can't change. Don't worry about who's alive and who's not. Don't worry about what you have no control over. Worry about staying alive, because, Dane, staying alive is what it's all about."

"I get it, Armstrong."

"Lay low, Dane," Armstrong says as he begins walking downstairs. "Getting too big too fast is not what you want."

"It's not, huh?"

Armstrong stops on the stairs and looks up at me, attempting to decipher my words. He rubs the back of his hand against the course cinder and gibes at me. "See, Dane," he says, holding his palm up to me, "not a scratch."

The jingling of his keys grows more distant as he marches down tier after tier, until, I hear the D block gate open and close.

The workday ends with yet another note, but this time the note is not on my timecard, but placed methodically on the shelf of my locker. The note seemed a dab more personal and malicious than the previous veiled attempts at humor. The note read: *"You're slowly fucking up!"*

York follows me from the locker room, dressed in his civilian clothes consisting of slacks and a white, button down, shirt.

Dutch Van Alstin – Murder in D Block

"Hey, Dane," York says. "There was a guy who came out of the supermarket a month ago who looked at you cross-eyed. I'll point him out to you today and you can *Bruce Lee* his ass up and down the parking lot."

"You're a sick bastard, Calvin," I say. "You'll make a fine warden someday."

"Not I," he says, pointing at himself.

"Why not? You couldn't do any worse than a clown like Edwards, and that's his goal someday."

"What happened now?"

"Oh, not much, just the old A.W. won't keep lock anyone."

"What did he do," York says with a grin, "give Ludlow a steak dinner for beating your fists with his face?"

"No, he keeps kicking Delgado loose."

"The coke dealer?"

"You do know him then?"

"Not really."

"He was the guy you were joking with at D block's gate the other day."

"I've got to grab my mail from my box and get home," York interjects. "Dinner is waiting and there's a knife and fork with my name on it."

A prisoner, with his back turned toward me, mops the foyer in front of the visit room. He turns toward me and gives me a rancid glare. It's Delgado. He sloshes his mop back and forth, as we maintain eye contact with each other until I walk up next to him, separated only by a wire gate.

"May I have a word with you, sir?" Delgado says with a smile.

I look over at the guard in the security booth and motion for him to let me through in the foyer. The gate creeks open and Delgado motions me to follow him into the visit room. I signal the guard, telling him everything is okay. I follow Delgado until he stops, turns, and leans on his mop handle, never losing the smile.

"You know, I've been in this joint awhile and I ain't had many problems." Delgado situates himself on the mop again and clears his throat. "But I'm in your block two days and I'm keep locked by some phantom guard and shanks appear out of thin air."

"What does that have to do with me?" I say.

"I'll tell you exactly what it has to do with you," he snaps back, "it seems as though you're trying to keep me from my conjugal with MY wife."

Dutch Van Alstin – Murder in D Block

"I don't kn--"

"Don't play that shit with me," Delgado says. We stay silent for a moment, eye-balling each other intently. "Let me tell you something," he says coldly as his smile vanishes. "No two-bit farm boy who danced around cow shit his whole life is going to fuck my wife."

My returning glare affects him none.

"You ain't gonna deny it?"

"Why should I?" I say boldly.

"You have no shame in bedding another man's wife?"

"There's more to it than that. Besides, you two are through, April loves me."

Delgado smirks. "Come on," he says dubiously while rolling his eyes, "April knows where her bread is buttered. She ain't going anywhere with you."

"She will, too."

"Nah, never happen, she may have gotten lonely one night and you were there, but that all. When it comes down to brass tacks, she'll stay with me."

"Why don't you let her decide instead of intimidating her?"

"I don't have to my friend," he says, tapping his chest. "She knows she's got it made with yours truly."

"Oh, you're a real catch all right."

"None of this matters, dirt ball, because your life ends before the sun hits the hills." Delgado throws his mop to the floor, steps close to me, and pokes my chest. "You will pay for what you did, you son of a bitch."

"Please, your eminence," I say, pretending to tip a hat. "Fill me in on how you plan on pulling off this miraculous stunt?"

"Oh, please," he says excitedly, "don't take me seriously.....please think I'm full of shit. It will be all the sweeter when your sorry ass is on a slab at the morgue. You don't have any idea the forces you are fucking with."

"You guys are all the same," I say. "Tough, bad ass gangsters, who threaten and threaten, but when it comes down to it, you're in here and I'm out there."

"Oh, my good man, my arms reach way out to those mother fucking streets. And believe you me, they're going to reach out and touch your ass, tonight."

"We can stand here and stick our tongues out at each other all day. Maybe I'll just have you *offed* inside here."

"You may have a few rat bastards who do chump shit for you, that's all. You ain't got the juice for anything more than that. You're a bush leaguer in with the big boys. Besides, you are on your way home now, unless you're scared. And since you'll be dead by tonight, my worries are gone."

"I'm not scared of you, Delgado."

"Oh…but you are," he says as his eyes grow big. "You most definitely are."

Small drops of sweat form up in a small scar under his chin. I scrutinize his face, trying to read the unreadable.

Poker player? I'm sure he is.

I turn slowly, never taking my eyes off him until I start to walk back to the gate. I tap on the bars alerting the guard in the booth.

"Are you going out?" The guard says.

I look up the stairs leading back to the prison, and then, back to the exit.

"How about it," the guard repeats, "in or out?"

I feel Delgado's piercing leer at me back.

"Out," I say, looking back at Delgado, "I'm going out."

Bluff?

Bona fide?

Pair of 3's or a flush?

I fumble with my keys as I get to my front door. The ride home was done with my eyes affixed to the rearview mirror, and now, the anxiety begins again. I open the door slowly, walk in, and shut it just as quickly. I gaze around the room at the Couch! Table! Chair!

Did they look like that when I left this morning?

Was the shirt lying on the floor like that?

I reach in the end table drawer and pull out my gun.

I listen to myself breath. I stand. I wait. I think.

I set my gun down to my side and sigh.

Paranoia.

Everything looks okay.

A pair of 3's, I call.

Bambino sleeps peacefully on my kitch--

Bambino? My heart races and my skin tightens. "Oh, my God," I scream, rushing over to scoop Bambino in my arms. I leap through the living room window as shattering glass flies in

Dutch Van Alstin – Murder in D Block

the air. I stagger, trying to maintain my balance, but fail as I drop to the earth. I crawl as fast as I can, shaking Bambino as he's cradles in my arms. I try to stand but in my panic, continue to fall, repeatedly slipping back on the ground.

I only crawl inches more before the stinging heat and charred glass tear into my flesh, inflicting inconceivable pain. I lie flat on the ground and bury my head in my arms to protect me from the thunderous explosion that sends my home into millions of pieces.

I roll over only to see a turbulent fire where my cottage once stood, where April and I once slept.

CHAPTER 16

The doctor pulls shards of glass from back. I am virtually catatonic. The nurse apologizes every time she has to rub the stinging salve into my burns. She need not apologize; I don't feel a thing. I know I am being unoriginal, but this whole mess seems like a dream. I don't know how else to sum up the situation, but it's akin to what Joey once said when we discussed the oddities of Donny's death: "things like this just don't happen."

Two Briersburg County sheriff's investigators stand outside my room in the hallway and haggle with a nurse to allow them access in to speak with me. Their anxiety and compulsion to conduct the interview finally wear down the frazzled, overworked nurse and she waves both detectives inside as she storms down the hallway.

One of the detectives appears to be a seasoned investigator with graying hair and pale skin. He dresses in a tan sport coat with a green tie that slightly covers the wrinkled blue shirt. The other plainclothesman seems to be the other's prodigy. He is outfitted in a blue blazer with a red silk tie, held in check by a brass clip fastened in to a white shirt that looks as though it had pins in it hours ago. The rookie stands erect and upright, eagerly holding a pen and pad in his hand. The veteran, however, does the talking in between sips of coffee from a Styrofoam cup.

"Mr. Erickson, I'm Sergeant Maldor of the Briersburg County Sheriff's Department and this is my partner Detective Vanderhaven."

Dutch Van Alstin – Murder in D Block

The rookie Vanderhaven nods his head courtly, still holding his pen firmly in his fist. I fight to return a minute greeting as well.

"Could you fill us in on what exactly happened, Mr. Erickson?" Maldor says.

"I, uh, smelled a whiff of gas when I walked in my cottage. And from there I, uh, grabbed my dog...MY DOG?"

"He's fine, sir," Maldor says reassuringly, "he's at the pound. You were saying you smelled gas?"

"Yeah, gas, I got a real strong whiff of it and when I did, I got real scared and ran out of there."

"Yes, sir," Maldor says nonchalantly. Vanderhaven scrambles to copy down my statement word for word, crossing all T's and dotting the I's.

"Now let me get this straight, Mr. Erickson, your cottage blew up into smithereens nearly the moment you entered it? Is that your story, sir?" Maldor says, laying out his skepticism for all to see.

"Yes."

"We mostly interested due to your line of work, sir," Vanderhaven chimes in. "Often people in law enforcement make enemies on the job and--"

"Also, sir," Maldor interjects, "nobody in the area smelled gas. And the Gas Company was repairing no leaks, nor have they located any leak."

Maldor awaits a reply from me but gets none.

"We're awaiting the results of the Fire Marshall, sir."

Keeping my prior *Columbo* mistake in mind, silence is my friend.

Maldor sighs in antipathy. "Mr. Erickson, I cannot help you if you don't help me."

"I'm telling you all I know, Sergeant."

"Fine, okay," Maldor says. A veteran like Maldor has been around long enough to recognize stonewalling when he sees it. He pulls out his business card, realizing the fruitlessness of his questioning.

"If you have anything else you want to tell me, sir, call me," Maldor says, flipping his card at me.

"Thanks," I say, taking his card.

"I'll, uh, talk with you again after I receive the Fire Marshall's report."

"Oh, Sergeant?"

"Yes."

Dutch Van Alstin – Murder in D Block

"Was anyone hurt at all?"

"No, sir," Maldor says as he walks out, "not as of yet."

The nurse continues working on my back and the doctor and I exchange a few words about my staying the night for observation. Considering the fact I have nowhere to go tonight, his offer sounds appealing but I decline just the same. Staying with April seems like a foolhardy thing to do considering the danger it would her place her. Although I am convinced the person, or persons, who planted the explosives are gone, I am not willing to risk April's safety. Most likely, the perpetrator planted the explosives, waited for the detonation, and took off out of town thinking I'm a dead duck.

Cassidy's rents rooms above the bar. The rooms are dingy and impersonal, but they do have a bed and a pillow, which is one-step above my present situation. My sentiments want me to call April, but my better judgment says to wait awhile. My phone shows several missed calls and a plethora of texts. Unanswered texts.

Chuck issues me room '13' for the night. I look down at the tag in resentment and thank him trenchantly for planting such an omen in my life.

Delgado's words were not a pair of 3's after all, I think to myself as I twirl my beer with my fingers. I have to assume he does not know the final outcome as of yet. Any phone calls going out are randomly monitored and recorded and it would be too risky to make a second call, the first being the setup of the whole cabal. The news filters in the walls slowly, especially during the upcoming baseball playoffs. Gambling is a major part of day-to-day life and all eyes and ears are on the money, not local news events.

Tomorrow, Mr. Raphael Delgado will be surprised to see my face.

The extra uniform in my locker is my last stitch of clothing available to me. I dress listlessly in an attempt to avoid lineup today. Averting the robot's inevitable crass insults is a must for me right now. The barbs will just have to be set aside for a future tragedy. Any last iota of patience I may still have would be vanquished by a full frontal assault by the robot's limited dialogue.

I stand at the top of the stairs and listen for the chart sergeant's dismissal of lineup. As I walk out into the foyer, I bump directly into the warden himself, James G. Frankhausen. "Mr. Erickson," he says, putting his hand on my chest, "we've been looking for you."

Frankhausen is a short man, no more than five feet seven inches but grossly overweight. His weight exceeds 300 pounds easily and his fat, round face is saggy and awkward. His hair recedes badly, leaving only a strip of black thatch around his ears. Pronounced liver spots cover his scalp, one shaped like a horseshoe catches my eye.

"Yes, sir," I say.

"We heard what happened to your home, son, here you go," he says, handing me an envelope. "You tell the quartermaster to issue you any uniform items you may need. And if you gives you any shit, tell him I said it was okay." Frankhausen says as he taps his chest spiritedly. I open the envelope and discover a check for *$4,000.00* from the union. "Why, thank you, sir," I say, somewhat stunned.

"I understand a collection was taken up for you as well. You'll find that money at the *employee support office.* You most likely find Mitchell the quartermaster hanging around there as well."

"I'm at a loss for words, sir. Thank you very much for everything."

"I'm not an ogre, son," Frankhausen says with a pat on my back.

The chart sergeant does not comment on my tardiness. He instead waves his arm at me and sends me to the main yard. "Do a let-in at nine o'clock in D block, Erickson and try to be on time."

In an attempt to kill two birds with one stone, I make the E.S.O. my first destination in hopes that Mitchell is in visiting with the director.

I knock. I listen as I hear a few schoolgirl giggles mixed with a couple of: "stop that" followed by more giggles. I knock again, only with more vigor.

"Oh, shit, stop it, Mitch, ah…come on in."

I walk in and look over at Karen Hyde, the E.S.O. director at her desk. Mitchell sits casually with his fingers interlocked behind his head.

"Hi, Mrs. Hyde," I say affably, "I'm Dane Erickson."

"Yes, I have something for you," she says, fumbling through some papers.

"If it was in that folder, Karen, you left it in the quartermaster room," Mitchell says.

"That actually works out well, Mitch, because Frankhausen said you could issue me some new clothes. I know you can't dig them all out right now, but how about just getting me a baton and a baton holder?"

Mitchell looks at his watch as if he actually something pressing to attend to immediately.

"Come on, Mitch," Karen says, "I need that folder anyway."

Mitchell grins devilishly. "All righty, then."

"Would you two like me to wait here by myself?"

Dutch Van Alstin – Murder in D Block

"Yes," they both say in near unison. They look at each other and giggle. "Jinx," Mitchell says. They walk down the hall and grab each other's backside as they chortle like adolescents.

I anticipate at least a fifteen-minute wait for the return of the two paramours. I take the opportunity to rummage through the E.S.O. personal files.

"O,P,Q…got it," I say softly to myself. I had a hunch Quinn may have visited the illustrious Mrs. Hyde at one time or another. The E.S.O. is a support center for the guards and their problems, whether they are work related or not.

I spread the papers in Donny's file out on her desk and rifle through the dates checking when Donny visited and how often.

I see six different visits; one was a mandatory referral by A.W. Edwards. Each visit seemed to have a particular dilemma. Karen wrote in her notes that Donny was very ambiguous during the interviewing. On one occasion, the last occasion, she referred him to outside assistance. Her notes also state Donny was suffering from 'conflicted homosexuality'. Every quirk has a name attached to it anymore.

The childish cackling of the two overgrown teenagers closes in on Karen's office. I grab the contents of Donny's file and stuff them quickly down my pants and put the folder back in the cabinet.

The door swings open and Karen hands me an envelope. "Here you are," she says buoyantly.

"And here is your authentic prisoner *tune-up* kit," Mitchell says.

"Thanks, thanks," I say to both quickly as I exit the office.

Nervously, I look around as I take Quinn's papers out from my pants. The E.S.O. file is not a personnel file and the day Pitt came in to snoop at Donny's file, it didn't include the E.S.O. I doubt Pitt even knew it existed. I had no idea either but I know guards do visit when they are at the end of their rope, and Donny had not a strand of twine left.

I know Red will be very angry that I am late for the yard, knowing this makes it easier for me to sneak back to the locker room to peruse the papers more closely.

Quinn was referred to an outside psychiatrist about six months ago, a Doctor Christian T. Baltz.

I think back to what Chuck said to me that night at Cassidy's and his words now make sense.

Chris! Dr. Christian T. Baltz… *Chris.*

Dutch Van Alstin – Murder in D Block

CHAPTER 17

Upsetting Red's steady day seems to nudge me along and speed me back to the main yard. The D block let in I am supposed to attend to is closing in and Red will not take kindly to me checking in and checking back out simultaneously.

"It's almost nine," Red says, looking at his watch, "where the hell you been?"

"Quartermaster."

"Hmm, okay," he says, looking again at his watch.

"I also am supposed to do a let-in at nine in D block."

"Then scoot on in there now," he says, "you only got a few minutes anyhow."

I walk up the steps leading into the corridor. While Red's back is turned, I step on the observation deck and look out through the sea of tan clothes for Delgado.

Over near the commissary door, I spot him. Those same cold, hate filled eyes seems calm and peaceful this beautiful, sun shining day.

Finally, Delgado looks up in my direction. His eyes connect with mine as he stops, stares, and does nothing. I stare back at him with a contentious grin.

Surprised?

Most likely.

Disappointed?

Dutch Van Alstin – Murder in D Block

I think he is.

Scared?

I know he is.

Delgado begins to walk again at his normal pace through the yard. His eyes still fixate on mine, but nothing like they did yesterday.

No, nothing like yesterday.

The tables?

Turned.

Delgado drops his eyes down as he drops from my sight, but not from my thoughts.

A countenance of near pleasantness gowned my face as I awoke from Cassidy's cheap, goose filled mattresses. My thoughts were of peace, closure and new beginnings.

My insurance check from the cottage will be cut today and subsequently signed by me soon after. I have mulled over the possibility of popping up a *pre-fab* house in place of my old cottage and since my old cottage is now debris, that time has arrived. The thought of a garage for my car and a hot tub for my bathroom appeals to my covetous and materialistic nature. Perhaps a new television to place in the bathroom would accentuate a hot tub nicely. The extra two thousand plus dollars I received at work went quickly, but I can soon say *sayonara* to Cassidy's ghastly rooms.

A visit to April today seems to be in order. I can't duck a meeting with her forever and I don't believe her, soon to be estranged, husband will be a source of contention any longer. If she and I are going to have any type of future, we need to hit this problem head on and wipe it out of our lives. I don't anticipate an overly warm greeting from her. I know if the roles were reversed, I would be irate that she hadn't contacted me.

I ring her buzzer. April nearly tears the door from its hinges as she opens it.

"Hi," I say.

"Hi? You can sit there with that stupid, shit-eating grin on your puss and say 'hi' to me?"

"What am I supposed to say?"

"How about: 'April, I'm such a piece of garbage for allowing you to hear my home burst into flames on the news and subsequently avoiding you for nearly twenty-four hours afterwards. Please, dear woman, allow me to buy you a very expensive, ostentatious piece of jewelry that will drain my paychecks for the next six months'. That, my good man, is what you should be saying to me right now."

Dutch Van Alstin – Murder in D Block

"I have a reason," I say pleadingly.

"I really doubt you can muster up a satisfactory explanation of your incredible self-absorbed, self-centered behavior of not allowing me the satisfaction of being with you during a tumultuous time in your life, you jerk."

"I'm going to use your own words against you," I say, growing impatient. "Don't say anything you will soon regret."

"You have one chance to explain this abject decision of yours to exclude me from your life."

"Can I come in?"

"Can means able, what you mean is 'may I'?"

"I'm starting to run short of poise and patience out here in the hallway. Either let me in the damn apartment, or we'll call it a day."

April opens the door wider and waves me inside to the living room.

"Let me start, April, by saying that I really wanted to call you."

"But?" April says calmly.

"I didn't want to entangle you in the whole mess."

"What mess?" she says anxiously, "the news said it was a gas leak."

"It was no gas leak. I just told the police that to because they were asking."

"Then why?"

"Okay, here it goes," I say lackadaisically, "your husband did it."

April's eyes grow large and her mouth struggles to say something. "Wha...you...wh...no way...I mean...how can...what on earth makes you say that?"

"On my home from work the day my house exploded, your husband stopped me in the hallway and said I would be dead before nightfall."

"Isn't that just idle threat? You told me you get that all the time?"

"No," I say, shaking my head fervidly. "He says I'll be dead and when I get home my cottage goes *blooey* and you want to chalk it up to idle threats?"

"Maybe it was just a coincidence? Maybe was just a gas leak? Maybe--"

"April, hello? Get real here! Somebody drugged my dog so they could plant whatever it is they planted. And speaking of which, the pound said you picked him up, is he here?"

"Yeah," she says despondently, "the vet put him on some medicine and he's sleeps a lot."

"Well he never sleeps when I get home and that day he was fast asleep."

Dutch Van Alstin – Murder in D Block

"Maybe he was just tired that day?"

I expel a frustrating sigh. "The vet told me he was poisoned."

"But how do you--"

"April!" I screech. "For God's sake, your husband says he'll kill me and my house explodes. Why are defending him so much? What the hell is the matter with you?"

April's excuses run dry. She turns and walks toward the porch and folds her arms tightly against her chest. "I...I just don't understand. He doesn't know anyone capable of that. He hasn't any friends with that type of clout."

"None," I say skeptically.

"No, Dane, when they convicted him, the state took all his money. You know how it works behind the walls, no cash means no power. Money is power and power is money, they go hand in hand, Dane."

"Then someone in his past owed him an enormous favor, April," I say agitatedly.

April looks over at me humbly. "Do you want some coffee?"

"I'm late anyway, why not?"

April pours two cups of coffee in mugs and hands me the fullest of the two. "I'm sorry, Dane."

"For what?"

"I feel responsible."

"Why would you," I say, sipping the hot brew, "he did it, not you."

"What are you going to do; obviously you can't report any of this?"

"Well, I could, but I'm not."

"What are we going to do?"

"Don't worry," I say, rubbing her shoulder, "I am arranging to have him shipped out of Briersburg today."

"How?"

"You needn't concern yourself with the details."

"But--"

"You said you loved me the other day. Did you mean it or not?"

"Of course I did," April says indignantly, "but I'm scared. Since he knows about us, he'll think I had something to do with it."

"I can't help that, April; we're talking about my life here. Besides, he'll be long gone and nobody's problem."

Dutch Van Alstin – Murder in D Block

"Okay," she says as her eyes well up, "I believe in you."

"I'll stop back tonight after work."

"Okay, please, be careful today," she kisses me softly on the forehead. "I mean it, be extra careful."

I walk in through the main gate, late again. I know the chart sergeant is going to go up one side of me and down the other this time. The guard at the entrance gate stops me. "Change into your dungarees, pal," he says, crushing out his cigarette.

"Why?"

"Briersburg is in complete lockdown today."

I cringe at the thought of a lockdown. A lockdown is synonymous with hard, dirty work and usually mandatory overtime. I guess it all depends on what particular job a guard has on that given day. A lockdown is when every prisoner is confined to his cell until the lockdown is lifted. In the mean time, every square inch, theoretically, is to be searched inside and out, including every prisoner and his cell. Lockdowns are done randomly, but an unusual situation can warrant one as well. All guard jobs, with the exception of towers, primary, gate entrances, are closed and those guards assist with the frisk. Some cells can take upwards of two to three hours to search thoroughly, depending on the amount of personal property he possesses. Some cells take a quick ten minutes. Usually the *big shots*, e.g., gang leaders, the toughs, have all the goods, whereas the poor, weak and dumb have very little.

Social Darwinism behind the gray walls.

"Why the lockdown?" I say. "Random?"

"Nope," he says energetically. "We got ourselves a murder."

Often the veterans, who hasten themselves out of general population, get ghoulishly excited at a murder.

"A murder? Big deal, since when do we lockdown over a shanking?"

"No shanking, this was an up close and personal murder. This guy was strangled and dumped in a trash can in D block."

"No shit, D block, maybe I know, I mean, *knew* him."

"The quirk here is they haven't caught the guy who done it. They found his dead ass after the 11:30 count last night."

"So what, whoever did it just made sure there was an extra cheeseburger at lunch today. By the way, who do we have to thank for this extra morsel of food?"

"Delgado," the guard says, floundering through his papers. "Yep, one Raphael Delgado of of G block."

"Oh...my...God."

"What's the matter? You know this stiff?"

"Know him?" I say with a stammer.

"Yeah, know him," he says, snapping his fingers in my face. "Hey, are you okay?"

"Me?"

"Yeah, you...unless you got a frog in your pocket."

I unwittingly feel my pockets.

"You're hung over, aren't you? I can tell these things," he says boastfully. "I got shitfaced last night too."

"No, I just...slept late."

"So did this lame fuck in G block," he says, grabbing his round belly and laughing. "You never answered me, did you know this cadaver or not?"

"No, I guess not too well, not really, too much anyway."

"Well, don't plan getting to know him any time soon," he says, laughing at his own joke again.

"I guess not."

The guard pulls out a fresh pack of cigarettes and taps them on his desk before he pulls off the foil. "I guess I can smoke my brains out today with the jail being closed down and all. That bullshit *No Smoking* in public places law is such crap anyway. I mean come on; a prison is a public place? I don't see these people flocking in here from the street for our tasty cuisine and superb entertainment. But that's the government today. They want to take care of you from womb to tomb. They want to tell you what to eat, what not to eat, what to do, how to do it, why to do it, what to wear, where to go, where not to go. And if you try arguing with them, they give you this *we know best* crap. I know what's best for me, not some overeducated underachiever who couldn't find any other job but leaching off the government's tit. I tell ya, pal, am I right or what?"

My catatonic state gives way. "...I'm sorry...did you say something to me?"

The guard shakes his head and sighs. "You better just go and get to work."

Dutch Van Alstin – Murder in D Block

CHAPTER 18

Panic is not an option. I have to bury any inclination that Delgado was anything more to me than another prisoner with another number. When the jokes abound, I'll just laugh. *'There's an extra cheeseburger for lunch today'*. *'His cell is empty, but we'll keep it open for his son next week'*. Or the ever-merciless jape: *'I have always admired his watch'*. It's *Oscar* time. I played Hamlet in high school, but the challenge of acting today rises up and above that. *Alas, poor Delgado, I knew him, NOT, Robotio.*

I peep in the chart office, showing the sergeant nothing more than one eye and my forehead. "I'm here, Sarge," I say.

"No you're not, Erickson." Pound says, much to my chagrin. "*Here* is in front of my desk. *There,* which is where you are, is out in the damn hallway, now get in here."

"Something wrong, Sergeant Pound," I say, slumping in the office.

Pound sits smugly with his chin resting on his hands. "Yes, you could say that." Pound sits silently, knowing I am waiting for him to speak. The pause he creates is an intentional attempt to unnerve me. Pound likes to make people squirm. To him, power, regardless of how petty, is Pound's whole reason for existing.

"First off, why are you under the belief you're exempt from lineup?"

"I ju--"

He jams his palm up in my face as he looks down and writes something on the charts. "Just, nothing, you start showing up for lineup. You do get paid for showing up, you know?"

"I know," I say courtly, "secondly?"

Pound sets his pencil down and glares up at me with a derisive grin. "I save the really big fuck-ups for last."

"And that would be?"

"Ludlow, the man you choked in the corridor the other day."

"That's hardly the way--"

Again, he rams his palm in my face. "Put your version in writing on my desk by three o'clock today," Pound says, dropping his head down to his charts. "Whatever that version may be."

"I'll have the memo on your desk today."

"I know," he says imperiously. "Now go read the Incident report on the murder and then go to your second home in D block and help tear the place apart."

I put my finger on my forehead and bestow him a bogus salute. Perhaps a full extension of my right arm at a forty five-degree angle would appease him more.

I take the clipboard out in the hallway and read the incident report away from Pound's peering eyes.

A prisoner locking in G-7-42 cell by the name of Raphael Antonio Delgado, was missing from the 11:30 PM count last night. G block was thoroughly searched to no avail. The emergency alarm was sounded at 11:49 PM and Acting Warden, Assistant warden Donovan Edwards, shut down the prison. The search was officially called off at 12:33 AM when the D block primary guard, Jonathan T. McCloud, spotted a piece of state issued orange prison clothing dangling from a trash can on the top tier. McCloud investigated and discovered the body of Delgado stuffed in the can. Nurse Ruth Lawson was summoned to the scene and Delgado was sent to Our Lady of Lourdes Hospital where he was pronounced dead by Dr. George Hodgkins at 1:03 AM. Probable cause of death was asphyxiation. An autopsy will be done by the County Coroner. At the time of this report, there were no named suspects.

Now what?

Dutch Van Alstin – Murder in D Block

I change into my dungarees and walk to D block. Joey sits with his feet high upon the desk with his hands tucked comfortably behind his neck. A piping hot cup of coffee sits next to his glasses, and a doughnut, still in the bakery wrapping, rests on top of his cup.

He spots me when I walk in and laughs. "Ho, Ho, Ho, here to...WORK?"

"Very funny, Santa," I say.

The most heinous job in Briersburg would be D block, primary guard, day shift. Being a primary guard is difficult enough. All the responsibility of the block falls on him. But in D block, the phone is constantly ringing, guards and prisoners hound the primary for favors and dubious questions, traffic in and out is maddening. However, during a lockdown, primary is golden. It is a coveted sinecure post anyone would want. The primary isn't crawling around the cell floors, running coat hangers around the toilet seals. The primary doesn't rummage through boxes filled with cock roaches and rat excretions, and he doesn't have to fight with other guards to get a lunch break. Today, Joey may as well be in Hawaii.

"Don't stick your hand on a dead cock roach or something," Joey says with a satirical smile.

"Some of us MEN have to make the prison safe for the rest of you guys." I say, trying to play on youthful ego.

Joey sips his coffee and stretches. "I can't be any safer than I am behind my big, comfy desk," he says, tapping the Formica.

Mack ambles downstairs with an embellished grin perched on his face. He empties his pockets and flips a cigarette in his mouth, lights it, and then slams the lighter closed. Mack takes a long, hard drag and exhales smoke amongst a sinister laugh.

"Get ready from some action, Dane," Mack says, stripping off his collar emblems, watch, and high school graduation ring.

Mack graduated? I think to myself. How?

"What are you talking about, Mack?" I say.

"I'll tell you," Mack says, handing his keys to Joey. "Some scum-bag won't come out of his cell and Red asked me to help, shall we say, *evict* his sorry ass."

If Red were on fire, he wouldn't ask Mack for a glass of water. The more likely scenario is Mack overheard Red talking about yanking a prisoner out of his cell.

I turn to Joey, furnish him my keys, and empty my pockets. "Duty calls, little boy."

"Ah, Dane," Joey says, leaping up from his chair, "Let me go. I'll switch with you today."

"Yeah," I say, taking off my gold cross, "that'll happen."

Dutch Van Alstin – Murder in D Block

Mack raises his hand for me to exchange a *high five* with him. I keep my hands busy and Mack eventually reaches over and itches his nose.

"Oh, come on, I'll switch for the whole day." Joey pleads.

"Welllll…let me think…" I rub my chin histrionically. "No!"

"Come on, Dane, I haven't had any action since I've been here."

"And today will be no different, sweetheart," I say, pinching his cheek. "I promised your mama I wouldn't let you get your hands dirty."

"Then I'll just eat this yummy, Bavarian cream," Joey says, rubbing his belly.

"Nice try, Junior," I say with a grin, "but I don't even like Bavarian cream."

Dateline conducted an episode on Briersburg. Joey was interviewed, but was the only guard unable to give a firsthand accounting of notorious mayhem plaguing Briersburg that justified their title of the episode, *The Brier Patch.* The robots taunted him ever since the episode aired.

Mack walks intrepidly up the stairs next to me. "It's time to ring the bell, Dane."

"The bell? Okay, Mack, the bell it is."

We slosh through the garbage; soaked with water and urine that has been tossed out on to the gallery. Globs of oatmeal from the morning meal, dangle and drip from the bars like stalagmites on a dank cave wall. Cartons of sour milk, mixed with grape juice, are slammed against the wall, creating a stench that only hurling cans of tuna through windowpanes can air out. Hand held mirrors pop out from cells with two eyeballs affixed on each polished glass to capture a glimpse of the action. An occasional insult is hurled at us from four or five cells back as we pass hands, flicking ashes on the galleries, from inside their cells.

Mack and I continue down the gallery until we see Red doubling back toward us. "Never mind, boys," Red says, waving us back down the gallery, "he decided to come out on his own. But he is going to slap some type of habeas corpus or a corpus delicatessen on me, I told him to put mine on rye."

Mack follows me downstairs and crushes his cigarette out on the stairwell and pulls out a fresh one. He taps the butt against the rail a few times and tosses it in his mouth, and then searches in vain for a lighter. "Ah, shit, gotta light, Dane?"

"Afraid, not," I say, tapping my pockets.

"With all that cash we gave you, you should be able to afford a lighter," he says with a laugh.

"That would be a bit incongruous since I don't smoke."

Dutch Van Alstin – Murder in D Block

"Huh?"

"That would be…*silly*, since I don't smoke."

"Oh," he says bewilderedly. "What did you spend all that money on, anyway?"

"I thought, since my house blew up and all, that I'd spend it on rectifying that dilemma in my life?"

"Yeah, I can see that, but, I'd a spent it on a whore."

"I know you would, Mack," I say, condescendingly patting him on the shoulder.

"You know, Dane, it's a good thing that mother fucker chickened out or I'd a crushed him into a fine pulp." Mack says, as the unlighted cigarette dangles in his mouth.

"I'm sure he doesn't appreciate how fortunate he is, Mack."

"Yeah…" Mack says as his eyes grow pale and distant, "he was scared to death of me."

I casually walk away from Mack and leave him to himself with his still yet unlighted cigarette in his mouth. Mack is own worst enemy sometimes. Before I discovered what an equivocator he was all the time, I actually was stupid enough to elicit his help concerning a rogue prisoner. A prisoner named *Spanky* was dropping his pants as the nurse made her daily rounds and grabbing his dick and yelling: "want it, bitch?" Spanky was going home in three weeks and writing him up was an abortive task. Mack and I brought Spanky into the storeroom and, me being under the assumption Mack's words matched his actions, awaited for him to make the first move. Finally, I dumped Spanky on the floor and pressed my boot in his groin until I could see he was in pain. I informed him to "leave it in his pants." Spanky knew what I meant and got the message. Mack did nothing all the while I roughed up Spanky. When we left the storeroom, Mack said to Spanky: "I don't want to see your balls out dangling no more!"

I bit my lip to keep from laughing.

A note on my time card read: "where a man sleeps at night is not nearly as important as *whom* he sleeps with at night." A grammatically correct letter from one of the robots? The note didn't smack of the usual childish antics resulting in petty wisecracks in regard to my cottage exploding. I heard a few of those gibes today, such as asking me if my heating bills have risen since I have no walls to insulate the warmth, and other samples of misdirected anger. But this note had a tinge of venom in it.

I change into some shorts and a tank top shirt to fight off the impending hotness of the day before I go to April's house. But unfortunately Mother Nature throws me a curve ball and dumps a cold September rain on me as I drive. The rain slams so hard on to the street that the

Dutch Van Alstin – Murder in D Block

drops seem to bounce off the pavement, causing steam to raise from the hot tar cooling amidst the downpour. April must have been notified about her husband by now. I believe I kept my composure well today concerning Delgado. Although the note leaves a queasy feeling in me, there is no guarantee the writer was referring to April and I. Who knows what motivates the robots; the note could have been some deviate form of sexual pleasure for whoever wrote it. I had better anticipate some emotional response from April. Divorce is one thing, but death is another matter altogether. My ego, along with my pride, needs to be quelled as I listen to her cry and grieve over C Block Delgado. I just need to take her words with a grain of salt and just be a good listener.

I wrap at her door and she immediately swings it open, wide. April hits me solidly in the chin with a clenched fist. Her prodigious wallop sends me crashing into the wall in the hallway. In a frantic haze of tears, she screams: "I hate you, I hate you, you bastard!" She stomps her foot with every spiteful word and spits on me as I lie on the hallway floor. Before I can move a muscle, April spits on me again and slams the door. Still awkward and dazed, I pull myself up from the floor and kick her door.

"Open up, April! Have you lost your mind?"

The door flies open and April hurls out a potted plant, smashing it against the wall. She attempts to lock the door and I slam my foot inside, ala, *pushy salesman*.

"Move your foot or I'll break it off at the knee," she shouts.

"Not until you talk to me and tell me what the hell you're babbling about here."

"Then I'll leave," April says, storming down the stairs. I stand and pursue her outside where the torrential downpour hasn't let up an iota.

"Why are you so mad at me? What the hell did I do?"

"What did you do?" She says rhetorically, "You're a killer, a killer, that's what you did."

"Me, you blame me? How could I have prevented it?"

"Prevented it?" April says in amazement. "You did it, you killed him!"

"What? How did arrive at that conclusion?"

"You said you had a plan, remember? Some secret, shrouded plan, now I know what it was." April begins walking down the street. A resounding crack of thunder alters her demeanor little as she continues the march down the street.

"I wasn't even there when he died."

"Oh, how convenient," she says, stopping in her tracks. "You're never present during your little transgressions. Raph told me about you. He told me the things you do; planting shanks, having prisoners beat up by other prisoners, and setting fires. Do you deny it? Any of it?"

"No, but that's comparing a stubbed toe with a broken neck."

"A very appropriate analogy."

"Oh, come on, murder? Me? That would make me no better than the garbage in Briersburg."

"Oh," April blurts out indignantly, "like Raph?"

"Would you stop twisting everything I say? Not for you, nor anyone, would I resort to murder."

She goosesteps over to me and kicks my knee, dropping me to the wet pavement. "Go to hell, you repulsive creep." April veers down the street in the rain, leaving me in a puddle clutching my kneecap.

Flashing red lights appear from behind me and a Briersburg City Policeman gets out of his car. He's a tall, thin man with jet-black hair, mismanaged from the rain. He tugs at his gun belt that seems to weigh him down some.

"I'm Officer McManus, Sir. Is there a problem here?"

"Problem?" I say, knowing he's probably weary from that reply.

"Yes, sir," he sighs, "problem. Is there a problem? You're lying in the middle of a rainy street, holding your knee. Besides that, I received a call of a disturbance. A woman was crying. Was that you?"

"Crying?"

"Let's start again, here," he says impatiently. "Were you involved in the disturbance with a woman? Your girlfriend perhaps?"

"Oh, her? She went home."

"Yes, sir," he sighs. "Can I see some I.D. please?"

I present my badge to him and he rubs the tin with his thumb. "Augustovson C. Erickson?"

"That would be me, yes."

"Working at the Briar Patch?"

"Forty three hours a week."

"That's about forty two and a half more than I would like to be there," he says, returning my badge to me. "Do you know Sammy Calhoun?"

"Yeah, a little bit. He works in the tower; I don't see those guys too much."

Dutch Van Alstin – Murder in D Block

"Sammy's my uncle."

"No kidding," I say, getting myself off the ground. "I'll give 'em your regards when I see him."

"How about Toby Sweet?"

"You're related to Toby?" I say inquiringly.

"Hell, no," McManus says. "I had to pull him off some guy the other night."

"Toby? Toby Sweet? Are you sure?" I say in disbelief.

"I doubt there are two guys with that name around this town?"

"I'm disappointed there's one."

"He's not a friend of yours I take it?"

"Hardly," I say, "I'm forced to work with him one day week. At least I think it's him, the Toby I know is a lily-livered marshmallow. I've never seen him get angry with anyone. What set him off?"

"From what I gathered, some guy didn't move his car far enough up at the gas pumps."

"You have got to be kidding me, for that he went off?"

"That he did, in fact, if the other guy pressed charges, ol' Toby would have been on the other side of the bars."

"*Bizarro* world."

"Excuse me?"

"Bizarro world, Superman comics had a story about a world where everything was opposite. Black was white, up was down, front was back, and now, Toby is a bad ass?"

"Let's get back to why I'm here, who was that girl? Your girlfriend? You two having a fight?"

"What guy doesn't fight with his girlfriend?" I say with a bit of a guffaw.

"Well, then is everything kosher now so I can get out of this rain?"

"Your end of it is kosher, my end however?"

"I can't help you there," he says jokingly. "Why don't you take it up with her tomorrow and just head on home."

"I will when it's rebuilt this week."

McManus laughs but isn't sure why.

I opt to bypass Cassidy's lumpy mattress for the night and saunter back to my…lot and take the boat out on the lake. I motor from one end of the lake to the other, only stopping once at the *Port Side Café* for gas and a quart of beer. The rain has nearly subsided and the sun is fighting to get past the graying of the sky. Mr. Moon has punched in as Mr. Sun has clocked out for the day.

I'm surprised, considering the day I've had that the sun isn't setting in the east. My girlfriend thinks I've become murderer; Toby Sweet is opening up cans of *whoop ass* on total strangers, what's next? Randy McPherson becomes a rocket scientist? Joey Gullo tells his mother to go to hell? Perhaps Bambino will acquire a taste for my blood and go for my throat when I get him back home? It's not a Superman comic fantasy any longer.

Bizarro world, AKA, Briersburg.

CHAPTER   19

The first cock-a-do flies pass me once again, for a grand total of three times in one week. I fight to focus my pupils, and the sunlight blocks the crystal of my watch. It looks as though lineup ended five minutes ago, so much for any chance I'll be at work on time.

A dream that invaded my sleep was particularly odd last night. April and I were going to a nearby car dealer to buy a new car and we argued about what state we were allowed to drive it in. Briersburg Prison was located in every state and April began singing softly every time we passed the rod Iron Gate in the front of the building.

Where is Dr. Sigmund Freud when you need him, or, at least Dr. Christian Baltz?

I decide not to *go quietly into the* chart office, but *rage against the* malevolent onslaught awaiting me. "I'm here," I say boldly, almost challenging Pound to get angry.

Pound lifts his head up slowly at me and then fixes his sights on Lieutenant Garrison.

"The A.W. wants to see you up in his office, before you report to work, Erickson." Garrison says unsettlingly

I, in paranoid fashion it seems, back out of the office into the hallway.

"And, Dane," Pound says, "when and if he's done, report to the main yard with Flannigan for the day."

Without another word by me, I leave and report to Edwards' office. I'm a little confused

Dutch Van Alstin – Murder in D Block

in what part an assistant warden plays when a guard is habitually tardy as I have been as of late. A sign displayed smugly on his door advertises Edwards' view of his own importance.

ASSISTANT WARDEN OF BRIERSBURG STATE PRISON

DONOVAN T. EDWARDS

KNOCK BEFORE ENTERING

How egotistical can one man possibly get? I knock.

"Good morning, Erickson," Edwards shouts from within his office, "come right on in."

There is no love lost between Edwards and myself. I was scratched from his Christmas card list a few years ago.

His office is large and ostentatiously decorated. The room looks as if it's in an octagon shape with awards from dubious departmental banquets plastered on each section of the walls. Across the wall, directly behind his over-priced oak desk, hang two large Japanese swords with some type of Oriental scrawl along the sheaths. On his desk, in the corner, is a picture of what appears to be his family, exaltedly placed on an old tattered Bible.

"Do you like those?" Edwards says, pointing at the swords.

"They're very chic, sir," I say.

Edwards squints his eyes at me, unable to discern whether he had just been insulted. "My father brought them back from Okinawa in 1946 when he was a P.O.W. They belonged to an actual samurai warrior who was in charge of the camp."

"Wow," I say disinterestedly. I'll make a wager that the name of the curio shop is still stamped somewhere under the sheaths. Although, I believe they were Made in Japan.

Edwards pulls off his tie and props his feet up on the desk. "Take your hat off, Dane, and have a seat."

I slide a chair over to myself and plop down in the mahogany leather.

"Care for a cup of coffee?"

"No, sir," I say, holding my hand up, "thanks anyway."

"How are you doing?"

"How am I doing…where?"

"In general," he says, flailing his hands.

"Why?"

Edwards springs up from his desk and tightly grabs the edges and sneers. As quickly as he angered, he calms himself and smiles as he taps out a mundane beat on his desk. "I'm inquiring because of an attack in the corridor the other day concerning you."

Dutch Van Alstin – Murder in D Block

"What of it, sir?"

"Well," he opens his arms outward, "what happened?"

"The prisoner, Ludlow, tried to punch me in the face and I grabbed hold of his collar and placed him in a headlock and dumped, well, *brought* him to the floor."

Edwards runs his tongue along the roof of his mouth a few times as he nods his head. He sits back down and continues the bobbing of his neck. "Okay, Dane, that's all."

I sit, motionless, leery of just walking out of the office at the drop of hat. "That's all, sir? I could have just written you a memo?"

He stands again and grits his teeth. "That's funny; I don't recall asking for a memo, do you?"

"No, sir, I don't," I say, vaulting myself out of the chair and out of the office.

Flannigan spots me walking toward him and whispers something to Armstrong. Armstrong waves me over to him at the observation deck. "Red wants you to go into D block and help with the keep lock recreation run again."

"Okay," I say, looking over at Red.

Gullo is engaged in a heated debate with Rook over whether Rook should be wearing his slippers as he paints the cellblock bars. I peer down my desolate gallery, saying nothing to Joey or Rook. "Yo, Rivera, get on up here," I shout.

"They done put him on a bus last night," Rook says.

"Was I talking to you, genius?" I say to Rook. He smirks and begins dipping his paintbrush in the can.

"Where is he, Joey?" I say.

"According to the logbook, they shipped him out around midnight."

"Midnight? Why all the cloak and dagger?"

Joey shrugs his shoulders as he continues reading the logbook.

"Had something to do with that guy getting killed up top," Rook says, pointing at the ceiling.

"Paint, or lock the hell in," Joey uncharacteristically shouts.

"All right, okay," Rook says, holding his hands up defensively.

"And go put some damn boots on, too." Joey says.

Joey and I stare at each other uncomfortably. "That's crap, Joey; Rivera had no problems with Delgado."

"How would you know?" Joey quickly snaps back.

Dutch Van Alstin – Murder in D Block

I falter in search of a quick answer. "I work here, remember?"

"Obviously someone had a problem with him, Dane."

I look for a flick of accusation in his tone but chalk my cynicism up to my growing trepidation.

The day languorously dragged on without anyone saying too much to anyone else. Conversations were strictly limited to imminent prison business. I have been in Briersburg during murder investigations and the aura that is occurring now is not the same as I remember. The deadening silence was rather eerie. When prisoners are this subdued and quiet, there's usually cause for concern. But trying to elucidate on why the robots are so taciturn and quiet is another matter altogether.

When three o'clock arrived, the day shift marched in symbolic lock-step to the time clock and went home. Everyone stared at one another, but nobody spoke a word. The night shift reported for work in their usual jocund and bantering self, jabbing each other in the ribs. All I can conclude is whatever made the day shift so reticent must have occurred in morning lineup. Before I go home, I walk back to the chart office to read any of the incident reports.

A guard in C block had urine thrown in his face and there was a prisoner on prisoner razor attack during supper, nothing out of the ordinary to generate such a macabre type atmosphere.

When I go to punch out my time card, Karen Hyde stands by the time clock reading through some papers.

"Hi, Mrs. Hyde," I say genially.

"Oh, good, Dane, I thought I wouldn't catch you before you went home."

"You're looking for me?"

Karen is a profoundly attractive woman in her late twenties. She has long, flowing auburn hair that curls at the top by her bangs. Her momentous beauty is in her shapely, yet very petit figure. She and Mitchell are married, just not to each other.

"Yes I was," she says affably. "The A.W. sent down a mandatory BR-60 file on you and I have to follow up on it."

"BR-60?"

"Stress management."

"Thanks," I say as I roll my eyes, "but I'm fine."

"I'm sorry, but the procedure is mandatory or your right to possess and carry an off duty

Dutch Van Alstin – Murder in D Block

weapon is revoked."

I look at my watch. "I…"

"The whole procedure takes about ten minutes."

I shrug my shoulders and motion her toward the E.S.O. office.

Karen hits me with many pre-printed questions concerning family life, upbringing, medications, and other meaningless drivel. We exchange a few smiles amidst some potentially embarrassing inquiries.

"Well, Mrs. Hyde, will I ever play the piano again?" I say.

She laughs. "I'm afraid that one is older than these walls."

"What's next, Mrs. Hyde?"

"First," she says, setting her pen on the desk, "you call me Karen."

"Okay, Karen," I say restlessly, "what's next?"

"I'll refer you to an outside assistance. But don't fret; it's your option to follow through if you wish."

"A shrink?"

"Well," she sighs, searching for words, "someone to help you deal with your feelings."

"Are you sending me to Dr. Baltz?"

Karen snaps her eyes up at me agitatedly. "Do you know Dr. Baltz?"

"By reputation only."

"Actually," she says uneasily, "he is no longer with the program."

"Why?"

"I, uh, we, the office, sent a referral to his house awhile back and the place was vacated. The employee drove all the way out to Mayfield for nothing."

"Mayfield? I say incredulously, "that's over eighty miles away?"

"True, but Dr. Baltz charged no fee for his services for our employees, and we felt the savings was worth the extra hassle."

"Was he any good?"

She looks up at me quizzically. "I thought you knew him by reputation?"

"Name only."

"Oh, well, you'll like Dr. Herman."

"Any idea where Dr. Baltz went to?"

She fidgets with her pencil and fixes her eyes on her papers. "No, not a clue." She sighs. "We haven't seen him or our files.

Dutch Van Alstin – Murder in D Block

My time card, again, is used for another cryptic note: "*I love the crisp air in September, what is your favorite month?*"

The notes are growing more and more intrusive and are harder for me to continue to dismiss them as insignificant. I actually find myself neurotically examining the back seat of my car before I drive anywhere.

The florist is on the way to my, soon to be, cottage. I send April some flowers with a note, imploring her to at least have a discussion with me in a calm, orderly fashion and hear my side of the story. I don't believe that is an unreasonable request on my part.

The cottage is coming along very nicely. The foreman at the work site assured me that the house will be livable in a matter of a day or two. The thought of any more than one more night at Cassidy's is, if you'll pardon my exaggeration, pure torture.

Therapy comes in all shapes and forms, not just in the shape of egg-headed psychiatrists. Mine arrives in the form of a fishing pole with a worm living on borrowed time attached to the hook. But before I drown a few innocent worms, my growling stomach navigates me to the Port Side Café to eat a plate full of their tuna casserole. Jenny, the waitress, informs me I am in effect the only patron who orders the tuna casserole and that's why the owner won't make up a fresh batch daily. Instead, she told me, he freezes several portions and actually writes my name on the containers. I gather that is an honor bestowed upon anyone who is brave enough to delve into the casserole.

The worm is hooked and ready to go to work. I toss my pole in the water and mull over the chaotic events surrounding my life. Two weeks ago, I was a semi-content civil service employee with a nice house, and a nice boat, and a nice dog. Now, my house is in eighty million pieces from a man who tried to kill me and the wife of that man, i.e., my girlfriend, accuses me of murdering him in retaliation. The A.W. believes I'm coming unhinged before his eyes, Joey Gullo thinks I'm a sinister clod, a deviate writes twisted, disturbing letters to me, via my time card, and Donny's mystery shrink runs off with all the personal files on his patients.

I don't wonder why Karen was a little embarrassed about my questions concerning the enigmatic Dr. Baltz. Not unlike most state employees, Karen was so zealous over saving her department a few dollars that she probably didn't bother to investigate the doctor's credentials all that extensively, if she did at all. Subsequently, the shadowy doctor took his labs rats and ran. Most likely he was used the guards as *guinea pigs* in some study or experiment. Some of these so-called scientists have no shame when it comes to research and believe anything they do to prove their hypothesis is okay as long as the motivations are well intentioned.

Dutch Van Alstin – Murder in D Block

The worm floats too close to the top and I know there are no fish on the surface. I reel in the line, weight it down with a sinker, and cast it out again. The worm sinks deeper into the lake and down into the murkiness. Two girls zip by on jet-skis, giggling and chasing each other, The one girl cuts the corner sharp, nearly dumping herself into the drink. She recovers and speeds off after the other girl, still laughing hysterically.

My line straightens complete out from the yank at the end of the pole. I pull the pole hard, matching it yank for yank. I reel the line in and catch a glimpse of a big, yet struggling catfish. The jerk of my pole snaps the line, sending the fish falling into the water where he swims off into the murky depth. He becomes another tale of how *the big one* got away.

I am comforted, at least, by the revelation that there is something in the lake to catch.

CHAPTER 20

The rain is crashing down on the pane of my paint chipped window, causing me to wake a half an hour before the alarm clock rings. I wrestle with the window, trying to get it open and allow some fresh air in to combat the musty odor. I then trudge down the hallway to the bathroom. I fill my percolator with the lime-laden water after throwing an extra scoop of coffee in it to give me an extra caffeine boost to face the day. The water smells of sulfur but the smell doesn't carry over to the final product. I'm fortunate that the water comes out of the tap at all, normally it requires me to bang on the pipes, ostensibly waking the tenant up who lives behind the bathroom. After a few curse words and vulgarities about my sister, he goes back to sleep.

I forced the contractor's hand a bit and he has guaranteed me my house will be livable by the end of the workday tomorrow. The thought of me spread out and comatose on my mattress, watching TV until I wonder off into slumber land, is more pleasure than I can bear to dream of. Chuck runs a great pub and a superlative kitchen, but these rooms should be featured on *Lifestyles of the Poor and Slovenly*.

Today's lineup, of which I was on time for, begins with a poignant plea by Garrison to further our efforts to clean the prison for accreditation. After the sermon by Garrison, Sergeant Green, the chart sergeant, reads off today's secondary news.

Dutch Van Alstin – Murder in D Block

"Listen up, gents," Green says from the podium. "We have valid information that today, in the box, there will be an attempt to grab a guard for, at minimum, a hostage situation. The rumor is that a staged allegation will take place in one of the recreation yards and when you guys enter to break up the fight, one of you will be grabbed. There is no pertinent information on who, when, or any solid details. What this breaks down to is this: be overly suspicious of anything today, especially you box boys," Green points to the box guys' area of the room. "I know we hear shit like this all the time but keep in mind, since the rumor Delgado was murdered by a guard has circulated in the general population, the A.W. is concerned some type of retaliation is imminent. To sum it all up, guys, be-very-careful." Green taps his folders and the lectern and steps down from the podium.

The bombshell that was apparently dropped on everyone yesterday finally reaches me. The lines have been drawn, but where those lines are and what they separate is up for grabs. A guard killed Delgado?

Green's most recent news will only feed the already paranoid fringe section of the robots. Maybe I am a bit more realistic and sensible then most of the robots, but the guard/murderer theory just doesn't make a whole lot of sense. The reserved nature that beleaguered the robots yesterday is now understandable. If anyone in their heart of hearts believes this cockamamie theory, then I am concerned what that belief is based on if not some delusional irrationality of fear.

Toby follows me out of the lineup room and into the yard jabbering all the way. I can't help but look at him differently ever since McManus told me about the escapade at the gas station.

"Wow, a guard, huh, Dane?" he says. "Who do you think could have done it?"

"First off, Toby, I don't think that is a question that will too welcome today. And secondly, did the notion that the rumor is erroneous ever come across that brain of yours? I mean, really, a guard a murderer, come on?"

"Just speculating, Dude," Toby says with his irritating two tiered grin.

Today's melody being sung from the corridor is York's version of the Ricky Ricardo song, Babaloo.

"Hi, Calvin," I say as I approach the gate.

"Aye, Bulldog," he says with a bogus Spanish accent.

By one o'clock, I notice the robots are not much more talkative than they were yesterday, maybe a little, but not much. My own dose of neurosis leaks out of me as I begin to scan the faces of the robots to see if there is an inkling of personal rejection toward me, perhaps concerning April, and not just a blanket silence everyone is embroiled in lately.

Red joshes with Armstrong about some woman they both know until a static filled screech trumpets out over Red's radio. "329 to 335" the tremulous voice from the box says.

Red snaps his radio from the holder. "335 here, go ahead 329."

"Call extension 968 ASAP."

Red springs from the sergeant's post and ambles quickly to the elevator. "Never mind the call, 329, we're on our way up now." Red snaps his radio back into the holder. "Let's move, boys, it's the box."

We climb in the elevator one by one, cramming in tightly. Red looks around at the crew and gives me a double look. He nods at me, as if in approval of my being there, and then continues looking at everyone.

"Enough," he shouts as more guards attempt to get on the elevator, "push the button." We all remain relatively silent on the way up to the box. One guard whistles a low tune to himself as he examines both sides of his hand. Mack somehow manages to climb aboard and stands stoically with an ominous leer on his face. "That bastard, Hopwah use to lock on my gallery," Mack says. "I've always wanted to shove this baton up his ass until it comes out his fucking nostril."

"Not a friend of yours, huh?" I say.

"A guy like me has no friends, Dane. We're like the wind, always moving on too fast to stop and get to know anyone."

"That's very deep, Mack."

The elevator climbs to the top floor and we are greeted by the near hysterical box sergeant, Sergeant Ginnan. "It's a setup, Red, it's a setup! Oh my God, it was true, it was true, it's a setup!" He shouts excitably.

"Settle down, Jeff," Red says. "How many and where are they?"

"Uh…six?…six, six! It's Bryndell and Shaunacy fighting though. The blood, oh, the blood is all over. They have shanks and they're cutting themselves to shreds."

"All right, Jeff, what yard are they in?"

"Number three, Red, yeah, it's number three. But you can't just go charging in there, Red. No, no, you can't just bull your way in, they're gunning for one of us."

"Relax, Jeff," Red says, "we got it from here." Red marches down the gallery with us close in tow. Mack stops to try and light a cigarette but when he realizes no one stopped with him, he throws the butt on the floor and scampers to catch back up with the others. We are all assailed with truculent taunts and pummeled with sour milk cartons and this afternoon's mashed potatoes. The debris smashes against the bars, splattering refuse as we attempt to shield our eyes.

Red continues walking.

We walk through the steel door leading to the yard corridor. The corridor is dark and barren, devoid of any sunlight. Red halts us in front of the yard entrance as Ginnan positions himself in the back of the assemblage.

"You have to take it slow, Red," Jeff says. "No batons drawn or any sign of aggression, they may react harshly. Just order them to cease and we'll come in and handcuff them, remember that they're gunning for you guys."

"Jeff, why don't you handle the yard door for us," Red says, ignoring his pleas for mercy. "When I say drop my arm, crack it open."

Red looks around at all of us as we catch our breath. He looks at each of us individually, sizing up the situation. He fixes his sights on a tall, lanky guard next to me and points at him. "Okay, you, you're going in first," Red says to him. "Go in along the right side and swing that hickory at what's ever in your way. "And you," Red points to me, changing my fear to pure adrenaline. "You're going to take up the left side and…" Red pauses and looks out upon the whole group of us. "Ah, fuck it," he shouts, "we're all going in, we're all swinging, and I want you to hit them bastards and hit 'em hard!"

Ginnan's eyes follow Red's arm as he raises it up over his head. "Red?" He says nervously.

"Jeff, I need you to be steady, Red says pressingly. "Are-you-okay?"

"I'll be fine, I'll be fine," Jeff replies.

Red looks back at us solemnly. "Ready, boys?"

We look at each other with false assuredness and nod our heads.

Red gapes at Jeff dictatorially. Jeff nods his head, still unconvinced in his mind, but prepared in the sum and substance of his spirit.

Red drops his hand and the Iron Gate opens, exposing the light of day sandwiched between the falling rain.

Dutch Van Alstin – Murder in D Block

CHAPTER 21

We rush the yard through the driving rain, swinging our hickory at everyone not gowned in blue. Earsplitting screams and shrills dominate the opening seconds after we cross the threshold. The guards are crying out to the prisoners to drop the shanks, the cries go unanswered. Upon Mack's ungainly advancement into the yard, he bumps my hip, sending me staggering to the concrete. I stand quickly, regaining my composure only to witness Shaunacy being the first to meet with the swinging hickory across his hip. The blow affects him little, if any, as he continues to draw blood from Bryndell's body.

Red blurts something completely inaudible to me, as his eyes grow big, pointing fervently behind me. Turning with my baton gripped in my hand, I am greeted with another set of unfamiliar hands grasped around my baton. An excruciating pain emanates at the base of my head and neck where the repeated thrusts are levied in an effort to get me to relinquish my baton. Another arm reaches from the other side and clasps my neck, choking off my air. I am forced to drop my baton in an attempt to pull the arm away from my throat. The sound of the hickory bouncing off the cement seems to happen in slow motion, deadening all other noises. My head is pulled tightly to the side. I lift my arm only to be greeted by searing, stinging twinge of agony as I watch my own blood drip down on to the pavement, assisted by the dripping rain. I hold my arm stationary, despite the repeated gouges into my skin, bringing forth new pools of

Dutch Van Alstin – Murder in D Block

blood with each gouge. "Razor!" I scream. "He's got a razor!"

The instinct to protect my neck somehow keeps my arm motionless despite the continued gashes.

The assailing prisoner being knocked to the pavement by an unknown guard's baton follows a thunderous crack, inches from my ear. The blood still drips from my arm, but I manage to grab the prisoner who now possess my baton. He swings it wildly in a crowd of chaos until I leap on his him, pulling him backwards as we land in the splash of a rain puddle, tinted red from my bleeding. The prisoner is pulled off me. I lie immobile, watching myself bleed continuously.

"Damn you, you piece of shit Hopwah," Red yells as he grabs the prisoner, who seconds ago wanted my life, and slams his head against the wall twice. Red then flings Hopwah to the pavement where he meets with several feet to his ribs and head. Hopwah puts little effort into protecting himself from the thrusts being driven into his body. More guards launch into a frenzied attack on Hopwah, flailing him up and down his body with hickory. The guards now and then look back at me and their anger is rejuvenated. Hopwah continues to endure the brunt of their anger over and over again. Hopwah continues his rant: "I hope he dies, dies, dies," as the battering on his person continues also.

By now a plethora of blue shirts have quelled the uproar and the prisoners involved are handcuffed, except for Hopwah who continues to be thrashed. Hopwah appears to have won the psychological war; he refuses to show pain or ask for mercy.

The rioters are carried, battered and bruised, back down the gallery. Only this trip, the prisoners remain very silent and still. One guard tears off his shirt and wraps it around my arm. They lift me up off the pavement and help me walk down the gallery. I stagger some through the rain as I exit the nightmare. Still dizzy and disoriented from losing blood, I walk down the gallery with as little assistance as possible. I receive a few pats on the back and a couple of consoling words. I, in a blood soaked shirt, am a sobering reminder of the reality that exists for all of them.

Our Lady of Lourdes' emergency room is inundated with people today. I would wager not a single person here has a similar injury, however. The doctor personally comes into my room to give me my discharge papers. "Here you are, Mr. Erickson," he says. "Keep those stitches dry and clean; all thirty-eight of them."

"Tell me, doc," I say, sliding myself off the examining table, "why do keep reminding me I how many stitches I have?"

"Because you are ignorant, nothing personal, I mean that in the literal sense, but you're ignorant about how serious your injuries truly are. What you really need is to spend the night for observation."

"I can't, doc, I have things to do."

He stands silently for a moment and then shakes his head pitifully, almost patronizingly. "How can you stand it, your line of work I mean?"

"Well, doc, actually our jobs are very similar, with one glaring exception."

"How so?" He says curiously.

"Both of us deal in human agony and misery; the difference is, in your job, you can do something to fix it."

My standard transmission presents a challenge since one arm is wrapped tightly around my waist. Bambino is still at April's. As pathetic and pitiful as this may be I believe I can elicit a dash of sympathy from April when I tell her of the *near death* experience I just had. Perhaps between the arm and the flowers I have sent, I can soften her up enough to where she'll at least listen to me for a minute or two.

My knock is preceded her hasty opening of the door. Her disposition grows reserved and inert; not to mention very surprised. She stands, saying nothing. She bears no sneer, but a smile is nowhere to be found either.

"Hello, April," I say.

She sighs agitatedly and leans on the doorframe. "Hello, Dane?" she says quickly to end the amenities, "what do you want? We have nothing to talk about anymore."

"Yes we do. My dog? My house will be ready Saturday. Can I come and get him around seven or so?"

"Seven P.M. on a Saturday night?" she says mockingly, "can you be a bit more obvious?"

"I just want my dog."

"He's your dog." She steps back away from the door and closes it in my face.

I knock again and vociferate through the door. "Can I come in and scratch his ears and say hello to him?"

No reply.

I knock, only harder. The door rattles at the thrust of my knocking.

Dutch Van Alstin – Murder in D Block

"Go away, Dane," she says.

I kick the base of her door relentlessly. "Open the damn door, April."

She flings the door open and raises her fist up to me. "I said, go away. What part of that sentence don't you understand?"

"You're a cold fish, April," I say. "You didn't even notice my arm wrapped up like a mummy?"

"Yes I did," she says tersely, "I just didn't mention it."

"Thirty-eight, count 'em, thirty-eight stitches I got from some lunatic who tried desperately to cut my throat."

"I'd never wish that upon you, but it makes no difference." April slams the door amid a perfunctory *"good night."*

I barrel into the door and holler: "April, open the God damn door now! I'm getting tired of this bullshit!"

"Get the hell away from my door," she shrieks.

"Not until you listen to what I have to say."

I leap so hard into the door that I leave a boot print at the base. The footsteps I hear traipsing up the stairs behind me belong to no other than Officer McManus. "Oh, I see!" I shrill. "Called the cops, did ya?" I say, staring at McManus.

"Not you again," McManus says, recognizing me as well.

"What the hell is your problem, April?"

"Look, Erickson wasn't it?" he says. "Get away from the door and come on outside with us." McManus arrives tonight with a partner, a bit older and more seasoned. "You no good bitch," I say, continuing my thrust upon her door.

"Look--" McManus says, walking toward me.

"Get away from me," I say, turning toward the both of them.

"I gave you a break the other night because you're a guard, but don't push it."

I kick at April's door again, cracking the base. Both cops grab me and pull me from the doorway. I struggle, futilely, causing them both to throw me to the floor. McManus's partner pulls out his nightstick and shoves it in my throat. "Shut up, right now," he says. "Guard or no guard, I'll haul you in tonight."

April finally opens the door and looks at the damaged door. "If that comes out of my deposit, Dane, I swear you'll regret it."

"Ma'am, are you pressing charges?" McManus asks.

Dutch Van Alstin – Murder in D Block

April ruthlessly glares down at me. "No," she says, looking back at McManus. "I'm sure he won't bother you," she stares back at me, "*or me*," she stresses, "for the rest of the night."

McManus reaches his hand to me and helps me off the floor. "Is your arm okay, what did you do to it?"

"Yeah," I say, looking at him and his partner. "Don't give it a second thought, I had it coming."

"I know that, but tonight I want to relax, eat doughnuts, play with the siren, you know, *cop stuff*. How about you leave her alone tonight and try to settle up with her another time, preferably my day off?"

"I will, and thanks, again." I extend a friendly salute to both McManus and his partner. April still stands in the doorway, staring coldly.

"I think I tore a stitch," I say to her.

She remains unflappable, saying nothing.

"Good night," I say with no reply returned. The contempt from her eyes pierces my soul; almost an eerie feeling comes over me from her ominous glare.

I walk down stairs and stop in the lobby. Finally, I hear her door close.

CHAPTER 22

The Furniture Company arrives early Saturday morning. I sit and wait as I hold a fresh cup of coffee brewed from my fresh, new percolator, plugged into my fresh, new electrical outlet, not that the outlet affects the taste, I'm just a bit giddy over being home.

My humble abode is complete to the point of where it is inhabitable. The current décor matches my present trifling lifestyle. There is no paint on the walls; no carpet sprawled from end to end, no drapes covering the windows, nor any type of bed linen. The cottage is a very basic style, not a Cape Cod type house, but more like a *box*. There isn't any fancy architectural structuring involved in the design, in fact, everything is much unadorned.

I shied away from any complexity or flamboyancy of any sort. Besides the fact the house was cheaper if it was simpler, my personal taste is practicality. I could, however, brag up some of the more contemporary features such as the poly-*somethingorother* bonded tiles affixed to the sides of the house in a pale, white glow.

The kitchen is larger than the old one and has an open entrance leading directly into a cozy living room. In the living room, I had the contractors install a majestic picturesque window seat overlooking the lake. Now I can enjoy the lake when it rains, and on those long, cold winter days.

A stone fireplace, that doesn't quite appear as old-fashioned as I had hoped, sits toward

Dutch Van Alstin – Murder in D Block

the rear of the living room. The fireplace is made up of all manufactured rocks and the shapes and sizes of the rocks take on a discernible pattern. The mantel is large enough for me to display my high school football trophy, and my *Stanley Templeton Academic Award* granted to the salutatorian at St. Alexandria high school since the early 1920's. The valedictorian of our class outdid my G.P.A. by a significant amount. The last I heard of her, and her name escapes me, she was an associate professor at some elite, Ivy League university.

The hallway is long and narrow, with just one bedroom and one bathroom breaking off at each end of the hallway. The bathroom is home to a 19" plasma TV mounted into the wall over the doorway. My bedroom is very spacious, but I requested a lot of that space be dedicated to closet. Due to a drainage problem in the area, I have no basement, leaving little room for storage. The closet actually spreads from one end of the room to the other.

A burly man, with greasy black hair, and another man, whose face is hidden behind the couch he is carrying, is walking up my, soon to be completed, sidewalk. I received a sweetheart of a deal on a four-piece living room set from *Dan-Dan, the Discount Man*. All four pieces are pasty yellow covered in huge green squares. The whole set cost me just a tad over *$400.00*. Since I have no paint or carpeting at the moment, I don't have to worry that about anything clashing.

"Where do you want it, fella?" The man with the greasy hair asks.

"I'll make it very easy on you," I say. "Just put all four pieces in the middle of the living room and I'll coordinate them later."

"That's fine with us, but what about your arm?"

"Oh, that," I say, looking at the sling. "It's actually worse that it looks."

"Surgery?"

"Well, I guess you could say that. I mean, there was a scalpel type instrument involved." The man just nods his head in agreement.

"Look, fellas, do you mind if I leave you to your work, I have errands to run today? I'd tell you lock up, but I have nothing to steal."

"It don't make no difference to us," he says.

"Help yourself to the coffee."

I grab a quick bite at a sub shop in town. I'm not a huge fan of stale rolls and compressed turkey, but the sub shop is adjacent to the florist, a place I have grown all too familiar with recently. After today, however, I am waving the proverbial white flag concerning

Dutch Van Alstin – Murder in D Block

April. Most of the flowers have been delivered with a card containing sentimental gibberish, but today, I plan on being contrite and submissive. I am writing a card in such a way where I outwardly give up hope for reconciliation, but furtively leave the door open for future chance at resurrection of our relationship. The embarrassment grows with every trip into the florist. I am actually on a first name basis with the owner.

The bell attached the door rings out as I enter. "Hello, Cameron," I shout, "it's just me, the pitiful loser in search of a dream."

"Oh, hello, Dane," he shouts from the storeroom, "I'll be right out."

I rub my fingers along the roses, trying to convince my wallet I can afford them.

"Still plugging away, hey, Dane?" He says, popping out from the storeroom.

"For the last time, I'm afraid."

"No more after today?"

"You guessed it?"

He begins cutting the stems of an arrangement next to him. "So much for my grandson's dream of a college education." He laughs. "By the way, what happen to the wing?"

"I tried to take a can of beer away from one of my co-workers."

I decide to buy the roses as one last hurrah and I phrase the card just right:

If proving my innocence takes forever, then forever it shall be.

My life needs closure at any cost and if it means giving you up,

then so be it. But you will know I am not a ruthless murderer.

Arriving at April's before seven o'clock will just make matters worse; I'll appear too pushy. I walk up the stairs, trying to decide exactly what I am going to say and how.

As I reach the top, I no longer need to contemplate my words. Bambino is tied up on her doorknob, twisting and turning. Obviously he has been in the hallway a great deal of time. Bambino gives forth a salvo of *yips* when he sees me. I untangle him and untie him from the door. All the while, he jumps at my chin, slobbering a sorely missed drool all over my face.

"Oh, Bambino," I say, scratching his ears feverishly, "you give unrequited love. I guess the least I can do for you is buy you a thick, juicy steak because the future is only you and I. It doesn't look as though mommy is going to come back to us."

Bambino ignores my words and continues the slobbering.

I've never understood why Sunday is considered the first day of the week. To me, it has always been the last day before the new week began. When I was a boy a Sunday consisted of a hearty breakfast, followed by a fist-pounding sermon at the Lutheran church topped off with a Minnesota Viking football game on T.V., if the antenna was picking up strong signals that day since my dad would not submit to cable. By Monday, my interpretation of the first day, mom and pop were back to work and sister and I was back to school.

Being that today is Sunday, I should look upon this as, if you'll pardon the stale cliché, *the first day of the rest of my life.* I had given into my hedonistic urges and dabbled in the illicit taboo lifestyle of danger and intrigue. It's odd, but now that April and I are kaput, my desire to delve into the maze of unanswered questions surrounding Donny's death has diminished greatly. I would now classify my former desire as an adventurous curiosity.

Delgado's death, regardless of the hype, will soon reveal itself to be a simple prison murder. He was a prominent cocaine dealer on the street and that nugatory talent normally manifests over into prison life. A sour drug deal is just one of a host of many reasons the prisoners kill each other. In fact, last year in D block there was a murder of someone over the theft of a pair of socks. Human life is worth very little behind the gray walls.

The shrouded life of Dr. Baltz still appears to my curios disposition. I'm sure my inference of what the doctor was up to, that I explained earlier, is true. He was most likely a pseudo-scientist looking for human guinea pigs. That notwithstanding, I plan on driving out to Mayfield today and track down the doctor's address that I found in Quinn'sfile. I am semi-familiar with the city of Mayfield. I've driven there a few times over the last couple of years for college football games and Baltz's street address sounds similar to a street near the stadium. If I'm right, that neighborhood around the stadium is quite seedy, not the locale one would expect a psychiatrist would keep an office.

Mayfield is overwhelmed with one-way streets causing me to distress more than one driver today. I try to look at the street light, stop signs, and the road simultaneously. The street Baltz's office was located, Mathius Avenue, is the street that I thought I remembered. And it is, in fact, in the ratty neighborhood that I remember as well. Mathius Avenue runs parallel to the railroad tracks and is besieged with pot holes and rudimentary patch work. There are about a dozen remaining structures on the street and approximately a third of those are boarded up and abandoned. Baltz's office is supposedly located at thirty-two Mathius Avenue, apartment three.

I reach the very end of the street and a dilapidated, broken-down house adjacent to the deserted railroad station has a number '3' hanging upside down on the porch, next to the number '2'. The house is a two-story, primer colored home with the attic window boarded. The driveway has weeds and shrubs protruding through cracked asphalt. At the end of the driveway is an old basketball pole, oddly, the net in the hoop looks brand new. I can only surmise that the house is abandoned also, or, at the very least, in extremely poor shape. There is a Dodge Omni out in front of the home with a valid registration and inspection, leading me to believe there is someone residing there.

As I knock on the front door, I contrive a last second scenario of how I am going to approach the subject of the doctor. A frail, sour woman walks to the door and peeks out at me cautiously.

"Good afternoon, madam," I say fetchingly.

"Okay," the woman replies.

"Yes, well, I was wondering if you could assist me in a matter of great importance."

"Okay."

"Can you direct me to the landlord of this dwelling?"

"You're looking at him," she says caustically.

I clear my throat and humble myself. "Oh, sorry about that, madam."

She continues to stare at me, saying nothing.

"Anyway, as I was saying--"

"I'm not buying, selling, giving, or lending and I don't owe anyone any money, and I already know Jesus, Buddha, and Allah." She grabs the doorknob and shuts the door.

"Please, wait; I'm neither a salesman, bill collector nor anything of the kind."

"Then what the hell are you?"

"That's a fair question, yes, that's a fair question."

"Well how about an answer then, buster," she says as she spits a mouthful of sunflower seeds on her porch. "I got things to do today."

"I understand, madam, I do. Allow me to get to the point at hand; my name is Joshua Herrnstein and I work for Dr. Baltz."

"You do, huh?" she barks. "Well you tell him to I got about five or six boxes of his crap in my garage and if he wants it, he'd better come get it."

"Exactly why I'm here," I say energetically, "I was sent by the good doctor to bring his stuff to him."

"Good? Ha!"

"Was there a problem with him?"

"I wouldn't know," she says, picking at her teeth, "I never met the bastard."

Dutch Van Alstin – Murder in D Block

"He rented from you though?"

"That he did, but all he did was mail a response to an ad I placed, and then mailed me a check for the first and last month's rent and a deposit, which he ain't getting back from me now."

"So you never did actually meet him?"

"Didn't I just say that?"

"Yes, madam, you did," I say. "But if he didn't stiff you on rent, then why the dislike?"

"Because I rent rooms cheaper than anyone in exchange for nobody bothering me. That man had people banging on my door at all hours of the night asking where he was. I told 'em all, he ain't here, he's never here!"

"How many different people?"

"There was this one fella in particular who use to come knocking a lot."

"A skinny guy, flat black hair, crooked nose?"

"That's the guy," she says, spitting again. "He drove me nuts."

Donny! I think to myself.

"I told that guy the same thing I tells the others, the doctor ain't here, he's never here."

"How do you know he moved out if he never really moved in?"

"Sent me a letter telling me to keep the last month's rent and he didn't need the place no more."

"Did he leave an address for the return of his deposit?"

"I told you he ain't getting it! I'm owed it for all the trouble he caused me."

"I'm sure, madam, the doctor doesn't care about the money; I was just wondering if he sent an address?"

"If you work with him, then hell, you should know where he is. Why ask me?"

"You're right, madam, I was wondering which of the two offices he wanted me to deliver his stuff."

"Mister, as long as you get that stuff out within two days, I don't care where you bring it. I wouldn't have kept it this long, but a damn state law says I gotta keep it thirty days at least."

"So it's been about that long now, huh?"

"Yep."

"I guess my showing up today was well timed?"

"Yep."

"Can you tell me where his stuff is and I'll get it out of your hair."

"In the garage, his name is on the boxes."

Dutch Van Alstin – Murder in D Block

"Thank you, madam, and I'm sorry that I bothered you and allow me to extend apologies from the doctor, too."

"Yep," she says as she shuts the door.

The old lady's garage is filled with junk. Baltz's boxes were buried under some National Geographic and some mason jars. I dump all the papers into one box and cram the contents in tightly. I leave the scant furnishings in the garage, with one exception. I needed a stapler.

Mayfield is a fairly large city, so finding a doughnut shop and a neighborhood park wasn't difficult. I sit, alone, under a big pavilion and rummage through Baltz's notes. The park is relatively barren, especially for a nice sunny Sunday afternoon. There are a few kids playing near the swing set and I see a wandering mutt, other than that, I'm alone.

Baltz had no filing system or organization whatsoever. He writes as most doctors do, in ancient chicken scratch. My only hope is to try to catch a glimpse of Donny's name somewhere.

I stumble across a few newspaper clippings from the want-ad section. One ad is for the apartment of the sassy old lady, and the other isn't discernible to me. Only in *Columbo* reruns are the ads circled. Here in the real world, I haven't a clue what the ad was cut out for, however, the exchange on the phone numbers tell me the newspaper was from Briersburg.

I finally spot Donny's name on the back of a computer printout. Nevertheless, after looking at the printout, I find it's more interesting than notes on Donny. Printed on the paper are the credentials of the clandestine Doctor Baltz. Included in the printout is where the doctor trained and interned, even a copy of his license to practice psychiatry. There is a host of information a person can get from such sources as the Internet, the library, and a multitude of others.

I even discover the date Doctor Baltz was born, 1933. And, also the date that he died, back in 1982.

CHAPTER 23

The sun peeks over the hill on a balmy Tuesday morning, the day I return to Briersburg. My window seat is worth every cent of the extra money it cost me. I watch from my window as the burnt orange glow struggles to find its place today. Every morning the sun seems to struggle more and more to be in its full blazing glory. The dark clouds that help introduce us to autumn are more prominent daily. My foolish male ego would never allow me to reveal this, but I actually make a point to wake two hours early just so I can see the sunrise. I can't help it, I love to watch the orange filter in more and more and watch as the darkness diminishes. I liken the whole process to a contest, a struggle within Mother Nature's kingdom on who will win the right to rule the day? The nighttime loses time after time.

The big Iron Gate is right where I remember it being. The night tower guard steps out on the platform and greets me with a salute. I wave back and motion for him to let me through. The first robot inside that I encounter can't seem to pass up the opportunity for a laugh at my expense. "Ooh, poor baby, didja mama kiss your boo-boo and make it all better," he says with his lips puckered.

"No, but yours did, genius," I say bitingly, "and it wasn't my boo-boo either."

"Get some fucking time on the job," he says as I walk through the main entrance.

The rest of the robots buzz about with each other within their respective cliques.

Dutch Van Alstin – Murder in D Block

Garrison rambles in to the room with his chin held high shouting for lineup to begin.
Sergeant Pound files in close behind Garrison, carrying Edwards' briefcase. Edwards struts in
the room seconds after the lineup is announced, giving him an opportunity to make a grandiose
entrance. Edwards nods at Pound and takes the briefcase from him.

Roll call is whizzed through at a lightning pace. Many guards didn't finish answering up,
"here" before the next name was called. Edwards is so obvious in his yearning to speak, he
repeatedly looks at his watch all through roll call. Pound looks up at us when he finishes
reading the last name on his list. "Men?" Pound says as he surveys the room, "the A.W. would
like to have a word with you all."

Pound may as well have said: *"and heeeeeere's, EDWARDS!"*

Edwards strolls up to the podium with a certain dab of haughtiness in his stride. He
removes his hat that sports a shiny, gold star and his eyes scan the room for anyone who
doesn't give him their full attention. "Men?" he pauses and continues his search. "The police,
and my sources as well, have the utmost reason to believe the murder last week of Raphael
Delgado was, in fact, an inside job." Edwards pauses again, seemingly for affect. "I can't begin
to tell you how this news sickens me, men. The thought that one of my guards has *turned* is
more than I can handle." Edwards rubs his brow and feigns fighting off tears, then, looks as
though he overcomes his melancholy with a sudden burst of ruggedness. "I want you to know
that many of you will be questioned today, but, I want it fully understood that any questioning is
to flush out potential witnesses. I want no speculation or rumor-mongering of why someone has
been called to my office. I repeat, you're all potential witnesses, not murder suspects."
Edwards places his hat back on his head and tugs at the brim. "Perhaps, only one of you fits
that bill." He stares over the assemblage briefly to leave his last words more impressionable,
and then, walks out of the room.

I have to wonder how many times he practiced that soliloquy. I can envision him
changing positions, altering hand gestures in front of his newly polished mirror, and finishing his
speech with: *"God bless you all, and God bless America!"*

We all begin to disperse from the lineup room. Garrison points at me, and summons me
over to him. As I walk toward him, he says: "A.W.'s office, now."

Garrison walks with me up the stairs to Edwards's office. He says not a word, nor gives
me a look all the way to the doorway of the office. "Wait here," Garrison says. He walks in the
office and closes the door, leaving me in the hall alone. I press my ear to the door and attempt
to decipher the mumbling voices.

Dutch Van Alstin – Murder in D Block

"Come in now, Erickson," Garrison yells from within the office.

A man with a conservative gray suit smiles as I walk in and he directs me to a chair in front of Edwards' desk. I sit and fold my arms neatly in my lap and look around at the unfamiliar faces. Edwards and Garrison are the only two people I recognize. Edwards sits near the corner on the armrest of a chair. Garrison stands with his arms folded by the door, not unlike a sentry.

The man who motioned me to sit is a tall man, at least six-foot, four, and solidly built. His matching gray pants are heavily starched and creased to perfection. His black, oxford style shoes are polished smartly. His face is steely and square, and clean-shaven, and a dimple caps off a very prominent chin. His eyes are brown or dark green, either way they do not open very wide and don't appear to be friendly.

Two other men are with him and they also have gray suits and stand on each side of him. He walks slowly around one of the gray suits and leans his backside against the desk. He presents a smug grin to me and extends his hand. "Hello, Mr. Erickson, I'm John Lafayette."

"Hello," I say, cautiously shaking his hand.

Lafayette stands back up, walks to the window, and peers out, shading his eyes from the sun. "Actually, my full title is Agent John Lafayette of the F.B.I., son."

He and I cannot be more than five years in age apart and he has the audacity to refer to me as *son*.

Lafayette turns to me and says nothing. He apparently waits to see my reaction.

"Oh, the F.B.I., huh?" I say disinterestedly

"That's right," he replies, sitting back on Edwards' desk.

"May I see a badge?" I say mostly out of curiosity, but he is clearly offended. He pulls out a billfold and taps it a few times. He smirks at the two gray suits and flips open the billfold and tosses it too me. "Here you go," he says with a spurious smile.

I peak at the golden badge and hand it back to him.

"May I see yours?" he says patronizingly.

I reach in my back pocket out my billfold and tap it a few times. I smile at the two gray suits and then toss it too Lafayette. "Here you go," I say.

Lafayette looks at the badge and emits a sarcastic whistle. "Wow," he says, "corrections department." He tosses the billfold back to me as he turns around and looks at Edwards.

"So, the name is Erickson?"

"Yes," I say.

"And that's *Dane*, right?"

Dutch Van Alstin – Murder in D Block

"Yes."

Lafayette, again, walks back to the window. The only view is the back alley of a Mexican restaurant. "That sounds Scandinavian…*Erickson*?"

"That's correct, I hail from Minnesota."

Lafayette hyperbolizes a smile as he opens his eyes widely. "I see." He walks back around to the front of the desk and sits again. "How's work going?" he says, cuffing his hands behind his neck.

I resituate myself in the chair, growing impatient. "Look, Agent Lafayette, may we just get to the point at hand?"

"Which would be what, Dane?"

"I don't know," I say. "This is your party, I'm only a guest."

"So, what you're trying to tell me is you don't know why you're here?"

"I hope I'm doing more than just trying," I say agitatedly.

Lafayette looks at one of the gray suits and then writes something down on a big legal pad. "I'm just interested in you, Dane."

"For what, John? We just meet and I don't know about you, but for me, the sparks just aren't flying."

"Okay, Dane," Lafayette says, "let's begin again. I guess I can see I'm not dealing with your average *shmoe* here?"

"Then why do keep talking down to me?"

"Talking down to you?"

"Yes, talking down to me, parroting every word I say?"

"What do you mean?"

"How you're talking to me now," I say, mimicking his tone of voice.

Lafayette forces a sigh out and stares back at the gray suits, as if he is being graded on his performance. He drops his head down and begins puttering with a pen. "We both have jobs to do and I am trying my damnedest to do mine." Lafayette pauses and then looks up at me. "Do you understand that?"

"I do," I reply. "But let's be straightforward, no more idiotic questions about my ethnicity or shit like that."

"Okay, that sounds fair," he says, yanking on his lapels and clearing his throat. "Delgado?"

"So it's about him?"

"Yes, are you surprised?"

"I guess not," I say, leaning back in my chair. "I mean, why else would you be here?"

Lafayette laughs. "That's true, unless you have some unpaid parking tickets out there I'm unaware of?"

"No, but then again, why would the F.B.I. be interested in parking tickets?" My own words cause me to pause in thought momentarily. "For that matter, why are they interested in a run of the mill prison murder? Isn't this a state concern?"

Lafayette wiggles uncomfortably. "Why don't you let me conduct the interviewing, okay? We have jobs to do and I'm doing mine; you just concentrate on yours. My job is to ask questions, got it?"

"A little defensive, aren't we?"

"You're quite the comedian, Erickson." Lafayette says.

"You mean I'm not 'son' any longer?"

Edwards explodes. "Damn it, Erickson, you--"

Lafayette throws his hand up in Edwards' face and halts Edwards in mid-sentence. "Do you want to go down this road, Dane? Okay, I'll bite, I'll play, we'll travel down any road you want to steer me down because I've been on 'em all, pal. I cannot be beaten at my own game. I conduct interviews on my terms; you can open and close fucking doors all day long your way. But right now, right here, we're going to discuss the deceased, Mr. Delgado and what you may or may not know about him. Is that okay with you?"

"You hurt me, not, with your petty insults."

Lafayette tosses his pencil in the air. "Is there a reason why you're being so uncooperative with me?"

"Yes there is," I say, leaping up from the chair and shoving my finger in Lafayette's face. "I don't care for your innuendoes that I am some sort of suspect!"

Lafayette leans forward, inches from my face. "I sat in the hallway this morning at your lineup and I listened to A.W. Edwards, and I specifically recall him saying we were flushing out potential witnesses, not suspects." Lafayette sits back on the desk and folds his arms. "Tell me, Dane," he says calmly, "why would you assume you're a suspect before anyone said anything to you about it?"

I recall when I was young and misbehaving, my mother used to put me in the corner. I don't need my mom today; I managed to back myself up rather nicely, thank you very much.

Dutch Van Alstin – Murder in D Block

CHAPTER 24

"Do you care to re-examine this comedic approach of yours, Dane?"

I fight off the feeling of a whipped puppy and sit upright in my chair. "Then why interview me first?"

"Because you were the last guard to write a ticket on him, well, sort of," Lafayette says, peering over at Edwards.

"Meaning what exactly?" I say.

Lafayette shuffles through some papers, stopping periodically and eyeballing them. His searching, still and all, seems to be merely for effect. It doesn't look as though he's even reading any of the papers whatsoever.

"Do you know a guard by the name of Brannigan?" he says probingly.

"No, I never heard of him."

"Neither have I," Edwards interjects. Edwards' words are, again, halted by Lafayette's stiff-arm move.

"The last person to write a ticket on Delgado was *S. Brannigan*," Lafayette says.

"Your point being?"

"The point is this, Dane," he says bitingly, "there is no such person."

Dutch Van Alstin – Murder in D Block

"Then I doubt the charge on Delgado would have stuck anyway."

"You're a real funny man, aren't you?"

"I'm just confused at how I'm supposed to know a man you say doesn't even exist? Frankly, Lafayette, I don't think you're making a whole lot of sense."

"Okay then, Brannigan, oops," Lafayette dramatically covers his mouth, "I mean, Erickson."

"I guess we both have a sense of humor, Agent Lafayette?"

"Oh, I can be very humorous," Lafayette says. "I'm just not now."

"I don't know about that, you're cracking me up here."

"May I continue?"

I gesture my hands for him to proceed.

"How well did you know Delgado, and I'm referring to Raphael?"

"Not too well," I say as I ignore his sarcasm.

"Any problems with him?" Lafayette rubs his chin. "Perhaps, personal problems?"

"No."

"No?"

"Yes…*no!*"

Lafayette reaches in his breast pocket and puts a pair of reading glasses on to make himself look more seasoned than his thirty-something year old self can possibly be. He rifles through more papers and plucks out a ticket that I wrote. "Filed only days ago by you," he says, as he tugs at his glasses, "a ticket for a shank found in Delgado's cell."

"So?"

"So, you just got through stating to me that you had no problems with him?"

"First off, you specified *personal* problems, and secondly, my finding a shank is not synonymous with having a problem."

"I guess that's just a coincidence, then?" Lafayette says as he takes off his glasses. "I mean, you finding a shank in his cell days before he's murdered?"

"You're a brilliant salesman, Lafayette," I say scathingly. "The statement you just made actually makes no sense, but the pitch in your voice and the way you phrased that question, makes anyone listening think: 'we got 'em now'."

Lafayette leans back in the chair and interlocks his fingers behind his neck. He pauses his words and looks toward Garrison and they nod their heads in unison. "Tell me, Dane," Lafayette says, returning his sights to me. "Is it true that you nicknamed your baton *Andrew*

Jackson?"

"What? Did we just make a left turn here?"

"If we did, Dane, keep in mind that I'm driving."

"Well at least next time click on your turn signal before you do."

One of the gray suits walks over to Lafayette and whispers into his ear, probably for effect as well. Lafayette nods his head periodically and then whispers something back to the gray suit.

"Where was I?" Lafayette says, looking up at the ceiling. "Oh, yes, Andrew Jackson. Did you do that?"

"No."

"No?" he pauses. "Andrew Jackson? No?"

"Why the hell would I do that?"

Lafayette smiles aloofly at the gray suits and then looks back at me. "Andrew Jackson's nickname was *old hickory*."

"What the hell does--"

"Never mind that," Lafayette interrupts, "let's return to Delgado."

"I didn't know we had left him?"

Lafayette stands and walks out into the hallway, leaving me alone to confront eight eyeballs staring down at me, but when he returns, the eyeballs shy away.

"Do you need some water?" Lafayette asks.

"No."

"Okay," he says, putting his glasses back on face. "I guess you're cool as a cucumber, huh?" He doesn't await a reply from me; he just digs bag into his papers and pulls out another report. "Tell me, Dane, what problem did you have with a man named Ludlow?"

"None, really," I say, scratching my head.

"None?" he says skeptically.

"No."

Lafayette snaps the paper in his hand and flattens out any wrinkles. "It says here that you violently choked Mr. Ludlow the other day in the corridor, correct?"

"You're being a bit melodramatic, don't you think?"

"Did you or did you not state the other day, and I quote: 'I grabbed him and put him in headlock and dropped him to the floor'?"

I look over to a grinning Edwards. "I *subdued* him," I say, still focusing my sights on

Edwards.

"Really, well the rumor is you grew angry as hell and choked, kicked, and punched him repeatedly. The cruelties of your character cracked in a callous display of violence!" he says sternly. "Not unlike how Mr. Delgado was murdered."

"Very good, Lafayette," I say high-handedly. "Now can you say: she sells sea shells by the sea shore?"

"If you give me a sarcastic, wise ass answer again, I'm just going to have you locked up for a day or two and we'll try these questions again afterwards."

"Look around you," I say softly. "Do you think jails frighten me?"

"I want to know why the manner of which you attacked Mr. Ludlow is similar to the way Mr. Delgado was murdered?"

"That's what you've been leading up to? All of this grandiose bit of theatrics and that's your *dénouement*, as it were? Is that what my tax dollars are going to at Quantico?"

"Interesting," he says, "you are aware of the training headquarters for the F.B.I.? Tell me, were you considering a career with the bureau at one time?"

"At one time, perhaps."

"Well, we lost ourselves a good man," Lafayette says with artificial sorrow. "Now if I may return to the choking at hand?"

"I-did-not-choke-him, as you so gallantly put it?"

"You're growing a little perturbed, aren't you, son?"

I grit my teeth and breathe deeply. "You're an arrogant, pompous, egotistical son of a bitch, do you know that?"

"My, but you are getting touchy, aren't you?" Lafayette says, eyeballing me intently.

I lean forward and close in on Lafayette's face. "I'll take that water now, Mr. F.B.I. man."

Lafayette motions for one of the gray suits to fetch me a glass of water. He dutifully obeys and walks out in the hall and fills me up a cup.

"Tell me, Dane," Lafayette says, leaning back in the chair again. "What do you know about April?"

"It rains too much."

Lafayette rolls his eyes and smirks. "You are really posing on me, you know that?"

"I don't pose," I say irately, "what you see is what you get."

"Well, my friend, as the song goes: *tell it like it is*," Lafayette says. "Were you and Delgado's wife engaged in carnal relations?"

Dutch Van Alstin – Murder in D Block

"Carnal relations?" I say, mimicking his semantics. "What are we, savages?"

"I'm sorry, let me try again, only in *street lingo* ease for you," he says derisively. "Where you: doing her, *boffing* her, humping her, fucking her, screwing her brains out, or any of the above aforementioned?"

"Oh that's tactful."

"That's not an answer."

"I don't like the wording, it's crass."

"Are you implying the relationship was more than sex?"

All five faces close in on mine and wait with baited breath for my answer. I stare out the window at the Mexican restaurant. "Those tacos over there are tasty."

"It's time to be straightforward, Dane," Lafayette says in a charitable tone. "Were you and she lovers?"

I look back at Lafayette, angry that his question is too candid and straightforward for me to just brush it off callously. "Why deny it, I'm sure you already have pictures or something?"

"Is that a yes?"

"It's not a no."

Lafayette stands and stretches as he glimpses at his Rolex. "All right, now we're getting somewhere. So you two are in love, is that it?"

"We broke up a while ago."

"Pity, really," he says with a wry face, "with her husband six foot under, you two are free to be together."

"You're way off base here, Lafayette. I had nothing to with his murder."

"Lafayette walks to the front of the desk once more, and sits facing me. "Oh I see, you're doing his wife and he ends up dead in the cellblock you primarily work at and you see nothing unusual about that?"

Stoically, I sit and look unabashedly at Lafayette. "You are in a class double 'A' maximum security prison, Agent Lafayette. Not only that, but you are in Briersburg State Prison where a certain infamous notoriety dwells. Within its walls reside desperate men, whose only chance at a degree of dignity, is to try and live up to, and surpass that infamous notoriety. Murders are commonplace here, sir. Extortion, drugs, weapon trafficking, prostitution, pimping, gambling, bribery, assault, robbery, arson, you name it and there's a motive behind it. To overlook all these possibilities is, well frankly, stupid on your part."

Lafayette purses his lips and nods his head, soaking in my tirade. "Interesting," he says.

Dutch Van Alstin – Murder in D Block

"It's very interesting, did you say arson?"

"Yes."

Lafayette, again, rifles through the papers. "It says here that number thirty five cell, on your gallery, was recently was set on fire?"

I sigh very exaggeratedly. "Surprise, surprise," I say, "an arson, in a prison no less? Good Lord, man, what are the odds?"

"Arson is commonplace too, huh?" he says disparagingly.

"Yes, Lafayette, yes it is. Don't you listen?"

"Arson, not unlike your...house?"

"You just bounce from topic to topic, just like that?" I say, snapping my fingers.

"Yes I do," he says, snapping his fingers as well. "Just like that."

"My house was--"

"I have the report right here," he says, yanking it out of his papers.

"Is there anything you don't have in that magic bag of papers?"

"Some things I don't, but a copy of an arson report by the Sheriff's office isn't one of them." Lafayette snaps the paper into place and begins reading. "It says here an incendiary device was placed under the kitchen sink and *BOOM!*"

"Does it really say 'BOOM' in that report?" I say glibly.

"How do you suppose that happened, Dane?"

"You mean the 'BOOM'?"

Lafayette tucks the papers back into the folder. "I see we're just not going to make any progress, let's call it a day."

"That's fine with me, Lafayette, because it sounds to me as though you already have a tentative theory in that little pea brain of yours and are trying to find certain evidence to coincide with that theory, whether it results in the truth or not."

"I'll say this much, wise guy, I do have a theory and my theories are never off base."

"Please, oh brilliant one, share this theory with little ol' me."

"Let me tell you what it is, slick," Lafayette rages. "I think a hot tempered prison guard, who gives deviant but revealing nicknames to his nightstick, like *old hickory,* and who likes to set fires, impersonate imaginary guards, and choke prisoners from behind when he's angry. I think that guard was screwing a prisoner's wife and when that prisoner found out, tried to kill the guard by having his house blown up. And, instead of that guard doing the right thing, like reporting the crime, he just thought he's commit one of his own like murder since he's an

Dutch Van Alstin – Murder in D Block

arrogant asshole who thinks he's above the law. That's my theory, tough guy, like it or not, I know it's true."

"Could you repeat that please?"

"We'll be talking soon," Lafayette says, grabbing his papers and storming out of the office.

"Don't bet on it," I shout down the hallway. "Leave me the hell out of your fantasies." Lafayette stops quickly in his tracks and hurls his body around toward me. "Too late for that because you're already in it up to your fucking eyeballs."

We stand eye-to-eye, toe to toe.

I win the stare down as Lafayette marches back headlong down the hall.

Edwards stands up slowly and pull his pants up to his waist. "Go home, Dane."

"Am I suspended or something?"

"No," he says, shaking his head. "But I could. Fraternizing with a prisoner's wife violates every rule, written and otherwise."

"I'm not any longer."

"I know, I know," he says patronizingly, "as soon as you discovered she was a prisoner's wife, you broke it off with her?"

"That's right," I say resolutely.

"And I'm sure the union would back you on that fable. So for now, take a couple days off with pay. Think of it as a *vacation*."

I look at Edwards and Garrison and mull over a response. I conclude saying nothing is better than saying something half-witted, and in my emotional state, that's not an unlikely scenario. I just walk away and go home.

Each day, the complexities of my life snowball out of control. When my life was drab and predictable, I was comforted in the notion that at least my life was safeguarded from the Pandemonium I undergo now. I miss playing it safe. I long for the time when the high point of my day was eating a tuna sandwich and watching Sunday Night Football. Maybe having April out of my life is a blessing in disguise. Maybe it's not too late to set right the predicament I have woven myself into.

I pull in my driveway and look forward to having Bambino leap on me, and relaxing by the fireplace. As I said earlier, familiarity doesn't breed contempt, at least not for me.

Upon swinging my door open, Bambino fails to jump on me. I spot him, sitting on the couch wagging his tail, as April scratches his ears.

Dutch Van Alstin – Murder in D Block

CHAPTER 25

In awe, I stand, as April casually scratches Bambino's ears. He slaps his tongue around as he repositions himself to make sure April scratches every inch of fur. April doesn't readily acknowledge that I'm even in the house; she sits, and talks quietly to Bambino. She dresses very casual in an oversized sweatshirt that hovers over her body. She ties the bottom of the shirt tightly, with the knot emanating outward on her waist in a fashionable style. Torn and tattered jeans cover her legs, a butterfly patch, also faded and frayed accompanies both knees.

April finally gazes at me with a brood look on her face. "I've really missed this old boy," she says, continuing to pet Bambino.

"April...what on earth?"

"You say that like you haven't seen me in forty years?"

"No, it's just that, well, you are the very last person I expected to see sitting on my couch. You've given me quite a shock."

April gives Bambino two final pats on his belly to signify that the massage is over with. She stands, pulls her sweatshirt down over her exposed navel, and walks toward me and stops. She crinkles her eyes, trying to read my expression. "Are you okay?" she says.

I rub her shoulders and she embraces me quickly. "I'm sorry," she whispers.

Dutch Van Alstin – Murder in D Block

"Don't be, I mean, I guess I can understand your anxiety over the whole thing."

"No, you're just being polite," she says, backing away, "I should have known better."

"What would anyone have thought?"

"We're not just *anyone*, Dane," she says apologetically. "I was wrong to say and do what I did."

"You're so young, April," I say, "anyone would be scared and confused."

"You aren't going to allow me to beat myself up over this, are you?"

"No, unless you're coming back was to just apologize briefly and move on?"

April grows a beguiling smile and leans in, throwing her arms around my neck. "No," she whispers, "that's not what I was going to do." April clutches the back of my neck and draws me in close, kissing me forcefully. Bambino nuzzles his nose between our intertwined legs and attempts to separate us. She withdraws from me slowly, intermittently kissing my neck and ear. "I'm not only going to *tell* you how sorry I am," she says, rubbing my thigh, "but I'm going to *show* you like you've never been showed anything in your life."

"Wow," I say passively. "And to think, all I was looking forward to was a tuna sandwich."

Bambino sits outside the bedroom door and waits...

"You know, that tuna sandwich I referred to when you first got here was only metaphorical," I say, "but now I am really hungry."

April peers down at her phone. "Holy shit, it is getting late, how about some supper? My treat."

"Supper, yes, your treat, no."

"Come off it, Dane, I've made some good tips at the salon this week."

"Then pay your rent or something, you're not buying."

"I need to make everything up to that I've done wrong," April says with true sincerity.

"I'm a man, April," I say with an impish grin, "we don't want food, we want...well, what you just gave me."

"And you didn't even have to buy my dinner beforehand?" She laughs. "But in retrospect, farm boy," she says, slinging her purse over her shoulder, "it is now officially *afterward*." She stretches her neck up and kisses me on the lips. "Get your wallet; I want whatever is extremely expensive and unnecessarily extravagant."

I snatch my keys off my entrance table and open the door for her. "By the way," I say to her, "you didn't mention whether or not you liked my new house?"

Dutch Van Alstin – Murder in D Block

"Oh," she says, looking around and absorbing all the newness, "I like it. I almost wasn't sure what house was yours when I walked up the sidewalk." April ceases his words.

"What?"

"Nothing, let's go eat."

I look down at my keys and squeeze them tightly. An abhorrent sneer grows on my face. "How did you get here?"

"I knew you were going to make a big deal of this," she replies, ignoring my question.

"I said, how did you get here, April?"

"Dane, I don't own a car. How the in the name of Sam Hill am I supposed to get from one place to another?"

"I don't care about that, I just want you stop hitchhiking! Are you aware how many deranged, maniacal madman are lurking out there, just waiting to rape stupid people who hitchhike?"

April scratches her eyebrow, hiding a smirk. "Okay, okay, you win," she says. "I solemnly promise not to stick my thumb out anywhere, unless it's to trim my nail or massage your prostate. I'm sorry. I just needed to see you today."

I throw my arm across the doorframe, stopping her. "I'm curious, why today?"

"Your flowers, every single day, were taking their toll on me. But it was your last card that did me in though."

"The last one?" I say skeptically, "why that one? I thought it was a bit drab?"

"I thought it was cute," she says, pinching my cheeks. "You wrote: you are what Veronica was to Archie, that unreachable star in the sky of love."

"Oh," I feel my face turn red, "that one. I drank a lot the night before and I think I was still a bit giddy."

"I laughed. I could just picture you writing that out, looking out of the corner of your eye to make sure nobody was watching."

"There's some truth to that," I say with a chuckle. "But that wasn't the last card I sent. Didn't you get the dozen red roses a few days ago?"

"Ooh, roses?" she says coyly, "I'd remember roses."

"You really didn't get 'em?"

"No, really, I'm not joking."

"If that cheap, crooked old bastard ripped me off, I'll--"

"Dane!" April interjects, "I'm hungry, can we go now?"

Dutch Van Alstin – Murder in D Block

"Sorry, let's go."

Bambino leaps upon my window seat as April and I back out of the driveway. He wags his tail in frenzied madness, as if he can't grasp why we keep leaving him home alone.

As we motor down the road, April subconsciously rubs my leg. Jokingly, I slap her hand and complain about the distraction. We laugh and tease one another, trying to re-establish the closeness and familiarity we once were on verge of arriving at. She toys with me by rubbing my leg and quickly removing it before I can slap her hand off me.

"How the hell am I supposed--"

"Dane, watch out!" April screams.

My car fishtails and screeches, and I am now facing north on a southbound lane. The driver of the tow truck that I nearly smashed into hurls several obscenities amidst several displays of his middle finger. I inherently grip the wheel tightly, still unsure what has occurred. April composes herself and releases her sturdy squeeze she has on my arm.

"Are you okay?" I say.

"Fine," she says hurriedly, "let's get out of the middle of the road."

I maneuver the car into the proper southbound direction. I try to extend a friendly, rueful greeting to the tow truck driver, but he responds with more derisive talk and *flips me off* with both hands. Thank heavens he's not an octopus.

"Come on, Dane, let's just get back to the evening at hand? I know you're getting uptight, but a nice, relaxing supper will soothe those jangled nerves of yours."

The alarm clock is whacked off the nightstand and into the wall with just one swoop of my fist. I shake the cobwebs from my mind and try to see through the glaze in my eyes. The familiar sound of pots and pans trickles out from the kitchen and into my bedroom.

I tingle my face with some ice-cold water and brush my teeth. Abortively, I search for a bathrobe, none can be found. A pair of old sweatpants snatched from the laundry will suffice. The smell from the kitchen is now reaching my nostrils. April stands in front of the stove cracking two eggs into a bowl. She has on one of my T-shirts as a nightgown and her hair is pulled back into a ponytail. April whistles a soft, harmonious tune as she sways her head back and forth, all the while, flipping the spatula in the air.

"Mozart?" I say as I walk in the living room.

"Oh, Dane," she says, looking at me disappointedly. "You ruined my surprise."

"Sorry about that."

Dutch Van Alstin – Murder in D Block

"I was going to make you breakfast in bed."

"I could always go lie back down and go to sleep?"

"Oh, would you do that for me, please?"

"April, I was only joking."

"I'm not," she says, shooing me back to the bedroom. "Get into bed and prepare yourself for a good, hot breakfast."

I lie down in bed and prop my head upon my arms. April strolls in the room with a tray of food filled with fried eggs, ham, buttered toast, and coffee. She tops the tray off with a dandelion from my front lawn. "Eat, enjoy," she says.

"That won't be too difficult for me." I say, digging into the ham. "I love to eat."

April rubs the crudely made tattoo on my biceps. "When did you do that, anyway?"

"When I was about fifteen or so. My friend Pete and I gave each other a tattoo with mom's sewing needle."

"Why?" She says curiously.

I force out a bogus laugh to cover my slight embarrassment. "I told my mom I did it to cover the TB scar."

"You had tuberculosis?"

"No, I got tested for it and the little prickly doohickey they use leaves a funny looking, brambly scar."

"I know, I got one too," April says, brandishing her near faded scar.

"At least yours isn't as noticeable."

"Did your mom buy that phony-baloney excuse?"

"Nobody fools mom," I say with a doting chuckle.

"You must have never gotten away with fibbing?"

"Not too often," I say, smelling the eggs.

"Speaking of fibs," April smiles and slaps me on the leg. "I called you in sick today."

"You probably shouldn't have done that," I say, cutting into the ham.

"Oh screw them! They can live without you one day."

"That's not what I meant," I say, fighting off a burp, "It's my day off today."

April snickers. "Oh well, either way your mine today."

"I do have to sneak in around six tonight and do some paperwork."

"Oh no you don't," she says reproachfully. "You're mine all day."

"April, all this is great," I say, pointing at the tray. "But yesterday the A.W. confronted me

Dutch Van Alstin – Murder in D Block

and said he knew about us."

"Oh, my," she pauses and looks down at my tray. "I didn't know that, I'm sorry."

"Don't be, I could care less what that horse's ass thinks about anything."

"But what does that have to do with why you have to go in tonight?"

"I didn't necessarily want to open this up again, but there's a rumor going around that a guard was involved in the murder." I dip my toast in the yolk and swallow the whole clump in one bite. "I don't want the news of us to go any further than Edwards' office; there's something quirky in the mix here?"

"What do you mean?"

"That's just it, April," I say, slurping my coffee. "I can't tell you what I mean; I can't explain it myself. I just know that usually by now the police arrest another prisoner. Why not this time? Why a guard? And why hasn't the murder seen any ink since the first day? No follow up story? The media thrives on sensationalism. Where are the dark, bleak stories concerning life in maddening domain of Briersburg?"

April shrugs her shoulders timidly. "I don't have a clue, Dane. This is out of my ballpark."

I cut the last piece of ham and toss it to a pleading Bambino. I feel somewhat guilty for *excluding* the detail that Lafayette interrogated me, but I don't want her suspicions about me aroused again.

"Well, if you don't have to go in until six or so, then your mine today, right?"

"Right."

"We could go for a swim; the warm air won't be here much longer."

"I'd like that."

"Is your arm up to it?"

"Yeah," I dip the last morsel of egg in the yolk. "The doctor at the hospital exaggerated my stitch count so as to convince me to stay the night."

April sighs in disgust. "Doctors are nothing but phony, duplicitous, shameful, arrogant gas bags who only worry about what their country-club contemporaries think! Oh, how I just hate them all!"

"Meow," I say playfully, "I wouldn't go that far…lawyers maybe."

"Well," she smiles, "be that as it may, you are able to splash around with me and have some fun, correct?"

"Try and stop me."

Dutch Van Alstin – Murder in D Block

April bends down and kisses me, smearing egg on my face. "After you get done playing detective tonight, are you coming straight home?"

"Yeah, I'll be here. I don't promise how long it will take though. I want to use the computers and dig into some files."

"I wish you would just let it go, Dane. I mean, we're together again. Isn't that enough?"

"I can't help it," I say, "something odd is happening and I don't want it to fall down on me, or us."

"Like I said, Dane, I'm out of my league. I'll just trust you when you say everything will be okay."

"I just wish everybody else shared your faith in me, April," I say. "Because, when it comes down to brass tacks, that's where it's going to count."

CHAPTER 26

As I search for my badge this morning, I lament some that the brief, yet pleasant two days off, courtesy of Edwards, are now winding down to nothingness. To complicate matters further with Edwards, I called in sick two days in a row also. As childish as this may be, I called in sick to counteract Edwards' flex of muscle by *vacationing* me for a couple of days. He'll take my exploit as a slap in his face and hopefully I left a welt. The main reason I chose to use the computers at work after six o'clock is because I know Edwards has a either a golf club, or a scotch and water in his hand by five-thirty.

The computer search on Delgado didn't give me any pertinent information. However, Briersburg's computers are not linked with any national database. They're limited to internal information only, like trouble he has been in since entering prison, who is on his visit list, names of visitors, package contents, prison duties and things of that nature. An episode of Columbo would have turned up something very noteworthy and unique, but here in the real world nothing out of the ordinary leaped out at me over the screen.

The more notable experience was observing the robot's reaction to my presence in the computer room. They looked at me out of the corner of their beady little eyes and let their conjecture filled delusions run amok in their mind.

Dutch Van Alstin – Murder in D Block

Why him?

Why was he the first one questioned?

I heard he's doing Delgado's wife?

Is he?

Did he?

They're all thinking it. They're all saying it. None of the robots, however, are saying one word to me about anything.

Edwards has the smile of a sadist this morning in lineup. I can't decipher the reason for his pretentious demeanor. Either he has let my sick day stunt get under his thin skin, or if it's just his natural abhorrence for me in general. Whatever the reason, I am confident I ruined his breakfast.

The morning rush from the breakfast meal ends in D block. I begin locking up the top gallery as the sound of synchronized footsteps, merged with the usual jangle of keys, clatter closer to me. A heavy hand slaps me on the shoulder and grasps hold of my shirt. I snap my head around and see the arm belongs to Officer T.J. Armstrong. Standing along with Armstrong is Red Flannigan and two other guards, their names escape me at the moment. None of the four men look as though they are sanguine about their presence here with me. I have seen that look on a myriad of faces before, many times on my own. And all of those occasions have had one consistent tenet, bad news.

"My instincts have never been wrong before," Armstrong says sternly. "For the first time in my life, I truly wish they were."

One guard seizes my radio and the other seizes my key ring. Red sighs, clearly disheartened over everything that is happening. Armstrong tugs at my shirt and leads me down the stairs. I am marched past Joey, who says nothing; he doesn't even lift his head to look at me. I halt my steps at the D block entrance and look at Armstrong. "You're going to believe whatever you want to believe, Armstrong, but at least allow me a little dignity and let me walk out of here on my own. I think I've earned that much."

Armstrong peeks out of the corner of his eye at Red. Red cues Armstrong approvingly and Armstrong releases his grip on my shirt. I straighten my apparel and smooth out the wrinkles before I enter into the corridor. Red and the other two guards stay put, but Armstrong shadows me closely. York mimics my tackle of Ludlow once more as I enter his domain. "We'll see you soon, Bulldog," York says reassuringly.

Dutch Van Alstin – Murder in D Block

Armstrong and I exit the corridor gate and step into a vacant main yard. We, alone, walk across the pavement, sharing the wide-open sphere with no one but the pigeons. A handful of crushed Styrofoam coffee cups lie outside the lookout posts and observation decks, accompanied only by a few forsaken cigarette butts. The wind kicks up the dust from the veneer of gravel and mud that permeates the asphalt. As we approach the Rooney building, the vexation and calamity escapes through the corridors and galleries encompassing Briersburg.

"You'll be back, pretty boy, only as my *bitch* this time!"

"You're going to look real sweet in them orange pants, mother fucker!"

A chorus of *murderer* and *killer cop* rumble through the cellblocks in a stentorian roar of venomous rage. A rage that could only be planted, nurtured, and harvested within the stone cold walls of Briersburg.

Throngs of perturbed and uneasy looks are launched at me until Armstrong and I finally reach the main gate. He still follows me outside and into the parking lot and waits for me to drive away. I slide my key in the door and fidget with the lock.

"You never really did fit in around here, did you?" Armstrong says.

"No, I guess not," I say bitterly. "But that doesn't add up to a mountain of evidence against me as a murder."

"No, I guess it doesn't necessarily do that. But then again, we're not the District Attorney and we don't need hard evidence, just the knowledge that you crossed the line."

"What line?" I say cynically.

"There's a line, Dane," Armstrong says, "and you crossed right on over it."

"Maybe so, Armstrong, but who decides where that line is drawn to begin with?"

"That line has always been there, right down the middle between right and wrong," Armstrong shouts. "Just because you get all hot and bothered over some filly from the visit room, doesn't give you the right to cross it!"

"It also doesn't make me a murderer."

"I'd like to believe you, Dane," Armstrong says. "But to tell you the truth, you're just not worth taking the risk of me being wrong. I tried to talk to you in D block the other day and explain to you what end is up, but obviously, you chose to ignore the warnings. You're too reckless, too wild; you don't know what you get yourself into, and now, it's too late for you here. God help you when the real trouble starts. I tried to warn you, Dane. And I walk away from you a man with a clear conscious because, as God as my witness, I did try." Armstrong casually strolls back across the street and in through Briersburg's main gate, never looking back once.

Dutch Van Alstin – Murder in D Block

I slam my car door and squeal my tires as I spit loose gravel every which way. Oh, how I long for the tuna sandwich right now. Everything in my life seems to keep spinning out of control. Nothing makes sense any longer with my one-step forwards and two steps backward lifestyle. My mom, in her own way, tried to comfort me when life would turn sour: she'd always tell me things couldn't get any worse. And at this juncture in my life, I don't know how they possibly could.

The light turns red as I zoom through the intersection. I swerve my car around a corner and coast into my driveway where I am greeted with one more step backwards. Legions of flashing lights saturate my home. They're parked in my driveway, in my yard; one car is even propped up against my deck. Charging for the door, I am subdued by two uniformed police. I struggle and toil with both of them, until one of the cops thrusts their nightstick across my throat, pinning me to the ground.

"Damn it, what's going on, that's my house," I protest loudly.

"You can't go in there, pal," one cop says.

"Why? I demand to know why?"

"If your name is Augustovson Erickson, then your house is undergoing an official search."

"Why? By whom?"

"By the--"

"Never mind," I say as I calm my emotions. "I already know who."

The two cops loosen their grip slightly as they stare down at me. "If you'll relax yourself, then we'll let you go?

I nod.

They both release their grip and gingerly stand up, still facing me.

Carefully, I pull myself up from the ground and dust the debris from my pants.

"Before you ask, Mr. Erickson, yes, they have warrant."

"I wasn't going to ask," I say, still brushing grass off me. "I'm sure Lafayette pulled one out from his magic bag of papers."

I watch helplessly as the gray suits and some uniformed personnel carry boxes of evidence from my house that I didn't know existed.

"Leave me the damn kitchen sink, will ya?" I shout into the mob scene.

"Shut up," a deputy yells, "or we'll cuff you and stuff you."

"I see you watched COPS last night, huh?" I reply.

Dutch Van Alstin – Murder in D Block

"I don't like your attitude, Buck."

Buck? I think to myself. "You guys are ransacking the home of an innocent man."

"Everyone's innocent, buddy-boy, little elves commit all the crime."

I have to wonder how often I've heard the prisoners make the statement I just made and how often I have given a similar reply.

Lafayette walks out my front door and says something to one of the uniforms. He pats the uniform on the back and points in the vicinity of my living room.

"Yoo-hoo, Commandant," I say, waving at Lafayette.

Lafayette grins; not unlike Edwards did this morning. He starts walking toward me, periodically barking out orders. He saunters over to me while carrying April's nightgown. "You think everything is a joke, don't you?" Lafayette says.

"I only spy one joke around here, secret agent man."

"Your humor…well, attempt at humor, is so obviously a facade hiding your anger."

"Is that so," I say rancorously. "You can file that diagnosis under the 'who gives a shit what you think' pile."

"Wearing nighties, Dane?" Lafayette says, holding up April's nightgown.

"No, the color scheme isn't for me, but on you it would be smashing."

"You just remember that old aphorism: he who laughs last…"

"Did you find anything besides a new nighty?"

"It's a sealed investigation."

"I didn't think so."

"We'll dig something concrete up on you, pal, just watch."

"I understand. The F.B.I. is great at finding evidence in crimes they can't manage to solve on their own."

"You're lecturing me on ethics?" Lafayette says smugly.

I lean in close to Lafayette and nearly bump noses with him. "Take the nightie home, John," I say gravely. "Just don't let Mrs. F.B.I. catch you sniffing the crotch."

"If I want a woman, Dane, I don't look near the bottom of the barrel, all the good ones are on top." Lafayette leans back and spits between my feet. "But how the hell would you know that?"

We stand, toe to toe, eye to eye, and man to man.

"I'll be seeing you soon, Augustovson." Lafayette walks over to a trashcan and tosses April's nightgown on the pile. "I just assumed this was an appropriate place to put her nighty, you know, being that she's so familiar with it." Lafayette walks back to my house, still barking out orders, still flexing his authoritative muscle.

Slowly the gray suits and uniforms trickle out and I am allowed access back in my house. The term *searching* would be inappropriate for the carnage Lafayette caused. Pillage, maybe, plundering, possibly, ransacking, perhaps, but searching? Not even close!

The gray suits dumped all my fresh coffee out on to the floor. Lafayette was probably imitating a James Bond movie he saw last night and thought he'd find some hidden microfilm. The cupboard is bare. All my canned goods are strewn all around with all the labels cut off. The elbow joints on all three of my sinks have been disassembled and the mucky contents dumped on the floor. He even felt the need to remove the mantel from my fireplace.

James Bond again?

I think so.

In the corner of the kitchen is a large manila envelope, propped up against the emptied out cookie jar. Written in big, bold letters across the side is my name. I pick the envelope up off the counter and suspiciously flip it over a few times before opening it.

Inside is an 8X10 glossy photo that causes me to smile roguishly. "So that's your plan, Agent Lafayette? Okay then, if that's what you want, I'm game."

I toss the photo down on the counter and look at the smiling face of John Lafayette. He is posed in a hunting outfit underneath a fifteen-point buck, mounted in priggish fashion upon his wall.

CHAPTER 27

Morning arrives and it brings with it the cool September air. The days of drinking ice-cold beer as I wade through the splashing water are being pushed aside by days of shore side views of the illustrious wonders of the fall season. Soon I will sit, wrapped in an old tattered sweatshirt, holding countless memories to only the one who wears it, and will be partaking in a steaming cup of hot coffee on my dock. The one living being, whose altruistic nature cannot be impugned, will romp through the yard and will bark at, and chase, the falling leaves. Only then will I be accepting at the changing of the guard.

Because summer's tour is dwindling is the reason April gives to sample one last morsel of summer in the form of a picnic. Picnics are enjoyable and I try to tell myself that as I drive to pick April up from her house. But I've never quite reasoned out to my satisfaction the enjoyment of packing food into a basket, and then, hauling that basket to another location and eating the food there, all the while, contending with insects. However, I need to stop letting the pragmatic aspects of my character beat up on the romantic side all the time. Being with April as we're sprawled out on a blanket, watching the sunset, has to be worth carting a few sandwiches to and from.

She waits outside in her apartment with a two bags of food in her hand. I receive a quick kiss as she slides in my front seat and tosses the goodies on the floor.

Dutch Van Alstin – Murder in D Block

"Hello, beautiful," I say buoyantly.

"Hello to you, too, handsome Harold." She replies.

I recall an old abandoned park that hasn't been host too many picnics in recent times. The park is off a secondary road, which was once the main road, near the riverbank. There are chewed up old picnic tables and two pieces of worn out playground equipment still standing. The grill was once filled with sizzling charcoals, cooking up rows of hotdogs by beer-bellied chefs. Now it sits with a gaping rust hole through the coal catcher and smashed glass and debris spread out along the ground.

April and I clasp hands and interlock our fingers as we roam the grounds, passing an antiquated backstop circuitously around two boarded up dugouts. The dugouts are glutted with weeds and scattering shrubs protruding in and around the structures.

Only the spirits of years gone by can still hear the clamor of young boys donned in button up wool uniforms with wide striped stirrups riding high on their legs. Now the obsolescent structures are called home by nesting pigeons vying for space among the rodents and insects. The bedraggled black scoreboard still has the numeral "3" hanging from the bottom of the fourth inning. The metal number plate is the last recognizable sign that the shabby steel mass was once a scoreboard. The *Teem* soda label spread across the top of the board is rotted and red from the corrosion. The board's contemporary function is limited to target practice for BB guns and a way to promulgate which girls in the neighborhood are *sluts* and who, besides Kilroy, was here. The dirt-covered infield that had those same clamorous boys sliding into home plate amid the roars and cheers of their parents now is infested with prolific plants and crabgrass, hiding any recognizable remnant of the diamond.

Down farther along the riverbank, I see four boys hurling rocks at the seagulls and pigeons. One boy was just pushed to the ground by another boy. The other two boys just laugh.

We continue our meandering walk, talking of nothing specific, the trees, last night's reruns, the squeak in my kitchen cupboard. Finally, the conversation takes an abrupt, solemn turn toward the serious.

"April," I stop and pull on her hand to halt her as well. "I need to tell you something."

Like most women, she grows distressed, expecting calamitous news. "Oh, no, what's the matter?"

"Remember when I mentioned that the A.W. found out about us?"

"Yes."

Dutch Van Alstin – Murder in D Block

"Well," I sigh, "he locked me out today."

"Locked out?" April says, seemingly perplexed by the guard jargon.

"*Locked out* is a euphemism for suspended."

"Oh, no," April releases her hold on my hand. "I feel so terrible, Dane. I've been exactly been a rabbit's foot in your pocket."

"A rabbit can't do for me what you've done," I say, walking up behind her and rubbing her shoulders.

"You know what, Dane?"

"What?"

April rotates around quickly and takes hold of both my hands. "Consider this a blessing in disguise."

"It's one hell of a disguise."

"No, I mean it; you never liked working at that hellhole anyway. And besides that, you just don't fit in with those guys you work with; you're a different type of person all together."

I walk backward, reaching behind me for the swing. I plunk myself down and begin to sway slightly. "Your point has some merit," I say. "To me, Briersburg has an aura of death around it, waiting to suck up the next person. I am tired of the ghosts I see every day, figuratively of course, but death and dying either way. I don't know if you heard, but recently we had a guard get killed in D block? I don't know if you remember him, but he threw a fit one day in the visit room when you were there."

"Yeah, I do," April nods her head slightly. "He was mad at Mrs. Hopewell. I guess he fell, or jumped, or something?"

"Everyone I have told this to thinks I'm crazy, but I think he was pushed."

"Why? It sounds to me like it was just some unfortunate accident?"

"I've been snooping around a bit and some pieces just don't fit into place."

April laughs. "You're a regular Charlie Chan. But, Dane, you need to start relaxing and not delving into every little oddity that comes your way. Why don't you just focus your life in a new direction. The word *us* comes to mind."

"I know, April. It's the first thought on my mind, too." I say with a smile. "I've just always had a curious mind and when something doesn't make sense, I have to make sense of it."

"Remember what happened to the cat?"

"I'm no cat," I say, as I begin swinging harder. "And a cat didn't drive all the way out to Mayfield the other day, no cat is that curious."

Dutch Van Alstin – Murder in D Block

"Mayfield? What's way out there?"

"Donny, the guard's name, was apparently a few clowns short of a circus. So naturally Briersburg's Cracker Jack ESO squad referred him to some quack named Doctor Baltz without ever checking his credentials. This wannabe doctor was probably too stupid for medical school so he thought he'd play with trained rats. He supposedly had an office in Mayfield, but when I got there, he was long gone."

"Dane," April says pensively, "I don't think that's fair that you refer to people who see a psychiatrist as *trained rats*. There are people with serious abnormalities and a psychiatrist is just as essential to the health industry as medical doctors. Because they don't treat tangible diseases, doesn't mean they don't exist."

"I, uh...was just...babbling. I didn't mean to, um, imply or infer, that a person who needs, uh, *assistance*, are less of a person. I'm sorry, if you, at a point in your life, needed to see someone, I know your life has been tumult from the get go, and, I know, I just mean, well, this quack that gave Donny the shaft--"

"Never mind, Dane," she says with a poignant smile, "I'm just a little too sensitive as well."

"I really am sorry."

She flings her hand at me casually. "To hell with it, don't give it a second thought. I don't want to ruin the rest of the night."

The sun descends quickly and the last sliver of red takes the last trace of warmth. April zips her jacket, wraps her arms around herself, and shivers. We both gaze up at an inchoate view of the moon, as the darkening skies begin to weigh in heavily. April, nearly in a catatonic state, fixates her sights on the moon. "It really is a beautiful sight, you know?"

"Yeah, it is."

"Mother Nature, you know, I mean how does she do it? How does that ball of rock that weighs enough to crush half our country float so majestically in the air?"

"I don't know."

"This may sound silly, but at night, Dane, I sometimes sit for hours out on the porch and just stare at it." She sighs. "When I was just a little girl, my daddy and I use to watch the moon and he'd tell me that the moon was a big diamond and someday, when I was bigger, I'd own it. I know he meant symbolically, but I still can't help but have this romantic childhood dream I'll own it still."

"Dreams are the root of hope."

Dutch Van Alstin – Murder in D Block

"Do you ever dream, Dane? I mean, dream of just more than the analytical world will allow you to dream?"

"We all do, somewhat," I say. "I just can't let the dream be my master."

"You see what I mean?" April laughs.

"What?"

"How many of those turnkeys you work with know the works of Rudyard Kipling?"

Silence invades our realm again. April grows chillier as she rubs her arms briskly, still swaying rhythmically on the swing along side of me. "What is it you really want to do, Dane? I mean, really? Who do you want to be? What are your dreams? I know you must have them, too?"

"Yeah, I guess I do."

"Share them with me, Dane, and make them our dreams also."

"I, I'm just not..." I rub my thumbs and sigh, "I just am not good at talking like this, April. I'm sorry; it's just another flaw in my already imperfect character. I've never been an open person to anyone."

"But we're not just *anyone*, Dane, and I'm not just anyone either. Don't be afraid to be a little sensitive around me."

"That's not the problem, April," I say, "I'm just a private person. I don't like putting myself out there."

"If we are considering a life together, Dane, than we need to feel comfortable around each other all the time and in any situation."

April and I continue swinging and she broaches the subject no more.

"I..."

April sprouts a smile on her face.

"I...guess, I, always wanted to load my truck with all the clothes and accessories I could fit and move south to some rural area not even a cartographer could find. Then I'd buy an inn or an old general store where people pay each other with chickens and pies and locked doors are something illusive to the thoughts of the townspeople. Besides running the store or inn, I'd like to write poems and short stories about the town and the people. People who remember each other's birthday and grandparents, where Briersburg is miles away with all its upheaval and anarchy and death in some other world. But, I am a realist, not a romantic. And I know nirvana doesn't exist, so I'd have to ask myself if such a town would exist, too?"

"Dane," she says softly, "that sounds like a lot of people's dream. But I think out of all the others, you can seek out such a town, and when you do, I'll be there with you."

I stare into her deep, green eyes and search for the person within her. "In my thirty some odd years, April, nobody has ever gotten me to speak of that. You got some power over me no other human has ever possessed."

"Dane, I feel good about being here with a guy like you. I'm glad you were locked out today, you just don't fit in with all those other guys."

I lapse in speech momentarily and absorb her words. April's statement speaks volumes into what I would like to believe too, but in my heart of hearts, I know I can't. "No, April," I sigh, "at one time you may have been correct. But the truth is, I'm no different and I realize that now."

"Oh you are," she says emphatically. "You have a warm, sensitive side that most men are afraid to let out of themselves."

"At one time, conceivably, what you said may have been true. But I have grown just as hardened and bitter as the rest of the guards.

April looks over at me inquisitively. "I just can't accept that, Dane."

"Let me tell you a story," I say, blowing warm air in my hands. "Two Christmases ago, I was reading the paper and I came across a story of an eleven year old boy killed in a car wreck five days before Christmas. His dad was driving and the car skidded off an icy road and the boy died instantly." I take a deep breath and rub my hands for warmth. "Anyway, his dad was trapped in the car for an hour, next to his dead son before help arrived."

"That is really very sad, Dane."

"Yeah, I know," I nod my head slightly. "As I read the story more, there was a picture of the boy, smiling, without a care in the world. In the story was how he played in a local hockey league and knowing some of those kids who play in that league, I wondered if any of them knew this boy. I wondered how good of a player he was and I thought about how his father must be beside himself with guilt for the rest of his life, and every Christmas only being a catalyst for that guilt from now on. The fact Christmas was near made it worse. I couldn't help but think about all the presents under the tree that wouldn't be opened by anyone. I wager those presents are still in a closet somewhere. I looked at the picture one more time and I just started crying uncontrollably like baby."

"Oh, Dane, that is so sad, really. But you just made my point don't you see? You are truly a caring, sensitive guy."

"No," I shake my head rabidly, "you didn't hear the rest of it. For months after that, I couldn't drive by the ice rink without breaking into tears again. Certain places or words or things would just bring the whole image back to me again and again."

"Dane, you're still giving my argument credence. I don't understand where you're going with this?"

I stretch my neck back and peer up at the night sky, forgoing any sight of the moon. "My point is this, April," I say faintly, "now; I don't even remember his name."

"Dane, that doesn't mean anything."

"It means more than you think, April. When Donny died all I could think of is how a few years back I would have tried to befriend him more. And now I never gave him a second thought."

"It's not your fault Donny died."

"But in a roundabout way, April, I may be responsible. Assume it was a suicide, maybe if he had a friend in Briersburg he wouldn't have had the helpless feeling."

April grabs my hand and rubs my palm with her thumb. "People are all unique, Dane. We all have demons in our psyche that need to be exercised and sometimes people exercise those demons in destructive ways that are out of anyone's control. This Donny was obviously disturbed or he wouldn't have been under psychiatric care. Trying to deny who and what you are is a destructive mechanism in the mind. He would have been dead any way you look at it and you couldn't do anything to stop it, or, most importantly, Dane, there is nothing you can do about it now. You're delving in too deep to an accident because you feel guilty and you're creating a situation that doesn't exist. Leave it alone, Dane." She says, tapping my hand.

"That's no answer, April."

"Dane," she sighs, "I've come to two inescapable conclusions in life. One is that there is a God and number two," she rubs my face and smiles sedately. "I'm not Him."

I secrete a token chuckle. "Neither am I? Is that what you're saying, April?"

"Yeah...in a way," she says with a smile, "but you're my savior, isn't that enough?"

CHAPTER 28

Bambino's slurping tongue wets my ears and my cheek. The alarm clock that once used to wake me has difficulty proving its worth since I now have nowhere to go. Bambino continues to nudge my arm in an attempt to make me get out of my nice, soft, cozy bed. My ignoring his pleas is unwelcome and he vociferates his objections with a loud, shrilled barking.

"Shut up, I have no place to go, let me sleep," I shout to him as if he woke this morning understanding English. Bambino's tenacity can only be interpreted one possible way; he needs to go to piss in the front bush that is no longer there. I falter some as I get out of bed. Looking around the house for April only yields a letter propped up against the percolator.

April writes that she didn't want to wake me this morning so she just took my car to work. Her taking my car is all well and good, but that leaves me with my old, beat up truck that I only use to haul garbage to the dump. Perhaps one day, I'll leave the truck there as well. Upon opening the door, Bambino tears outside like a shot, nearly running into the neighbor's mailbox. I run my fingers through my gnarled hair believing somehow that it will work as well as a comb.

The paper has no ink dedicated to the murder again nor does the local news sites, fortunately though that includes no news of my home being ransacked. The percolator sits empty triggering my memory about Lafayette's search for a secret decoder ring. My only one true *addiction,* i.e., coffee, compels me to slide an old pair of slippers on my feet and brave the

Dutch Van Alstin – Murder in D Block

perils of my truck for a short-lived drive to the corner store.

The old bomb of a truck cranks slowly but the motor generates enough fire to start the archaic engine amid a cloud of black smoke. The truck's frame shakes so severely that the last few specks of the dull brown paint fall to the ground. With a few more pings and rattles, the outmoded relic arrives at the store.

I grab the first can of coffee I see off the shelf and wait in the checkout line. A tap on my shoulder from behind draws my attention away from the chagrin I feel when I see the brand name of the coffee, *"Drink Me!" Fresh Coffee From The Fields of Latin!*

"Hello, Dane," a friendly voice says to me. I spin my neck around and am greeted by Ann Shelby, a nurse from Briersburg.

"Hi, Ann," I reply, trying to straighten my rumpled hair.

"I haven't seen you in a while, Dane."

"Nor will you for a while, I'm afraid."

Ann grows bewildered. "Why? What happened to you?"

"I see Briersburg's grapevine hasn't caught up with you," I say, handing the cashier a ten-dollar bill. "I was locked-out yesterday."

"Oh, my" she says sympathetically, "no, I hadn't heard."

The cashier holds out her hand. "I need twenty-three more cents, sir."

"You're joking," I retort, holding a nine ounce can.

"Sorry," the young cashier says, slightly embarrassed.

"Here, Dane," Ann reaches in her purse and begins rummaging for change.

"No, no, that's nice of you, but I'm fine." I slide a quarter along the register.

"Golly, Dane, I hope your suspension didn't stem from that Ludlow man you…I mean, who was bruised up the other day, because the A.W. inquired about him to me?"

"Oh he did, did he?"

"Yes, and that Ludlow was pretty banged up along his neck and back. But I remember what you did for me when that Spanky fellow kept exposing himself to me, so I told the A.W. he didn't have a scratch."

"Ann," I exclaim with a mixture of gratitude and concern, "you can get fired for falsifying records."

"Oh, pish-posh, you stuck your neck out for me, why can't I reciprocate?"

"I am truly obliged, Ann, but the A.W.'s scandalous witch hunts don't end because he hits a road block. He managed to find another reason."

Dutch Van Alstin – Murder in D Block

"That Ludlow fellow was nothing compared to what those guards did to that man who sliced you."

"Hopwah?"

"That's him," she says," they absolutely beat the tar out of that man. I'm talking broken femur, broken pelvis, fractured skull, and three broken ribs, not to mention a myriad of cuts and bruises."

"Wow, I had no idea they beat him that badly. I guess I'll sit by my mailbox and wait for that lawsuit to reveal itself."

"From Hopwah?" she says incredulously, "that thumping was like a trip to Hawaii for him."

"He enjoys pain?" I say sarcastically.

"Yes, he does. Mr. Hopwah is a true blue masochist, and I don't mean that in an axiomatic tone either. That man thrives on physical pain; he receives a sexual thrill from injury. What your cohorts did to him was akin to locking you in the Playboy mansion, alone, for a year."

"You have got to be kidding?" I say with obvious incredulity

"No, Hopwah was orgasmic during the beating. I'm telling you, the man is a sicko."

"Does suicide coincide with that behavior?"

"Huh, suicide? No, why do you ask?"

"I recall him having rope marks around his neck in D block."

"He is also into *auto-eroticism*. Are you aware of what that is?"

"Yeah, I think so, it's where a man ties rope around his neck until he nearly suffocates for arousal purposes?"

"You got it; he's a sick man, Dane."

"And I thought I had troubles."

"I am sorry for your troubles, Dane."

"You needn't be."

"But you're not missing much anyway. We are in the beginnings of a tuberculosis epidemic and I've been giving tests by the hundreds."

"Like this?" I say, showing her the prickly scar under my tattoo.

"Heavens no, we don't use the Tine test anymore. How old are you?"

"I'm thirty-one."

"Oh, then I bet you received one of the last tests ever given. Anyone younger than you doesn't have that scar anymore. We now use a............"

Dutch Van Alstin – Murder in D Block

My lack of interest causes Ann's voice to fade away. I have always liked Ann Shelby very much. She is one of the few sensible voices in Briersburg. She is smart, well mannered, and very attractive. However, she is also loquacious and just plain gabby. I stand before her with a pair of slippers, an old sweatshirt bearing a faded emblem of *St Alexandria High Class of '01,* and a head of hair that looks as though an eggbeater combed it. Still she besets me with a boring dissertation on TB, causes, effects, testing, treatments, and other ho-hum details.

After a few *uh-huhs* and a couple of nods of my head, I return home with my very expensive coffee.

The last drop perks in the pot and a loud, brusque knock is levied at my front door. I slide the curtain back and catch sight of John Lafayette on my porch. He is apparently attempting a new approach of casualness with me. He is donned in blue jeans and a gray, cardigan sweater over top a white dress shirt.

Reluctantly I open the door, look Lafayette up and down, and sit on my couch. I leave the door open, not officially inviting him inside.

"May I come in?" he says cordially.

"If I say no, will you go away?"

Lafayette walks in and looks around the room. "Nice place, Dane."

"Ah, are we forgetting you were here yesterday ripping the place apart? Does that ring any bells in that *room for rent* brain of yours?"

Lafayette scorches his nose, hiding a smirk of embarrassment. "Look, Dane, we got off on the wrong foot."

"*Dane?*" Are we buddies now? Would you like a cup of coffee to celebrate our new found friendship...John?"

"Thanks, I would."

"Goody, McDonalds is open and the coffee is good and fresh."

Lafayette emits a large sigh of disgust and helps himself to my coffee.

"I had to buy that fresh this morning, you know?" I say from my living room. "Your lackeys dumped all mine out on the floor. By the way, did you find the microfilm, Mr. Bond?"

"No warming up in the bullpen, huh Dane? Just coming right out to the mound and hurling the hard stuff?"

Bambino finally notices Lafayette and utters a low growl as Lafayette sits on my couch. "Is that dog friendly?" He asks.

"Please don't tell me a big, tough G-man like you is afraid of a little pooch?"

Dutch Van Alstin – Murder in D Block

"No, but I just want to sit and relax and talk with you."

"I'll tell you what he likes, John: Just spread some bacon grease along your throat and he'll be your friend and won't bother you. Really, I mean it! Just try it."

"May we can the hostility and your rank attempts at satire, and just talk?"

"Certainly, John," I say, gulping my coffee. "Or do you prefer *Jack* as Kennedy did?"

"John is fine."

"John it is," I toast my mug to him and sip the coffee again.

"You're a bit hostile this morning?" Lafayette says, pinching his thumb and forefinger together.

"Oh, excuse me if I seem a bit upset at the fact I have lost my job, my home, and I'm being hounded by a slapstick F.B.I. man for a murder I know less about then he does. So if I sound a trifle bit curt, brusque or churlish, then you'll have to forgive me."

"Look at from my side," Lafayette says, setting his coffee on my table. "I got a dead prisoner and the guy who was having an illicit affair with his wife is a prison guard in the very cell block he is murdered in. I just can't get passed that, Dane."

"Are you just hell bent on getting me for some reason? Was Delgado a golfing partner of yours at one time? Why are you so obsessed with the death of some slug?"

"Delgado was last counted at noon and--"

"Hold it; hold it," I interject, "answer me. What is your angle here?"

"My angle?" He says verbosely.

"Yes, John, your angle. Now stop stalling and answer me."

Lafayette sips his coffee and forges a cough. "Well, there's a new civil rights law enacted by congress concerning--"

"Racism? You're kidding, right? You think Delgado was killed because of racial reasons?"

"Are you going to tell me there aren't any racist guards?"

"I'm telling you a sundry of guards strip off their white hood and robe before they clock in, but that makes them empty-headed, not killers."

"Since when does being a racist exclude anyone from murder?"

I slam my mug on the table, spilling my coffee on the table. "Since you just said he was murdered because of a love triangle, now stop the bullshit!"

"What bullshit?"

"The reason you're here is bullshit. You're not here because of some bogus civil rights

Dutch Van Alstin – Murder in D Block

law, now start talking?"

"May I continue?" Lafayette says placidly.

"By all means."

"Delgado was last counted at noon, and by 11:30 that night, he was dead."

"Briersburg has a five o'clock count too, spy boy."

"That's a little touchy," Lafayette says. He helps himself to another cup of coffee and this time, stirs in some sugar and cream.

"Touchy?"

"Yes, you see, Delgado was in the toilet during the five o'clock count at one of the upholstery shops and the guard there never actually saw Delgado. The guard only heard his voice."

"How the hell was Delgado counted then?"

"The guard in the upholstery shop walked up to the toilet and said a voice called out to him and said, *'I'm here'*."

"A living, breathing body."

"Huh?"

"In the academy, not Quantico," I stipulate. Lafayette rolls his eyes. "We were told that you only count a living, breathing body. You don't officially count a voice, a proxy, or a hand waving high atop the gallery. Only a living, breathing body was to be counted. They drove that point in our head from day one."

"This guy didn't."

"Who was it?"

"I can't tell you off the top of my head, I need my notebook."

"I can't believe you got whoever it was to admit he didn't count Delgado. Screwing up the count is a social faux pas behind the walls."

"This guy wasn't the brightest star in the sky. I think he fell out of a stupid tree and managed to hit every branch."

"That doesn't narrow it down much. That could be any of them."

"Yeah, but he was...McPherson," Lafayette blurts, "Randy McPherson."

"Mack?" I say inquiringly.

"Does that ring any bells?"

"No, not really, he is the leader of the idiot movement though."

"Well, anyway, Delgado may have been dead well before five o'clock."

Dutch Van Alstin – Murder in D Block

"Whereas he came in contact with hundreds of convicted felons, several of which are murderers, and yet here you sit, in my living room, sipping my coffee."

Lafayette swallows the last of his coffee and leans back and props his feet up on my table. "I need to get to the bottom of things here, Dane."

"Why? Do you have a pay raise riding on it?"

"Dane," Lafayette leans forward, "let me help you."

"I'm touched, John, really very touched at your philanthropic concern for my well-being." I slide my mug across the mahogany, bumping his foot off my table.

"You don't when to quit, do you? Let me tell you, mister, this is serious, very, very serious." Lafayette says, jamming his finger into his palm.

"Let me tell, *you,* Mr. G-man: you have tried intimidating on my turf with your underlings surrounding you. You've plundered my home in some ambiguous search for evidence that doesn't exist. And now you show up here, dressed like Mr. Rogers, and are trying the *'my buddy'* routine. And you have the nerve to want me to cooperate?"

"Do you know why I know you're involved in the murder?"

"Tell me, I forgot."

"Because that little diatribe you just delivered sounds like something one of those prisoners you hold in so much disdain would say. You, sonny boy, bullshit your words like common criminal."

I stir my empty cup with my finger and remain silent.

"Do you want to help me or not?" Lafayette says.

"You're barking up the wrong tree here, Lafayette. I didn't have anything to do with Delgado's death."

"Don't you think I want to believe you? Do you think I take comfort in believing a fellow law-enforcement officer has turned?"

I laugh caustically. "How did I go from a guy who opens and closes doors all day to a, if my quote you, *a fellow law enforcement officer?"*

"I apologize for that comment, Dane, but you were smacking me around pretty good that day, too. I know you don't know why we don't pursue a prisoner, but our sources say it was a blue shirt."

"Did your source formally lock on my gallery and make yummy tuna turnovers?"

"I can't reveal details of an ongoing investigation."

"Apparently not," I say, "I haven't seen a word about it in any news outlets. But I still

Dutch Van Alstin – Murder in D Block

can't help envisioning my former porter sitting in some cushy federal cell, watching round the clock TV and eating all the taco dip and salsa to his heart desires."

"Be that is at may, Dane, our sources say the murderer was a guard and you're the only guard who was doing his wife."

"That is really crude," I say. "There is a lot more than *doing her* as your schoolboy lingo puts it."

"Doing?"

"Huh?"

"Doing, you said '*doing*'. I thought there was a schism in the relationship?"

"Oh, please, as if you didn't know. You probably have my bedroom bugged as part of the N.S.A. That'll make some erogenous nights for you and Mrs. F.B.I. to listen to."

"The fact she is, shall I say, more than just a concubine to you, makes my situation more problematic."

"I'm getting hungry, Lafayette," I say, looking up at the clock. "So if there's nothing else?" I motion toward the door.

"No, not unless you have something to add?"

"Yes I do, why don't you--" I stop and pause. "I'm hungry."

"Go ahead," Lafayette waves his hands.

"No," I groan, "I have nothing more to say."

"Are you sure?"

I grab each side of my head and squeeze my eyes closed. "Yes, yes, I'm sure. Just get out, please."

"Okay, Dane," Lafayette says, handing me his card. "If you want to talk, call me." Lafayette walks down my sidewalk and gets in his car. I wait until I see him drive off down the road and out of my sight.

"What the hell am I doing?" I say aloud. "Remember Columbo, Dane. Remember Columbo."

CHAPTER 29

Another fork is stacked in my already overflowing sink of dirty dishes. April has commandeered my car once again leaving me with my truck. Customarily what I like to do when I need to put my thoughts in focus is drive my car and listen to some music. Since April makes that synopsis unworkable, I will settle for the rhythmic backfiring of my truck and fire and brimstone A.M. radio.

I arouse the sleeping motor with the key and watch helplessly as the exhaust fumes grow thick around me, sending me into a coughing spasm. The radio picks up two stations clear enough for me to listen. One show promulgates the philosophy of Watergate burglar/ex-convict, G. Gordon Liddy as he verbally berates the intelligence of prison guards. The other show consists of a discussion concerning the proper care and planting of tulips.

Tulips are out of season anyway.

To every door, there is a key. A horribly stodgy cliché I admit, but the cliché matches my thoughts at the moment.

Delgado is the *door* to all my recent woes.

Who is he?

Where did he come from?

Where do I start?

Dutch Van Alstin – Murder in D Block

I have a copy of the information from the computer at work concerning his prison career. That information was minimal, I agree, but little information is stronger than no information. Before I proceed with anymore digging into facts, I need two things.

One: a picture of Delgado...picture? That's what has been eating at my insides lately. That damn picture I discovered the first night I spent with April. I don't mean because she hid the picture on me, although that didn't warm the cockles of heart, but who was, or wasn't, in the photo is what bothers me. That particular picture was taken during one of Briersburg's many family festivals. April was family. Where was she?

Mother?

Father?

Sister?

Brother?

Any trace of Delgado lineage anywhere?

Do any of these keys fit? It doesn't emerge as a profound discovery, but perhaps it is a beginning. For now, the wrong puzzle piece will work better than a nonexistent puzzle piece.

Again, another bad cliché. My dad was full of them.

I drive by Briersburg and childishly spit on Edwards' car. Certainly, my intention to drive into town was not to lay a *hocker* on Edwards' Cadillac, but since I was passing by anyway?

The time has arrived for my mom to be told about April and how serious we're getting. Besides the onslaught of personal questions she will levy at me, her first request will be to see a picture of April. Mom is one of these people who profess to be an amateur clairvoyant and is able to judge people's character by their appearances. The clairvoyance yarn usually flows out of mom after she and my Aunt are finished *testing* certain wines in conjunction with their duties as caterers.

After making arrangements at a local photography shop for a formal photo, my next stop is at a jeweler. *Compass Jewelry* is adjacent to the photographer's shop. I inquired of the clerk for the reason for the name Compass. The answer was that the owner always *points* his customers in the proper direction.

There is another jeweler located uptown a few blocks from my initial staring point. The rings were superlative, but the prices ranged from very expensive to WOW$$$$! The clerk showed me a *special* collection of rings for people with paltry assets and a meager cash flow, i.e., guys like me. He had a nice array of repossessed rings and all with negotiable prices.

The door's security buzzer sounds alerting the clerk someone has entered. The whirring sound is loud and annoying, causing me to turn my head to the door. If Elvis walked in arm and arm with Big Foot, I' think I'd be less surprised than what I actually do witness. Mack swaggers up to the counter with a glamorous young lady on his arm.

"Dane?" He says surprisingly.

I extend my hand out to him as I give his lady friend a look-see. Mack grabs my hand with both of his and gives me it a boisterous shake. "How the hell are you?" He says.

"I'm glad someone from Briersburg is speaking to me."

"Ah, fuck that joint," Mack bellows. The store clerk lowers his glasses and glares at Mack disapprovingly.

"My sentiments exactly," I reply.

"No, I really mean it."

"So do I, Mack."

"No, no, no, not the way you're thinking," Mack pulls out a cigarette and fumbles for a lighter.

"There's no smoking in the store, sir," the clerk says.

"Stick your store policy," Mack remarks, "I just MIGHT be buying something."

The clerk looks covetously at the wad of cash Mack waves around in the air. "Ah, yes, but if you light a cigarette in here, the sprinkler system will activate, so if you don't mind?" The clerk points at the door.

"That's more like it," Mack says as he walks out the door.

I follow Mack outside and his lady friend brushes against my backside while walking out behind me.

Mack fires up his cigarette and inhales so hard that I can see his cheekbones. He hands a cigarette to his lady friend. She smiles at him and lights it.

Mack's playmate is taller than he is, at least by an inch. Her hair is long and scattering, and the reddish flow progresses past her waist. She has a petit face she covers with a massive amount of make-up that seems to have been applied professionally. Her lime green dress *V's* downward in front, intentionally exposing her large, and recently purchased, bosoms. In each ear she sports a long chain affixed to a charm in the shape of an eagle's talon. One ear is home to several pierces and one hole is filled with a diamond stud.

She hits off her cigarette and blows the smoke upward, stretching her neck demonstrably.

"What are talking about, Mack? What's going on in Briersburg?"

Dutch Van Alstin – Murder in D Block

"I told 'em to shove their job up their ass and tossed 'em my tin." Mack laughs amongst a cloud of blue smoke.

"You quit?"

"Damn straight, fuck 'em, I got better plans anyhow?"

"Good for you, what are they?"

"Wendy and I are heading out west."

"Hello, Wendy," I say politely.

"Oh, yeah," Mack says mundanely, "Wendy, Dane, Dane, Wendy."

"Hello again, Wendy."

She responds by raising her eyebrows at me a few times.

"West, huh?" I say, turning back toward Mack.

"Yep," Mack hits his cigarette again. "I got a chance to be co-owner of a motorcycle shop with Wendy's cousin."

"Good for you, Mack. By the way, how long have you two…" I scurry my finger by the both of them.

"Three days," Mack boasts as he throws his arm around her shoulder.

"I see."

"What brings you to the jewelry store, Dane?" Mack says.

"Uh, mother's day gift?"

"For your mom?"

"Yeah, that's the general idea."

A disconcerted countenance crosses over Mack. "Mother's day is in May, this September?"

"Mother's day is in September in Minnesota."

"Oh," he says if that were common knowledge for everyone.

"Out of curiosity, Mack, any news about the murder?"

"I thought you did it?" Mack says with a laugh.

"Well, you know the rumor mill?" I say.

"I'm just fucking around; I know you didn't do it. But that's the scuttlebutt." Mack takes another long drag of his cigarette and coughs as he exhales. "Who cares who done it anyway? I mean, there's one less mouth to feed, that's my opinion."

"That's one way to look at it."

"The whole place is in chaos, that's the biggest reason why I quit."

Dutch Van Alstin – Murder in D Block

"Meaning?"

"For one thing, they went around and tore into every guard's locker looking for something."

"Looking for what?"

"Anything," Mack takes his last puff of his cigarette and crushes it into the sidewalk. "Anything they could get their grimy little hands on and when I saw all my shit thrown all over the place, that when I says enough was enough. I'd already had some dickhead F.B.I. agent hounding me about a count slip I made. He insisted that Delgado was dead by three o'clock and I couldn't have counted him at five."

"How does this F.B.I. guy know that?"

"The autopsy said Delgado's time of death was between noon and three and this F.B.I. asshole was set on saying the same thing."

"You sound sure Delgado was alive at five o'clock?"

"Damn straight."

"You're positive?"

"Does a bear shit in the woods?" Mack declares, tossing his arms out in the air.

"I guess he'd have to."

Mack pulls another cigarette out of his shirt pocket and taps the tip against his palm.

"Randall," Wendy says, yanking the cigarette from his hand, "you're supposed to be cutting down on these?"

"Give that back to me," he says, snatching it back out of her hand.

"Mack, you're telling me Delgado was definitely alive at five o'clock?" I say.

"I opened the toilet door for him personally just a few minutes before I counted."

"Couldn't he have been murdered inside right afterwards?"

"And his dead ass carcass carried five hundred yards through four security gates, six checkpoints, and then carried to the top of D block and dumped?"

"You got me there," I say, slightly embarrassed.

"I'll tell you the way it happened from the time I let Delgado in the bathroom. I didn't see Delgado when I counted so I banged on the bathroom door and said: 'hey taco boy! Are you in there'?"

Wendy slaps Mack on the arm and chortles, "Oh, Randall."

"Anyway, Delgado said back to me: 'yeah, be right out in a minute'."

"Did he come right out?"

"It was five o'clock, I went home! I ain't waiting to see if some spick is done in the crapper."

"I see. Anyway, nothing personal here, but why did you admit to Lafayette you never saw Delgado's face?"

"How'd you know this F.B.I. guy's name?" Mack says, squinting his eyes.

"Uh, I saw his name tag."

"Oh," Mack nods his head. "Anyway, this Lafayette character tells me the security cameras were on me at about five minutes before five with a count slip in my hand--"

"Cameras?"

"Yeah, I guess there are cameras in the upholstery shop."

"No," I shake my head, "there aren't any cameras in there at all."

"What?" Mack says in astonishment.

"Don't feel bad, it's an old ploy."

"What is?"

"For investigators to claim they have a recording, or a picture, or some type of irrefutable evidence to counter your story to check its validity. Lafayette, well…tricked you."

"That fucking pig."

"That's the guy."

"It don't matter though, because even if I didn't see Delgado at five, I seen him five minutes before when I let him in the shithouse and you can take that to the trunk!"

"Bank."

"Huh?"

"Bank," I say, correcting him. "The adage is: you can take that to the *bank*, not trunk."

"Whatever! All I know is that I saw the guy five minutes before the five o'clock count and then I went home."

"Okay, Mack, I don't doubt you for a minute man, really," I say, extending my hand again. "You take good care of yourself and I wish you all the finest out west with your motorcycle shop."

"Damn straight," Mack exclaims, "gonna call it *Randy's Motorcycle Shop*."

"Very creative," I say as I begin walking away. "By the way, Mack, what brand of motorcycles are you selling?"

Mack scratches his ear and looks over at Wendy, and then back toward me. "Uh, I'm not sure."

Dutch Van Alstin – Murder in D Block

CHAPTER   30

The produce section doesn't have any melons without my fingerprints all over it. After finally discovering a fresh melon, I rummage through the lettuce bin searching for the perfect green, leafy head. My grocery cart is full to compensate for my cupboards being empty.

I rush back to my cottage where I throw a rudimentary supper together as quickly as I can. The name "Chicken *ala'* Dane" is bestowed upon a few pieces of breasts with some barbecue sauce spread evenly across and grilled to perfection, or whenever the timer buzzes on my new outdoor hibachi. The chicken sizzles and the sauce drips on to the hot coals, sending smoke into my face. I wave it away with a perforated spatula in hopes somehow it will still be effective. Some melted cheese and milk are boiled and dumped into a tub of macaroni and presented with the title of "Mother Erickson's old fashioned macaroni casserole." A few pieces of toasted breadcrumbs are spread evenly across the casserole dish to give it that *down home* semblance.

Tires squeal around the corner near my driveway. April has the top down on my convertible and is moving up the driveway at a record pace. The weather is not overtly warm out today, but since I've managed to get that convertible top repaired, I can't convince April to leave it up for a minute.

After a quick peck on the lips, she walks in sniffing her nose like a bloodhound.   "What is that enchanting aroma?"

"Chicken *ala'* Dane and Mother Erickson's old fashioned macaroni casserole."

"Barbecued chicken and macaroni and cheese?"

"It sounded better when I said it."

April drapes her around me and drops her body downward, dangling her body from my neck. "As long as you're the cook, I don't care what it's called."

"Do you get the feeling our gender roles have been reversed?" I say, sporting an oven mitt on my hand.

"Hell no, it's the 21st century," April says, stripping off her coat.

I have always wondered why the phrase: *it's the 21st century* explains everything in a nice neat package.

"Any coffee, Hon?" She says, rubbing her palms together.

"In the pot, fresh too."

April pours herself a cup and sips it slowly. "Ooh that feels good," she sips again and licks her lips. "I needed that burst of heat."

"I have to get out on the porch in that smoke factory and locate my chicken."

"I'm jumping in the shower and wrapping myself in a quilt."

"Uh…no you're not I'm afraid."

"Why?"

I tread back into the kitchen, grab a platter, and carry myself out to the grill. "Well, we're getting our picture taken tonight in town."

"Pardon me, Mr. Erickson," she says skittishly, "we're doing what, when, and where?"

"Pictures? We're going to have our picture taken tonight."

"And why are we doing that when my hair looks like a bird's nest and you can just whip out your iPhone and snap it?"

"I want to send my mom a picture of you and she's very formal."

April acts demure and coquettish about the whole plan, but after supper, she dresses exquisitely, as if she could do otherwise. She outfits herself in a lacy maroon blouse with a suede-matching vest. The blouse is conservative, yet still stylish. She leaves the two top buttons undone and had her golden crucifix dangling from her neck.

The lipstick she chooses is a touch darker shade than she normally wears; and a light dusting of green eye shadow is spread thinly above her eyes. Her hair is combed out with just an inkling of wave to it and she brushes her bangs down slightly, just above her eyes.

Dutch Van Alstin – Murder in D Block

"Wow," I say, grabbing her arm and pulling her toward me. "You are sumptuous beyond belief."

Her face grows red, "Oh, stop, you're just being gentlemanly."

"I don't even know what that means," I say as I bite her neck.

"Stop it you savage," she laughs, "you'll smudge my makeup and your mom will think that I look like a whore."

"All right, all right…party pooper."

The photographer is overdoing his job at making April feel comfortable and relaxed for the shoot. His hands are all over her body in an attempt to *position* her just so. The playful come-ons are so obvious and if refers to her as "sensuous" one more time, I may flog him with his own camera. I believe the photographer forgot the first rule of business: never flirt with the paying customer's girlfriend. For a business that is dying with the advent of quality photo equipment available to the public, this guy is pssing off a paying customer.

When the photographer finishes groping April, she and I duck into a coffee boutique for a quick sip of some hot brew and some nonchalant chat. We grab a booth toward the rear of the shop after I signal the waitress for two cups. Unfortunately, we are not completely alone in the coffeehouse; two drunks sit only a few tables away being loud and obnoxious. I recognize them both. They're guards at Briersburg; both work the evening shift. I am not completely sure of their names, but I think its Fran Kelly and the other I only know as Cherryhill. Both men look over at April and I and are pointing and snickering. I don't know either of them all that well, just enough to discern whether I like them or not, and I do not. The clock has barely ticked at seven and these two are sloshed beyond reason. Guys like Kelly and Cherryhill can smell out cheap drink specials with the skill of a bloodhound.

I begin phasing out what April is saying to me as I stare tenaciously at Kelly and Cherryhill. Their childish chortling slowly ceases as they begin looking back and forth between themselves and me. Cherryhill pokes Kelly in the shoulder and smirks. He then stands up and wipes his hands on his napkin and walks toward April and me.

"Hello, Dane," Cherryhill says.

"Goodbye, Cherryhill," I reply.

Cherryhill glances back at Kelly and laughs. He turns back to April and winks at her. "She is cute, Dane," he says, still fixating his sights on her. "It's no wonder you're chasing her around."

Dutch Van Alstin – Murder in D Block

I stand slowly and lean into Cherryhill's face. April stands as well and grabs my hand, simultaneously rubbing it gently, and she pulls me out the door.

"Please forgive me, *seniorita'*," Cherryhill says as he bows at her feet.

April tugs at me more forcefully, trying to pull me out the door.

"Hey," Kelly roars, "we're talking to you guys!"

Both drunkards begin following us out the back door and into the alley. "Is she the one, Dane?" Cherryhill says. "Is she the one that made you turn?"

"Chica grande puta, Dane," Kelly says, grabbing his oversized belly and laughing so hard that drool runs down his two-day growth of whiskers.

I hurl my body around and swing my fist wildly, connecting with Kelly's ear. Kelly falls back and falls into some trashcans. Cherryhill quickly reacts by clenching both fists together and knocking me in the back of my head, sending me to the pavement. Kelly recovers from my shot to his ear and assists Cherryhill as they both kick me, lying in the alley.

April grabs a steel trashcan lid and begins pummeling both Kelly and Cherryhill relentlessly over and over without a second's pause between blows. They cover their heads, cower to their knees, and scream. "Stop it, bitch, stop it now!" April continues to mash their heads with the lid until flashing red lights appear from a police car whizzing up the alley.

"Break it up," the cop yells as he leaps out of the car.

I lift my head up only to spot McManus once more. April drops the lid and runs to me, bursting into tears. McManus scrambles over to the fray with his nightstick drawn. He freezes in his tracks as he scrutinizes the sight of me again. "Haven't we danced this tune enough already?" He says.

Still groggy from the thump to my skull, I waver some as I try to stand. "How do you think I feel?" I say facetiously. "Eighty cops in this city and I always manage to run into you."

"Is she okay?" McManus says, looking at a still emotional April.

April continues the sobbing but manages to produce a faint nod of her head.

"What the hell is going on with you two geniuses?" McManus squawks at Cherryhill and Kelly.

"They...they..." April continues to bawl.

"Calm down, Miss," McManus says soothingly, "everything's okay."

"Officer?" A voice chimes from the alley, "I saw it all."

"Sir?"

The waiter from the coffeehouse walks out with his apron still draped over his portly

Dutch Van Alstin – Murder in D Block

body. "These two nice folks here," he points at April and I, "were just sitting and sipping until these two gorillas followed 'em in the alley and attacked 'em both for no reason."

"Would you two washouts care to elucidate on that scenario?" McManus remarks.

"She beat us with a trashcan lid," Kelly whines pathetically, nearly in tears.

"Trashcan, huh?" McManus says. "How very appropriate."

"The fact is these two beer swilling losers were kicking me while I was down and she helped me out with that lid there."

McManus tries, but no longer is able to fight off his grin. "Do you want to press charges?" He says to me.

"You can't arrest us," Kelly cries out, "we're prison guards."

"So what?" McManus shouts. "I ask the questions here, not you two cement heads."

Kelly rubs his head and stares down at the pavement.

"No, I don't want to press any charges. I think having a woman kick both their asses is punishment enough. But please, Officer McManus, don't let that fact get spread around town or anything."

"Heaven forbid," he replies sarcastically. McManus peers down at the two whipped puppy dogs and kicks some pebbles at them. "Beat it, you emasculated doormats before I sick her on you again."

Cherryhill and Kelly stand slowly, still licking their wounds as they walk laggardly down the alleyway.

"Good to see you two together, but I guess that didn't keep me from being called here, now did it?"

I laugh. "Why do you keep cutting me so much slack?"

McManus shrugs his shoulders lackadaisically. "I know those two lamebrains all too well. They've been guests of the back seat of my car a few times. So have a lot of you guards for that matter and they all whine about how they'll lose their job if I arrest them. You on the other hand, you never tried pulling that shit with me."

"Thanks, I try not to be too much of a…ah… well, one of those."

"Good, there's enough of 'those'." McManus waves at us as he gets in his car. "Goodnight folks, go home now so I can rest."

"Do you know him?" April says.

"Well…sort of, I guess."

"Are you okay?"

Dutch Van Alstin – Murder in D Block

"Just a sore neck, how about you?"

April snaps her fingers flippantly. "Piece of cake for a tough street girl,"

"I can't say I've seen you that pissed since you walloped me."

"Me?" she says with skepticism, "what about you?"

"I know, but I wasn't about to stand idly by while some redneck calls the woman I love a whore."

"Whore? I thought he called me a bitch?"

"Actually he said them both. But he called you a whore as we were walking in the alley, don't you remember?"

"He did?"

"Yeah, *puta*, remember? *Prostituta*, or *puta*, however you want to say it, the meaning is still the same."

"No, I guess I didn't hear him."

"Let's go home. I want a cheeseburger."

April stops and lets go of my hand. "Dane?"

"What?"

"What does *turn* mean?"

"Huh?"

"Turn? Those guys asked if she was the one that made you *turn*, what does that mean?"

"Okay," I sigh, "I'll tell you everything. But you have to promise not to jump to conclusions about what I'm going to tell you. There's a little more to what I told about why I was locked out the other day."

CHAPTER 31

April shakes her head at me disappointedly. "You should have filled me in on all the details before, Dane."

"But how could I have when you just started believing I had nothing to do with your husband's death? What was supposed to say to you then: 'oh, by the way, the F.B.I. believes I killed your husband, too'."

"F.B.I.?" April says, visibly stunned.

"Yeah, go figure."

"The F.B.I.?" She repeats, looking blankly.

"Yes," I say, growing more curious, "is that ringing any bells? Do you know why they're interested in this whole fiasco?"

April looks at me pensively, not saying a word.

"April...are you okay?"

"Yeah," she says placidly, "I'm fine."

"You didn't answer me."

"Yes I did, I said I'm fine."

"Not about that, about the F.B.I.? Do you know why they're investigating?"

"No, no bells here, Dane."

"I thought we were being honest here?"

"We are," she smiles.

"Come on, April; give me some credit for a smidgen of smarts?"

"Okay, Dane," April says, tugging fiercely at her shirt. "Why is the F.B.I. involved? What are you hiding from me? Are you being honest with me?"

"Hey, whoa, we're past all that, remember?"

April drops her head and runs her tongue along the inside of her lip.

"April?"

She smiles empathetically. "I'm sorry, Dane, I know you didn't do it. I didn't mean anything by what I said, forgive me?"

"I'm sorry, too."

"For what?"

"For not laying all this shit out in the open, the F.B.I., the ransacking of my house, all that."

"Never mind, I know I acted a little crazy after Raph died. I let my emotions get to me. I should have known better than to think you were involved, but our relationship has been a little odd from the start. I mean, we didn't have the most auspicious beginning, did we?"

"No, I guess not."

April pouts her lips and moans out a kittenish whine. "Is that where he hit you?" she says, rubbing the back of my neck.

"Yeah, but don't worry, I'm okay."

"Are you sure, sweetheart?"

"Maybe you better drive, I am a bit dizzy."

April giggles. "How do you think those two bozos feel?"

We arrive home and April unlocks my front door and tosses the keys into her purse. She comports herself as a nursemaid to my seemingly minor wound by helping me to the couch and making me some popcorn. I am not allowed to anything but go to the bathroom; that is one task that cannot be handled vicariously.

The remainder of the night is a cozy milieu of watching old reruns and laughing at corny old episodes of *I Love Lucy*. The yawns accumulate quicker and quicker on April until she finally surrenders.

"I can't stay awake any longer, are you coming to bed soon?"

"Maybe soon, there's an old episode of Columbo on I haven't seen in a while."

Dutch Van Alstin – Murder in D Block

April gives me a friendly peck on the forehead and musses up my hair. "All right," she says with a snicker. "I obviously can't entice you away from Columbo."

"I'll be in a bit, I promise."

As soon as I assume a horizontal position on the couch, the yawns begin to infiltrate me too. I fight a few yawns myself as I watch Peter Falk chew on that odious cigar as he unravels the case of the *vanishing magician*. A magician commits a murder concurrently with an ongoing vanishing act that he is in the middle of performing. Columbo is obliterating the magicians, supposedly, *airtight* alibi.

Maybe, if I smoked a cigar? Maybe then, the wisdom of Columbo would saturate my brain as well. Maybe if I trade Bambino in for a near comatose basset hound? Maybe added shrewdness would help me sort out what has been bothering about April's apartment.

I have always despised those sham family festivals. The themes created by Briersburg's family festival coordinator are truly deranged when considering where these festivals are hosted. The coordinator, Mr. Hopper, failed to grasp the concept he was inside an enormous structure with a huge wall encompassing the whole area. And those nice, well bred, compassionate men in those tall, thin towers? You know the ones armed with the M-16 rifles? They keep the prisoners from scaling the wall to freedom. Mr. Hopper contrived themes such as *Autumn Sounds* and *Musical Muse* and the ever farcical: *Arts in the Park*. The prisoners would pose for photos and send them home with their wives. I'm sure these photos looked phenomenal displayed above the fireplace, until their boyfriends visited, of course, then they have to hide the picture…

I sigh.

Underneath a plant stand!

I need that picture, tonight.

The credits running along the TV screen and four empty *Dr. Pepper* bottles tell me the night is growing late. April sleeps soundly, cuddling up to my pillow. I fumble through her purse and grab the keys. Bambino notices me putting on my coat and begins leaping from side to side, wagging his tail frantically.

"Easy, boy," I say, scratching his ears. "You have to stay here and take care of mama."

Bambino sits obediently at my feet to offer me his version of a goodbye through the drooling of his tongue. I reach up in the pantry and toss him a biscuit. He devours it up in the blink of an eye and sits, awaiting another treat.

"Go lie down," I say quietly.

Dutch Van Alstin – Murder in D Block

Bambino walks to the couch, circles a few times, and plops to the floor amidst a grunt.

Three more Pepsis and a half a tank of gas later, I return home. Bambino greets me and licks my hand repeatedly.

"Okay now, boy, I'm home. Now please go lie down now?"

I climb into bed gently, not disturbing April's peaceful slumber. I kiss her lightly on the cheek and she subconsciously smiles. The clock hands click on the four o'clock hour, and yet, I fight the urge to sleep. The weight on my eyes grows.

One.

Two.

Asleep.

"Yip! Yip! Yip!" Bambino barks. The clock hands near the eleven o'clock chime. I seem to increase my propensity for laziness daily.

Bambino charges out the door as I help myself to some of the coffee April left for me in the percolator. She also leaves me a note explaining that she took my car to work and that she'll be bringing home a pizza. She signs the note with an *I Love You* written in red ink. How can a person not love someone who takes an extra second to dig out another color pen to just write, "I love you"?

April glued a St. Christopher medal on the dashboard of my truck. I told her I didn't believe there was any hope for that death trap on four wheels disguised as my truck, not to mention the fact I'm a Lutheran.

Despite the pings, rattles and occasional backfires, my truck motors into town safely. Money is scarce since my unfortunate suspension, but I manage to convince myself the need for a Ford Mustang when I reach the rental office. I have always had a knack for convincing myself of things that are ostensibly untrue to, in fact, be true. And as I hand over all that extra cash for a Mustang convertible, I remind myself that I am taking a long, arduous journey and comfort is of the utmost importance.

After draining my savings account from the credit union, I cruise down the main street to the jewelers I visited yesterday. The clerk immediately recognizes me and affords me a mixed greeting.

"Ah, good afternoon, sir," he says, peeking behind me.

"That other guy isn't with me, in fact, he's never with me. We just unfortunately bumped into one another here."

"I see," he says mundanely. "Well then, sir, how may I assist you today?"

"The ring you showed me yesterday?"

"I remember it well, sir."

"I'll take it."

"Very good, sir," he scrambles underneath the counter looking for the ring. "I guess this means you're going through with your plans?"

"You bet. She's a great girl and I'm going to snatch her up before someone else does."

"I'm sure she's very special, sir," the clerk says, most likely for the twentieth time today.

"That she is." I hand over two thousand dollars in cash and he bestows upon me a five-minute lecture on the proper care of diamonds.

"Please, sir," he says, placing the cash in a drawer. "I would appreciate you keep us in mind for the wedding bands."

"I'll do that," I say, "just one thing?"

"Sir?" he says as he lowers his glasses.

"That, ah, gentleman that was in here yesterday?"

"I remember him well, sir."

The clerk is in his late fifties with a strip of gray hair around his ears and some loose hairs wavering around on top of his head. He wears glasses that he keeps on a gold chain around his neck, most likely to give him that *jeweler* look.

"Did he buy anything at all?"

"I'll say," the clerk grabs the computer screen and swings it around toward him. "He purchased a two and half carat diamond stud earring. Frankly, I was shocked that he purchased anything at all, not to mention he paid in cash."

"One earring?"

"Yes," he says dryly. "Apparently the diamond was for Miss Wendy's, ah, well, how shall I phrase this, not her navel, but a little *south* as it were."

"They're a class act."

"Anyone who hands me $4,500 cash is worthy of my respect," he says with a smug titter. "Present company excluded from my impudence, sir, I assure you."

"No offense taken, but I do have to go. I have many things to take care of today, thanks for everything."

"Please, sir, the wedding bands?" He shouts as I walk out the door.

Dutch Van Alstin – Murder in D Block

The bells over the photographer's shop rings as I open the door.

"One minute!" he shouts from the back room. He walks out wiping his hands on a rag, stopping dead in his tracks when he catches sight of me. "Hello," he says with false confidence.

"Hello," I say curtly.

"Please, Mr. Erickson, about yesterday. Please accept my apology for my lack of professionalism, it was uncalled for."

"Yes it was, but that's not why I'm here."

"Oh?"

"I want to know if you can have the proofs ready by four o'clock today; I'm going out of town?"

He finishes wiping his hands and tosses the rag in the back room. "I'll tell you what, since I behaved so poorly yesterday, I'll have them within the hour."

"Even better."

The photographer is in his late forties, but strives to appear youthful. His hair is blonde and tied back into a small ponytail. I see a small scar under his eye that he seems to attempt to hide in some makeup. "Again, I am sorry." He says.

"You're a photographer second and a man first, what man can resist her?" I say proudly.

"I'm glad you understand, I mean, she really is gorgeous."

I return a pixilated, but stern grin.

"Oops, there I go again. Sorry, I'll see you in an hour."

"An hour it is."

Packing is a chore. Especially when I attempt to cram so much luggage in a miniscule trunk and no backseat to speak of. My attempts to call April at the salon are going straight to voice mail. Her phone does not receive texts due to the fact it is a *free* phone given by social services. Nonetheless, I prefer a cowardly note full of falsehoods to a phone call anyway.

Dear April,

I tried to call you but the phone went straight to voicemail. I have to drive to Minnesota for a few days because of an unforeseen family crisis. I'll call you about six o'clock and fill you in on the details. Sorry I was unable to wait and explain in person. Feed Bambino for me.

Love,

Dane

Dutch Van Alstin – Murder in D Block

The flirtatious but talented photographer was true to his word concerning the pictures. Six photos, delicately framed were waiting for me when I arrived. So now it's a twelve- pack of Pepsi, a thermos of coffee and it's on to the expressway.

Next stop: St. Alexandria, Minnesota. Home of the *me!*

CHAPTER   32

Natural body functions and gasoline are the only rests I allow myself until nearly seven o'clock. The clock is ticking and I really don't foresee delaying my promised phone call to April a moment longer. I find myself in a small borough somewhere in Ohio, but large enough to have a mini-mart with a clean bathroom.

I pull out the cell phone for the inevitable call.

"Hello! Hello! Hello!?" April shrieks.

"Hey, honey," I say.

"What's going on? Is everyone okay? Nobody is ill, are they? Your mom? Is she okay?"

"Ah, let me try and wing this: nothing serious, not really, not physically, no, mom is fine. How did I do?"

"Can you please be serious for once in your life?"

"April," I say airily, "everything's okay, calm yourself. The problem stems from a cousin I grew up with. Last night he attempted suicide and my aunt is a basket case and wants me to talk with him, ASAP."

"Oh my Lord! Your cousin is in the hospital I assume?"

"Yes, but a friendly face, you know?"

Dutch Van Alstin – Murder in D Block

"Most definitely, family intervention and support is imperative. Has he a history of depression?"

"Who?"

"Your cousin, silly?"

"No, I guess not, just the usual hardships we all face."

"Is he on medication?"

"Medication?"

"Yes, medication? Is he on any anti-depressants? Zoloft? Prozac? Effexor?"

"Not that I'm aware of, I'm not sure," I stammer slightly. "Is that important?"

"Possibly, but from what you're telling me, the family support sounds solid. Has that been the case his whole life?"

"He didn't grow up with Ward and June as parents, but yes, a good family."

April's inquisitive interrogation is making me feel guiltier about my minor prevaricating, particularly with our talks about *honesty* and such. "Look, honey, if I'm going to make St. Alexandria before the rooster crow, I need to be heading back out on that highway."

"The rooster crow?" April says with a giggle.

"I guess I'm starting to talk like an ol' country bumpkin already."

"Hmm, sounds *Mayberryish*."

"You'd love Minnesota, April."

Silence.

"In fact, next trip out here; I think you need to come along with me."

"Oh, Dane," she starts whimpering softly, "I'd like that more than anything."

"I'll be home soon."

"I love you, Dane."

"I love you too, April, bye."

"Bye."

Four A.M. comes near and I am singing deliriously to myself and occasionally landing a punch to my face. I cross the Wisconsin border and into the twin cities of Minneapolis and St. Paul, still keeping myself awake with every little trick of the trade I can conjure. At this very moment, there is a rooster in St. Alexandria wiping the sandman out of his eyes, preparing his voice for the morning crow. St. Alexandria is only about a half an hour from the twin cities. I rarely visited the city as a boy. My father did bring me to a Twins game one time, years ago, and I recall an episode where dad needed a much-needed part for the tractor from a shop in Minneapolis. Except for those two occasions, I haven't seen much of the area at all.

The rooster is on the fence post crowing up a storm. I stop my car in front of the old farmhouse and soak the whole scene in briefly. The sun's orange cracks over the east through the slope of a hill I sled road as a boy. I still envision my dad walking out of the barn, wearing that old red engineer's cap, tilted to one side of his head. And there I would be, running behind him with one strap of my overalls undone, slapping me in the head with every step. Mom would be getting bacon out of the refrigerator and slicing it nice and thick as my sister Carol Ann fumbled with our cantankerous old wood stove, trying to get it light.

I alert the dogs as I pull my car in the driveway. Mom steps out on the porch and stares at the unfamiliar car. Mom's silver hair, with the two curlers on top, blow in the wind and she squints her aging, gray eyes, trying to see in the window.

Her eyes grow like saucers as I walk toward her. "Oh my Lord! Pepper, is that really you? Why didn't you tell me you were coming, I would have breakfast ready." She scrambles down the driveway in her yellow housecoat, and a pair of dilapidated slippers that she refuses to throw in the trash.

'Pepper'! I had almost forgotten about that name. The reasons behind that particular nickname run the gamut. My grandfather claims I was dubbed the nickname because I resembled his grandfather with the same nickname. Mom says it was because I always dumped pepper on my food when I was a baby. And my grandmother makes a less exacting assertion of the names origin; her reason was because the name just *suited* my personality.

I am subjected the normal rigmarole of hugs and small talk that transcend into cusses and curses of how I never write or call, how I need to find a nice girl, and how I need to get a safer job. The entire diatribe takes less than five minutes. I am transformed from the beloved son to the Prodigal son in a matter of moments.

"Please, mom, I've been driving all night. I have to get some sleep."

"Sleep?" she says irascibly, "I haven't heard nor seen you in--"

"Mom, please, didn't we just travel down this road a minute ago?"

"Don't you dare sass me, young man, I'm still your mama."

"Yes 'em."

"But I suppose you do need a few winks before chores."

"Chores?"

"Yes, chores, things need to get done, don't they?"

Dutch Van Alstin – Murder in D Block

I sigh. "Yes, ma'am."

"But as I said, I guess you need a little shuteye, use your old bedroom, it's still the same."

"You mean you moved the still?"

"Very funny."

My room looks the same as the way I left it, with a fat down pillow and a soft mattress. There was always a lump underneath my hip too.

I climb on top and pull down the comforter. The lump is still there.

"Get up!" Mom shouts, kicking my bed.

"Huh, wha.., what's going on?"

"I said get up, can't you hear? For the love of God, Pepper, it's almost noon! You can't lounge around in bed until noon."

"You can when you crawled into bed at six this morning," I say, hiding under my covers.

"You sound like you're ten years old again. Now get yourself out of that bed and chop me some firewood."

"Who's been chopping for you since I've been gone?"

"That nice Mr. Calvetti who lives next door."

"If he's so damn nice then let him do it."

"Don't you cuss in my house," she says, kicking my bed repeatedly."

"Sorry."

"Besides, he's been acting funny as of late. I believe he's getting a notion to begin calling on me."

"So go to a matinee with him or something."

"An *Italian*?" Mom says, using the *"I"* in long form. "I can't cook any Italian meals of any kind."

"Come on, ma, learn to cook some Italian meals and let me sleep."

"Only an Italian can teach a non-Italian how to cook them meals."

"Where did you hear that malarkey?"

"It's common knowledge."

"Common to whom?"

"To everyone who watches Oprah!"

"Boil spaghetti, open a jar of Ragu, rub garlic on your fingertips, anything! Just let me sleep for twenty more minutes?"

"Get up!" She shrills once more.

"Okay," I sit up and rub my eyes, "I surrender, you win."

"Was there any doubt?"

"No," I sigh, "I guess not."

Mom has a pot of coffee percolating on the stove and pours me a fresh cup. No sooner does the last drop splash than she begins the *nice girl* and *safer job* homily.

"You sound like a broken record, mom."

"There's nothing wrong with meeting a nice girl, Pepper. Mrs. Nylan's boy found himself-_"

I toss the photo of April, rendering mom speechless, for a moment that is.

"What's that?" Mom says.

"Not *what,* but who?"

"Very well then, who is that?"

"Her name is April Delgado, soon to be April Erickson."

Mom picks the photo up off the table and covers her mouth, fighting off tears. "Oh, my, Pepper, I..I..I'm not sure what to say."

"Say you're happy about it."

"Oh I am, son, I truly am. I didn't know you were seeing anyone. She's beautiful."

"I'll bring her next trip out so you can meet her."

"*Grandma,*" she says tenderly.

"Huh?"

"I'm just trying the name on for size."

I set my mug back on the table. "I think you better just put it back on the shelf for now."

"Surely you plan on having children?" She says defensively. "Your gal is fertile ain't she?"

"Yes, mom, but before you submit your grandchildren's application to Minnesota U, can we take things one step at a time?"

Mom steps back to the stove and pours herself another cup of coffee. She fumbles with her apron and sits back at the table. "That wood is out back."

"I'll chop wood, mom, I promise. But first I need to see Pete."

"Pete?" she says surprisingly. "Why Pete?"

"Do I need a reason? I mean, he was my best friend all the while we were growing up?"

Dutch Van Alstin – Murder in D Block

"It's just the way you said it, so quick and urgent: *PETE!*"

"Why are you always so suspicious?"

Mom looks at me out of the corner of her eye, sipping coffee.

"I just need...correction, *want* to see Pete, okay?"

"Fine," she says, setting her coffee down, spooning another heap of sugar in it. "If you want to go visit a boy you use to steal apples with from Tucker's orchard instead of your mama then go ahead. I seen his mama at the trade show a spell back and she mentioned Pete was transferred to the barracks near *Anoka.*"

"Anoka?" I say, checking her accuracy.

"I ain't senile! Anoka! Anoka!" Mom sets her coffee down and rubs her chin. "What are you up to?" She says, squinting her eyes at me.

"Nothing."

"Hmmm, is this girl of yours nice?"

"We're back to April?"

"Did we ever leave?" she says harshly.

"I laugh as I get up and snatch my jacket. "She's a good girl, mom, you'll like her."

"Uh-huh, and is she going to teach you all those fancy Italian dishes?"

"She's not Italian, mom, she's Spanish."

"Spanish? But I cook no Spaniard suppers?"

"That's okay, mom," I laugh. "She'll eat whatever it is you cook."

Mom sips her coffee again. "She looks Italian to me."

"I believe you have nice Mr. Calvetti on your mind."

Mom blushes. "Nonsense."

CHAPTER 33

The Hansen farm is very close to our farm. That short distance was very convenient when Pete and I were boys. Obviously, Pete no longer lives with his parents, but I'm sure Mrs. Hansen will gladly tell me where he is living. Anoka isn't too far from St. Alexandria and I don't envision Pete as being a person who would stray too far from home at any course of his life. I don't mean to insinuate Pete is a *mama's boy* of any sort, but he has never shown any interest in leaving the general area of St. Alexandria. I attempted to coax him into traveling out east with me, but he balked, citing family *issues*. Pete has done well for himself. He snared a job with the State Police and has recently been promoted to an investigator of minor felonies.

Pete's mother fawns over me and offers me coffee on three separate occasions, a taste of pie, and a piece of fudge, all within five minutes. Fudge is my *Achilles heel*.

Mrs. Hansen informs me that my boyhood pal, former apple thief turned state trooper, is supposed to be stopping by their house after supper to deliver some antiques.

"Thank you, Mrs. Hansen," I say, chewing the fudge heartily.

"Don't be speaking with mouth full of food, young man." She says in a saucy tone.

"I'm sorry, Mrs. Hansen."

"Why don't you sit a spell and have some more fudge? Petey will be here soon."

"I'm sorry, Mrs. Hansen" I say, "but there's a woodpile waiting back at mom's."

Dutch Van Alstin – Murder in D Block

"Well then, you tend to your mama's needs."

"Yes 'em, but I was wondering if you could do me a favor."

"Certainly, Pepper."

"Could you give Pete this?" I hand over a large, sealed manila folder. Pete's mom flips it over a few times and glares mistrustfully at its furtive appearance. "Hmm, I can give it to him, Pepper, but he'll be sorry he missed you."

"Tell him I'll see him tomorrow sometime."

"It was good seeing you, boy."

The woodpile hadn't disappeared as I had hoped it would. The chopping is only a sad reminder of the dismal physical shape I have allowed myself to slip into lately. Every wheeze and every grunt is a punishment for every greasy cheeseburger and fried chicken eaten at Briersburg.

Mom and I spend most of the remaining night talking about Carol Ann, the cows, new types of fertilizer, the town drunk, that *damn clerk at the bakery who can't seem to find time for a proper bathing*, and stories of our family tree that are bordering on myth.

The yawns weigh in heavily cutting our night shorter than I would like. But the lump on the mattress seems to be calling out to me and I drop into bed. I don't even move Rufus, my mom's shepherd dog. He lies diagonal across the bed and emits a low growl as I move the pillow from his head. Somehow, even though he takes up most of the bed, he leaves me the lump.

Cumbrous pounding is levied on the front door. Rufus raises his snout some but drops it back down to the bed just as quick. A quick glimpse of the clock tells me midnight is nearly upon us and it is this reason, I hustle to the door before mom wakes. I flick on the porch light and see Pete, shielding his eyes from the unwelcome light.

"Pete," I say excitedly, but quietly.

Pete has changed very little since I saw him last. He stands well over six-foot tall and weighs in at a solid two hundred fifty pounds of hay tossing muscle. His blonde hair is thin and stringy and he combs it straight down with no particular styling in mind. He has dark blue eyes, moderately oblong in shape, topped off with thick bushy eyebrows. His face is clean-shaven and his nose is big with the septum arched to one side.

"We have trouble," Pete blurts out, "and we have to talk, now."

"We haven't spoken in six years and that's the first thing you say?"

Dutch Van Alstin – Murder in D Block

"I wish I could be--"

A noise from the kitchen hushes Pete's words. "Pepper, is that you?" Mom says.

"Uh, yes 'em," I say restlessly.

"We need to go somewhere," Pete whispers. "This shit is big!"

"What's going on out here?" Mom peeps her eyes around the corner and into the foyer.

"Nothing, mom, Pete just stopped by for a visit."

She stretches her neck out like an ostrich. "Oh, hello, Peter."

"Evening, Miss Erickson," he says.

"I'm a widow, Peter," she says sternly. "It's still proper to be calling me a '*Missus*.'"

"Of course, ma'am, yes, I meant no disrespect."

"Come in out of the cold, young man." Mom opens the door and motions Pete inside to the entrance. She looks at Pete up and down as he nervously scratches his ear. He quickly removes his hat remembering mom's long-standing rule of *no hats* indoors.

"Thank you, ma'am." Pete fidgets. "It's growing colder as the harvest season winds down."

Mom looks Pete squarely in the eye and then directly to her wrist, where a watch normally would reside. "What are you doing here so late?"

"Just, ah, visiting, ma'am." Pete sheepishly turns his hat over and over in his hands.

"At midnight? I know your mama taught you better manners?"

"She did, ma'am, but, ah, I'm sorry about the time." Pete glances over at me and then looks at the floor.

"Peter?" Mom says.

"I am truly sorry about the time."

"Pete is just visiting, mom," I say, looking at the floor as well.

"Peter Matthew Hansen, I know your mama!"

"I know, ma'am, but there's nothing going on."

"Do you have a guilty conscious or something? I didn't say there was, did I?"

"No, no you didn't."

"Augustovson Caleb Erickson?"

Pete snickers at my true name.

"Come on, mom, Pete's just visiting."

"I remember when you boys were fifteen and you returned from the fair with wine on your breath and you thought if you keep your head low, I wouldn't smell it. I'll tell you right now, boys, I smelled it then and I'm smelling it now!"

"Would," Pete clears his throat. "Would you like it if I returned at a more respectable hour, Miss…ah, Mrs. Erickson?"

Mom pushes her glasses up on the bridge of her nose and looks at the both of us. "I guess you two can go now," she says, bouncing her foreboding glare from eye to eye. "You just stay out of trouble, you hear?"

"We will, ma'am, yes ma'am, we will."

"Well then…" she darts her eyes back and forth one last time, "be off with you."

I follow Pete outside into his truck as mom peeks through the living room window. Pete backs out the driveway slowly and cruises at a leisurely pace until we see my porch light go out. "I'm sorry I wasn't a bit friendlier, old buddy, but this whole deal you laid on me is one big mess."

I sigh. "Give it to me straight."

"Let's go have a beer at that old tavern over the bend."

"Which one?"

"That place old man Pickman never named, we all call it *that old tavern over the bend.*"

"Oh, that place."

"I can't wait until you fill me in on the details, Pepper because all this shit sounds bizarre."

Pete's driving can't be blamed for my body being jostled around against the dashboard. These old country roads are replete with potholes and trying to drive between them is like trying to run between the raindrops.

There are only three trucks in the tavern's parking lot and one rusted, rotted Dodge Aspen that I have to believe has been abandoned. The tavern rests in a pastoral section of the county with only a handful of farmhouses in close proximity. The owner lives in one of the upper floors of the gray-shingled edifice, with a nearly collapsed porch, only supported by some ropes, hooks and a few prayers.

Pete cradles the folder tightly under his arm and raises two fingers to the grizzled, wintry bartender. The bartender nods then wipes his nose with the sleeve of his torn flannel shirt.

My impatience grows as Pete lackadaisically sits at a booth and stares at a painting of *dogs playing poker.* "Hey, Pete, what do you got?"

"Oh." Pete revives himself from the reverie created by the photo. He resituates himself in the torn vinyl seats, making a queer noise with every move. "I read your letter and I did all the things you wanted me to do. All I can say, Pepper, is you must have been one desperate fellow to drive all the way out here. You could have just mailed this to me?"

"No I couldn't. I needed an answer, tonight on the prints," I say, hurrying him along. And I didn't want any trace of it on the Internet. I have some asshole Gendarme skulking me. Which reminds me," I say, pulling out my cell phone. "I better shut this off".

"I took that photo you gave me and I picked all the prints off it that I could find."

"Good, good," I say, still trying to scoot him along quicker.

"I ended up finding five different sets, that's why it took me so long. One set, apparently male, judging by the size, has no file on record. I'm not sure who that could be. It could be anyone--"

"That doesn't matter, Pete," I say abruptly, "no files means no criminal record. I'm interested in criminal records only."

"Two sets are apparently these two guys on either side of the guy in the middle. Their prints kicked back all the information needed, including a photo. Here," Pete hands me the pictures, "they match these two guys, agreed?"

"Agreed."

The bartender slides the two cans of beer on the table and then digs his fingernail in his ear. "You boys need mugs?"

"Not me," I say.

"Suit yourself," he says, while simultaneously burping.

"As I said, these two are eliminated." Pete reiterates.

"Yes, yes, come on; let's get to the deep dark secrets here."

"I know. I'm just approaching this methodically so we don't get confused."

"Okay, sorry, we're in your camp now. I'll shut my mouth."

"That means two prints remain, correct? Five minus the unknown and these two guys leave two?"

"Only if five minus three still equals two, Pete. I follow your logic, but can speed up that logic some?"

"I guess I'll approach it this way, Pepper. I have five extraordinarily pieces of bad news for you."

"Good approach, Pete." I say scathingly.

"I'm trying to give it to you straight."

I gulp my first swig from the can and wince at the flat, warm liquid they pass off as beer. "Sorry, proceed."

Dutch Van Alstin – Murder in D Block

"Let's put the print issue aside momentarily."

"Why?"

"Because the prints will tie into the news I'm going to read to you." Pete wades through a stack of papers and slides out a computer sheet. "I ran the name of *Raphael Antonio Delgado,* the date of birth, social security, and NCIC number in the computer. Now before I divulge any of this, I have to ask: are you sure the data you gave me is correct?"

"All of it came from the computer system Briersburg Prison; I sure as hell hope so."

Pete swigs his beer but seems unaffected by the taste. "Here goes: *Raphael Delgado was killed when he was stabbed to death in Auburn State Prison in upstate New York in June of 1985 in the bathhouse during a--*"

"Killed?"

"According to the name, DOB, SSN, and NCIC, he was killed nearly thirty years ago."

"Do you have a photo?"

Pete slides one of the photos from his folder out on to the table. "Not even a close match to the guy in your picture, is it?"

"Nope."

"The question before us, Pepper is who the hell is this guy?" Pete says, pointing to the Delgado that I know.

"Don't look at me for an answer."

"Pepper, I also ran this April girl's name too." Pete wiggles the empty can and motions to the bartender for another. "I know you didn't specifically ask me to, but I did anyway."

"And?"

"I ran her married and maiden name with her D.O.B. and the computer found no criminal record, but three different driver's licenses issued. There was one in Florida, one in Arkansas and one in the state of Washington, here's the pictures." Pete hands me a montage of photos, none that even remotely resemble April.

"None are her." I slide the photos back to Pete and sense a little bit of judgment in his eyes.

"However, the maiden name *April Cruz* did kick back an alias used--"

"That's not her, come on, get back to the topic at hand."

"Pepper?" Pete persists, "we need to cover--"

"We'll come back to her in a minute. Please, can we just move on to Delgado?"

"Fine, but the news doesn't get much better. In fact, these next two things are going to blow your mind. I'm waiting for Rod Serling to come walking out of that men's room with a cigarette lodged between his fingers."

I lean back in the booth and laugh.

Pete looks at me with bewilderment. "What's so funny?"

"Nothing," I sigh, "I just want a tuna sandwich right about now."

CHAPTER 34

"Tuna sandwich?"

"Never mind," I groan, laying my head flat upon the table, "it's a private joke."

Pete swigs the last portion of beer and shakes the empty can at the bartender. "How about you, Pepper? Thirsty?"

I shake my head as I continue burrowing it into the table.

"Where was I?" Pete says.

"All over the place, Pete. You're all over the fucking map here. Will you please get to Delgado and what it has to do with the fingerprints?"

"Right." Pete shakes the cobwebs from his thoughts. He begins rifling through his papers and produces another printout. "The results of the third prints are what are so strange. One set, presumably belonging to this Delgado fellow, or whatever his name is, came back with a security block on them."

That bit of irregular news compels me to perk my eyes and peek out over my arms. "Security block?"

"Yep," Pete grabs the can of beer from the bartender's hand and nods to him in thanks. "Anyway, I never heard of such a thing either. But be that as it may, it happened. The computer refused to run the prints and when I tried to circumvent the authorization, a screen

Dutch Van Alstin – Murder in D Block

popped up on my computer reading: *fingerprints not accessible from this unit.*"

"A State Trooper's computer? Do you have any idea why?"

"Not why, but *who* on the other hand, I can tell you."

An uncontrollable snicker emerges from my mouth.

"What's so funny?"

"I already know who."

"How would you know?"

"The F.B.I., right?"

"How did you know?" Pete says skeptically.

Inadvertently, I ignore his question. "All I have is more questions, not answers."

"Hey," Pete tugs my arm, "what's going on here? How did you know it was the F.B.I. blocking Delgado's fingerprints?"

"Because, Pete, the F.B.I. has been hounding me since Delgado's murder."

"The F.B.I.?" Pete says incredulously, almost as if he thinks I'm delusional. "The F.B.I. doesn't care about some prison murder, what are you babbling about?"

"I wish I knew, Pete. There's this Keystone Cop by the name of Lafayette--"

"Lafayette?" Pete digs his fingernails deeper into my skin. "That's the guy, Pepper, that's the guy."

"What guy? Now what are you babbling about?"

"He called me minutes after I tried to run the prints and was giving me the third degree about what I was doing and why. I felt like a criminal."

"He has that knack."

"Pepper," Pete picks up Delgado's picture. "Who is this guy and why is some F.B.I. zealot so interested in finding out who killed him?"

I sit silent as I watch Pete examine Delgado's picture from all possible angles. He even turns the photo upside down and rubs the surface with his finger.

"See anything I may have missed?" I ask.

"No," Pete remains tenaciously fixated on the photo. "But what the hell is *Arts in the Park day* all about?"

"That's where the prisoners show off their *undiscovered artistic talents* and share their new found gift with the world."

"So Delgado and his cronies painted these? I thought the day was a showing of sorts?"

"They show 'em, but they also paint 'em. The truth is, some of these guys are very good

Dutch Van Alstin – Murder in D Block

painters. One prisoner painted this huge panoramic scene on the wall of G block, but most prisoners paint shit like this guy here." I say, pointing to Delgado's comrade.

Pete scoffs. "You mean the skeleton hands wrapped in chains and blood from behind iron bars?"

"Those paintings are more common. The ones that scream *martyrdom* as if they awoke one morning to find themselves in Briersburg."

"What's Delgado's painting mean? Half-moon merged with a half sun? What's so big about that?"

"Some prisoners just paint scenery and have delusions of grandeur that they'll be the next great Renaissance artists."

"I think the only painting he'd ever have done would be someone's kitchen."

"Yeah, maybe," I say disinterestedly. I retrieve the photo from Pete, lay it flat on the table, and prop my chin under my arms.

"I tried that." Pete says glibly.

"Yeah, but…"

"But what?"

"Delgado's face, it bothers me. What do you think of his face, Pete?"

"Meaning?"

"What stands out in your mind when you first see it?"

Pete shrugs his shoulders. "I don't know…the scar?"

"That's not what I was thinking, but that's puzzling to me, too."

"Why? How uncommon is a slash to the face in Briersburg?"

"That's the problem, I see two or three of these a day. They're called *telephone* slashes because of the way they are cut. Do you see how it runs from his ear to his lip?"

"Uh-huh."

"What happens is this: someone sneaks up from behind--"

"What are you staring at?" Pete queries.

"Nothing, stand up for me though. I can demonstrate this better than I can explain it."

Pete indulges my whimsy by leaping up and posing in a boxing stance.

"You're not supposed to be expecting the attack, Pete. That's the whole point of the experiment."

"How the hell did I know?" Pete turns around and places his back to me. I slide my body in near him and reach up to his face.

Dutch Van Alstin – Murder in D Block

"Now keep in mind that Delgado is shorter than you. Now what happens is this: a prisoner comes from behind and reaches over and jabs the tip of the razor by the lip and pulls it up through the face to the ear. The scar is usually straight from the point of impact until the ear. Then the cut curves slightly because the attacker is simultaneously running away, hence the name telephone."

"What's your point?"

"His scar," I snatch the photo from the table and shake it. "Look at it. It's perfectly straight, not one iota of deviation whatsoever. You need a damn ruler to cut that straight. That doesn't look like a *cut and run* job at all."

Pete sits back down and mulls over the photo one more time. "Nothing personal, Pepper, but that doesn't mean a thing. Granted, we're in your field of expertise here, but I can give you a dozen explanations. How about a deep cut into the face? That would keep the razor from straying?"

"Then the scar would reflect the deepness. If the cut requires longer, wider stitches, then the scar is always swollen and thick. Delgado's scar is rather tiny. I've seen the scars from attacks you mention and they're normally from actual razor fights where the prisoners have several gashes. This gash is from a sneak attack from behind."

"Okay, but you're still not sending a chill up my spine with any of this?"

"How about his nose then? If I only had a nose like that, hell, if you only had a nose like that? You only broke your nose once and it's all fucked up and crooked."

"Well, la de da, Mel Gibson. Besides, I broke it twice."

"High school football game against Pierpoint and where else?"

"When we were ten, you shoved me out of a tree-fort, remember? I said I could fly and you said 'prove it'?"

"Oh…yeah, twice. Anyway, look at Delgado's nose? That is an elegant nose. It's perfect in size, shape, symmetry, that's the nose I want."

"Are you saying he should possess a hideous mass of cartilage like mine, Dane?"

"Seriously, do you think Delgado could have been despised enough by someone enough to where they slashed his face but nowhere in his illustrious career as a criminal had he pissed anyone enough for them to bop his beak?"

Pete, again, swallows the last of his beer and signals the bartender for another. The bartender sluggishly saunters over to the table with two more cans. "We got two chili dogs left over from breakfast, you two want 'em?"

Dutch Van Alstin – Murder in D Block

"Sounds mouth-watering," Pete says, smacking his lips. "How about it, Pepper?"

"I'll, ah, have to take a rain check."

"Okay, Pepper, I see your point, but there's no guarantee that someone busted his nose at any point? You can't assume facts not in evidence."

"I know, Pete. But I can't believe he's never had it smacked, kicked, bashed, hit, slapped, something at one point and time. That nose of his is perfect. Even the good Lord doesn't make 'em that perfect?"

"Okay," Pete peruses the photo again, "plastic surgery? So what? My spine still doesn't tingle."

"If you were going to have plastic surgery, wouldn't you have the scar removed?"

"Not if I already got the surgery and then got slashed in prison. Wasn't that the point of your little demonstration?"

I scrutinize the top of the beer can and wince at the crud formulated at the top and in the crease around the lip. "According to the internal files at Briersburg," I say, scrubbing the top of the beer can with my T-shirt, "Delgado never received stitches, at least from this stint he was doing now. Either way you look at it, he had that scar before he came to prison. He also has a tiny scar under his chin that you can't make out in the photo, but why keep that one too?"

"I don't follow," Pete crams the greasy chili dog in his mouth, dripping sauce all over the table and on his chin.

"Put all these facts together and see if something in that melon of yours doesn't click? First, we know this guy isn't Raphael Delgado, agreed?"

"Agreed, (burp)."

"Secondly, this guy is at a family festival and he poses with two prisoners? He doesn't pose with Aunt Lucille or Cousin Rosa? No family at all? I checked his visit log and April has been his only visitor, ever; including these so called family festivals, understand?"

"Yes, just my nose is fucked up, not my brain."

"Thirdly, and perhaps most crucially, his murder is the focal point of an F.B.I. inquiry? His prints are secretly sealed? Lafayette is obsessed with protecting the--"

"Protection?" Pete declares as he digshis nails into his leg. "Pepper, now my spine does have a chill."

"Protection, Pete?" I say, wheedling the final words from his mouth.

"Witness-Protection-Program."

Pete and I sit silently. We stare at each other and smirk like the cat that ate the canary.

Dutch Van Alstin – Murder in D Block

"Think about it, Pete. Combine all this stuff together: the phony scars, the nose job, Lafayette, even that painting?"

"What of it?" Pete retrieves the photo and looks blankly upon it.

"A rising sun replacing a moon? New life taking place of the old?"

"That's a bit of stretch, don't you think?"

"To base my entire theory on, yes. But the painting can be just another penny in the fountain."

"Maybe so, but this whole thing is weird. Stuff like this doesn't happen?"

"That's too easy of an explanation, Pete. Something is happening and I'm not just going to deny it because the reality of it unnerves me some. Give me another concrete reason why a federal agency is probing into this mess so deeply?"

"Someone didn't protect Delgado to well, did they?" Pete says with a satirical grin.

"I guess not," I say, as I sip some more beer and crush the can with my fist. "That bastard Lafayette tips my life upside down because he doesn't want bad PR with the bureau."

"Before you float away on cloud nine, remember, I have more bad news."

"Thanks for reminding me."

"Fortunately, or unfortunately, depending on how you view the matter, I ran the fifth set of prints on that picture."

"Where is this going?" I say, apprehensive of the answer.

"I can't find any words to say this gently so, here you go." Pete slides a folder at me across the table. "Read it, Pepper. That alias I mentioned? I found the match and you're not going to like it. Pepper, her name isn't Delgado or Cruz."

I bat the folder away; hoping all the bad news will just disappear if I don't read it.

"Her real name is April Salvano and she doesn't hail from Philadelphia either. She's from the Los Angeles area and she's thirty-two years-old."

"Then it ain't her, Pete." I say caustically. "April is only twenty-two and she's a good kid. She's just had a tough life."

"Nobody from Sherman Oaks has a tough life." Pete slides the folder to me delicately. "Pepper, it's her," he says, almost apologetically. "The prints match and so does the photo."

"Why do you have her fingerprints on file?"

Pete sighs and dumps the contents of the folder out before my eyes. "Read it, damn it! You need to know what you're getting yourself into. She did two years at Goffstown prison in New Hampshire for a fraud conviction."

Dutch Van Alstin – Murder in D Block

I glide the photo out from the pile and place it in front of me. Senses can lie. Everyone knows that your eyes can, and do, play tricks on you. I searched deep inside myself to find a reason not to doubt my eyes. There was picture showing a woman with straight black hair, dark pursed lips and cold, dead eyes. Her knuckles were white from where she gripped the sign reading *Goffstown State Correctional* and an ID number.

I probed the picture for a girl with big green eyes and a crowning smile. I failed to see any of the exuberance and exhilaration being emitted from her face. But no matter what, behind that countenance of hate and despair, I saw April.

CHAPTER 35

"You may as well give me the rest of that chili dog, Pete, because my life isn't worth shit anymore."

"Don't beat yourself up over this, Pepper."

"I should just go up to that big ox of a bartender and kick him square in the balls. Maybe he'll do me a favor and beat some sense into me."

Pete rubs his fingernail in the can and chews on his lip. He looks up a few times, thinking he has something comforting to say, but demurs at the idea of actually saying a word.

"*Salvano*," I say callously. "There is a bit of humor here?"

"Where is it hiding?"

"My mom saw a picture of April and said she thought April was Italian."

"Your mama is a shrewd cookie, Pepper."

"I know she is; I should have taken her remark as a clue also."

"Also?"

"Huh?"

"You said *also*, as if there's been more reasons for you to suspect something was up with her from the start?"

"I brush off Pete's comment with a wave of my hand.

Dutch Van Alstin – Murder in D Block

Pete glares at me immutably.

"What are you staring at?" I say, restlessly squirming in my chair.

"This is me, Pepper, not some twerp you've only known for ten minutes. I know when you're hiding something and you're hiding something. Admit it; you had doubts about her before this bombshell dropped, didn't you?"

"Pete! How can you say that? You don't--"

"Knock it off!" Pete barks. "You could have just sent me the photo but instead you furnished me with all the personal information on her as well. You even made it a point to tell me her fingerprints were on the photo so I could 'eliminate' them from everyone else. Face it, Pepper, in your own furtive style, you wanted me to check her out from the get go."

I spin the can on its side and plink it around in circles with my thumb. Pete's grilling stare persists. "Didn't you?" He says, undaunted by my reticence.

"Okay, Columbo," I hold up my empty can to salute him, "you're a master of how people think too."

"Well, I am a detective, Pepper. I actually get paid to do this. Not much, perhaps, but I do get a paycheck for deciphering things."

"LAST CALL!" The bartender screams, startling some old boozehound sleeping at the bar.

"Another cold one?" Pete says.

"They've all been piss warm. Why do you come to this dump anyway?"

"I've got a sometime girlfriend one farm away from here. She's a substitute school teacher and divorcee."

"Define sometime?"

"Like tonight, when I can't drive home."

"Well, unfortunately I have a lot of driving to do."

"You know, I've been thinking?"

"About what in particular?"

"When I first kicked up the file on this April lady, I thought you were mixed up with a bad apple. But now that you and have been talking..."

"Yeah...so?"

"If this Delgado character was really in the W.P.P., then so was his wife."

"You mean..."

"Maybe she wasn't trying to deceive you intentionally. She couldn't tell you anything

Dutch Van Alstin – Murder in D Block

about her past no matter how badly she may have wanted."

"But Pete, she and I were talking marriage. I can't believe she'd keep something so momentous from me."

"I'm not an expert on the W.P.P., but I do know some things about it and the most important rule is absolute secrecy at all times, with all people, in all circumstances, regardless of the status of a personal relationship. You don't tell your father, mother, daughter, son, whatever! There really was no benefit to you, or her, if she brought to light anything concerning her involvement in the program."

"You're overlooking the obvious, Pete. Delgado is now a name on a tombstone in Potter's field. Evidently there was a big leak somewhere?"

Pete exhales very softly and rubs the drowsiness from his eyes. "I'm afraid you're more right than you think, Pepper," he says, almost apocalyptic in nature.

"Pete," I say growing panicky by the minute. "That tingle you felt earlier? It's now up my spine."

"I know. If she was in the program with him, she's in danger, too."

"I don't know what to do, Pete. I'm all out of answers here."

"I know what you'll be doing in the next five minutes," Pete unfolds a paper he had tucked in his jeans. "You forgot number five, pal."

"Believe me, I haven't forgotten. Lay it on me."

Pete clears his throat as if he's at a high school recital, reading some monotonous speech. "An arrest warrant has been issued for Augustovson Caleb Erickson, believed to have family in the area. He is wanted in connection with blah, blah, blah, blah, and a bunch of other nonsensical bullshit." Pete crumples the paper and tosses it on the floor. "As a duly sworn police officer for the state of Minnesota I immediately drove out to his mama's farm, but he had already gone. He was *heading north to moose country in Canada*, according to his mama."

"Pete, what can I say? You're the best."

"Just promise me my son can toss your son from a tree-fort someday?"

I laugh. "It's a promise."

"One last thing: you need to talk with that Lafayette guy."

"Are you crazy?" I say. "He's the reason I'm in this mess?"

"Think clearly here," Pete stands up from the table and paws at his jacket. "You need to talk with him about what you know and make sure he's watching out for April. Threaten to blow the whistle on everything, do something to get his attention, because he seems to be the type of guy only worried about covering his ass."

"That's been my impression."

"Then tell him you'll strip him of his pants and expose his bare ass to the world."

"I guess it's about time for him and me to speak." I fervently shake my head in disgust. "That son of a bitch has been lying to me since day one and now I'm calling him on it. He either talks to me or I talk to C.N.N."

"There is one more thing--"

"Oh for the love of--"

"No, no, no, nothing like that." Pete says mildly. "It's about that car you rented. The *frammistam* misalign with the muffler bearings and the whole car went blooey so I rented you an Audi. I may have left an *illegal* radar jamming device, effective in almost every state I know, underneath the dashboard. And here is a Minnesota driver's license of a guy that looks a lot like you that I took last week from a drunk driver. Use it to catch a flight. I know you, Pepper and I know you're going to L.A., aren't you?"

"You keep coming through for me, Pete. I'll never be able to make it up to you."

"That's why we're friends, Pepper...you don't have to."

"Explain to my mom for me, will you?"

Pete shivers at the thought. "Damn, Bro, now you're are asking too much."

"I assure you, the berating will be over before you can't count to ten...thousand."

"You better go," Pete looks at his watch, "time is not on your side."

"Where's the Audi?"

"At my parent's farm," Pete tosses me some keys. "Take my truck and leave it there. The keys to the Audi are in the ashtray."

"Where are you staying?"

"With that divorcee."

"Does she have a name?"

"Probably."

The motor idles slowly as I back the car out of the Hansen's driveway. I pass by a boarded up fruit stand along the old gravel road. Minnesota in the fall is timeless. If I were to pass by here in a horse and buggy a hundred years ago, I doubt the view was any different than it is now. The memories I have of this hamlet are very far reaching.

I pass by my old farmhouse. The gravel roads slowly morph into asphalt.

Dutch Van Alstin – Murder in D Block

CHAPTER 36

The bathroom door is missing and the colors of the towels are a cross between dingy brown and grimy gray. The motel in a little jerkwater berg just inside the Wisconsin border still charges me $98.00 to stay the night. The clerk was gowned in a tank top shirt with two holes in the former iron-on patch of a peace symbol, and yet, looked at my shabby attire and was seemingly offended that I was renting a room. He changed his coarse manner when I slipped him an extra twenty and a promise of another twenty-dollar bill if he forgets that he ever laid on eyes on me.

The disheveled man nearly salivates at the thought of an additional twenty; he even calls me *sir.*

The morning arrives too soon for me. The frantic clerk who is importunate for his promised cash greets me with a phone call before the six o'clock hour.

"For God's sake, give me some time to wake up and get a shower."

"Hurry," he says briskly, "I leave in a half an hour."

The minutia of drizzle sprinkling from the showerhead makes lathering any shampoo nearly hopeless.

Quickly I dry, comb, shave, dress and exit out of the room. I toss the clerk the key and fasten the twenty to it with a rubber band. He pounces on the greenback and shoves it in his pocket without so much as a second glance. I drive back north over the border to the twin cities once again to catch a flight.

The airport parking lot is very crowded. The valet ushers me to the rear of the lot next to a Checker cab that appears to have been abandoned.

I locate the perfect flight from the various manifests before I punch in a few numbers in one of the rare payphones left in the world and give my nemesis, John Lafayette, a collect call in Briersburg.

"Agent Jonathan T. Lafayette speaking. How may I be of assistance?"

"You really are an arrogant bastard, you know that?"

"Erickson? Is that you?" Lafayette says eagerly.

"Do you even need to ask or have you managed to piss someone else off as much as you have me?"

"Where are you?"

"Where am I?" I say with incredulity. "Where am I? I'll tell you where I am. I'm off exit eighty-three near Bowling Green, Kentucky. No, wait, wait, I'm really in Bangor, Maine eyeballing Bullwinkle himself. No, I'll be serious this time. I'm in Jacksonville, Florida sucking down a Tutti Frutti shake at the local *Dairy Queen*. I mean, you can believe that, right? After all, that's how stupid you think I am."

"Are you quite finished, Dane?"

"No, Lafayette," I clear my throat as if I'm announcing a Grammy winner. "You dirty, rotten, no good, *sonofabitching* asswipe mother fucking liar. How dare you?" Upon the completion of my tirade, I peek up at all the staring passerby of whom I have drawn their attention toward me. "Now I'm finished."

"How dare me? You have the audacity to be angry at me?"

"At least I've been up front with you, unlike *some* people I know."

"How do arrive at that conclusion?"

"Simple as pie, Mr. Johnny-Cake. I know all about Delgado, and I know he was in the W.P.P. and I know you screwed up in the *keeping him alive* department and I know how much that must have really pissed you off."

"Who told you that?"

"Nobody told me, John. I figured it all out myself. I'm not as stupid as you make me out to be you know?"

Dutch Van Alstin – Murder in D Block

"I never said I thought you were stupid."

"And I know a lot more too, pal."

"Where are you, for real now?"

"You don't know when to quit, do you? Are you trying to tell me you're not tracing this call as we speak? Because, Jonathan T. Lafayette the ass, I know all about the arrest warrant, too."

"You have my word, Dane; I am not tracing this call. Turn yourself in and we'll talk. You've only got half the story."

"I got the half I need."

"Dane, don't go off halfcocked here? Turn yourself in and we'll talk."

"Talk with you? Are you nuts, you've done nothing but lie to me since day one?"

"No, I'm on the up and up here. Turn yourself in and we'll talk."

"Oh we'll talk, G-man, but under my terms."

"Hold on there, slick, I don't take orders from you."

"Then consider it an offer you cannot turn down. Perhaps that will smooth over that ruffled ego of yours?"

"Turn yourself--"

"Is your needle stuck or something? I said no! I'm not going to do that! We're going to talk but it's going to be my way."

"And that would be what?"

"First off, I have pertinent information that April is in danger. I want assurance from you that your little mass of storm troopers will protect her."

"Lafayette scoffs aloud. "She's hardly in any danger."

"Humor me briefly, Lafayette and consider the possibility I am innocent. Isn't my little request worth a face to face?"

"All right," he forces out an exaggerated sigh. "Consider yourself humored."

"I'm serious about that, John. Don't double-cross me here or I'll kick your ass."

"I said I'll do it and I will. Now you need to turn yourself in right now."

"Secondly--"

"Secondly, nothing," Lafayette howls. "I've humored you all I'm going to. I am not playing anymore parlor games with you, Dane, and that's that."

"Okay," I say squarely, "I have to go now and hold a press conference and announce how the F.B.I. screwed up again and who screwed it up. Combine this fiasco with Ruby Ridge,

Waco and the laboratory scandals, you spying on everyone, and the F.B.I.'s budget will consist of enough money for two sling shots and a few chewed up pencils." I hang up amidst Lafayette's pleas of *"Wait! Wait!"*

I rub a dab of smudge of my watch crystal and yawn.

The phone rings for the fourth time and I answer, "Mike's Meat Market, what's your beef?"

"Very funny."

"That was quite a feat of magic you pulled there, Lafayette. Calling me so quickly like you did because I believe your exact words were: 'I give you my word, (cough, cough), that I'm not tracing this call."

Lafayette pauses and says, "Okay, your way."

"Listen well, John, because I'm only saying this once. There is a plane landing here in three hours, be on it. When it lands, and I'm convinced there are no other junior Nazis roaming about, I'll page you and tell you where to go from there."

"I don't like this, Dane."

"I don't rightly care, John."

Silence...

"Okay. I'll be on it, alone."

"Oh don't come alone," I say tauntingly, "bring your self-respect and humor with you. I'm sure they miss you very much after all these years."

"Fine, I will. Why don't you bring along your honor and integrity, they haven't seen the light of day in years either."

"See you in three, Johnny."

"Wait!"

"What now?"

"Nothing, but you didn't tell me what airport?"

"This is Minnesota, Lafayette, we only have one."

One task completed. A second daunting task requires the assistance of a *certain* type of janitor.

A gaunt man with greasy black hair and days of whisker growth cloaking his face pops out from the corner with his cleaning cart. His body shakes and his brow is saturated with sweat as he dips his mop in his bucket. With ever swipe of his mop, he grabs his chest and emits a toilsome exhale.

Dutch Van Alstin – Murder in D Block

I slip the man a twenty, knowing in the back of my mind my twenties are running low, for him to place an OUT OF ORDER sign on a bathroom door away from the baggage claim area.

He bites his lip and mutters some words not in English. But the universal language, i.e., money, does all my talking.

The remainder of the day is spent with me watching reruns on the pay TVs since I do not dare turn my cell phone back on, all the while keeping one eye out for anyone in a gray suit and skinny tie. Attire that shouts to the world: *"I am the F.B.I.!"* I believe Lafayette is not going to attempt to pull anything on me today. He knows my patience is wearing thin and this case seems too important for him to risk blundering our meeting.

Lafayette's plane touches down and is announced over the loud speaker. I sit, meshed in the crowd, watching the departing passengers.

Lafayette is the eighth or ninth man out of the gate. His head gyrates, achieving at least three pirouettes as if I will be waiting for him with open arms, offering to carry his luggage.

"Mr. Bond, pick up the courtesy phone, please. Mr. Bond, courtesy phone."

Lafayette dashes over to a ticket agent and she points to a row of phones near the snack bar. He glances at his watch and scurries toward the phone.

"Hello, hello!"

"Hello, Lafayette."

"Is that you, Erickson?"

"Why?" I say, growing suspicious. "Who else are you expecting?"

"Nobody, it was just an icebreaker."

"You better be up front with me because I am watching you as we speak."

His neck stretches like a giraffe's, peering out over the sea of faces hoping to capture of glimpse of mine.

"Start walking to the snack bar until you see some blue arrows on the floor. Follow them until you reach a corridor on your right."

"Blue arrows?" He says, snapping his eyes back and forth. "Okay, I see 'em."

"After you reach that corridor, follow the orange arrows until you see a men's room on your left. There will be an out of order sign on it but just ignore it and go on in."

"Out of order?"

"Yes, I greased a janitor's palm so we may have a little privacy."

"Now who's being James Bond here?"

Dutch Van Alstin – Murder in D Block

"Afraid, John?"

"Stuff your second grade psychology, mister." Lafayette slams the phone down and sashays quickly down the hallway.

I rush to the men's room the back way, remove my boots, and place them in the last stall. I then dart back to the first stall and stand on the toilet seat and wait, in silence, for the inevitable.

The eerie cessation of sound is broken with the slow creaking noise of Lafayette pushing the door open. His footsteps stop and the door closes completely.

The silence resumes. I stand, motionless, even too afraid to breathe for fear of making a sound. Lafayette's stillness ends as I hear his oxfords squeak with every stride, pausing momentarily between steps. He squats down slightly and eyes my boots in the last stall. Pulling out his pistol, he traipses, slowly. The squeak of shoes passes by me and I leap out of the stall, jamming my finger in his back.

"Freeze." I remain very tranquil and inert.

Lafayette halts his steps and keeps his arms out to the side.

"Place your gun in the sink and walk slowly to the trashcan."

"This is a stupid move, Dane."

"Keep your two-cents in your pocket and do what I say. Remember, you think I'm a killer."

"I trusted you not to pull something like this, Dane."

"Now you know how it feels to be lied to, my mendacious friend." I retrieve his gun from the sink and grasp it firmly. "Now you may turn around, nice and slow."

Lafayette complies with little enthusiasm. His rancorous glare is exposed to me as he turns his body toward me. "I cannot believe you're doing this."

"And I can't believe you fell for this?" I hold out my fingers in a makeshift gun. "And that boot trick?" I laugh, rubbing the humiliation into him deeper. "That's an old *Three Stooges* ploy. In fact, if you didn't fall for it, I was going to claim it was only a joke the idea was so corny." I laugh again as his rank stare grows more acrimonious. "But, I see it didn't."

"He who laughs last, Dane…"

"It'll still be me, G-man and we can make sure of that by you pulling out that phone and calling off the dogs."

"Hey," Lafayette opens up his jacket, exposing his vulnerability; "I came clean. I kept my word."

Dutch Van Alstin – Murder in D Block

"Don't go getting so self-righteous with me, John. You've done nothing but lie to me from the beginning."

"I didn't have any choice in the matter."

"That's too easy of an excuse."

"Maybe so, but it's the truth."

"I'm going to give you the benefit of the doubt here. I'm going to assume that your recent bout of stupidity is uncharacteristic of you and this mess with Delgado's murder has you shaken up a bit. Obviously Delgado dying is of great importance to you?"

"Sounds true enough," he says. "I can't over emphasize the significant ramifications of his death."

"Okay then, why?"

Lafayette looks at his floor and jostles his feet.

"I'm waiting, John?"

"What do you know already?"

"I know I didn't do it, but I'm your scapegoat so nobody finds out the goof up in W.P.P."

"That's not true, Dane." Lafayette says adamantly. "You're nobody's scapegoat; I want the truth, too."

"...Lafayette says while picturing Dane with a tin can in his mouth." I quip.

"Knock of the witticism and get in the game with the rest of us. What do you already know?"

"Okay, I'll start with this: I know the identity of Raphael Delgado was stolen from some dead convict killed in New York some time ago. I know the corpse stuffed in Briersburg's trashcan was under your watchful eye at the time of his unfortunate departing of the earth. What I don't know is why a guy in W.P.P. was in prison to begin with and why you can't assume someone found out he was a snitch and iced him? That is a much more plausible scenario than the twisted, obscure love triangle you concocted?"

"You're right and wrong."

"Not this route again?"

"No, wait," Lafayette slides the trashcan under him and sits. "You got the bull by the balls and I know it. I'll come clean."

"Finally."

Lafayette scratches his forehead and snickers simultaneously.

"Out with it, John."

Dutch Van Alstin – Murder in D Block

"Okay," Lafayette tosses his hands in the air in defeat. "Here it goes: Raphael Delgado, as you knew him, was under F.B.I. watch."

"I knew it!" I shout victoriously.

"No, I'm afraid you still don't."

"What do you mean? You're sounding like your old double talk again?"

"No, Dane," Lafayette stares at me, trying to read my thoughts. "What I mean is Raphael Delgado was under F.B.I. watch, but, he was not involved in the witness protection program at all."

CHAPTER 37

"Now you are really double-talking."

"No I'm not." Lafayette says harshly, obviously losing patients with my accusations.

"Then I don't follow."

"That's because it's a difficult script to follow along with."

"Then get out your copy and start narrating for me."

"Where do I begin?"

"Uhhhh.....? The beginning?" My sarcasm is laid out plainly for Lafayette.

"Not everything is as simple as milking a cow, Dane."

I shrug off Lafayette's stale insult and bore into him harder. "Start somewhere. Anywhere. As long as it's a beginning." I say amid gritting teeth.

He again sighs, trying desperately to stall. "Delgado was helping us, in a way."

"Oh, Lord, don't tell me he was a Fed?"

"No, he helped in an unofficial capacity."

I roll my eyes and scratch my ear with the gun. "Every time you attempt to clear things up, you murky the waters of logic even more. Will-you-get-to-the-point?"

"Dane, I don't know what you're into and I don't what your angle is. I do know you're a prison guard whose integrity and intentions are very suspect. At the risk of appearing aloof or elitist, I got to say something to you. You are in way over your head. The F.B.I., in conjunction with the DEA, is involved in a project that has been in the works for over four years."

"Was Delgado's death part of the plan?"

Although my question is sincere, Lafayette looks at me, searching for acerbity.

"If you're asking if Delgado's death was part of some *evil, ominous* plot," Lafayette uses his fingers to quote his words, "then you're wrong. In fact, Delgado's death screws up almost everything we worked for." Lafayette rubs his forehead and snickers derisively again. "I can't help but thinking the effort is pointless now."

"What big plan are we talking about?"

Lafayette stands and points at the sink, seeking permission. I thrust my hand out at him letting him now he being a bit histrionic. He splashes cold water on his face, breathes some water in his nose, and coughs.

"Look, Dane, I can't accentuate the importance of secrecy here. The people who all know about this are only the people involved. I don't blurt out details to every Tom, Dick, and Harry."

"I don't give a fuck if Tom's dick is hairy. I don't think you have a whole lot of choices here, John, but I assure you, and I won't go out to the bars tonight and start shooting my mouth off like some rube. Now let's hear it."

Lafayette sighs and scratches his nose. "Angelo, AKA, Angel Carbone. Heard of him? Do you know who he is?"

"Yeah...I think so, a mob lawyer?"

"That's him."

"Then you mean *was,* don't you? I remember that now, Angelo Carbone was gunned down in New York City a few years back."

"Wrong on two counts, Dane." Lafayette remains focused on the floor, rubbing his head fervently.

"What two counts are they?"

"First off, he was more than just a mob lawyer; he ran the books in several operations. Secondly, he was never killed in New York City."

"What are you talking about?" I laugh sardonically. "I remember that shootout well. In fact, it was one of your boys from the bureau..."

Lafayette peeks up over his arm at me as I stop in mid-sentence. "Bingo!" He says, pointing his finger at me.

Dutch Van Alstin – Murder in D Block

"You mean…oh come on…stuff like this doesn't happen?"

"I told you it was too intricate to explain to you."

"You're telling me that shootout was a setup?"

"Well…" he sighs. "Yes and no."

"Oh for the love of…fasten your seatbelts, ladies and gentlemen, here we go again."

"Shut up and listen." Lafayette's hands begin to shake as he fosters more anger. "The hit on the family member was real. Carbone was skimming cash off the books until he got wind he was a target of a hit. And instead of him waiting around with a bulls-eye on his backside, he decided to strike first."

"And?"

Lafayette grumbles and rolls his eyes. "Let me spell it out for you, hayseed. The hit on the family member was genuine. The shootout with us was genuine. Carbone being shot was genuine. These facts notwithstanding, Carbone's death was NOT genuine. Do you follow along? Or do you need me to draw you pictures in crayon?"

"You're not saying Delgado and Carbone were one and the same?"

"Congratulations, tiller of the soil, you didn't even need the crayons."

I lean into Lafayette and press the point of his gun against his lapel, grinding the barrel into his chest. "You're telling me the gun battle wasn't staged? Are you sure about that?"

"Yes, Dane," he says bitterly, "now try and follow along with me."

"Oh, I get it." I lean back on the trashcan and rest the pistol on my lap. "The shootout between Carbone and your boys was real. So that means you and your posse of Elliot Ness wannabes just, *happened* to be there?"

Lafayette grows visibly angered and disconcerted. "You…" he tugs at his lapels and wriggles his body on the trashcan. "That's not the point. Let's stay focused here."

"Oh, no, I think we're on cue. Let's see if this ol' bumpkin with a fourth grade education and an affinity for watching the pigs copulate can sum this up for you. You tailed a man knowing he was about to dust off a mobster and you let him do it so you could capture him? Is that about right? Does this hillbilly understand the big city slicker F.B.I. man?"

"No."

"Oh, I see. It just…well, worked out that way, huh?"

"Do you want to continue, or do want to pass judgment on the bureau?"

"I have a feeling we'll do both."

Lafayette spits between my feet and snarls at me. "You're a real piece of shit, Erickson."

Dutch Van Alstin – Murder in D Block

"Continue your lovely chronicle of events, John." I whisper hauntingly. "You left off where you allowed a murder to be committed so you could snare the culprit."

Lafayette closes in my face, still leery of my tenuous hold on his gun. "You just don't understand the way things work, Dane."

"Oh, but I'm receiving quite an education today, John."

"We had a sharpshooter posted close by." Lafayette leans back on the trashcan and cuffs his fingers behind his neck. "He hit Carbone in the leg and we then created the illusion of Carbone's death."

"I'm still confused at why you went to all the trouble to, for lack of a better phrase, capture him, and then fake his death, give him a new face, and then put him in prison anyway? Didn't he end up cooperating?"

"Again, you're in left field, Dane. Carbone did cooperate, that's why we sent him to Briersburg."

"Huh? You sent Carbone, or Delgado, whatever the hell his name was, to prison on purpose? Why?"

"Did I say prison?" Lafayette snaps. "You don't listen too well, do you, Dane? I said Briersburg, not just any old prison."

"The difference being?"

"The difference being, Mr. Erickson, that your warden, James Frankhausen, is trafficking cocaine by the barrel full."

"Frankhausen?" I remark skeptically.

"That's the guy." Lafayette slumps his body on the trashcan and moans. "Frankhausen is alleged to be involved in funneling massive amounts of cocaine through the prisoner's families and we're convinced Frankhausen isn't even the top banana. We have reason to believe the corruption of drugs and money-laundering goes up the ladder and into the State Department of Corrections itself and Frankhausen is a conduit to the prisoners and their families. The distribution is the largest in history spreading all throughout New England, New York, Jersey, Pennsylvania and right on down I-95." Lafayette shakes his head, disgusted at his own words. "And all of this hard work, Dane went down the shitter because some naïve, neophyte, horned up, pig breeding, shit for brains, redneck prison guard couldn't keep it in his pants."

"You mean me?"

"Oh brother," Lafayette drops his head down again and sighs. "You just don't know when to take things seriously, do you? You need to grow up, sonny-boy."

"If what you're telling me is true, John--"

"Everything is true, Dane." Lafayette grows unnerved and angry. He slaps his leg and digs his nails into his skin. "I'm not playing around here. I live in the *real* world, Dane, not some capricious, jocular world where life is full of chimerical anecdotes and witty comebacks."

"You're talking about me again, aren't you?"

"Oh what's the use?"

"As I was saying, if all this is true then isn't more likely someone found out and killed him? That seems more credible than some quirky romantic beef?"

"Nobody knew!" Lafayette barks as if my theory was some sort of accusation of his incompetence. "We had an agent stashed inside and he reported no rumors or troubles concerning Carbone's identity."

"You had an agent posing as a guard? Who was it?"

Lafayette shakes his head. "That's not pertinent information."

"I know everything else?"

"I guess it doesn't matter." Lafayette shrugs. "We pulled him out today anyway."

"Then who was it?"

"His real name is of no concern to you, but you knew him as Toby Sweet."

"Toby?" I say, taken aback some by the revelation. "That sissy boy?"

"Let me tell you: Toby's no sissy. That whole *pantywaist* portrayal is just an act."

"Toby?"

"Yes, Toby, as you know him at least."

"That explains the cop."

"What cop?"

"A city cop I know said he pulled your man Toby off some guy in a gas station." I whistle lowly and snicker. "Some temper on your boy."

"Funny you say that," Lafayette perks his head upward and throws me a toplofty grin, "he said the same thing about you."

"Oh he did? Well don't believe everything he told you, he and I didn't like each other to well."

"You have that way about you, Dane. My friend B.J. said you were an asshole, too."

"Who?"

"Bryce Pitt. He told me you gave him a rash of shit during his visit. I guess I shouldn't take your petty insults too seriously."

"You sent that Pitt fellow to Briersburg? Why?"

"We wanted to be sure that guard, what's his name...Quinn. We wanted to make sure his death wasn't linked to our project."

"Was it, because I have been--"

"Didn't have a damn thing to do with it, Dane. Not a God Damn thing!" Lafayette interjects. "This Quinn guy just took the plunge, that's all. Anyone who has to work around dickheads like you all day is bound to be severely depressed."

"So what all did Toby tell you?"

"Like your assault on Ludlow? The one you denied to the fullest? And he also told me you gave Delgado the raspberries as soon as he entered your cellblock."

"Raspberries?"

"Excuse me, professor. I was trying to put it in *Minnesota ease* for you. Toby said you harangued Delgado the first day he walked in the block."

"So? I do that to all of the prisoners?"

"Yeah, and the fact you were creating skin friction with his wife never played a part, did it?" He says sarcastically.

"Speaking of which, why didn't you guys make Carbone and April split? Why, if this project was so important, didn't you tell him he had to give all of his ties to his old life?"

Lafayette laughs at me. He stares at my face as if I just told him I was a space alien. "What the hell are babbling about? They were never married beforehand. He married her while he was in prison."

"What?"

"Yeah, genius, he married her after he was in prison. I thought you knew what end of the cow to milk? Carbone wanted to do the mattress mambo while he was in Briersburg. So he called *dial-a-whore* and found himself a sperm bank with tits that he could make bimonthly deposits in."

"I know..." the shortness of breath causes me to gasp slightly. I sit down at the edge of the sink and swallow, hoping to moisten my arid throat. "I know you're purposely making disparaging remarks about the woman I love, so I've decide not to kick your uppity ass all over this here powder room. That fact notwithstanding, I don't believe you anyway. I find it doubtful you would allow him to marry and jeopardize your project."

"Look, Dane," Lafayette fights to keep from smiling, "he only wanted to fuck her once a

Dutch Van Alstin – Murder in D Block

while. He wasn't about to have any conversation with her beyond, 'does this fasten from the front or back'?"

"I don't…I just don't believe you at all."

Lafayette again chuckles at my anxiety. "You're right. He may have also said, 'more baby, more'."

Lafayette's tie serves as a mechanism for me to slam him on the floor. The can falls, causing a loud crash. His feet catch in the plumbing fixtures causing his leg to be twisted. He lies, nearly upside down, in a puddle of water and pile of debris from the fallen trashcan. Still, Lafayette looks up at me placate, nearly laughing. "What's the matter, big boy? You found out your April isn't Mother Theresa?"

"She's got more to her than that, you bloated gas bag. You're lying about everything. I don't believe this whole horseshit about Carbone or anything."

"I'm going to say it once more, Dane. I don't care whether you believe me or not."

"Why would a guy like Carbone go along with all this shit anyhow?"

"Because," Lafayette scoffs, "he was looking at life in Marion, that's why."

"What's the difference? Marion? Briersburg? Tomato, *tomato*! Prison is prison, isn't it?"

"Delgado was his new name. We were going to release him after the project was done and he was a free man to live as he saw fit and mate with who he saw fit."

I shake my head more vigorously, searching in vain for an explanation to convince myself I am right. "I would rather live the life of a mobster in prison, trying for an appeal, than to live in some broken down trailer with a few hundred dollars allowance every month."

"Now what are you crowing about, Dane? Trailer? Allowance? The man had a new face; he could do what the hell he wanted to do."

"And do what? Work at the *Buy-N-Bag* for eight bucks an hour? Paint those yellow lines along the highway for some municipal paycheck and dried up 401K?"

"Have you come completely unglued?" Lafayette props his hand under his head as if he's watching TV while lying on the floor eating popcorn. "I just told you the man skimmed mob money? Weren't you listening? The son of a bitch had millions!"

"Wh…huh…that money…that money gets seized, doesn't it?"

"Normally, but him keeping his money was agreed to beforehand. That's how important this deal was. Are you trying to tell me you didn't know your little girlfriend got a raise in her allowance? Like by a few million? Come on, Dane, I was born on Tuesday, but it wasn't last

Tuesday."

"Damn it!" I shout, driving my fist into shattered glass where a mirror once resided. I reach down and pull Lafayette up by his necktie. The blood from my hand drips down my palm and on to his coat. For the first time today, I see a tinge of alarm in Lafayette's eyes. He is now witnessing the nonsensical ravings of a madman, a madman with a gun.

A madman with the wool lifted from his eyes.

"Tell me, you big mouth piece of shit. Tell me!" I shove Lafayette's pistol in his throat. He gasps at the pressure in his windpipe, but tries desperately to speak.

"For God's sake, man, tell you what? I tell you whatever it is you want to know?"

"Just how much cash did Carbone have?"

"You really didn't know, did you?"

"I said how much?" I shake his necktie feverishly, jostling his body against the sink and the toilet stall.

"Close to…thirty million."

"I was wrong." I throw Lafayette against the sink, releasing my grip. He grabs his necktie and nervously tucks it back into his jacket.

"Wrong about what?"

"I was wrong about what I said about you earlier. You are just as stupid as I thought you were."

CHAPTER 38

Lafayette stares at me uneasily, trying to predict my next move. A bead of sweat forms under his eyes and drips sluggishly down the bridge of his nose and rests on the edge. He purses his lips some and sighs gently. "Okay, Dane, we're adults here."

"Slowly, Lafayette, and I do mean *slowly* reach in your jacket pocket and take out your handcuffs."

"Sure thing, Dane." Lafayette perches a scant smile on his face. He reaches in his coat slowly and nods his head at me. "Whatever you want, Dane. Cooler heads need to prevail now, don't you think?"

"I don't think." I snatch his handcuffs from him and open them up. "Remember? I'm just a redneck hillbilly capable of anything, ala, *Deliverance.*"

"Yeah," Lafayette expels a nervous laugh, not believing my subtle threat, but still goosey and apprehensive over the uncertainty he faces. "I didn't mean any of that. It's just an investigative ploy, you know? You're a law enforcement guy? You do investigative--"

"Oh would you stop kissing up and just turn around?"

"Why?"

"Just do it or prepare to squeal like a pig, you handsome devil."

"Okay, now, that's just not funny. Let's be professionals here. We're both professionals,

Dutch Van Alstin – Murder in D Block

aren't--"

"You're kissing up again," I say, gesturing for him to do a pirouette. "And I'm starting to hear banjo music in the background."

"What's next, Dane?" Lafayette scrupulously turns his body around but still cranks his neck backward to make eye contact. "You need to keep a cool head, Dane."

"Squat down and put these on," I hand him the handcuffs, "and fasten yourself to the sink pipes. And do it correctly, John, I'll be checking your work."

"Okay, Dane, you're the boss here." Lafayette, still making eye contact, hunkers down to the floor and complies.

"John, I believe we took the same course in hostage survival. In fact, the course I took at the academy was from Quantico's training films. So never mind all the humanizing with eye contact, the passive, submissive tone in your voice, and the general ass kissing. I have no intention of hurting you because I haven't hurt anyone yet, contrary to what you think."

"Okay, Dane, you're right again. I believe you when you say you're going to be sagacious and sensible here."

"Good. Now to celebrate, I'll just take your cell phone from your coat and take it with me. You don't need to be making any calls for a while."

I empty the magazine of all the bullets, eject the round in the chamber, and dump them all in the bullets in the trash along with the handcuff keys.

I return Lafayette's gun and give him a perfunctory apology and Nazi salute as I walk out the door.

With great alacrity and speed, I hasten to the car and rummage through April's file Pete put together for me.

The last known address for Miss April Salvano is of the home of Dr. and Mrs. Salvon' of Sherman Oaks, California. I will have to assume the deletion of the "O" in Pete's file was erroneous, or the Salvono's augmented their name. Perhaps an Italian isn't exactly greeted with warm accolades in a neighborhood like Sherman Oaks. How will they feel about a Scandinavian visiting their turf?

I punch in the phone number on the report and await several rings of the phone.

A gallant voice answers, "Dr. Salvon's residence, Bernard speaking?"

Knowing this conversation cannot be done over the phone, I simply hang up with the reassurance I have the correct home. I don't dare to take a chance on a flight. There are too many high tech spying cameras in the airports these days.

Dutch Van Alstin – Murder in D Block

Pete's radar *jammer* is fired up and I speed south to Missouri to the famed Route 66, now interstate four lanes, and turn right.

Next stop, California.

At four A.M. I cross the New Mexico border. My eyes are weighted from fatigue and my kidneys are filled with coffee. The Audi begins veering across the centerline, signifying to me that exhaustion has won over my zeal to reach California as soon as possible.

The Audi's backseat would leave young lovers to be very creative in the positioning of their bodies. There is scarcely room for me to lie down, not to mention how two clunky, awkward teenagers, not really sure how to *do it* to begin with, would manage.

My feet drape over the neck rest of the driver's seat and I am able to tuck my hands underneath my neck to cushion the harshness of the inevitable stiff neck when the sun rises.

The traffic is relatively light leaving the noise to a minimum. I miss the sound of the lake rustling up to the shore. I miss my dog annoying me at three A.M. with a tennis ball in his mouth, thinking I'm going to play catch. I miss the way the paperboy could never manage to get my paper on my porch and out of the rain. And I even miss the bad tasting coffee in the lineup room.

My life today is what it is and only since yesterday, an eternity has passed me by.

California looks no different than Nevada, which looked no different than Arizona or New Mexico. The ocean is still blue, the sun still rises and sets at certain intervals, all the McDonald's have golden arches, and nobody in this state can drive a car worth a damn either.

I take refuge at a nearby truck stop and fuel up the Audi. Before I partake some supper, I wash my hands and face and wish I could scrape my whiskers off with my fingernails.

The waitress, between the snapping of her gum and her ceaseless spilling of my coffee, gives me directions to Sherman Oaks. A few different times she stopped in mid-sentence and stared at my grubby attire, gleaming suspiciously at me, but gives me directions nonetheless. I have no idea how to program the GPS in this car and I'm still not turning on my cell phone until I am back in Briersburg.

As I cruise north on route 405, I plot how I can approach the Salvon's. Every ploy and trick full of guile had to have been tossed there way at some point and time. Between salesman, save the Whales, save the coyote and save the sewer rats, I can imagine a person is constantly knocking upon the Salvon's door with their palm showing. I guess there is no substitute for the truth, although the truth may not be a welcome scenario either.

Dutch Van Alstin – Murder in D Block

A few people shout: "go back to Minnesota you *Oakie*" as I make a quick dash from lane to lane. The irksome trip through a part of the country I've only read about comes to an end when I drive upon a large, rod Iron Gate. Traveling alongside of the seemingly never-ending wall, I at last come on to a stone wall consisting of vertically aligned bricks and precut stones. Engraved in majestic fashion is a brass name plate with the name *Salvon' Estate* engraved. The gate is unmanned. Only a call button, in what seems to be an old fire alarm box restored to its former condition, operates as a buffer between the public and the Salvon's.

I press the button and receive some static in return. The pause seems endless until the static ceases.

"May I be of some assistance?" A regal voice responds.

"Uh...yes," I clear my throat, "I...uh, need to talk, uh, confer with Mr. Salvon'."

"*Doctor* Salvon' is not receiving any visitors today." The static vanishes at the completion of the smug reply.

"Wait, please, sir. I'm not a crackpot nor a salesman or anything of the kind. I need to speak to the doctor with regards to his daughter...sir?" The cessation of sound continues.

Strike one. I back the car around and start to pull out.

The gate begins to rattle, not unlike Briersburg's yard gate. The static reappears briefly and is replaced by the gallant voice once more.

"Sir, please pull your vehicle up to the east entrance and I'll meet you there."

"Uh...east?"

"Just pull your car along the driveway, sir. Turn left at the...I'll tell you what, sir, I'll send an escort down and he'll assist you."

"Thanks."

A man gowned in traditional butler's attire motors down the driveway in a large golf cart. The man may be dressed appropriately, but he does not fit the quintessential image of the ideal butler. He is a muscular man with flaming orange hair and a full beard. His horned rim glasses lack the nobility of manner and sense of distinction one expects of a butler of an obviously stately manor.

He pulls next to me and looks at my grungy appearance with understandable apprehension and mistrust.

"Leave the keys in your vehicle, sir, and I'll have it tended to right away. If you don't mind, sir, just climb aboard the rear seat and I'll escort you to the residence."

"Sure thing." I say with the enthusiasm of a child. "I'm glad the coach decided to let me

Dutch Van Alstin – Murder in D Block

pitch this late in the game. I've been working on my curve ball."

"Pardon?"

"Uh, it's just a vain attempt at humor, sir. Remember when the relief pitchers use to be escorted on to the field with little golf carts?"

"That's a…baseball term?"

"Yes." I say sheepishly, broadcasting to him my overt lack of refinement and culture. "Aren't the *Dodgers* big news out here?"

"Not particularly, sir," he replies. "Now hold on to the railing, sir. We'll be at the manor momentarily."

The butler zips back up the driveway exposing to me a sight unimagined to me before. Hollywood's Epicurean vision of mansions comes to life with the pulchritude of manicured lawns. Each individual blade of grass looks so symmetrical and taut. The lime green texture expands over the rolling hillside and unfolds to a large stone fountain at an archway on top of the drive. The water spurts from each end of the structure into a two separate pools, filled with some type of exotic fish. As we reach the tiptop of the entrance, a mammoth brick structure seems to pop out of the ground. The estate stretches into the open three stories high with the top story actually bowing outward as it rises.

Small handcrafted angels inundate the skirt surrounding the base of the home. Although my glance is brief, I don't see any repeating design or lay out of the angels.

The butler stops the vehicle and motions me toward the entryway. Resting down beneath the manor is two large kidney shaped pools. The one pool has water that looks unruffled and smooth. A man with a powder blue uniform and a *milkman* style hat swishes his net through the other in a routine fashion, cleaning up an occasional blade of grass or perhaps a runaway tree leave.

The driveway circles back down the mansion away from the direction I arrived. It curves and meanders downward until it's conclusion can no longer be determined.

I follow the butler to the doorway with my sights affixed everywhere but the sidewalk. He peeks back at me periodically, still unsure of who I am and what my intentions are. He intentionally escorts me to a side entrance where a mastiff of a breed I don't recognize snarls at me as I walk by. A muffled growl can be heard as the butler stops to scratch his ears momentarily just before tossing him some type of biscuit. The mastiff devours the morsel immediately and paws into the ground searching for crumbs.

"The poor beast has an insatiable appetite for meat," he says.

Dutch Van Alstin – Murder in D Block

"I've lost a few pounds recently," I counter, "the only meat I have is in my fridge."

"Yes...*fridge*." The butler pulls open both doors and motions me in. I stand, unsure if his gesture is what I perceive.

"Please, sir, go right on in. I'll summon the doctor for you."

I take one giant step and poise myself in the foyer. The butler slams both doors and locks them from the inside.

"This way, sir." He walks down a thin, marbled hallway that causes my boots to echo with each step.

My neck spins around like some sappy tourists popping light bulbs at every nook and cranny of some celebrity's home. The hallway seems to never end. There are doors off to the sides but they are all sealed shut. I cannot spot any servants, any openings. The hallway is devoid of any paintings, knick-knacks, statues, or anything of the kind. The butler walks beside me peering at me from the corner of his eye.

Finally we stop. The butler smiles and points his finger up at the corner of the ceiling. There mounted on the wall is a camera.

"If you will, sir. Please look into the camera for a few seconds while we snap a few security shots for our records?"

"Your records?"

"Please, sir. Surely you understand. The Doctor and his wife must be careful of security measures?"

"Yeah," I sigh, knowing his point is valid. "Certainly. I'll cooperate in any way."

"Thank you, sir."

I stare up into the camera briefly while my mug shot is taken.

The home reeks of opulence but manages, somehow, in a way I can't explain, to shy away from ostentatious. The furnishings, the décor, they all seem personal and individual, not merely for show.

Whether the house is pretentious or not, it's still a long way off from the mean streets of Philly where April claims she hails from.

Oh be it ever so humble...

Dutch Van Alstin – Murder in D Block

CHAPTER   39

"Sir?" The butler says in a haughty intonation. "I'm afraid I must require you to, uh, some of your apparel is…well…" The butler shrugs off anymore of his vain attempt at a benevolent tone and blurts: "your boots, sir. I need for you to remove your boots."

"Oh," I glance down at my boots caked in Minnesota mud. "Of course." I slide each of them off all the while affixing a pleasant smile to the butler. "Here you go."

"Uh…they'll be fine where they are, sir." The butler draws his hands back away from my boots as if they were saturated with the plague. "Just place them neatly at the library foyer."

"Of course."

"Dr. Salvon' is in the library. I will announce you, if you wish, Mr.…?

"Erickson," I say, amidst the clearing of my throat once more. "Dane Erickson."

"Certainly. Follow me if you will," he looks me up and down once more, "Mr. Erickson."

"Dane is fine."

"Hmmm, yes," the butler emits a mechanical laugh. "I appreciate your amiable manner, sir, but I, as an attendant to the doctor, refer to his entire guest list, even you, by their surnames."

"I see. How very…let's call it *ill-bred* of me to think otherwise."

"Don't give it a second thought, sir. The first was ample enough for me."

Dutch Van Alstin – Murder in D Block

"Quite. Now can you please tell Mr...., oh my, that old hick talk we use in the hills is bubbling to the surface again, I mean *Doctor* Salvon he has a guest?"

"Of course." The butler opens the door and announces my arrival. He then steps back and waves me inside.

"Hey, Mack?"

"It's 'Stockman,' sir," he says, fighting off a curt tone.

"Yes, the old surname thing. Perhaps a cool, crisp *Perrier* with a twist of lemon would be very delightful? In a pre-frosted glass of course."

"Of course, sir. I'll bring it forthwith."

"And tell me, which way to the outhouse?"

Stockman ignores my snide comment, backs out of the room, and closes the double doors behind him.

An older, distinguished gentleman leans against a fireplace toward the rear of the room. He lights a pipe sending puffs of smoke clouding about his head. Just like the movies: rich guy smokes a pipe dressed in a robe. It's quite obvious this is Dr. Salvon.

"Hello, young man." The man says, waving me toward him. "Please, step over here and join me. I'm Doctor Salvon." He extends his hand out to me graciously and smiles. "I'm sorry; I didn't catch your name in full."

"I'm Mr. Erickson, Doctor Salvon."

"Please," he holds his palm up to me, "in my home, a guest calls me Richard."

"Thank you," I say, knowing I'll be referring to him as Doctor anyhow, "please call me Dane."

"Dane it is."

The doctor stands taut and proudly. I estimate his age as *sixtyish* or so, but in superior physical shape. His hair is predominately black but a trace of silver is spread out through it giving him a very genteel semblance. His eyes are large and round but seemingly very friendly. His mustache, a bit bushier than I'd expect for the blueblood sect, is completely silver. He drapes himself in a red silk robe with some type of banal design across the chest, and the sleeves bow outward, not unlike a boxer's robe.

"Would you like a cappuccino, or perhaps some coffee?"

"Coffee sounds splendid, sir." *Splendid?* think to myself.

"I'll have Stockman bring us some latte and pastries."

"He should be right back momentarily. He was gracious enough to fetch me some water."

"A good man that Stockman," he says. "If he was brusque with you in anyway, please accept my expression of regret."

"He was okay. I'm sure he is just doing his job and watching out for you."

"Yes, he was a linebacker for the Washington Federals of the now defunct U.S.F.L. from the 1980's. His actual tenure here is to protect Mrs. Salvon when I am out of town. As you can see, he is rough around the edges, but he is a fine man and very protective."

"I'm sure."

"So," the doctor walks back to the fireplace and pokes the ice cold coals in the fire, "Erickson? A Viking name. Fierce warriors they were, but proud and noble people, even though they were quite brutal. Tell me, Dane, do your roots stem from Denmark?"

"No, Norway for the most part."

"Really? I assumed the sobriquet *Dane* was primarily Danish?"

"Well, yes it is, normally, but my coworkers bestowed upon me that little nickname and they aren't the most incisive bunch of people. To them, all Scandinavian people, whether from Finland, Sweden, Switzerland, Norway or Denmark, all know how to yodel, wear wooden shoes, are proficient at hockey, play the Hardanger fiddle and can polka all night long."

The doctor utters a laugh. "You're very witty, Dane. But still, you seem proud of your lineage. That's a quality in people that is fading and I respect immensely those who are not ashamed to proclaim where they hail from."

"Thank you, Doctor Salvon'."

"I had an 'O' at the end of my surname originally and I deleted it for strictly business reasons. I'm a surgeon by trade," he holds his hands up as if a surgeon's hands can be distinguished between that of a mailman. "I went into plastic surgery some thirty ago." He laughs again, but at what I am not sure. "I use to work on these phony-baloney Hollywood people. You know the type? The ones who measure your integrity by what color ribbon you wear on your lapels? Anyway, with all their rhetoric for tolerance and diversity I can tell you this; an Italian doctor is an elitist's no-no." The doctor elongates the "I" in Italian just as my mother does.

He slides a book off the shelf, thumbs through the contents, and forces himself to mount a smile on his face. "We opted to drop the 'O' to give our name a more acceptable European name, i.e., French. These Hollywood hypocrites are all the same. They don't mind if a Frenchman or German does their tummy tucks, but an Italian?"

Dutch Van Alstin – Murder in D Block

The doctor turns the book's cover toward me and taps on the binding. "The famous Fredrick Douglass letter to Thomas Auld. Tell me, young man; are you familiar with it at all?"

"Actually, I am, sir," I say, unintentionally boastful. "The letter was written to Douglass' former slave master after Douglass was free. If I recall correctly, the letter appeared in a local newspaper."

"Quite sharp, Dane," the doctor declares, "I'm impressed."

"Thank you."

"Do you know the most impressive element of Douglass' letter, Dane?"

"No."

"It's where he begins writing about his children. The letter's tone seems to change from one of understandable ire to one of mercy. I can envision Mr. Douglass writing, digging his quill into the parchment until he begins writing about his children."

The doctor slides the book back on to the shelf and sighs.

"Then he releases his rigid grip on his quill and writes tenderly of his children. He even alludes to Auld being welcome in his home and how he would be treated hospitably. There's a man, Douglass of course, who was not ashamed of his ancestry."

I stand, actually twiddling my thumbs, intimidated slightly by the Doctor's rambling. I think of some type of reply, but none surfaces to my brain.

He breaks the tense silence and offers me a seat. My weary body happily accepts the offer and I plunk myself down in a soft leather chair.

"My daughter…April," he pauses slightly. "When she first began to lose touch with the family, she had come across evidence of my changing the family surname. She ranted and raved about we were no better than the snobs I operated on. I'm not sure, Dane, but perhaps she's correct?" The doctor stares bewilderedly into an empty fireplace. I, again, do not know what to say.

Stockman returns with a tray of drinks and even some coffee and pastries. He hands me the water personally leaving me to ponder how the prisoners use to spit and urinate in food they knew the guards would eat.

I credit Stockman to have more class than that of the pitiless animals I dealt with in Briersburg and I sip the entire contents down quickly.

"A toasty fire appeals to me, Dane. How about you?"

"Sounds nice, Sir."

"Stockman? If you will, please?"

Dutch Van Alstin – Murder in D Block

Stockman cracks some kindling and lights some papers ablaze. "Will there be anything else, Doctor Salvon'?"

"No thank you, Stockman. Just summon Mrs. Salvon' in approximately five minutes or so."

"Very good, sir." Stockman manages to glare at me invidiously before he exits.

"Dane, before I can allow Mrs. Salvon' in, I must know about April."

"What specifically would you like to know?"

"Well..." he sighs, "is she, I mean, is her health up to par?"

"Sir, are you questioning me whether she's alive?" I say intriguingly.

The doctor looks down at his feet and smiles defensively. "Yes, Dane," he says. "I'm afraid that is exactly what I am asking you."

"Yes, sir, she's alive and well."

"Thank God," he sighs. "Thank the sweet Lord."

"Has it been that long since you've heard from her?"

"I'm afraid so, Dane. That's why I had to inquire into her well-being. I couldn't possibly allow anyone to spring such morose news to Mrs. Salvon' about her little angel."

A woman, unannounced by Stockman, opens the double doors, walks in, and smiles at me. "Good morning, young man." She says to me.

"Good morning, Ma'am."

"Please," she raises her hands defensively, as if the term *ma'am* was offensive to her, "my name is Theresa."

Mrs. Salvon' also looks to be in her late fifties or early sixties, but like her husband, her physical shape is marvelous as well. I cannot detect one trace of silver in her wavy black hair and if she colors any of her hair, it is very subtle and unnoticeable. She is very shapely and trim and her girlish figure is easily discernible in the silky maroon dress she gowns herself in this morning. Her nose crests upwards some, but on her the curvature is fashionable. And her eyes are April's.

"Darling, this is Dane Erickson," the doctor says.

I begin to rise and she motions me to remain seated.

"Welcome to our home, Dane."

"Thank you, Ma'am, uh...Mrs. Salvon'."

"Theresa?" The doctor says.

She snaps her neck at the doctor and smiles.

Dutch Van Alstin – Murder in D Block

"Dane is here to discuss April, dear."

Her eyes well up and she bites at her fingernail. "Oh my...April? April? Is she okay? Is she well?"

"She's fit as a fiddle, Mrs. Salvon'."

"Oh, Richard, our baby."

"Yes, Theresa, now we both need to sit down and calm ourselves."

"Where is she, Dane? Has she told you about us? What is she doing now? Is she working anywhere?"

"She's doing well, Mrs. Salvon'." She lives way out east--"

"Dane," she interjects, please tell me what she said about us? I need to know, Dane."

Mrs. Salvon's façade at a courageous front seems to be chipped away with every parcel of information about April, regardless of how innocuous that information may be.

"Well, Mrs. Salvon'...I--" I gape at the doctor hoping he will rescue me.

The doctor, seemingly knowing what I'm about to say, nods at me reassuringly and rubs Mrs. Salvon's leg.

"Well, she told me," I clear my throat, "she, uh, hailed from Philadelphia and she was, well, for the lack of a better word, poor."

Dr. And Mrs. Salvon' look at each other, and then, embarrassment causes them to look away from each other.

"She told me she grew up with her dad because her mom died when she was--"

"Damn it, Richard!" Mrs. Salvon shrieks as she leaps up from the couch. "Damn her, Richard! Damn her again! Why is every time someone comes to this door with a story about April and one of her little schemes, I'm always the one dead in her scenarios? She must wish it on me, Richard, she must. Why else would she say the same thing over and over again? What did I do, what did I say to cause these deep acrimonious feelings from her to me?"

"Please, Theresa. I know this isn't easy for you, but please let Dane finish or we'll never be able to help April."

Mrs. Salvon continues her sobbing on the doctor's shoulder. "I'm sorry, Dane. I should be use to this torture by now. I'm very sorry I've made you feel uncomfortable in my home."

"Oh, Ma'am, please," I say imploringly, "don't concern yourself with me. I'm okay, I promise."

"Every night I look at her beautiful face before I go to bed and remember when she was happy with us and I just cry all over again."

Dutch Van Alstin – Murder in D Block

"Grandma? Are you okay? A soft voice from behind me prattles.

Now all beauty has its roots and when I turn my head, and view this angelic, precious face staring helplessly at her grandma, I know what April's roots looked like.

Mrs. Salvon' pops up from the couch, wiping her eyes, and hugs the little girl. "No, no, grandma is fine, sweetheart," she wipes her eyes again and perches on a spurious smile on her face. "You go back into the kitchen and have Alec make you some French toast. You know the kind? The one with all the vanilla and cinnamon?"

The little girl darts her head toward me, and smiles. "Hi, Mister."

"Hi, sweetie," I say.

She waves at me and dashes down the hallway shouting for her French toast.

"Yes, Dane," the doctor says evenly, "that's April's daughter."

I force out a prolonged sigh and drop my spiritless body down on the chair.

"Perhaps we should begin from ground zero, Dane," Mrs. Salvon' says. "We know you're here with regards to April, but what specifically did you want to ask?"

"I don't where to start. I'm afraid anything I say will upset you."

Mrs. Salvon' closes her face in on mine and rubs my cheek. As I look at her up close, her radiance is no less striking then from a far.

"Dane, whatever you say will presumably disturb us, but we won't blame you. We know where the fault lies, so please tell us whatever you want." She says.

"April was married," I pause and check the Salvon's reaction, or lack thereof. "Anyhow, her husband was killed and ever since he died, my life has been chaos times ten."

"Oh, Lord," Mrs. Salvon' leans backward, visibly stunned. "What happened to him?"

"There is no euphemism in the thesaurus that can say this delicately: he was murdered and the police believe I did it."

The Salvon's look at one another and then back toward me.

"Dane? I'm just going to be brazenly forward here. Are you alluding to the idea April killed this man?" The doctor says.

"I'll confess, sir, that I did believe that at one time. I had heard April inherited his money and I jumped to all sorts of conclusions. But the realities surrounding the entire situation make it virtually impossible for her to have known about this man's money."

"That's a relief," the doctor sighs. "I can't believe I am asking such questions about my own daughter."

"Dane?" Mrs. Salvon' says skeptically. "How can't a woman know her future husband

Dutch Van Alstin – Murder in D Block

has money?"

"Because their relationship didn't have a real advantageous origin." I laugh some, realizing too late the Salvon's may fail to see any humor in the whole mess. "As it turns out, April's husband was a prisoner where I worked as a guard."

"What?" the Doctor says, clearly flabbergasted.

"Yes, sir. She married him after he was incarcerated, for whatever reason, but the only motive to kill him would have been for money and there's no way she could had prior knowledge of his money."

"Dane, I find this very implausible." Mrs. Salvon' says.

"I understand your--"

"Dane?" The doctor shouts.

"Yes, sir?" I say skittishly.

He sighs, calming himself, as he rubs her fingertips in his eyes, covering his face. "What prison did you say you were a guard at?"

"Briersburg State Prison, sir. It's back east in--"

"Oh, Lord, forgive me," he bellows. "It's my fault; the whole thing is my fault. Oh my, God, what have I done?" The doctor continues burying his face in his hands as he rattles his head hysterically.

"Richard? Are you okay? What's the matter, Richard?" Mrs. Salvon attempts to pull the doctor's hands away from his face but his grip remains strong.

"I'm sorry, Theresa," he says, "but April did have a motive."

"How, dear? You heard what Dane said? She couldn't have known anything?"

"But she did," he sighs heavily, fighting off tears. "April knew all about Mr. Delgado."

Dutch Van Alstin – Murder in D Block

CHAPTER 40

"Oh, Richard, you didn't?" Mrs. Salvon' exclaims.

"Oh, no, what have I done?" The doctor continues jabbering.

"Oh, no, Richard, not April? She couldn't have?"

"I realize this is a bit self-serving of me, but I'd like to know, Doctor, just how you knew the man's name was Delgado? I didn't reveal that detail?"

"Richard, this Delgado man was one of yours?" She queries.

"Yes, Theresa," the Doctor lifts his head up and runs his palms across his face, trying to hide his tears. "He was here two or three years ago, just about when April was released from Betty Ford."

"Betty Ford?" I burst out loudly. "What on earth is going on here? I am completely lost. Sir, what did your wife mean by the phrase *one of yours*? One of your what? I don't want to appear unsympathetic to your pain, sir, but you've hurled a lot of stimuli at me and I'm finding it hard to digest it?"

"I know, son," the doctor rattles his head and sighs. "I apologize. Where would like for me to begin?"

"I'm not sure what connects with what? How about we start with the Betty Ford clinic? Is April's stint there related to how you knew Delgado?"

Dutch Van Alstin – Murder in D Block

"No, not directly at least."

"Is Betty Ford related to how you knew Delgado? Were you a doctor there at one time?"

"No, no, no, nothing like that," the doctor shutters his head ardently. "April being in Betty Ford had nothing to do with how I met Mr. Delgado."

"Did April meet him as well?"

"No, just myself. April never met the man while he was here."

"Let's begin with how you met him, doctor. What did Mrs. Salvon' mean by what she said? One of your what? Did he work for you at some time?"

"Dane," he looks at me thoughtfully and purses his lips, preparing his thoughts into words. "What I am about to tell you cannot go further than the three of us. In fact, it's gone too far as it is."

"Sir, my confidentiality is sound, but why are being so furtive here? What's going on?"

"As I said earlier, Dane, I'm a plastic surgeon by trade. I no longer cut into the Hollywood sect, the pressure was unbearable.

"However," he clears his throat and rings his hands, "I'm not exactly retired either. I'm contracted by certain government agencies to perform surgery on some law enforcement people, persons in the witness protection program and Mr. Delgado was a patient of mine."

I expel a misgiving laugh and stammer. "You have to be joking, Sir. With all due respect, doctor, that statement sounds like a *"B"* movie they show at three A.M. on channel 999."

"That's because you're reading too deeply into what I've just said, Dane. What I do may sound comparable to underground spy stuff but actually, it's not uncommon. I'm not implying I have some secret laboratory with bubbling test tubes and overflowing beakers. All of my surgery is very common practice; it's just not promulgated to the nation for obvious reasons. We're talking about minor surgery here, Dane. Pad the eyes, drain the cheeks, and touch up the nose, not some metamorphosis where their own mother will not recognize them. The government contracts my services on an as needed basis. That way I don't need to appear on a payroll and my services come under the discretionary spending accounts all agencies have. Secrecy is a must. Agents need to change their appearances, witnesses lives are in danger if they're recognized. Every precaution is taken to protect confidentiality."

"Then it's probably obvious what my next question is, Doctor?"

The Doctor looks at me abashed and chagrined. "I believe so."

"Delgado was one of your patients and you told April? Why, sir? Why would you breech that security? And for that matter, sir, how did you become privy to such information clearly outside of your realm as a plastic surgeon? It's not as though you needed to know his name to carve him up?"

"That's where the story has a touch of age old sin, Dane."

"Can you elucidate for me, sir?"

"Certainly," he says, refocusing his attention. He pours himself another cup of coffee and warms up Mrs. Salvon's mug. "Would you like some more coffee, Dane?"

"Thank you, no," I say, masking my rudeness.

"It's obvious that I'm never aware of my patients identities, pseudo or otherwise. And, frankly, I never gave it a second thought. I never had any interest in knowing who they were or why I was operating on them. I just did my job, collected my fee and forgot all about them.

"However," he leans back on the chair and balances his cup delicately on his lap, "my vainglorious side reared its ugly head. Oh no, it wasn't enough for me to be a plastic surgeon for the government, operating on G-men, mobsters, witnesses, I had to push the envelope. I had to feed my need for power too. I had to—"

"Doctor?" I say, interrupting his soliloquy, "can you just get to the crux of your thoughts?"

"Yes, Dane," he sighs once more. "My apologies for rambling, it's just that I am so disappointed in my behavior. On one occasion, the occasion when I operated on Mr. Delgado, I sat with Mr. Delgado's escort and we shared some wine in the den. Oh he was a brash young man, full of pomposity and the wine began to procure his judgment some. He began divulging little tidbits of information on what Delgado was doing and who he was and why he was being operated on to begin with. Now I should have stifled him as soon as he began revealing such top secret information. But unfortunately, the wine seemed to be hindering my better judgment as well. I admit, I reveled in the thought I was being let in on a clandestine operation and I was intrigued by the surreptitious nature of our government. I was actually part of it. I could feel it. I was *in the loop*, as it were. My machismo raced to the ends of my soul, feeding my curiosity. Oh what a fool I have been. Just an old fool."

Mrs. Salvon' rubs the doctor's leg and smiles affectionately, trying to sooth his humiliation.

"I thought nothing of it all as the months progressed. I merely chalked the experience up to the intoxicating effects of the alcohol and went about my business. Here, Dane is the part where the Betty Ford clinic comes in."

"Richard, I'm not sure what you mean?" Mrs. Salvon' says.

Dutch Van Alstin – Murder in D Block

"Just explain to our friend, dear, why April was there and I'll tie up the loose ends for you."

"If you would, Mrs. Salvon'? I'd appreciate a little clarity in why April was there and for how long? Perhaps I can make sense of this nightmare I put myself into?"

"Certainly, Dane," she releases the doctor's hand and shifts her body toward me. She folds her legs and resituates herself on the couch, telling me I'm in for a lengthy account of April's fall from grace.

"April was a normal, healthy child. Growing up, she laughed, she sang, she played, she learned, she did all those things and more. She went to college at Berkley and received two Master's degrees. One in English literature and the other in psychology. She then went to UCLA Medical School to become a doctor and that's when the roof caved in."

"How so?" I say.

"There's no Kafkaesque reason why April began to falter. She started using and abusing drugs. Her grades plummeted and she flunked out of medical school. Now I guess I could ask myself the old chicken and egg question, but whether the drugs lead to failing or vice-versa is irrelevant. April began making all sorts of wild accusations, claiming two different professors raped her when she declined their sexual advances. She said that was why she failed because the doctors there were against her and they wanted her to fail. She even alleged that Richard was involved in seeing that she failed because he was afraid of the family competition. She began accusing her sisters of similar things."

"Sisters? April has sisters?"

"Three," Mrs. Salvon' shakes her head and groans. "They're all professionals; one is even a Doctor herself. As you can surmise, the paranoia was consuming April rapidly. She became very promiscuous and there was even talk she was prostituting herself for drugs. Any which way, that's around the time she became pregnant. Richard actually had to pay her $50,000 not to abort Christie, that's our granddaughter."

Mrs. Salvon' pauses and tries to sip some coffee. Her obvious nervousness and agitation causes her to shake, spilling some of the hot brew on her lap.

"April made an attempt, albeit a dispassionate one, to turn her life around. She wrote her dissertation, trying to obtain a PhD in psychology, and she entitled it <u>Convincing People the Sky is Green and the Moon is Made of Cheese</u>."

"What?" I say with open-mouthed wonder. "This is not my area of expertise but that is ridiculous."

Dutch Van Alstin – Murder in D Block

"I know," she nods at me, concurring my dubiousness. "But it's true. And the board had the same reaction and they denied her a doctorate outright. They called it a 'nonsensical rambling of perverted facts and unsubstantiated theories'. That's when she went back to, if she ever really left, her old ways. She began holding Christie over our heads. She threatened to take her away forever if we didn't cater to her in every way shape and form."

"What did you do?"

Mrs. Salvon' stares at me and shrugs. "We catered to her," she says placidly. "We didn't know what to do. She actually threatened to sell Christie to a black market baby ring at one time."

Mrs. Salvon's unwarranted shame surfaces again as she glances back over at the Doctor, trying to fight off tears.

"Continue, dear," the doctor says.

"Richard finally offered her one final chance. He told her she could live in the guest house and return to college, if she successfully completed a stay at Betty Ford."

"Did she?"

"We thought she did," Mrs. Salvon', a trifle calmer now, sips some more coffee. "I mean, she completed the program and all and stayed with us for a while. She was, however very despondent and very depressed all the time. Soon after that, she left and we never heard from her again."

"And I'm afraid I know why," the doctor chimes in.

"Please, Doctor, continue," I say pleadingly.

The Doctor places his cup on the tray and pulls at his robe, searching for a modicum of dignity. "I told April about the whole Delgado plan."

"Why, sir?" I say, shaking my head in disgust. "Why would you do such a thing?"

The Doctor rubs his chin and stares blankly in the fire, looking at the fiery red embers. He tries to make sense out what has happened, without really knowing what has happened. What happened to his little girl? Why did she go so awry? What happened to the vibrancy, the love, and the spirit? All those qualities that I saw in her myself. The Doctor remembers when all those qualities were truly hers and were part of her makeup, not some façade she used to manipulate and beguile me. All the zeros in his checkbook can't buy him the peace of mind and self-satisfaction he once knew as a father. All the zeros in his checkbook can't pay to replace April's soul.

"A father's love is intrinsic in his character, Theresa. I…I just couldn't stand seeing her so depressed, so ashamed. She'd look at me as if she was afraid I hated her or thought she was some type of monster. I thought the guilt of what she had done was taking its toll on her and her fear of losing our respect was too much. But obviously I over read her emotions because, although she was depressed, it wasn't because of what she did to us."

"She and I sat in this very room one night sipping some Jamaican bean coffee that we purchased. I knew how she loved exotic coffees and teas and I bought it just for her, Theresa, truly I did."

Mrs. Salvon', again, smiles and rubs his hand comfortingly.

"I remembered how important and how powerful I felt after being let in on the covert operations of our government. And, I confess out of pure desperation, I thought she'd feel that energy too if she knew. She'd know I trusted her like a father trusts his daughter. She seemed so very much intrigued as I laid the plan all out for her. She was asking follow up questions and listening so intently. I actually saw that sparkle in her eyes again, Theresa. Even if was just for a moment, I saw it. That's how I have to remember her, with that sparkle. Oh, Lord," he buries his face in his hands. "What have I done?"

"Richard," she says soothingly, "you can't blame yourself. You did what you thought was right."

"I do blame myself, Theresa, I do."

"I only have one more question, sir. I'm sorry, I don't want to appear apathetic to your pain and forgive the harshness of the question I'm about to ask."

"No, that's okay, Dane," he says. "Ask whatever you wish. I guess I owe you that much."

"You are obviously well off financially. Why would April go to such lengths for money when she had millions at her disposal?"

"Because that's what type of person she had become, Dane." Mrs. Salvon' says. "The money wasn't her underlying desire it was the course upon how she acquired the money. She had become cruel and ruthless. The cocaine destroyed her sense of decency. Her undiagnosed mental illness masked who she once was. She began thriving on manipulation and delighted in how she could wangle people. She told Richard he may have been able to shape a nose and drain a cheek but she could shape a mind and drain the spirit." Mrs. Salvon' shivers. "That was such an ominous statement she made. It was the beginning of the end for her. To April, money was nothing unless it could wield power. To her money and power were commensurate. We could offer her the money but what she wanted, we couldn't offer. She wanted to be able to act as a puppeteer to people. I don't know, Dane," she says, stirring her coffee. "I've failed as a mother with April. She harbors contempt for me that I will never understand."

"Mrs. Salvon'…Theresa?"

"Yes."

"Did you once teach a manicotti recipe to April?"

"Yes," she says fondly. "Yes I did."

Mrs. Salvon' drifts off in her thoughts. She remembers a little girl standing on a stool, spreading noodles evenly throughout a pan. She watches as the little girl pours the sauce while spilling drops of tomato paste on her chin but nearby is a loving mother to wipe it clean with a kiss.

"I just thought you should know April made it for me one night and she was very proud that her mom had taught her the recipe. And may I add that the dish was delicious. I ate three portions of it myself."

"You're a sweet boy," she says, rubbing my face delicately. "I wish April met you a few years ago."

"I've taken too much time from your day as it is. You two have been very gracious in the face of adversity. I am sorry for your pain."

"Dane," she smiles and takes my hands. "Maybe all of this will work out and you and April will return here, married, and I'll make you that manicotti recipe. You'd like that wouldn't you, Dane?"

"I think that would be marvelous."

"Don't you think there's a chance it will happen? Don't you?" She says excitedly.

"I think so, Theresa," I squeeze her hands tightly. "Hope is something that can never diminish if we keep it alive."

"Goodbye, Dane," the doctor says, extending his hand out. "I've enjoyed meting you. Your altruism and sense of decency radiate on you, son. Please take care of yourself."

"Thank you, sir. Coming from a man of your stature, that means a lot to me."

"Allow me to escort you back outside, Dane. The maze of hallways may throw you off some."

"Thank you, sir."

The Doctor and I walk out as he periodically stops to explain a piece of artwork or a portrait. He offers me some polite invitations to return "sometime" and visit he and his wife.

Dutch Van Alstin – Murder in D Block

Finally, the maze of hallways and corridors end and my car sits at the top of the driveway, running and freshly washed.

"If only my hubris hadn't seized me that night, Dane. I should have told that cocky little F.B.I. man I wasn't interested in his braggadocio confabulation and to just do his damn job."

"F.B.I.?" I say pensively. "The man who told you all these secrets was from the F.B.I.?"

"Yes."

"Do you recall his name, Doctor?"

"Yes," he chuckles slightly. "He had a very snobby elitist attitude and his name matched him implicitly. That's why I remember it so well.

"Lafayette it was. Yes, that was his name, John Lafayette."

CHAPTER   41

LAX is crowded with angry, frustrated travelers, exhausted from their pressure-filled day of tumult and mayhem. Given my present mood, I could be their king. I would have no difficulty feeling their pain and understanding their plight. Because there is no botched board meeting, nosy in-law, nor rude cab driver that is any match for my hostility. Today, I am the epitome of a 'weary traveler'. I pity the poor sap that crosses my path today in anything less than a congenial manner.

The clerk at the rental counter smiles ungainly but manages not to set me off when she accepts the Audi with a few unplanned scratches along the door. She benevolently directs me to the ticket office that has the most forthwith flight to Briersburg.

The ticket agent promises me I'll be on Briersburg's soil by six o'clock tonight, Eastern Time. Of course, to accomplish this task means there is no stopping, and crowded bathrooms and a supper consisting of stale bread and a vain attempt at meatloaf.

The flight leaves LAX in forty minutes. I take advantage of the small lapse in time to place two calls to Briersburg. I phone a friend in the parole office and the guard who replaces Bob Andover on his days off.

The flight attendant offers to take my carryon bag, but I politely decline her proposition. My luggage will do me no good sitting on a cart in Hong Kong.

Dutch Van Alstin – Murder in D Block

The flight is long and tedious and I attempt to use the time to sort matters out in my mind. But unfortunately, I am saddled sitting next to an old man who claims he was once engaged to Angie Dickinson. The old man critiques their entire tenuous relationship of how, where they meet and what caused the schism between them.

As the flight progressed and the man downed seven Scotch and sodas, light on the soda, he began to come clean with a more plausible story. The truth of the matter was that the old man was a paid extra on Miss Dickinson's 1970's TV series "Police Woman."

The old man's stultifying tale of a Hollywood love story gone askew did awaken me to a long held belief that I have always held. Nestled deep down inside every lie, is a tinge of truth that supports the lie.

The old man was, in fact, an extra on the show, i.e., the truth. That bit of truth gives the support for his whimsical tale of love and betrayal of a Hollywood starlet: the lie. The dab of truth gives the old man some credence to perpetuate his story.

April murdered her husband. When I finally understood that fact and accepted it as genuine, some of the puzzle pieces began to fall into place. I admit, I use a stale cliché, but my objective is to sort out facts, not to sound clever.

The actual act of strangulating Raphael Delgado was, of course, was not performed by April. I mean how could she? He's in there and she's out here?

However, that is the same course of thought I bought into when I was confronted with, what I wrongly perceived as, a perfunctory threat by Delgado. My cocksureness of Delgado's inability to harm me was vanquished the day my home exploded, seconds after I leaped out my window.

Regardless of April's inability to commit the actual strangulation does not preclude her from being the murderer. She masterminded it, followed through on it, and subsequently framed me.

Lafayette's incredible stupidity in divulging such secretive, stalwart information about his job proves just that: he is incredibly stupid.

I now understand his overwhelming obsession to pin this murder on me at any cost. I may never know whether Lafayette truly believed that I, did in fact, kill Delgado. But, if he could prove I did it, or chump up a bogus charge on me, then the murder would have been chalked up to an unforeseen romantic quarrel gone askew. Who Delgado really was and why he was in Briersburg would not need to be made public. And, most importantly for Lafayette, a potentially embarrassing and career threatening conversation, steeped in machismo, arrogance and a

Dutch Van Alstin – Murder in D Block

snifter of wine, could remain hidden, and hidden forever.

Lafayette's mistake lain in the way he viewed Delgado's murder. He viewed the murder and its surroundings as one would a law-enforcement officer on the street. However, what we have here is a prison murder. The two are not mutually exclusive.

Since Lafayette had convinced himself, or wanted it to appear that I was the murderer, Delgado had to have been dead by three o' clock, the time I went home. The problem with Lafayette's theory is that someone who views murder from behind the prison walls, e.g., prisoners, views it from a completely different angle. For me to have looked like the guilty party, the murder would have to have been done while I *wasn't* in the prison. The appearance of Delgado being alive after three o' clock was a must for April to frame me.

But, he wasn't. Delgado was dead by three o'clock.

A guard who would even contemplate such a crime would never actually commit the actual murder. The opportunities just do not exist. The confinement and lack of privacy make this scenario realistically impossible.

A guard would enlist a prisoner to commit the murder long after that guard went home for the day.

A prisoner would know that. An F.B.I. agent would not.

What about the rumors that a guard was the murderer? Was that rumor intentionally spread by the killer? After all, rumors grow and multiply like wildfires.

But the answer is no. The rumor, or lie, has a dab of truth underneath. That small bit of truth supports the lie. A guard did not kill Delgado. But although a prisoner knows the inner workings of a prison murder, so would a guard.

For the first time that I know of, the cat and the dog worked hand in hand.

The plane touches down in Briersburg and I give the old man a hearty handshake as I depart. I also allude to him that I believe his tale of Angie Dickinson. Somebody believing him seemed so important to his fragile ego.

I hail a cab and jaunt back to my cottage. My car sits in the driveway but I have a sinking feeling my house is empty.

Bambino charges at me eagerly, covering my face with his toilet water coated tongue.

"April?" I shout, not expecting a reply.

I locate no letter or any sign she's been here recently. Even Bambino food dish is empty, not to mention his water. And my new carpeted living room now resembles the cow

Dutch Van Alstin – Murder in D Block

pastures back in Minnesota.

After gracing Bambino's dish with some expired cold meat from my fridge, I trek out to my car and travel to the salon where April works.

The only people I see through the salon window are two young ladies giggling and slapping at each other in a frolicsome manner. The one girl spots me and waves me inside.

"I'm sorry, sir," she says, "but we're just about ready to close."

"That's okay," I reply. "I'm just looking for April? Has she been in today?"

"April?"

"Yes, April Delgado? She works…here?" my eyes dart back and forth between the ladies, knowing I will momentarily be embarrassed.

The two look at one another confusedly. "No, we don't have any employee by that name. Are you sure you have the right girl?"

I laugh aloud at the irony in her query. "No, Ma'am, I believe I don't."

My last resort is April's apartment. The very least I would like to leave her a letter and an imploration for her to call me.

I wrap at the door briskly. "April? It's me. I know you're in there."

"Miss Delgado is gone." A voice says from behind me.

"Huh?" I say, spinning my torso about.

An aging white haired woman steps closer to me. "Gone."

"Where?"

"Don't know, young man," she shakes her in a pitiful manner. "She paid me the rent she owed and took off."

"Not a word of where or why?"

"Nope," she shakes her head more fervently. "She just said she was movin' on, wherever that is. I did ask her why she was leaving so quickly."

"What did she say?"

"She said she was done and she was movin' on, wherever that is."

I drop my hands to my side and then into my pocket.

"She did sound as though she'll miss our little burg though."

"Really?" I say enthusiastically. "Why? What did she say?"

"Said it was a real pretty town," the woman scratches her chin and nods. "Yepper, said it was real pretty, with the lakes and all."

"Did she leave any type of message…for anyone?"

Dutch Van Alstin – Murder in D Block

"No, young man, she didn't." She says gently, sensing my disappointment.

"Well, then," I expel a loud, exaggerative sigh, "I guess that's that. I thank you for your time, Ma'am."

"I'm sorry young fella, she was sure a nice gal."

"One in 17.1 million Ma'am." I smile politely and wave goodbye.

In a state of melancholy, I ramble down the road and turn my car by the prison.

I stop the car, get out, and gape up at the icy hard walls of Briersburg. I stare up at the twin towers of stone and brick, stretching up high in the sky, unable to reach the sun.

I may have lost my heart to April but I lost my soul inside the walls. I fell prey to the weakness of the weak-minded and allowed the misery and pain to cloud who I was and where I came from, what I was supposed to be and who I was supposed to be. I permitted my dignity to be stripped from me right from under my nose by malicious men with vicious agendas. An agenda of prolonging the anguish that nests within and cultivating it to a pool of seething hate. A pool where I went in so deeply I could no longer keep myself afloat until the inevitable happened: I reached my hand up and went down for the last time.

I finally drowned.

I close my car door and close a chapter in my life that should never have been written.

The water streaks my windows from the intermittent drops of rain. The clouds grow dense and gray and the remaining leaves on the trees sway harder in the sudden gust of wind.

"Yep," I say aloud to myself. "Looks real pretty out there now, you bitch!" Are you enjoying the wondrous scenery of little burg, Ap--"

I slam on my car breaks, my entire car in a tailspin. Several cross words and a folio of middle fingers are hurled at me from the drivers I nearly smash into.

I jam the car in reverse and spin around, squealing my tires as I dash off in the opposite direction through red lights and stop signs.

Kingfish Lake is my destination. I leap from the car and charge up the embankment.

I ascend to the top of the knoll where April and I once walked hand in hand and peer down at the misty waters on this cold September evening. The waters begin to shape into larger waves as the last hint of orange escapes over the hillside. The leaves begin to oscillate rapidly, some being pulled from the branches from the increasing gale, trying to kick up a storm.

Underneath that tree is a woman with long black hair, sitting neatly with arms folded around her knees. As she focuses her sights up and down the lake, I can plainly see it is April.

April gazes up at the knoll, staring intently at me through her raven black sunglasses that

Dutch Van Alstin – Murder in D Block

cover her eyes. A sour grimace covers her smile.

Her hair begins to whip harder in the continuing surge of a growing wind, determined to bring forth the upcoming storm.

CHAPTER   42

Our eyes lock like two strangers in a strange land. We stare coldly and emotionless, knowing the trouble that lies in each other's hearts and minds.

Her countenance grows grimmer and piqued the longer her eyes fixate on me. I stare back, trying to appear bitter. But deep down, I am unable to experience anything but the yearning for who I thought she was. Standing before me now is a soulless chasm, a mockery of human nature and a thief of the spirit.

There is nothing left of the person I exposed all my vulnerabilities to only days ago. The girl I knew only existed in my thoughts and dreams, and I made the crucial mistake of allowing the dream to become my master.

Her stock-still stationary glare ceases as she rises up from the ground and methodically brushes away the debris that clings to her. A slow, grim march follows as April promenades at a laggard's pace along the shoreline and begins her ascension up the knoll.

She stops momentarily and retrieves a cigarette that was cloistered inside her shirt. Several flicks of a butane lighter bare no results until she shields the unwelcome draft from the flint. She exhales her smoke upwards as a gust catches it, sending it back around her face.

The trudge continues with random pauses as April catches hold of her windblown hair and tries to pull it back around her neck.

Dutch Van Alstin – Murder in D Block

She takes a drag of her cigarette and pushes the rim of her sunglasses forward. The wind causes her, once again, to frolic wildly. April, growing more irate, pulls at her locks abruptly and tucks them down her long, suede jacket.

Her procession ends inches from my face. She exhales the last of her smoke and hurls the butt at my feet.

"Tell me, Dane," she says mockingly, "is your cousin dead yet?"

I shuffle my feet some as I gaze at my mirthless expression in her sunglasses. "Your attitude is a bit hypocritical, don't you think?"

"Me?" she says amidst an incredulous laugh.

"Yes, you. I tell a small fib and you, the Machiavellian queen, dare to criticize?"

April rubs her nose quickly in attempt to shield her haughty grin. She steps around me and walks slowly down the knoll toward the parking lot.

I pursue her at a leisurely pace until she comes to a white Lexus parked by a phone pole. "Nice car," I say.

She returns a sardonic grin at me and leaps her backside upon the hood. "Before I go, Dane, I have to ask you something."

"What?"

"Did you really drive out to Minnesota at all?"

"Before I answer that, I want to know why?"

"Why, what?"

"Why me?" I reach back and feel a park bench and lean my body against the railing. "I mean, what did I ever do to you?"

"I don't follow you, Dane."

I close my eyes tightly and emit a heedless laugh. "I'm not going down this road with you. I went to Minnesota to check you out and judging by your hasty departure from our fair city, I gather you knew the jig was up?"

"I must confess, I don't get the connection between driving to Minnesota and checking me out, but I admit, the jig is up and I know it. That's why it's time for me to move on. But before I do, I have a question."

"And that would be...?"

"What made you suspicious of me to begin with?"

"Several things," I say. "Little, tiny unexplainable obscurities that didn't fit your personality."

Dutch Van Alstin – Murder in D Block

"Fill me in, please," she says mid a narcissistic chuckle. "I am very intrigued."

"First off, why me?"

"Why you ...what?"

"Knock it off, April," I exclaim, growing impatient with her flippancy. "What the hell did I ever do to you?"

"The question is, Dane, what the hell did you do *for* me?"

"It was the little things," I say, ignoring her comment.

"Such as?"

"We'll start with your age?"

"Okay. What of it?"

"You lied about your age."

"All women lie about their age, Dane. It's what we women do best."

"Not hardly. You lied because you had to portray the helpless little girl, lost in a turbulent world. In fact, you lying about your age was the straw that broke the camel's back."

"Before you mention all those other pieces of straw, how did you know I was really twenty-nine?"

"Try thirty-two."

"I'd rather be twenty-nine," she says with a smile.

"I ran into a nurse at work who gave me a twenty minute dissertation on TB. The causes, effects, cure, and the test."

"So? You say that like the world just stopped."

"It was when you showed me your vaccination scar from the old Tine tests for TB. The nurse told me that she was surprised I had one of those scars because people my age received a Mantoux test, leaving no scar. That meant you were my age at least, but probably older."

"That's rather petty, don't you think? You have to be a little neurotic to pick up on something so trivial. Are you neurotic, Dane? Are you one of those people who think everybody is against you? Are there microphones planted in your Cheerios by the government, Dane?"

"As I was saying, you also called me *farm boy* in the visit room one day and I had never told you of my background?"

"Big deal. Raph told me all about you."

"Oh, I already know your hubby filled you in on me."

"Meaning?"

Dutch Van Alstin – Murder in D Block

"In due time, sugar plum, in due time."

"Any way you slice it, Dane, these two 'cold hard' facts seem pretty lame to me. You are really paranoid. Do you have anything worth its salt?"

"As a matter of fact, I do. This may seem rather ambiguous, but you didn't carry yourself off as a tough street girl raised on the mean streets of Philly. You were to well bred, too uppity in your mannerisms. You used fifteen letter words, you listened to Mozart, and you quoted literature. For God's sake, April, you offered me cappuccino. You just didn't fit the profile."

"You are such a smug bastard, Dane," she says, shuffling her feet. "What profile? Who the hell are you to say what people fit what profile? *You* recognized Mozart. *You* quoted Kipling. *You* used fifteen letter words, too. What the hell makes you so damn special? Are you a blue blood? Do you know which fork to use for salad and which one to use for your filet mignon? Why can't everyone enjoy some cultural and intellectual pursuits without you dubbing them some sort of snob? Well let me tell you something, you're the snob. If people don't fit your narrow-minded, hackneyed images, then they're some type of weirdo. Because a person enjoys different pleasures in life than you do, doesn't make them inferior to you, just different."

"Okay, April," I say candidly, "you win that round. But maybe if I weren't such a snob, I would never have noticed all the other things. But since I have substantial supporting evidence in my favor, I'll stick my original theory about you."

"What 'supporting evidence' do you have, Dane?" She says, finger quoting her words.

"I met a nice met a nice couple recently, you may like them too. Their names were Dr. and Mrs. Richard Salvon' of Sherman Oaks, California."

April's eyes grow agape. "You bastard," she stomps her foot in the rocks beneath her feet, kicking some pebbles into my face. "You son of a bitching bastard! How dare you?" April charges at me, flailing her arms at me. "You have no right to do that."

Instinctively, I grab her and thrust her against her car, pinning her shoulders to the door. "I have no right? I have no right? You are making me look at life in prison and you say I have no right? You bitch! You cold-hearted, cynical bitch."

"Those people beat me, Dane. My father molested me for years and years, and you think I owe them a thing?"

"Oh yeah? What about your daughter? What did she do to you?"

"You son of a..." April wriggles in a futile attempt to break loose from my grip.

I grab her chin and snap her neck back against the hood of the car. "You will shut your God damn mouth, April and you will listen to me."

Dutch Van Alstin – Murder in D Block

"Oh yeah? Who do you think you are? Do you think your some big city detective manhandling some street trash whore?"

"Not street trash, but a hard-boiled, unfeeling conniver who uses people and spits them out when she's done." I impart one more thrust to April's face against the hood of the car and pull away from her.

She stands, regains her composure and shakes her head disapprovingly at me. "Me?" She says skeptically. "I use people? Me? How about you, Mr. Perfect? How about how you used me?"

"How or why or what for did I use you?"

"What did you think when you first saw me, Dane? What did you think? Did you wonder what I was like underneath, or just underneath the sheets? Did you ever ponder what was inside of me? Or did you just want to put 'it' inside me? Did you ever cogitate on what was in my head, or, did you just want to see if I *gave it*? Just another slutty wife of a prisoner, hey, Dane?"

"You're comparing lightning to the lightning bug, April. Yeah, I admit that's what I was after when you 'conveniently' ran into me that night at Cassidy's. Oh you were dressed to kill, so it seems."

"Oh that's so clever. How long have you been waiting to work that into the conversation? And why are you being so sarcastic about 'casually' meeting you?"

"Cassidy's is a guard hangout. Everyone in town knows that and all you had to do was go there and wait for me to show up."

"And why would I do that? You weren't all that 'great', if you know what I mean?"

"When a man is in competition from the hundreds of ghosts that have been there before him he tends to come up short as a lover."

"Implying I'm a whore in a roundabout way doesn't explain why I would be waiting for you."

"Because I'm the guy you husband told you about. I'm the one he said was sneaky, corrupt, and dishonest."

"You finally got something right tonight, Dane."

"And so you set your sights on me. All you had to do is flaunt your feminine wiles on me and make me fall in love..." I pause and collect my thoughts amidst a sigh. "...fall in love with you and when your husband is murdered in my block, who better to take the blame? Certainly not the poor little Latina girl who cooks manicotti."

Dutch Van Alstin – Murder in D Block

"The manicotti was a faux pas as well, dear? Greasy spicks only eat tacos and salsa? Is that it, your lordship?"

"That's not what I said. I'm referring to the time that asshole guard called you *'puta'* and you didn't even know what it meant? How does a Latina girl not understand the Spanish language? That's all I meant; don't lump me in with some Klansman. Besides, you have a lot of nerve. You snuff out a person's life and don't bat an eyelid? And you didn't just do it for the money either, you like the power trips and mind control."

"You're psychoanalyzing me, Dane."

"No," I say cantankerously. "I speak from experience. The night at the old abandoned park when you persuaded me to spill my guts out to you; you ate that up, didn't you?"

"Like yesterday's pizza, Dane," she remarks. "But all that proves is you're easily duped, nothing else."

"You're all heart."

"If this drivel is all you have, then you don't have much. In fact, I could still make a good case that you did it."

"That's another thing," I say. "If you truly thought I did it, then why didn't you ever call the police?"

"I didn't have a quarter."

"You have a smart ass quip for everything, don't you?"

"Yes and it's very annoying, isn't it?" She snaps back.

"At least when I do it, it's for humorous reasons, not to try and maintain control. You like to control things, don't you, April?"

"Are you back to psychoanalyzing again?"

"No, that's your department."

"Is this an introduction to your next point?" April leaps back upon the hood of her car and winks at me. "Do you mind if I smoke?"

"It's your life."

"Isn't it though." April slides out a cigarette and lights it.

"As I was saying, you not only can manipulate other's emotions, but yours as well."

"More psychoanalysis?" April yawns histrionically.

"No, I'm just thinking about the time you pounded those two clods with the trashcan lid. You were absolutely ferocious that day."

"Someone had to keep you from getting your ass kicked, Dane?"

Dutch Van Alstin – Murder in D Block

"And I thank you for that to this day, but that's not my point. My point is this: you were a pit bull one second and a defenseless waif the next. With the snap of your fingers you went from a powerful rage to little Miss Helpless."

"And there you were, Dane, ready to exploit that weakness for your gain."

"The topper was when you pounded me with all those questions concerning my cousin. I felt guilty for lying to you so I never noticed that the questions you were pummeling with were something you shouldn't be asking? I had to ask myself how you knew all that stuff? Only a psychiatrists asks such questions, huh, April?"

April turns her head away and lies it flat on the car. I stretch my neck out and look down at her. She fights to keep from making eye contact with me.

"A psychiatrist similar to *Dr. Christian Baltz*?"

April snaps her face at me and stutters her words. "You...you bastard."

"That's right, April," I nod my head affirmatively. "I guess you can add *sexist pig* to my repertoire. Because I just assumed that Dr. Baltz was a 'he'. My chauvinistic side never let me entertain the thought that the 'he', could actually be a 'she'."

CHAPTER 43

"Get the hell out of my way, Dane. I'm not finding a bit of this funny anymore." April shoves me aside and grabs the handle on her car door.

I wrest the handle from her hand and slam the door. "I think you'll listen to what I have to say first."

April tries to shove me and I grab her coat and twist the lapel, pulling her toward me. "I'm not letting you go until you hear me out completely."

"Who the hell are you to tell me when I can or can't go somewhere? Let go of me now!" She demands, trying unsuccessfully to squirm free.

"Not yet, April. I have a great deal more to tell you. We have only scratched the surface here."

"I don't know what you're trying to prove with this Dr. Baltz shit, because I have no idea what you're saying."

"Oh yes you do. I believe the psychiatrist ploy was your first plan of entry into the prison, vicariously of course. I was very suspicious of anyone who would offer free services to any state run agency; they're notorious for massive spending. A Doctor could make a nice chunk of change from referrals by the corrections department. But money from fees wasn't in your plans. You searched through the various *specimens* that were sent your way looking for your ideal

Dutch Van Alstin – Murder in D Block

patsy. The list was endless. Guards with drinking problems, drugs, marriage, depression, personal problems, vulnerability you could exploit."

I relax my grip on April's coat. She yanks the lapel from my coat and smoothes the wrinkles. "Are you going macho on me now, Dane? Does that make you feel tough and ferocious?"

"You're off duty, Dr. Baltz. Stop analyzing me so much."

"You're such a fool, Dane. You just prove it whenever you open your mouth."

"As I was saying, April. You can justify in your mind that I am some sort of racist, sexist snob and framing me and trying to kill me--"

"Kill you? When did I do that? I had nothing to do with your house blowing up."

"I know. That's not what I meant and you know it. We'll get to that soon enough. But as I was saying, before you interrupted, you can justify what you've done to me and the murder of two prisoners--"

"Two? Where do you get two? Where is all this bullshit coming from? Have you gone completely crazy, Dane?"

"If you'll shut your mouth momentarily, I'll fill you in on how I knew. As I was saying, for a third time, you can justify all that you did, except for what you did to Donny Quinn. What did that poor, pathetic guy ever do to you to justify his dying?"

April folds her arms and leans against the car in an almost childlike pout.

"I know Donny was referred to the lovely and charming Dr. Baltz for some type of counseling. Donny was gay and he didn't want to be and ESO did what they do best and that is passing the buck. When you got Donny in your sights, you saw a perfect sample of a screwed up man and an easy mark for manipulation. There were several angles you could approach him from. A gay prison guard is like a window washer afraid of heights, the two cannot go together. His cohorts would have eaten him alive, worse than they were already. You made him ashamed he was gay. You alluded to him that it was choice and he was who he was because of some defect in his character. Donny must have confided in you about being blackmailed by a prisoner called Toes, the same prisoner who attempted to blackmail me, too. You knew Donny was smuggling in booze by leaving it in the unlocked fireboxes and you figured if Donny would smuggle in booze because a prisoner threatened to expose his gay life style, then what would he do if someone more respectable and reliable, such as a psychiatrist with recorded interviews and documentation, blackmailed him? The desperate measures he might take could be all you needed. Maybe Donny would kill your husband and inadvertently take the fall. How am I doing so far?"

"At making an ass of yourself? You're superb."

"Then it occurred to me, you still needed a point man inside the prison to help you setup Donny. Tell me, April, who did you meet first? Was it Donny Quinn? Or was it Randy McPherson? Mack was constantly in trouble with bar brawls, three divorces, and two drunken driving charges. I know he was sent to ESO and then I'm sure he was sent to the curvaceous and sexy Dr. Baltz."

"Why thank you, sir." April retorts with a whimsical curtsy.

"If I may continue. Mack thrived on thinking he was some type of arcane, mystical man involved in top-secret agendas. How hard would it be for a master of manipulation, such as yourself, to equate murder with being a secret agent of sorts? I'm sure Mack jumped at the chance to work *incognito* in your plan. Mack did the legwork for you inside the prison. He covered up your hubby's time of death so as to frame me. But Mack's first role was to setup the blackmail attempt on Donny. You gave a recording from your sessions with Donny where he talked about being gay to Mack to play for Donny and when he played them, a scuffle ensued. Donny panicked. Unfortunately, Donny didn't react the way you thought he would. I always thought his death was shrouded in some manifold, complex duplicitous plot. But the truth is when Mack played the recording, they scuffled a bit, but then Donny became so distraught, he jumped. He just plain jumped to his death."

"I think you're living in some fictitious world where you think *you're* a spy of some sort." April says.

"No, what I said makes sense. I couldn't help but think something was up because nobody saw or heard when Donny fell. But the truth was, sure the prisoners heard it. But what the hell are they going to do? As far as they knew, Mack had thrown Donny off the tier after an argument. If Mack would kill a guard, as the prisoners thought he had, then what would he do to them if they talked? A prison is like an airplane, where are they going to run? Where can they hide from Mack?" I step a bit closer to April and pull her face toward me.

"But Mack did other things too, didn't he, April?"

April crosses her arms and childishly rolls her eyes. She opens her mouth as to speak but merely flings her hand at me instead.

"I shall, with your blessing, continue. Mack also served as your personal post office. When the attempt to have Donny murder Raphael failed, you needed another inlet. So you changed your direction to setting up a guard to take the rap, but letting a prisoner commit the murder. You skulked through the personal ads and found the Prisoner Pen Pal directory. Mack delivered your love…well, let's call them what they were, *lust letters* to a prisoner at Briersburg. Mack convinced this man that all of his correspondence was subject to censorship and he would act as a personal courier between you and him."

"Tell me, Dane? Who is this mythical 'man' you speak of? Do you have any idea of what you are talking about?"

"Yes I do," I snap back. "There was a prisoner named Vinetto that had no visitors for years and years. He was the quintessential lonely convict and he was in search for love, and there you were, April, with so much love to share."

"Jealous?"

"No, of course not. I shared all I want to with you. The giving and receiving theory in the concept of sharing is a bit slanted in your eyes. But Vinetto didn't know who you were. He figured Mack was just corrupt and to keep that appearance, Mack was probably taking some nominal fee from Vinetto to deliver letters. Certainly Vinetto had no idea he was the target of an ominous plot by Lady Lucifer herself."

"Oh, that wit of yours again. It's so clever, Dane. I mean, you are just so clever."

"Your sarcasm notwithstanding, I have a point I'd like to make. You corresponded with Vinetto and convinced him you would be all his if he got rid of Raphael. The day that guard took Vinetto up to the visit room and came back with that erotic tale of you and Raphael was your way of *advertising.*"

"Advertising?" She says with a chuckle. "I went from Lady Lucifer to Darrin Stevens?"

"I'm sure some of those letters you wrote to Vinetto got hot and steamy, not like the nettlesome letters that Mack placed on my time card for you. After all, you wanted to entice Vinetto erotically, you only wanted to tweak my mind and keep me looking paranoid."

"You don't need my help in that area, Dane. You are the cardinal example of paranoia."

"Paranoia or skepticism? I guess there is a fine line there, April. We can debate where that line is, later. Anyway, when you visited Raphael that day, Vinetto got to see you in action. I bet Vinetto headed for the showers after that visit, huh? All Vinetto needed to do was to kill Raphael and all that licentious sex was his. What a parole present for a guy who hasn't felt a woman's touch in ten years. Tell me, April? How was sex with a man who hasn't had it in ten years?"

"Real good, Dane," she says in a malignant tone. She looks down at her hand and rubs her thumb against her fingernail. "One time? We did it in your bed. Think about that tonight as

Dutch Van Alstin – Murder in D Block

you're lying there next to that stupid dog."

"Ooh, a counter-punch?"

"No, just having fun as I wait for you to make some sense."

"Then I'll continue on the short lived parole of Mr. Vinetto. Because, alas, poor Vinetto was killed in an apparent car crash soon after his release from prison. I hear his car went over a cliff and he was dead instantly. I called a friend I have in the parole office to see if any recent parolees had died or jumped. He informed me Vinetto was recently killed while driving drunk. Tell me, April, how much Sangria did you dump down his throat before you pushed him off the ledge? Did Mack help you on that one?"

"Randy wanted to show me how strong he was, Dane." April says with a pseudo-harrowing grin. "I tried to stop him, really I did."

"I'm sure you did."

April looks at the sky when she hears the rumbling. "Here comes the rain," she says calmly.

"Yep," I say, "so it is."

"Are you done, yet?"

"Just about. All except how you tried to kill me."

"I already told you I had nothing to do with your house--"

"April...enough already. I know what you did and you know what you did. Good old Mack was there for you again. You must have paid him well because he is throwing cash around like a madman."

"An analogy I'm sure you're all too familiar with."

"Mack set up the attempt on my life. The one you had set up in theory, Mack set it up in actuality. The brawl in the box where I was sliced up was no coincidence. Your husband was dead and suspicion was zeroing in on me by that time. If I was killed, then you were free and clear."

"But Mack made a mistake when we were on our way to the box to break the fight up. He said how much he had hated Hopwah and how he wanted to get him. Since we had not arrived at the box yet, how did Mack know Hopwah was even involved in the fight? And it was no accident that lummox bumping me when we charged in the yard, he knocked me down on purpose knowing Hopwah was going to try and cut my throat. You, posing as Baltz, had access to state files on all the prisoners. You knew about Hopwah's bizarre fetishes and sexual practices. Mack had Hopwah on his gallery at one time. How hard was it for Mack to convince

Hopwah to kill me? He's doing life in prison and this state has no actual death penalty. What does he have to lose? Hopwah could be a martyr, a hero, and a celebrity of sorts? Hopwah's life is ostensibly over; why not have his five minutes of fame? That explains why you gave me such an eerie look the day I showed up at your apartment with my arm in a sling. You expected me to be dead. You were angry that I was alive. That was the second time something went awry in your plans."

"If that were true, then why did I bother coming back to you? You have an answer for everything, so how about an answer for this? Do you have one?"

"As a matter of fact, I do. You lied when you said you didn't receive my last bunch of roses. You did receive them. In fact, they're the reason you came back to me. The card read that I was going to find out who killed Raphael and clear my name. Your inheritance wasn't finalized yet, you couldn't afford to have me out there running around like that. You came back to me to divert my time and attention away from the murder."

April shakes her head and smiles. "You don't miss a thing, do you? You really are neurotic, Dane."

"Did you really harbor that much hate for me where you wanted me dead?"

"Wanted and needed are two different things, Dane. You take things too personally."

"Excuse me," I utter a defensive laugh. "Murder isn't personal? You wanted to cease my breathing forever, lay me in a cardboard box and you don't feel I should take that personally?"

"What does it matter, Dane? You figured it all out, you win?"

"I won a Pyrrhic victory at best. Knowing who and what you are now doesn't change that I am in love with who I mistakenly thought you were."

"That person doesn't exist, Dane. You can't possibly be in love with a phantom."

"When people die, April, that doesn't stop them from being loved by someone still. I love a woman who doesn't exist, and I hate the one that does, but to me they're the same thing."

"They're not, Dane." April reaches her hand out and fells the droplets of rain.

"Are you proud of yourself, April?"

"Does it matter?"

"No, I guess not. The whole thing, me and you, us, the dreams I had, the dreams I thought we had, they all just seem such a waste."

"All in all, Dane, I enjoyed being with you. You were fun to be around sometimes and you cooked pretty well, too." April laughs. "Don't sell yourself too short."

Dutch Van Alstin – Murder in D Block

"Perhaps they'll put that moving tribute on my tombstone someday."

April laughs again because she doesn't know what else to do. "You need to listen to your own advice better; you let the dream become your master, Dane."

"I know I did."

"And I'm sorry you did." April takes hold of my face and kisses me softly on the lips. "Goodbye," she says in a ruffled voice.

The rain begins falling harder to the ground, matting my hair to my head.

April reaches for the door handle as the thunder rumbles louder and the lightning flashes across the sky.

"April?"

She turns toward the door and looks at me uneasily, sensing a connotation of urgency in my voice.

"You're not leaving here."

April drapes a cluster of hair from her face and lays it back around her ears. She fixes her sights on her hands, still clasping the door handle. "Oh yes I am, Dane. I most certainly am leaving here."

She pops the handle and opens the door while I, simultaneously, kick the car door shut.

She stands, resolute and unruffled and perches a haunting smile on her face. She raises her eyes at me and rubs my face gently. "You have to move out of my way, Dane, because I am leaving with or without your permission."

"I will not just stand here and watch you walk off."

"Then," April kisses my cheek. "Get in the car and go with me."

"Are you insane? Or do just think I am?"

"Not insane, just realistic. Face it, Dane; you know you want to go with me. So, go with me. I have over seventeen million dollars and we can have lots of fun with that much cash."

"I'm not even taking that offer seriously. I am not that stupid, you know?"

"I didn't say you were," April slides off her sunglasses and flips her drenched, flat hair from her face. "As long as you don't have any unrealistic expectations of us hand in hand through a field of posies, then you're not stupid. Now either get in the car, or, get out of my way."

"The answer is no on both counts. I'm staying, and, you're staying. You don't deserve to be free."

"I deserve whatever it is I can get, Dane. You aren't the judge of who gets what and

Dutch Van Alstin – Murder in D Block

who's allowed to be free. Who do you think you are?"

"Me?" I say, running low on stupefaction, "you tried to kill me, remember?"

"That was business, Dane!" She shrills. "That is so egotistical of you! It wasn't you, specifically, it was business, stop taking it so damn personally. You don't know what it's been like for me? I never measured up in anyone's eyes. I was never a daddy's girl. I was never a mama's girl, I was nobody's girl. People just want to use me, Dane. They all just want something from me. Why should I wait around and let people take from me and use me? They're going to do it to me anyway; I'm just beating them all to it. I'm just better at it than they are, that's all. I've beaten 'em all at their game and none of 'em can handle it. They can't handle the fact they've been beaten at their own game. That's not my fault they can't handle that. That's their fault. I didn't make the rules, I didn't make 'em, they were already there and they were working against me. All I did is turn the rules around in my favor, that's it. I just changed the course of my life to something better and that bothers them all. Everybody who wanted to see me fail, everybody who lived to humiliate me. I know they all wanted me to fail. They all just take and take from me. Nobody ever wanted anything from me unless they were using me, that's all. So I finally quit being the world's doormat. What's wrong with that? Huh? What's wrong with that? April is nobody's fool any longer, Dane. I am tired of being used and treated like shit. It's my way from now on and nobody is ever going to treat me badly again. I promised myself nobody would ever make a fool of me again and nobody has. Take! Take! Take! That's all they ever did and I say no more taking from April! I've had it! I'm going to start taking before I get taken. I owe nobody nothing! They all wanted me to fail in life, Dane. What was I supposed to do with my life? After all, it is *my* life! My fucking life! And I don't need the approval of some backwoods rube to live it how I want to live it. Now I'm telling you again for the last fucking time, get out of my way. I'm not asking you, I'm telling you. Get away from the damn car, now! Do you understand me, Dane? Do you?"

"As God as my witness, April," I rest my hands on her face and rub the droplets of tears away from her already saturated face, "I don't. I don't understand. But, I confess, I believe for the first time since we met, you are being sincere."

And with a crack of thunder, I knew my future was going to be forever unsure, and forever uncertain.

Only one thing was definite, my future was forever unchangeable.

Dutch Van Alstin – Murder in D Block

EPILOGUE

Floating off shore in the lake is a handful of shingles from my cottage, ripped from their perch from the tumultuous storm last night. With every ripple of the waves, the shingles float closer to shore.

The sun still refuses to shine through the gray sky, a telltale sign of the destruction that whisked through the air hours ago, creating havoc only I can understand.

My allegiant dog lies next to me on the dock, wagging his tail rhythmically with sound of the waves slapping against the hull of my boat. My fishing line drifts off to the left with the current of the water, sending my hook nearer to my neighbor's dock and away from mine.

There are inescapable facets of life that are immutable:

Dark hair imperceptibly turns silver and the strong bones wither away as the once sleek skin grows dried and scarred. Without so much as a tick of the clock, the young and vibrant grow old and cynical, watching life in a holding pattern as the sands of time dribble out crystal by crystal.

But how I travel to that undeniable destination is strictly up to me to decide on a day-to-day basis. And today, I sit eating a tuna sandwich as I scratch the ears of my dog.

The fishing line jerks, causing me to grab the pole with both hands. I fight the force that pulls away from me and heave the line with every ounce of strength I can muster.

Dutch Van Alstin – Murder in D Block

Flying out of the water at the end of a hook is a catfish so large that my dog pops his ears up and scrutinizes the struggle between man and nature. I lurch the line once more in a desperate attempt to launch the fish back on to my dock.

The fish splashes back into the water, still fighting to release his mouth from the hook. I reel the line in with my hand and pull the remarkably large catfish on to my dock.

I drop him into the water bucket as he smashes his face against the sides repeatedly. I wipe my hands and send a smile toward my dog who fails to appreciate my victorious struggle. I attribute the fish's unusually large size to his age and his years swimming about in the water.

I wrap up the line and place the lures back in my tackle box while watching my dog trot aimlessly back to the cottage. A reflex chuckle emits from my mouth as I watch the struggling fish, importunate for his release.

With one swipe of my boot, I kick over the pail and drop the fish back into the lake. The fish darts out through the water and out into the deep murk. I wish it well and say a tacit little prayer that it never ends up on another angler's hook. The fish has swum for decades in freedom, unscathed and untouched by human hands, bothering nobody in his daily pursuit.

Perhaps I cannot be the sole judge of who deserves freedom, but I can apply my wisdom to the situations as they arise. I look out at the lake and wish the denizen of the deep God speed.

Because, in this life, there are certain living things that deserve to be *free*.

Dutch Van Alstin – Murder in D Block